Song of the Sea Maid

Also by Rebecca Mascull

The Visitors

REBECCA MASCULL

Song of the Sea Maid

HODDER &
STOUGHTON

First published in Great Britain in 2015 by Hodder & Stoughton

An Hachette UK company

1

Copyright © Rebecca Mascull 2015

A CIP catalogue record for this title is available from the British Library

Hardback ISBN 978 1 473 60435 3
Trade Paperback ISBN 978 1 473 60436 0
eBook ISBN 978 1 473 60434 6

Printed and bound by Clays Ltd, St Ives plc

Hodder & Stoughton policy is to use papers that are natural,
renewable and recyclable products and made from wood grown in
sustainable forests. The logging and manufacturing processes are expected
to conform to the environmental regulations of the country of origin.

Hodder & Stoughton Ltd
338 Euston Road
London NW1 3BH

www.hodder.co.uk

To Simon my port
and Poppy my starboard.

I

I think I had a brother once.

We sit in the road below the window of a pie shop, his face obscure in the cat-black of a London alley past midnight. We poke at the mortar with sharp sticks, then scrape away till the bricks come loose. He grunts as he manoeuvres the first one from its rest. A voice cries the hour; it is the Watch in the next street and we stop, waiting to see if the old man will turn into our alley and catch us. We hurry. I watch my brother's hands grasp the slackened bricks and pull them free, dry mortar crumbling dusty and mysterious in the dark air. When the hole is large enough, he shoves me through and I spy two fat pies on the counter. In my littleness, I can barely reach them and do so on tiptoe, my brother fretting in whispers lest I drop them. I entice each pie on fingertips and pass them through to him. There is one for each of us, my brother and me, and once I have scrambled back out we fall to eating them, face-first, the red berries like gore on our dirty cheeks. He finishes first and wipes his fingers about his shirt. He takes my pie plate, licked clean, and tosses both in through the hole. A brisk breeze whistles up the alley and flings litter in our faces. We giggle and grab at it, my brother catching a slip of paper with neat writing on it. I know I cannot read and I do not think he is able, but he scans it and passes it to me.

'For you, from me,' says he.

'What does it say?' I reply.

He runs a finger along the letters. '*All thy life be happiness and love.*'

There is a commotion behind us. I see a bad set of men
with wicked faces, looming towards us. I reach for my brother.

He shouts at me: 'Run!' He shouts again, 'Run!'

And I run. Down the alley, around the corner, out into the
thoroughfare. But I am thunderstruck. I will lose him, I think.
My brother. Thus I turn on my heel and race back to the pie
shop. All is quiet. I see a woman leaning by the wall and ask
if she saw the gang. She points down yonder and I quit her,
not knowing where I am going. But I hear the men before I
see them, laughing till they are like to split their sides. I find
them striding along the footpath ahead, one holding my brother
who fights and chafes like a trapped rat, but it is a vain struggle.
The man bangs my brother's legs against a post and he hops
quieter thereafter. I follow behind for streets and streets, till
the brackish smell of the docks fills my nose and we come in
sight of the vessels bobbing on the Thames. They drag him
on board a boat and though I wait and wait all through the
night, he does not reappear. At morning light, the boat leaves
the wharf, my brother hidden below. I stand on the quay and
shout at the men on deck, yet my reedy voice is lost in the
dockside hubbub and the boat drifts away, my brother and
my happiness with it.

The days after his loss are a heart-searching time. I take
out his note to me and gaze at it often. I beg for food and
gain little. I stare in at shop windows and consider how to
rob from them. But I do not have my brother's guile and fear
I will be caught and beaten. One sun-shining day late in the
afternoon, I trail behind a gentleman in a brocade coat, his
cocked hat under his arm and a bag wig keeping the powder
from his collar. I think, A wig like that would fetch some
coins. He stops and raises his arm to call a chair-man and I
jump high, grabbing the bag and whisking the wig from his
shaved head. I turn to run but he is so quick and grabs my
arm, his grip too strong for me to wrench away and I am
fairly caught and cannot budge.

'Is it a boy or a girl?' asks he, peering at me. I wear breeches my brother gave me yet my hair hangs long about my shoulders. 'Where is your mother?'

I do not speak. I jut out my lip and stare the gentleman hard in the eye. I am told since that my grimy face, petulant and proud, and my clothes all tatters and hair matted grey with dirt awaken a pity long dormant in this busy merchant.

'Do you wish to eat, child?'

I nod. I still have his wig in my fist. My arm held fast, he bends down to pick up his fallen hat and leads me to a hackney coach, whose driver refuses the fare at the sight of a bare-headed gentleman attached to such a ragged bundle as me, yet is persuaded by double the rate. Inside, we are most cruelly shaken up as the pavement is uneven and the horses are fast trotters.

When we slow to our destination, the gentleman says, 'May I have my wig?'

I oblige and we step out. We stand before a great edifice, a white-stoned building with a towering front door topped by a broad plaque. I cannot read the letters engraved in the inscription, yet above them stand stone effigies of a boy and girl, heads bowed and hands clasped in gratitude. The gentleman has pulled the bell and as we wait, he tells me: 'This is the Asylum for the Destitute Wretches of the Streets of London. I am a business associate of the founder of this institution. With any luck, this will be your new home.'

A woman appears at the door. Her mob cap and pinner are bright white, as if laundered in ice. Her face is set in a hard pattern but when she looks at me, there are wrinkles about her eyes I like. She talks with the gentleman for a time. She nods and I am told to enter.

'You will do well with Matron,' says the gentleman. 'Good luck to you, orphan, if such you be,' and, adjusting his wig slightly, he leaves.

The front door is closed and bolted, the only light leaking

dimly from a slim window above, a spiked iron bar clamped across it.

'What is that for?' I ask.

Says Matron, 'Have you never lived in a house?'

I shrug.

''Tis there to stop rogues like you from smashing the glass and being thrust through by blackguards who use children for their thievery.'

She ushers me towards a door and we go into a room wherein stands a circular table and chairs, brown panelling on the walls and a bow-window to the street, before which I am positioned that the woman may regard me fully.

'Perhaps you are three years of age. Or just four. Yet you are so malnourished 'tis possible you could be five, six or twenty.' She shakes her head in disgust. 'A child so filthy, it's more monkey than mankind.'

I am taken to a kitchen in an outhouse, across a muddy yard. There we find two maidservants who gape at me. I am told to take off my clothes. I will not do it. I clamp my hand around my brother's note in my pocket and close my eyes tight.

'You are eaten up with vermin, child,' says Matron. 'You must wash.' Hands tear my clothes from me, stand me in a tin bucket before a crackling fire and pour water on me. They scrub me with soap for an eternity and find a little girl. I do not open my eyes this whole time or release my fist. When I am done, Matron tells the maidservants to go and ready the other children for prayers and I open my eyes.

'Come now,' says she, holding up a pair of scissors. 'I must dress your hair.'

I let her tug my head this way and that, watching the tangled clumps fall to the floor and feeling a sudden lightness about the ears.

'What is your name?' she asks. But I do not know it. I cannot remember my brother calling me a name. I only know he found food for me. Perhaps he called me 'sister', though I could not swear it. She continues, 'No matter. All foundlings here are given new names.'

She opens a cupboard filled with piles of clothes, girls' to the left, boys' to the right. I have never conceived of so many clean clothes together in one place. To possess more than a shirt, jacket and one pair of breeches seems luxury to me. She retrieves a shift, stays, stockings, petticoat, apron and cap. She helps me dress and ends with a green jacket bodice, an image of a flower sewn on its front with white thread for the petals and a golden heart. I am found sturdy shoes from a shelf of many pairs and told to sit on a stool by the fire. With only a shift and skirt to cover my legs, my underparts feel cool and vulnerable. I wrap my skirts about my thighs, my hand still closed around my treasured note.

'Will you open your fist for me?'

I shake my head.

'For meat, will you do it?'

I am torn. The long-lost taste of flesh! She opens the safe, brings out dabs of meat on string and passes one to me. She shows me how to hold it before the fire to cook it. As I gobble it down, the precious slip of paper drifts to the floor on the warm air and is snatched by Matron, who reads aloud: '*Price 1d.*'

'No,' say I. 'Those are not the words.'

'Yes, they are. See? Price, a penny. Is that your worth, child?'

'You are wrong. The devil burn you, for you are *wrong*!' I shout and cry my bellyful for the first time in that orphanage, and not for the last.

Matron wipes my blubbering face with her handkerchief and observes me.

'A bold little miss. A clever one too, for your size. I shall give you the surname Price, from the only scrap of identity you own. As for a Christian name, the gentleman who found

you was a Mr Dawnay, first name Jacob not suitable. But
Dawnay, now. A prettyish sort of a name that would do, would
it not? Eat up then, as it is evening and time for bed.'

Other foundlings named here have received such as Julius
Caesar, William Shakespeare and Theodosia Rainbow. So my
name is not as foolish as it might be. And that is how I become
Miss Dawnay Price.

2

Matron leads me up two pairs of stairs. Halfway, I hear the sound of boys larking behind a closed door, past which I am hurried. I peer down at the awkward angles of the banisters that form a square spiral to the hallway below. Ascending the last few steps, the laughter of girls emanates from above. My throat aches with fear and I clutch at my clothes. I have no memory of sleeping in a room or sharing any space with so many females. I think on my brother and wish to weep, but I prevent myself and determine to face whatever is in this room with defiance. At the very top, we enter a garret and I discover my dormitory and meet my fellow inmates. There are two rows of beds, amid which there is a covey of girls, from around my age to perhaps double it. All are dressed neatly in the same green jackets and white caps, some sitting in pairs holding hands, others standing with linked arms. At our appearance, all stop still and some cock their heads to look past Matron and stare at me. Some eyes show interest, while others betray suspicion in their frowns.

'This is Dawnay Price. She has no family we know of and was found today on the street. Be charitable to her for she is different from you and has no one to recommend her. Now, ready yourselves for bed.'

Matron stands while we undress in solemn silence and place our clothes at the base of our beds. We lie in our shifts on low, hard cots on thin, straw mattresses with one sheet and one blanket each, the warmest and most comfortable I believe

I have ever been for sleep. There are even the vestiges of a small fire in our room – I discover later this is only lit for one hour every evening – but enough to feel like a furnace to me. It transpires that all seventeen girls are in this one room, while all fourteen boys sleep in the other on the second floor. Presently, that is our entire number and Matron says there is no room for more, until someone leaves. We are forbidden from speaking once the candle is snuffed and placed on a stool by the door, but I lie awake in my bed opposite the one window and hear the other girls whispering.

I sit up in my bed and say, 'Does anyone here have a brother?' and the whispering stops, but no one answers me. It is in my character to ask questions. I persevere. 'I had a brother but men came and took him on a boat.'

Then a voice speaks, a low flat voice of an older girl. She says, 'He was pressed.'

'What?' say I.

'Taken by the press gang. You won't be seeing him again. *Ever.*'

Then another girl speaks, this voice high and chiding: 'We all came here as babies. We were not street rats. Not like you.'

'I am not a rat.'

Another says, 'Our mothers could not keep us, so they brought us here for a better life. Where was your mother?'

'Giving your father a favour under a thick hedge!' cries the first and then all the girls are jeering at me, I know not why. I listen to them without a word. In my sensitive soul, I take this as a declaration of war and from that moment on, I determine I will not have friends in this place.

We are woken at dawn by Matron, the others say prayers I do not know and we wash our faces from a hand-basin. I am shoved about by those beside me as I do it, spilling water and attracting tuts and sighs. They dress quickly but I forget the order of clothing and am laughed at for my ignorance. Matron assists me and finally – glared at smugly by each girl long since finished as they file past me – I pull on the last item, the jacket adorned with the asylum's emblem.

'Why do we wear a flower?' I ask Matron.

''Tis the daisy. I suppose you have never seen one.'

I shake my head.

'The daisy means innocence.'

'In-sun-se?'

'Purity. Now stop testing me and get yourself to the refectory. You will miss your meal.'

After a taciturn breakfast of bread and cheese and a cup of water, Matron takes me aside and leads me down the long corridor to the front hall. We stand outside a grand door and Matron straightens my cap, which will not sit neatly.

'This is called the court room. 'Tis where the meetings are held, guests are received and the master works, and is a room you will never set foot in again after this day. You are about to meet the founder, child. Speak not one word, a graceful sink when you are introduced and when you are dismissed.'

'How do I sink?'

'Oh, my eyes! You *were* born in a field. A sink, a curtsey? Watch me.' Matron joins her hands at the waist, slides one foot forward, takes a sideways step and slides her first foot to join the other foot. Her heels touch, toes turned out, then she bends her knees outward and sinks.

'I cannot do it!' I cry. It would take a month of lessons to master its intricacies.

'You *will* do it because you *must*,' says she and knocks on the door.

A man's voice from within calls, 'Enter,' and the great door opens to reveal heaven on earth in all its wonderment.

My young eyes have never seen such a room, my unformed mind never dreamed of such a place. It is the white ceiling that captures my eye first: adorned with intricate carvings of branches, leaves and flowers twisting among themselves in joyous writhing. The walls are green and hung with paintings of fat women and burly men, of naked flesh and flowing robes, and the enacting of mighty and important deeds. Smaller pictures show buildings of white stone surrounded by trees and acres of land. A massive hearth is charmed by a hearty fire and above it another imposing scene in white plasterwork tells of boys reaping amid sheaves of corn, girls sweeping and washing clothes and a giant man standing above all smiling down on them, ships of the navy swaying to the horizon behind one shoulder and an ox bellowing beside the other. Before all this embellishment a real gentleman sits in a high-backed chair, wearing a neat periwig, his arms resting on a polished table before him and a long feather in his hand. He places it down, slowly shifts back his seat and stands up, immensely tall.

I am brought before him. He comes out from behind his grand table and looks down upon me, an ant at his feet.

'Sir, this is Dawnay Price, our newest foundling,' says Matron. She glares at me and I know I must do it.

I stare at my feet and cross one before the other and begin to bend, yet find myself bowing forward like a man and thereafter decide I have nowhere else to go but back up.

'A fine gentleman!' jests the founder, his eyebrows arched. 'Named for a very good friend of mine, also a fine gentleman. If you honour that name, you will go far in life. So, child, welcome to your new abode. All who enter here are fortunate base-born objects. Those who have been saved from the streets, alleys and rubbish heaps of London, the abandoned vagabonds of the poor. Here you will be provided with shelter and sustenance. And furthermore, a virtuous education to make you useful – on the land, on the sea or in the home – instead of falling into rough ways and becoming swindlers and cutpurses, or else molls and jades, ending your portion shackled in a coffle of prisoners shuffling through the streets to be transported on ships to foreign lands or to break your necks on the gibbet. Is that what you want, child?'

I have listened to each word and surmise I understood perhaps one quarter. But I know what the gibbet is and shake my head.

'I do not want to hang, sir.'

'Quite. But there are fates worse than death, Dawnay Price. If you were not the luckiest wretch alive to be found by my good friend and brought to this sanctuary, it is likely you would have ended up in the hell they call the workhouse, that den of disease where the weak go to die in misery. You are fortunate that I have saved you from such a fate and you will work hard for me every day you pass here, Dawnay Price, to thank me for my charity. Here you will learn a trade and your catechism. We will prepare you for a life of service to society, where instead of fouling the streets with your poverty, you will be reformed. All children come into the world unblemished. It is the cruel world itself that stains the child and turns it to roguery. We are here to save the child, turn it from sin and render it beneficial to the public. Do you understand me?'

I have been looking at the feather on the table. Beside it is paper and a pot of black liquid. On the paper are words, black words. Beneath it is a board stretched with cream-coloured paper with dark stains on it. On a side table behind the founder there are more pots and feathers too, stacked in a vase. What can they possibly be for? I have never seen such curious and lovely things.

I ask, 'What does the feather do?' I feel a sharp cuff to the back of my head. I forget myself and try to sink, this time tripping forward and almost knocking the founder's knees with my head.

'It is a fool!' he cries and I am swiftly removed from this handsome room.

★

In the months that follow, I become accustomed to our rigid routine. After breakfast, we spend the morning in the schoolroom on the ground floor. Our schoolmaster is a young man I discover is Matron's nephew, who also looks to the welfare of all boys in this institution, as Matron does with us girls. We are put to school in a trifling manner, with reading and arithmetic. Once I learn my letters, I can read my brother's note and I know then that Matron was right. But I am grateful to him for his kindly deception. I look it over often and if I squint hard and long enough, I believe I can see the words he spoke writ on the paper and it comforts me. At the very least, his hands have touched the paper I touch. At times I weep over it for so long that my eyes smart afterwards and my head aches like a beating drum. I hide the note from the others in a crack in the dormitory wall behind my cot.

I consider my brother often, or the fact of him. After all, he claims all my infant memories. I call him up into my fancy and recall his features or a kind word. I picture him aboard ship, a resourceful sailor I imagine, considering how he kept us thriving in those early days. Perhaps he was drowned at sea or caught the yellow fever in some distant port. If he lived, I hope he resides in a warm place, with victuals and drink and some portion of love or friendship. I want that at least for the one who fed me, who told me to run those many moons ago. He was a boy of a free and merry turn and I loved him.

Every Sunday, we gather in the schoolroom for a lengthy sermon by our founder. Here we are read stories from the Bible and are taught of hell, omens and to be suspicious of fanatics, as they began our civil war after all, not so very long past. He makes quite clear to us his views on the poor.

'When you leave this place in apprenticeship, we will have chosen a place for you in a respectable and useful profession, to be nurtured by those of the working classes who appreciate religious moderation and our noble nation. Together we will make good citizens of you and force the kingdom of darkness to totter. And hear this: never shall a child from my institution be sent to fester with porters, higlers, chair-men, day-labourers or market folk, as these people are one and all an insolent rabble who encourage revolt and, what is more, they never go to church on Sundays.'

I ask Matron afterwards if poor people have a day off from work.

'Sundays for some.'

Say I, 'No wonder they do not go to church if it is their only day free from work. They might want to go for an airing or sport and play.' I am smacked on my leg for this, for blasphemy and cheek. But I notice Matron fidgets during churchtime and always disappears after for a little and I wager she would welcome the extra morning of freedom.

Lunch is the same as breakfast – bread and cheese – for five days of the week, with boiled tripe on Saturdays and some sort of brown soup on Sundays. Supper is bread and cheese again, though at times we have boiled greens if someone has found some dandelions to pick. Once a month we have one small potato each with our Friday supper. After lunch, we are given a brief period of fresh air, whatever the weather may bring, in the walled yard behind our building. There are grey walls and a dusty floor to it. Not quite room enough to run and jump, so some of the girls skip about, little ones play pat-a-cake, and the older boys form animated knots and brag of exploits. Sometimes I creep along each of the four walls, counting my steps, and thereby roughly calculate the area of the yard. Most often, I find a corner and watch. I am alone, yet surrounded by others. From my first day, I continue my silent stand against them and feign to revel in my solitude. The boys ignore me anyway, and the older girls ensure the younger ones have nothing to do with the street rat. One time in this yard I find a magpie with a broken wing. I cup it in my hands and take it to Matron who says, 'One for sorrow, two for mirth, three for a wedding and four for death,' and promptly breaks its neck. 'You orphans have enough room for sorrow in your lives, without inviting it in.'

In the afternoons, we are instructed in trade. The girls are split into small groups and assigned to a maidservant, where we are taught the art of domestic service, the hundred small skills it takes to become a charwoman or laundry maid. The boys are permitted to leave the building to pursue grander trades, such as boot black or sweep. It is hard, busy work and the only junctures at which we stop are mealtimes, but I am so empty when I sit to eat that I do not enjoy this moment of stillness but think only of my belly and the food that barely fills it. It is never enough and we are always hungry, all of us.

Our only moments of rest are the minutes in bed before sleep steals our minds till morning. I lie and think of my brother and where he may be; I think who my mother and father might have been and if they are dead or in the work-house or hanged from the gibbet; I think of how the window in our dormitory is split into four squares and that each pane has four sides and I multiply the four sides by the number of panes and I imagine if the room had four windows or eight or sixteen or thirty-two windows how many panes of glass there would be altogether and how such as glass is manufac-tured and what ingredients might be needed to make glass and whether it is a material one finds in the ground or the fields or the mountains or if it is something that is made by the hands as bread or cheese are and how light and cheerful our room would be with such a prolific number of glass panes letting in the sunlight all the long day. This is but one of the many ruminations my mind considers each night in the quiet and the darkness before sleep. Yet these thoughts move so fleetly I never have the chance to grasp them and by the next night they are gone and replaced by more and new ones, so many it hurts my head.

One evening after dinner, Matron summons me to the kitchen and bids me sit before the fire, as I did that very first day with her.

'You have been with us for one year now, Dawnay. We ask each of our new arrivals how they are settled in their new life after this period. 'Tis part of my role so I do it. How is it with you, child?'

'What is the feather for?'

Matron's eyes grow wide. 'Still harping on this?'

'Is it for writing? I think it must be for writing.'

'Yes, for writing. 'Tis named a quill.'

'Quill.'

'Quill,' says Matron.

'Do we learn to write? Will we learn to use the feather, the quill?'

'Oh no, child. You do not learn to write here. Reading and numbers is all foundlings need. Writing is not necessary in your future forms of employment. Whoever heard of a cabin boy who could write, or a milkmaid? A charwoman does not even need her numbers, as she is not paid in coin but in broken meat and cinders. What need has she for a quill?'

'I need one.'

'Whatever for?'

'To write down my thoughts so I cannot forget them.'

'And what does an orphan need to think about?'

'Everything.'

'Is that so?'

'Yes, Matron.'

She is frowning at me. She is thinking. 'I said you were a clever one. My nephew says it too.'

'That I am clever?'

'Indeed.' I grin. Matron cannot help herself and she smiles also. Yet she stifles it. 'But there is nothing to be done about it, child. The founder is resolute on the matter. Orphans are not to learn to write. And the idea of a girl receiving an

education would never be borne. He has three daughters
himself and no sons and has given them all the same sage
advice in order to secure matrimony, namely, that they should
hide any vestige of a lively mind if they are to catch a husband.
Wives who are cleverer than their husbands are unnecessary,
as are clever servants likewise. Thinking never cleaned a floor.
Better put it out of mind.'

But I do not put it out of mind, as I cannot. The following
morning I hide a reading primer from the schoolroom inside
my jacket. I carry it round all day – its weight a delicious
secret against my heart – and hide it beneath my bedclothes
that night. I wait in bed while the other girls whisper, then,
one by one, their whispers cease and they all breathe heavy.
I get up and creep across the room; the floorboards creak but
everyone is too spent to waken. I fetch the candlestick from
the stool and use the fire's embers to light the wick. I make
my way downstairs and along the hallway to the grand door
and listen carefully. No sound emits, thus I deduce it is empty.
I turn the handle to the court room and enter. There is no
one inside, yet the dying fire throws shadows dancing on the
walls that make me start. I am watched by the exalted ones
from the wall paintings as I go to the side table and remove
one quill from the vase, take one of the two inkpots and
retrieve sheets of paper from the large table.

For a moment, I consider staying in this room to do my
work, but cannot risk the double punishment for not only
thievery but also inhabiting Eden when God has banished
me from it. I carry my treasures back up the staircase and
into the dormitory. There is a table beside the fire where our
water jug is stored. I remove it to the floor and set up at the
table, using the candle stool to sit on. The stolen book open
before me, I dip the stolen quill in the stolen inkpot and try
to imitate the shapes I see on the pages. My first attempts at
writing are poor, scratchy efforts. The ink splashes and spills
and resembles the murder of a pen across the paper. But I

persevere and make a passable letter A through to E, after much effort. I look at the quill and think of its life as a feather, which bird dropped it in its moulting – perhaps a goose – and what sights this feather saw on its journeys across the skies, winging past treetops below and clouds above.

I work every night for weeks and teach myself to write. If the embers are not warm enough to light a candle, I write by moonlight if it be full. I hear the night soil collectors on their jolly route from pit to pit. Twice, I see a cartload of people pass by on the road, who all stand shoved together in the cart's bed; by their clothes they look very poor, all rags and filth, as I was when found. Yet on their sleeves each wears a matching badge, with the letters SG sewn on. They trundle past in the middle of the night, one calling, 'Where do we go?' and I ponder this myself. I tell Matron it woke me one night; she explains they are the paupers of our parish of St Giles. These poorest of the poor are entitled to some paltry handouts only if they reside in the area, thus the parish regularly deserts cartloads of paupers outside its boundaries so that it has no responsibility for them. One woman she heard of was heavy with child and the parish did not want another pauper child born within its boundaries, says Matron, 'and when the big-bellied woman was abandoned beyond the parish border, she fell to pieces and died moments later.' On these long nights, I think of the woman who fell to pieces and comfort myself that by learning to write, I obtain a skill that could make me a living one day, and thus will prevent me from riding that benighted cart. I listen for the Watch as he passes our windows and I count the hours down. I leave three hours at the end of the night to pack away my tools and sleep till dawn, so that I receive the minimum of rest to feed my body what it needs.

The days pass in routine: schooling, meals, service. Some of the orphans leave us, three boys and two girls, apprenticed to those in trade. One girl is thirteen years, a lumpish thing who no one would take for a time, yet the others are much younger, from ten down to one of seven years only, the brightest boy here. The gifted ones go soonest. Matron holds a solemn ceremony of farewell to mark each orphan's entry into apprenticeship, the boys to a cobbler, butcher and calico printer, the girls to household business. The best thing is that the leaver is given a final meal of fat bacon and the rest of us watch with wet mouths; the worst is that none of us knows how our new master or mistress will treat us. There are frightful stories whispered of apprentices beaten, starved, bound and worse. It fills me with shuddersome fear.

I estimate I have at the most three years left before I am apprenticed – nobody knows my precise age, but Matron estimates gone six or seven years by now. Perchance I have fewer years remaining here, as they say I am very sharp and forward, so I must make progress with my writing before I am gone and have even less freedom than the wretched amount I have now, the portion I steal of it after dark. The nights are where I become myself. In the long days, I have come to an unspoken truce with my fellow occupants and they leave me be, though I sometimes find one or two staring at me at bedtime. Perhaps they know what I am about in the night. I hide my scribblings, the quill and the inkpot beneath my cot. I am forced to steal again, as my quill needs sharpening, and thus I pilfer a knife from the kitchen. Nobody has discovered my treasures, or, at the least, disturbed them. But I cannot sustain this progress with so little sleep. During the day, I am chastised for falling asleep at my desk in the schoolroom, falling asleep at the needle when practising my stitches, falling asleep even at mealtime over our long-awaited weekly soup. And finally one night I fall asleep at my writing and am awoken with a clout about the head and a clump of crowing inmates surrounding the furious face of Matron, who hits me again and cries, 'Get up, girl!' I am made to stand facing the corner of the room while I listen to the others dress and wash their faces without a word and leave.

Once we are alone, Matron says in a quiet, cold voice I have not heard her use before, 'I fear the founder will send you to the workhouse for this.'

I turn from my corner and cry, 'Oh please, Matron. Not that, *please*!'

'No use in begging me. You should have thought ere committing the crime of theft. And from the founder himself? 'Tis unheard of. I know not *what* he will do.'

'Will you not help me, Matron?'

'I have tried, believe me. When you slept at your work, the other girls knew I would have beaten them about the ears for less, but I let you go with a harsh word. And there are things of which you know nothing. I have argued for you, more times than you could imagine. When I saw your hunger for learning, I went myself to the founder and asked him, Cannot the Price child have a little extra time for school work? My nephew I persuaded to give up his free time to help you, but the founder refused. No foundling would waste the precious God-given day on learning to write when there is real work to be done. He knows wastage of time is a sin and would not have a wretch wasting its time under his beneficence. But I asked again, another time, and another. The Price child is a prodigy, sir, and would perhaps do better in life with some learning to quiet her restless mind, but no. He is adamant and I cannot tell you how far I pushed his goodwill to me as his employee, to the point where he raised his voice to me and said that no girl ever possessed a brain for learning, no more than a bear that performs tricks, and that I must stop this minute from asking and asking for such a wretch or he would have to find another housekeeper. There, you had no idea of that, did you, girl? And now this? Oh, what is to be *done* with you?'

'Keep my secret, Matron. Please. Keep it our secret and do not tell the founder.'

'You are crack-brained! An inhabitant of Bedlam stands before me! Every orphan in this place knows about it by now. The founder would hear of it ere luncheon. And how long do you think my post here would be mine if he knew I sanctioned theft from his room and hid it from him? And a knife too? What havoc did you plan with that?'

'To sharpen my quill, that is all. I had no evil intent. Believe me, I beg you! Protect me!'

'No, you are discovered and that is the end of it. Get dressed now and prepare yourself for what is to come.'

Matron turns to leave the room but I touch her arm.

'Thank you for all the times you spoke for me.'

'You must stay here in this room until you are called for. Sit on your bed and *do not move one inch.*'

3

I dress slowly, wash my face with care and sit down as I am
told. My empty stomach grumbles. I wait all morning. These
will be my final hours beneath this roof. By this evening, I
may be in hell. Yet even this does not break me, nor bring
a tear to my eye. I consider this. I do not weep because I
have no fear. Something has changed in me since I taught
myself to write. This is my armour and protects me from
the blows life may deal me. As the sun reaches its noontime
zenith in the sky, Matron calls up the stairs for me to come.
As I descend, I hold my head up and prepare to meet the
founder's fury.

Matron awaits me in the hall.

'I have met with the founder this morning. He has considered your case. He has just this very minute summoned to
see you in his room. There are people there. But he says he
wishes to see you now.'

'What people?' I ask but she does not answer.

She grasps my hand and leads me briskly down to the court
room, where she knocks at the door. It opens immediately.

Once inside, I almost stumble with amazement. The walls
are lined with chairs, upon which are seated gentlemen and
ladies dressed in every type of finery, fluttering fans and
nodding and smiling. To one side waits a patient line of poor
women – I estimate twelve of them, no, thirteen – all holding
babies, some of whom sleep and some cry and the mothers
are shushing them, rocking them or simply staring into space
as if the baby makes no noise, as if they are deaf to it. All

eyes turn on me as I enter, then immediately dismiss me as
an object of no interest. Matron leads me to a corner, to await
the founder, who is perambulating along the chairs of the
quality and offering witty comments to make the ladies titter,
his wig powdered white for this formal occasion. The side-
board where he keeps his ink and quills has been cleared and
in their place are plates of food and jugs of wine, luxurious
food I have never set eyes upon before: tarts of all sorts and
sweetmeats and fruits; sea creatures – the like of which I have
only seen in books – are seated quite dead on ice alongside
peas and salad; and every kind of meat and poultry piled up
glistening in silver dishes. I am astounded to discover that
food comes in so many colours other than shades of brown
or grey. The appetising scents waft about the room, admixed
with pomade and powder. The quality do not regard the table
of treats, but many of the poor women ogle that food, even
while their babies squeal ignored in their arms.

The founder finishes his round and claps his hands, at
which all the poor women turn their heads to him expectantly.
The room hushes. The founder gestures to my schoolmaster
who stands beside the table. He fetches a cloth bag and hands
it to the founder, who takes it to the first poor woman in the
line. Holding her mewling babe on one arm, she reaches in
and takes something from inside. It is a ball, a black ball, and
she frowns. The founder shakes his head. There is an audible
sigh from the audience. The next woman is offered the bag,
and she too takes a ball, this time white. She smiles and looks
behind her at the next woman, who will not meet her face.
This one takes a ball and it too is white and they smile together
and pet their babies and jiggle them. Some of the quality clap
their hands together and nod approvingly. The next takes a
black ball, the next black and the next. Then appears a red
ball, and the mother looks quizzical, but no one answers her
questioning face. There are three more white balls and smiles,
one black and three red. The mothers with the black balls are

led across the room by a maidservant; dejected and wordless, they are shown out and the door closed behind them. The whites huddle and mutter to each other, joined in success. The red wait, separate, alert. The founder speaks to these.

'You are hereby upon the list of reserves. Leave the details of your place of abode with my secretary and he will be in contact with you in due course if a lot becomes available.'

Another maidservant is there to lead away the victors. Matron steps over to her and says, 'Can you administer the medical tests for these five yourself? I must stay here with the child,' to which the maidservant nods and leads them on. The founder continues his jolly banter with the guests, while Matron and I stand in the corner waiting.

I tug at her sleeve. 'What game was this?' I whisper hoarsely.

''Tis no game. 'Tis a ballot. These women sue to be admitted to the orphanage. Those with the white balls have won a place for their babies here.'

So this is how they come. An orphan lottery. Yet it strikes me that there are no babies living here. I am one of the youngest. The orphans range from four years or so to fourteen.

I ask Matron, 'Where do the babies go?'

'They are sent away to wet-nurses until they are four or so, then they are returned and live here till apprenticed.'

How very hard it must be for the children to leave their wet-nurse 'mothers', those women who have fed them from the breast and have filled their unformed early minds with every close memory one would call Mother, only to discover somewhat younger than I am now, that this is not their mother, not their home, and not their life. And they are to be sent away for good to an orphanage, their real home, where their desperate mothers left them years before, the true mothers, the ones they do not remember, abandoned for a second time. But this is the worst betrayal of the two, for this one they are old enough to understand, and they will always remember. I think of my mother and father, of how I have not one memory of them, of their faces, of their voices – and I decide it would be better to have a recollection of affection and to suffer the loss of it, than to have no remembrance of love at all.

I ask Matron, 'Why are the ladies and gentlemen here?'

'Child, such questions! They come to watch the spectacle, for entertainment. Now hush!'

As they leave the room, the chosen mothers hold their babies tight and pet them, gaze upon the unformed faces and fingers with blank eyes, and I feel a hollow of sadness at the thought of what these mothers are about to do, when they must give up their babes for good; a sorry scene played offstage, as the company may not find this part so very *entertaining*.

Once the show has concluded, the ladies and gentlemen applaud and gossip. Some stand and make their way to the refreshments, which they pass around and gobble politely from tiny china plates. The men all wear the same kind of frock-coat, stiff and full-skirted, yet each one is a different colour and pattern – one striped in pink satin, another encircled in red and gold embroidered apples – as if they engage in an elaborate competition of design on a theme. The ladies are far more varied – mantuas, sack dresses and circular hooped skirts – all with caps yet many are topped with fancy hats, some with long lace lappets hanging down their backs, all set about with jewels and spangled shoes. Several wear richly decorated filmy aprons, a kind of mockery of their high station in life, that they will never, ever be required to muddy that apron with something as vulgar as work. Some of the ladies wear a gauzy scarf at their neckline, while others seem to have tugged down their stays to show as much as is decent of their bosom. All is cotton, silk and velvet, no linen or wool as we orphans wear. Every person in the room rustles and creaks as they move. It is the sound of money.

'Price,' says the founder, scowling, and his stern tone shocks me back into recollection of my situation. 'Come with me.'

I glance at Matron, who nods, and I follow him to an old gentleman who is seated alone, holding a large glass of golden liquid. He wears a full-bottomed peruke wig with curls that smother his shoulders and looks mightily uncomfortable in it. As we approach he stands and reveals that he reaches only to the chest of the founder, who bends down to address him. 'This is the object of which I spoke. Dawnay Price.'

I recall my manners and sink, something I have practised since my first disastrous attempt. The gentleman finds his seat and says, 'Sit beside me, child.' The founder has moved on and a thousand questions race through my mind: is this gentleman to be the instrument of my punishment? Is he perhaps a magistrate to take me to the courthouse or to the pillory or even to the gallows? Or worse than all of these, worse even than death, is he from the workhouse?

'I did not mean to steal it, sir. I am no common thief. I meant only to educate myself. The good Lord gave us free will, did He not? And I used mine to better myself. Is this a crime, sir?'

The old gentleman smiles at me and his small dark eyes disappear in good-natured crinkles.

'You speak well, my dear. There is a niceness in your turn of phrase. I understand from your schoolmaster that your particular strength is mathematics, yet clearly your mind extends to the power of the word also. Is it truly so that you taught yourself to write alone, at night, by candlelight?'

'It is true, sir.'

'An extraordinary child, it is. Let me explain to you my presence here, as I perceive you are frightened of me, or what you believe I may represent. Yet calm yourself, as I represent no organisation but myself. My name is Markham Woods. I am a merchant, a trader in madeira and port and other beverages. I was raised in a modest home, left it at a young age and travelled the seas to make my fortune. And make it I did, returning home from the New World a rich man. I now inhabit a place on the margin of polite society. I am tolerated by the ladies and gentlemen you see here because I am so very wealthy. They cannot afford to ignore me, particularly when they fall into debt – as many of them do – and require my financial assistance. Thus, I am welcomed into this circle by my friend, Mr Beelsby – your founder here – yet, as you see, I sit alone, as the quality may acknowledge my right to be admitted, but they do not deign to speak with me.'

'I believe you have a rightful place here, sir. You have all the proper clothes and such. And your wig is remarkable.'

Mr Woods chuckles and replies, 'I do like you, Miss Price, very much! I am afraid I overheard a lady here remark that I found my hairpiece in a wig dip.'

My heart is at ease with this gentleman. Yet I still cannot quite believe my good fortune and continue to fear the founder's intent.

I ask, 'What is to become of me, sir?'

'I understand there will be some punishment for your actions: of removal of your tripe ration for one month. I believe a strong lass such as yourself will bear this well. However, your crime has alerted the founder to an understanding of precisely how keenly your ravenous mind cries out for learning, and that is to your great advantage. Some time ago, on my entry into society and acquaintance with your founder, I offered to sponsor one orphan from this establishment who he deemed worthy of a full education, so that the child might rise above its unfortunate origins and achieve something in this life of trials. I asked him to look out for such a child. He has shown me two boys so far who I felt had nothing special about them whatsoever and who did not inspire my mind or my pocket. But when he told me today about a girl who had stolen a quill and ink from his very desk and taught herself to write? Well, I knew this child was the one. He was not easily convinced that a girl should receive any further education at all, as it is common knowledge that a woman's mind is but a shadow of a man's. But I have travelled across the world, my dear, and seen many a strange thing perhaps unthought-of by your venerable founder, and I have somewhat differing views about what is common knowledge and what can and cannot be achieved in this life. I asked to meet you, and persuaded him with a generous donation to the asylum's funds that if I chose Miss Price, then Miss Price it would be.'

'Choose me for what end, sir?'

'Why, to afford you a decent education, my child. In the week to come, you will be introduced to a very dear friend of mine, a tutor somewhat down on his luck who also happens to be the most learned and intellectual man I have ever met. He will be your teacher in all things academic; he will visit you early every morning and will continue your mastery of writing, teach you the sciences, geography, history and Latin, as well as all manner of logic, rhetoric and ethics. We are going to train that extraordinary mind of yours, child, and thereby discover what treasures it contains.'

I am staring at Mr Woods. My mouth is dry and cannot move.

'Can you speak?' says he. 'Are you happy?'

'I believe you have seen into the heart of me, sir.'

'Not your heart, child. Your *mind*.'

4

My tutor's coat is shabby and his shoes are muddy. Matron tuts at him as she wipes the floor with a rag behind his steps.

'I do apologise, madam.'

Matron ignores him and I suspect that to be a tutor is not a very high station in life.

Once we are left alone in the front room, the one with the broad bow-window, I see with a gasp that the table is furnished with a stack of paper, several quills and enough ink that I believe my pen will never run dry. I have been plucked from obscurity by the hand of fate and placed at this table to learn my fill. To work no longer in secret, at night, by moonlight! I am eager to begin. My tutor bids me sit and I notice his cuffs are frayed.

I ask, 'Are you poor, sir?'

My tutor smiles. 'I knew your benefactor, Mr Woods, since boyhood, when we attended the same ridiculous day-school. We were beaten daily, you know, for forgetting a book, or sneezing, or blinking, or *breathing*. Mr Woods escaped it all at a young age by going off to sea, but I had not his courage or adventurous spirit and stayed to be beaten. I did learn a bit more than him though, so now we are in our proper places: he is a rich man with life-learning his legacy, and I am not a rich man yet my head is filled with bookish knowledge. Which is best, do you think?'

'To be rich *and* clever.'

He guffaws and holds out his hand, my first handshake.

'I am Mr Stephen Applebee. My wife is called Susan and

works as the cook at Mr Woods's house. Our son Owen serves in the army as an ensign, his commission having been bought for us by Mr Woods; Owen from a boy did insist on his intention to wear the preposterous red coat and would have run away to be a common soldier had we not had the good fortune to be aided by our generous friend. I am a master at a boys' school in Marylebone at which I teach Latin, algebra, mathematics and the use of the globes. I walk over there four afternoons a week and teach from two till five. It does not pay exceedingly well. Thus, I supplement it with tutelage of which you are one of my charges.'

'You do talk a lot.'

'I do, I do. But that is a good thing, for a tutor, I think, don't you? You would not be too impressed if I stood silently and glared at you.'

'That is true. And you do own more knowledge than me and have more experience of thinking. Therefore, it will be good for me to listen to you.'

'Thank you for that condescension, Dawnay.'

He is a thin man, with dark shadows beneath his eyes. His wig is tidy, though, and his cravat has such neat stitching on it. I think his wife Susan must look after him very well and that is why he possesses such a jovial turn. I wonder if they miss the company of their son and that is what makes his wide brown eyes seem melancholy.

'Has your son killed any foreigners?'

'I can see one must be quick-witted with you. You are always listening, aren't you? Even when it seems you are bored. My son was like you, but he squandered it all by joining those infernal idiots in the army. He had a nomadic soul, you see, which could not be cured by reading to him from *The Arabian Nights* each bedtime, as I hoped. No, he has not killed any foreigners, as he has not left the British Isles as yet. He very much hopes for a war some time soon, and I very much hope we will never have another.'

'What means nomadic?'

'A nomad is one who wishes to roam about from place to place.'

'I am that, sir. At night, I sometimes lean from the window in the dormitory to see further, but I can only see the lamp before the last house in this street. I would very much like to walk beyond it one day.'

'You mean, you have never seen the end of this street?'

'No, sir. I have not left the orphanage since I was brought here. I would like to see St Giles.'

'You would not like it, my dear, if you did. I mean to say, St Giles is a carbuncle. But there are other parts of London – oh, visions to behold!'

I sit up straight and clasp my hands, my heart soaring at the thought of it, to see London; to pass through these walls; to be free. 'From my window I often think I should dearly love to sprout wings and rise above the rooftops and see beyond the buildings, the city and the river. I should like to see whence the moon rises. I want to go where the sun sets.'

My tutor looks at me for some moments, curiously. 'Do you get sick in hackney coaches?'

'I do not believe so, sir, but in truth I do not have enough experience of them to know.'

'Then come, child. I am sure Mr Woods would not object to funding a little trip. Our first lesson will be conducted in a mobile fashion. Thus, we take to the streets.'

'Where are we going, sir?'

'The marvellous Menagerie!' he cries with a flourish and stands.

I have no clue as to what a menagerie may be, but the word fills me with the spirit of enquiry.

London, in all its variety, flows past our carriage. It is a hot summer day and the streets stink to high heaven. As the images fleet past my eyes, dim memories of my time before the orphanage gather in my mind: running along the road behind my brother, dodging down an alley – that is all I can recall. Today I see ox-waggons and herds of sheep. Chair-men trotting through the traffic shouting, 'By your leave, sir,' as they elbow and shove their way, pushing unaware pedestrians into the walls and puddles as they rush on. A polluted channel runs down the middle of the road and this emits the worst stench of all, fetid and rotten. Another memory of my brother: the two of us sitting on a wall, a fancy gentleman walks beneath us in the street, his sword hanging from his hip swaying as he strides, and we throw bits of mouldy apple into his wig as he passes and we hoot with laughter. Then the memory is gone again.

'The streets spark pictures in my mind!' I tell Mr Applebee.

'What kind of pictures?'

'Of my brother.'

'Where is he now?'

'Pressed. Gone, who knows where. Most likely dead.'

'No, not dead.'

'How do you know that?'

'If he be only half as keen as you, he'll have talked his way out of any trouble.'

The coach slows and I think of my brother – perchance alive at sea – and am happy. We come almost to a stop as we approach a massive waggon pulled ponderously by eight horses. It is so broad it takes up almost the entire thoroughfare. No carriage can get past it.

Says Mr Applebee, 'How many hooves?'

'Thirty-two, of course.' And my tutor smiles, pleased with me, and I discover I am thrilled with his approbation. I have just met this man with the threadbare coat, and yet already I find I am so very keen to impress him.

'Come, we will be stuck here for centuries. Let us walk the last stretch.' Mr Applebee pays the driver and we dismount.

At the same moment, we see a very well-dressed young

man alight from a chair and take a step on to the path beside us. There his satin shoe finds a loose stone and rank black water shoots from beneath it all the way up his white stockings in a scummy splash. He cries out in disgust and looks about him, as if someone nearby is to blame, not Providence.

'A beau-trap,' Mr Applebee smirks. 'One of the joys of a-walking the streets of London: watching the quality grapple with our domain.'

The ways are crowded here by the river, almost as busy as the waterway itself, jostling boats filling its choppy waters with oars and scullers and cutters, the watermen shouting their prices to the customers on the shore, calling them over for a ride across the dirty old river. We walk past countless women sitting in chairs in the streets beside their front doors – engaging in gossip and complaints – watching the people, eyeing us as we walk by. A milkmaid has stopped at a house, her pails on a yoke about her shoulders, chalking up debts on a customer's doorpost. So Matron was mistaken, think I: a milkmaid does need to write. Other street vendors carry their food atop their heads, shouting and singing their wares: ox cheeks, live lobsters and gingerbread – and my stomach yearns for them. Porters stride everywhere wearing big pewter badges, carrying goods of all sorts through the arteries of London. A constant barrage of sound assaults the ears, from the road and the river packed with vehicles, the street musicians – here bagpipes, there a trumpet – the knife grinders and stonemasons, the oxen bellowing, the horses whinnying and, above it all, the many hundreds and thousands of people everywhere raising each voice to be heard above the din, as if to say, Here I am, this is my business and I will see it done, by your leave! I see a fat man drag off his sweaty wig and thrust it in his pocket, then he trips over a dead cat and the sweat flies from his shaved head in fat droplets. We swim through a watercourse of humanity, of all shapes and types, from dukes to beggars. All life and all death are here.

'I shall have that,' says Mr Applebee. He scoops up the dead cat and, removing a cloth bag from his pocket, stuffs the mangy corpse inside.

'What will you do with it?' I cry.

'I will gain entry.'

'To where?'

'To the Tower of London!' announces Mr Applebee and I look up to see an imposing building frowning down at me: a castle rising from the river, proud in its turrets and round-houses and narrow-windowed eyes. My sense had been so busy with the life of the street I had barely looked above my cap for many steps and had not seen the Tower as we approached. My tutor leads me through the gates and approaches a gatekeeper; he opens his sack and the keeper nods. The latter pulls out the dead cat and gives it to a lad, who runs round the side of the building, through a side gate and into a garden beyond. We follow him and find ourselves shuffling behind a crowd of onlookers filing in before us through the narrow gate. The smell beyond is immediate and as hard as a stone wall. A stench of old meat and something else, something alien to me, something pungent and rank. Then a sound – the most extraordinary sound, the like of which is unheard of in my life and so strange to my ears I almost run and hide from it, so great is my natural fear and revulsion of it. A roaring, a kind of shouting but from the belly not the throat, bawling in anger and fierce rage, a fuming yet empty kind of a sound, inhuman, unknown.

'The Menagerie,' Mr Applebee whispers by my ear with ceremony and we leave the garden to enter a row of cages in which sit, stand or pace squarely a collection of beasts and birds so outlandish, so utterly foreign that they may as well have leapt from the pages of a storybook. Their animal move-ments are uncanny and vital and to see them alerts my senses to the very life in me. The monstrous noise comes again and I spot its maker. I recognise the beast from my schoolroom picture books. I thought once that to read and write could teach you the world, yet at this moment I appreciate for the first time that one must seek out the world, in order to truly know it. 'Marco, the lion. And this one is Caesar,' says my tutor and we stand before the cages of the two lions. Caesar sleeps and Marco is awake and alert, padding the four steps from one end of his cage to the other, glaring at us in silent fury, his shaggy head as wide as a door, thick tail thrashing and prominent ribs jutting from his pale brown flank. Behind him, the boy we saw earlier opens a hatchway into the cage and tosses in our poor dead cat. Marco sets about it and after some grisly minutes the diminutive corpse is no more. I am glad to see him eat. He looks hungered.

Says Mr Applebee, 'They are of the same family, you know. The lion and the cat. Both feline.'

'Cats are friendlier.'

'True. Lions are to cats what wolves are to dogs.'

'Wild and tame?' I ask.

'Precisely. Here are more felines: the tiger, the leopard and the panther.'

The next three cages contain the variations upon the theme of cat: stripes, spots and full black; the tiger, heavyset and broad like a fighter, sleeps with one eye flickering open every time a child cries out; the other two are lean and muscular, watchful and restless. Next we see an eagle tied by thongs to its beam; a porcupine snuffling, its quills quivering on its back as it shuffles about its pen; a vulture, its ugly bare head sleeping in the sunshine, dreaming of carcasses no doubt. I know all their names as there is an animal A through to Z in one of my schoolroom books and vulture is V, lion is L, even porcupine is P. There are monkeys for M in the book – my favourite, as they are naughty in stories. They always looked to me like hairy people, cheeky people, with no sense of decorum.

Say I, 'Are there no monkeys?'

'There was an ape here the last I knew. It must have died or been sold on.'

'I should very much like to see a monkey one day.'

'Noted,' says my tutor.

And then it is time to go. I wish to stay for hours but I follow him and, in truth, I am glad to leave the smell behind me. All the way back I think on the eyes of the wakeful animals, who rarely meet your glance, but if one does, it leaves you with the burning message: *I am captive, but you are free to go.* Not me: my chain is but a little longer than yours, bound as I am by my poverty and my youth, nameless and friendless as I have been. Yet I know Mr Woods and Mr Applebee now and they have slackened my rope and given me a taste of the world beyond my fence. And I will have more of it, *mark my words*.

5

Thus I begin my education. Every morning is spent at the table by the bow-window, where we grapple with mathematics and the English language primarily, with a little about the natural world and some logic when we can. The afternoons are spent with Matron; the reason being, when I returned from the Menagerie that day, I was set upon by some other inmates for my special treatment, who gave me very rough words and bid me begone. They put upon me and used me very ill, pulled me by the nose and struck at me. Thereafter, I remain with Matron, she my protector and I her pet.

The founder insists I must continue to learn the skills of housekeeping, as, despite my education, I may well attract a husband one day or, if not, require such skills to earn my keep. So Matron keeps me with her each afternoon and we go through the playact of learning domestic service, yet she sometimes turns to me and pinches my cheek saying, 'You'll not need this, eh, my clever chick? You'll be no oyster-wench. You will make your way in the world and be done for very nicely.'

I begin my forays into that world in my first geography lesson. One day Mr Applebee rolls out a map for me to peruse. It contains all the known continents and seas. There is an area in the Southern Ocean where the vague outline of a land mass is painted but not completed. Beside it in elaborate script is written the phrase: *Terra Incognita*.

'What does it mean?'

'It means "unknown land". Mapmakers use this phrase when they do not know what lies beyond.'

'Beyond where?'

'Beyond here,' and he points to the boundary, surrounding which is a decorated border, yet no more land or sea.

'What is beyond the edge of the map?'

'Ah, now that is the mystery. It is believed there lies the Great Southern Continent, yet no one has discovered it thus far.'

'Will it be found one day? Will the mystery be solved?'

'Man is a celebrated explorer and he will answer it one day.'

Geography becomes my favoured subject and I pester my tutor to unfurl the map for me often. My other favourite pastime in lessons is to ask my tutor for puzzles. He gives me problems in geometry or a conundrum in logic and has learned to give me the time to complete it. At first, he would wait a little, then ask if I required assistance, then begin to tell me the solution and make me fume so hotly I would go red in the face and more than once answered back in anger, though swiftly apologised, which he graciously accepted. Now he understands that it may take me many minutes, or a half-hour, or more, yet once I take my first step upon the puzzle I will not descend till I scale it myself. I work through it methodically, step by step, yet once in a while there is a moment when I simply see the solution laid before me, complete, as if I had lifted into the air like a bird and looked down upon the earth and saw the pattern of the maze as God would see it. Those days are rare at first, yet as we work on puzzles more and more, these moments increase. And it is a tremendous sense of accomplishment when the answer reveals itself to me. I have taken on the problem and I have conquered it.

After some months of our studies, Mr Applebee informs me we are to walk to Bloomsbury, where we will visit the home of my benefactor, Mr Markham Woods.

'You have been invited for luncheon to be had in the kitchen.

Thereafter, upstairs for a conference with Mr Woods. He wishes to discern your progress, so you must speak up and be heard, or Mr Woods will believe I have been slack and taught you nonsense. Will you speak up, Dawnay?'

'If I can take some meat home for the other children, or some other food, I will say whatever you like.'

'Will you indeed! Well, we shall see about that. Perhaps something can be arranged,' says Mr Applebee, and I am happy that I can offer some benefit to the others here, though they despise me in their jealousy. I do not hate them, as I see them like myself as the caged animals in the Tower, pacing their small lot. I have been given the promise of a key, and I would hate myself too for such a gift. I cannot give them my good fortune, but I can perhaps use it to ease their empty bellies.

As we leave the orphanage, my tutor informs me: 'Your institution is on the better edge of the hole that is the parish of St Giles. Walk further that way and you will find one of the worst areas of the country, let alone London. A cesspit of humanity and degradation. Here we are on the boundaries of a quality area, within which your benefactor lives in Bloomsbury Square. Thus poverty and wealth are uncomfortable bedfellows in this city.'

Some way towards my benefactor's house, we come across a spectacle in the street. A man has been put in the pillory and a crowd are gathering to throw missiles at him. The crowd is serviced by a woman selling oranges, a ballad singer screeching tunelessly and two boy pickpockets doing a good trade at the back. My tutor tries to hurry me along, but I overhear a woman in the crowd call out, 'What are you in for?'

The man wears a tidy wig, a clean shirt and a stock tie. He looks rather affluent to be a criminal. 'I am a publisher,' he shouts. 'My only crime is that I printed an essay on how the Church does not help the poor.'

A cheer goes up, a hat is passed round and, rather than throw rotten food and stones at the man, a small collection of coins is made and drink given him.

'A publisher is a man who prints words?' I ask my tutor.

'Yes, it is. A writer writes the words, then the publisher arranges them in print and then books are made.'

'Does this happy event occur with all publishers punished so?'

'Certainly not. Only last month I saw another publisher near here, who had published ideas against the King, stoned almost to death. It is illegal to throw stones at the pillory, but who is there to stop it?'

We walk on and I wonder at a world where words can be so dangerous. We reach Bloomsbury Square and a tall, picturesque house with a total of thirteen windows – one row of three, then two of four and at the top there are two more. We go around the side and enter a courtyard through a gate. We cross the yard to a brick outhouse and my tutor knocks gently on the door. It is opened by a woman slender of face and figure in a plain gown and apron. Tendrils of auburn hair peep from a mob cap topped with a black bow, which is prettier than Matron's·cap. Her nose and cheeks are scattered with freckles.

'You remember that my wife is Mr Woods's cook. Well, here she is, child. You may call her Mrs Applebee.'

'She may call me Susan and be done with it,' says Mrs Applebee, and sees us in. The kitchen is roomy with red-brick walls and a lovely fire, which I run to. I can never resist a fire, even in summer. The room is dominated by a broad table, upon which sits a variety of vegetables and fruit of assorted colours in wooden bowls, many of which I have never seen and could not name. The range looks enormous to me, with a considerable roasting spit and beneath it a metal plate to catch dripping. Beside it there is a separate bread oven, from which Mrs Applebee removes a just-baked loaf and places it on the table. On every wall are shelves stacked with pots, jugs, mugs and plate racks, filled with pewter and copper platters, while there are silver dishes displayed in a glass-fronted cabinet. From the ceiling on hooks hang meat and game to keep them safe from vermin. It is a kitchen from the realms of angels and I stare open-mouthed at all its glories.

I see Mr Applebee give his wife a quick kiss on the cheek and she smiles with her eyes. Then she turns and squints at me.

'They don't feed them much there, do they?' says she. 'This one is as skinny as a pipe, and she favoured too. Come now, sit and eat.'

Mrs Applebee brings me pigeon pie and potatoes in a rich dark gravy, with a pile of hot greens beside it that look for all the world like miniature trees. Hot food never graces our dishes at the asylum, only soup and tripe that are barely warm by the time they reach our mouths. The comfort induced by hot meat, hot vegetables and hot gravy and the taste of more than one distinct flavour in the mouth at once is delectable. I eat so fast I burn my tongue and nearly gag.

'She will be sick!' cries Mr Applebee.

'Do slow down, child,' says his wife. 'There is no hurry to be had. You can take your time with it. She has never seen food like it, Stephen, I warrant. Poor lamb.'

After, I am given a bowl of a creamy mixture, yellow and steaming hot; I am told it is called rice custard and it is the food they must serve in paradise, so delicious is it and soft in the mouth.

'I was to ask for meat for the other orphans. But I think they would rather have sugary matter, as we never do have it, except a kind of fruit cake at Christmas time, only once a year, you see. Can I take some for them? Please, Mrs Applebee?'

'What's this?' she says, and her husband has quiet words with her as I gobble down every scrap from my plate and use my fingers to wipe up the last vestiges of sweetness.

'A kind child it is,' says Mrs Applebee and sits beside me on the bench. 'But food for a score of children would be immediately missed here, my dear. I would be rightly accused of stealing and be sent away. You know this is true, Stephen. I am sorry, my dear. But I cannot give you food to take for the others.'

Say I, 'Matron says orphans' legs bow naturally, that their teeth fall out because they talk too much. But I have learned from Mr Applebee that plants need light to make their food and soil and water to grow, and I think that children need their own medium similarly, that bread and cheese is not enough to make a child grow straight with strong teeth. And I think our simple food is making us ill. Mr Applebee agrees with me, is that not right, sir?'

'It is possible, Dawnay. There is no proof for it. It is most likely an imbalance in the four humours within your bodies, and nothing to do with food. We would have to test it, by experiment. Let us think on it, but now we must go, as Mr Woods awaits you.'

We leave the kitchen and cross the yard to a back door into the house, whereupon we wipe our feet carefully on the mat, proceed along an airy corridor to the front hallway and then ascend the main staircase. The walls are the light blue of spring sky, ornamented with the plaster heads of important men on plinths surrounded by garlands. I am led upstairs to the withdrawing room. A quick knock, and then another, is greeted with silence, so after a wait of some time, my tutor chooses to enter in any case. It is a room as spacious in size as the court room at the asylum, and yet its soft furnishings, canvases of ships and knick-knacks of china and carved wood serve to create a homely and welcoming atmosphere. The walls are covered with a deep red swirling silk, the fire warms every corner and three squat cabinets, one placed against each wall, all have circular designs on each door like eyes inlaid with subtle wooden shades of beige and copper and long legs that curve outwards, all of which serve to make them appear like three friendly toads waiting to greet me. There is nothing of grandeur here and everything of comfort and ease.

We find Mr Woods asleep, propped up in the corner of a high-sided settee. My tutor nudges his employer's shoulder, warily at first, then more roughly, and speaks into his ear, 'Wake up, man! The child is here.'

Mr Woods starts up and cries, 'I think never to exceed the bounds of moderation more!', his wig askew and his eyes wet with emotion. Mr Applebee helps him compose himself and then my benefactor looks upon me.

'Why, it is Dawnay Price!' He bids me sit opposite him upon a stool embroidered with an exotic boat. 'So here we are, in my home. What do you make of it, Dawnay? Is it not a nice house?'

'Very nice, sir. Full of ornament and colour. And you have the best cook in London, to be sure.'

'Ah, you have eaten? Good, good. That old rogue Beelsby . . .'

'Sir?' questions my tutor and clears his throat as if needing drink.

'Yes, yes, Stephen. Of course. Dawnay, your distinguished founder has your best interests at heart, I am sure – in keeping you half starved, the dog-hearted intermeddler – but never mind it, for you are to come each sennight here and eat a good luncheon with Susan. We shall have you fat in no time. Now, what have you been learning, child? What has this old friend of mine here been teaching you? Anything, anything at all?'

'I know all my letters and grammar. And numbers, sir, with addition, subtraction, multiplication and division of them.'

'Excellent!' says my benefactor. 'With clever Stephen here as your guide, you will stick to your course and not be put out of your latitude by contrary winds. What else have you learned?'

'A little geography where we study a map of the known world. And natural philosophy too, sir. Namely, some of the science of plants and how they grow. In fact, there is an experiment we wish to carry out, with your permission.'

'And what is this, now?' he asks my tutor, who is glaring at me.

Say I, 'Where one tests an idea, to see if it be true. We think the children grow crooked at our asylum as they eat the wrong food. But if we could provide fruit and vegetable matter, some meat and sugar, from your kitchen, each week, we could try it, and see if the children improve. A worthy test, wouldn't you say, sir?'

Mr Woods thinks on it, then says, 'So I am to feed all the wretches now, is that it?'

'In the interests of science?' adds my tutor quietly, picking at his nails, and I watch my benefactor's frown consider it and hold my breath. My mind wishes to test our hypothesis, but my forsaken heart desires to use this food to win friends.

'We shall see, we shall see. I suppose if I spent less on port and more on foundlings' suppers, I would find my way to heaven more surely. And after last night's excesses, Stephen, I simply must refrain. I must change my ways. I will, old friend, I will.'

'As you say, moderation is the key, Markham.'

'Yes, yes,' says Mr Woods, swabbing his brow with his kerchief and standing up. 'Come, child. Speaking of science, I have something of much interest to show you. It is in the next room. A room, my dear, filled with *wonderful things*.'

I follow with inquisitiveness, my tutor behind me. Mr Woods opens a double door through to a capacious room with a bright white ceiling decorated with the plasterwork shapes of musical instruments, sheets of notation, books and quills. Yet the room itself is darkened by the collection of an inordinate number of objects displayed on shelves almost obscuring all four olive-green walls, with tables in the centre of the room

also covered with artefacts in glass display cases and, beside
them, two chests filled with tiny drawers, brass panels fronting
each one with a card and neat handwriting upon it, naming
its contents.

Says my benefactor in a grand voice, 'This is my Cabinet
of Curiosities! Or at least, it began as a cabinet. And now, as
you can see, it has taken over what was the saloon. I have
even sold the spinet to make room for it all! I collected many
of these objects on my travels, Dawnay, and brought them
back for fun. Yet Stephen here taught me the value of such
curios and encouraged me to use my fortune to seek out
more. Now I am older and too stout for adventures – other
than the drinking kind – all right, Stephen! I know! But the
child must be aware of such things as liquor? She is not, you
say? Ah, well, protect the innocent, of course. Now, where
was I? Yes, the age of adventure is over for me, but not my
curiosity. So these days I pay young men to travel for me and
bring back these odds and ends. And now, I can finally make
use of them, as you are to come here with your tutor each
week and study them all, make a list of them and – well, you
know, catalogue them for posterity and the good of your own
learning. You have nothing to say, my dear?'

But I have stopped listening. I am stepping about the room
in shock, my eyes dry with astonishment at the jostling shapes
before me – skeletons and horns, shells and dried beans,
carvings and sculptures, brass instruments and engraved silver
objects – all of them exotic and not at all English, not at all
of my experience, but all of them outlandish and queer and
remarkable. There are beautiful pebbles patterned and swirled
in rainbow colours, and whorled shapes from a thumb's breadth
to a dinner-plate's size, laid in long lines, beside strange stone-
like plants in twisted forms, these by labels reading *Minerals,
Fossils, Corals*; glass containers with tiny creatures or grey
bodily parts suspended in liquid of yellow and orange; dozens
of visitors' cards have been turned up at each edge and filled

with brown seeds in this one, red nuts in another; a frame criss-crossed with partitions, each neat triangle filled with piles of minute shells in purple, black, green and shiny white; here a small table topped with a glass jar turned upside down, labelled a *Double-Barrel Air Pump* and there a dried-out wedge shape labelled *Shark's Fin*, beneath it a tray of sharp teeth-like objects named *Tongue-Stones: the Petrified Tongues of Sea-Monsters*; a jar with a cork stopper houses a miniature reptile, mouth open as if surprised at the winglike structures on its back, called *Baby Dragon Preserved in Spirits*; beside it, laid out on a desk, a spiralled tusk, as long as the desk itself, its label declaring it a *Unicorn Horn*; and a hefty book opened at a page headed *A Table of Antiquities*, with line drawings of hairy ape-like men with big pot bellies and women with long ears and fish tails; and more, more, a myriad of objects of peculiar spectacle.

The world has come here, to this room. And I will study it and know it. These objects that have been brought from so far, one day will lead me away beyond them, to the realms whence they came. For my mind is opened this day, to the richness of this globe, this life, to the spaces beyond the map. And nothing will contain my capacity for wonderment.

6

The year is 1740, I am presumed to be circa eight years of age and winter is here. It brings the most chilling cold anyone can recall, where we girls put on petticoats and stockings abed to prevent our shivering the whole night. One morning, we wake and find the chamber pots frozen. Once downstairs, my tutor and I come to our classroom to find the ink solid ice in the glass on the standish. He tells me, 'The Thames River is frozen too and presently they hold a frost fair on the ice. Let us wrap ourselves up and go there. We shall tread in the footsteps of King Henry VIII and Queen Bess, who travelled and sported upon the frozen Thames in their own times.'

Outside, the cold seizes me like a footpad, while the fog that wraps up London almost entirely in these months hangs lowly, thick and white about us, and I almost step into a pile of fresh horse dung shoved up against our wall, keeping our lead pipes warm and free from cracks. We travel down to the river by coach, at a snail's pace through the murk. We crawl through Covent Garden, where I see looming from the fog towards us the faces of many handsome women with much colour upon their cheeks and lips, joking and japing in the street in gaudy clothes. They are brighter and louder than the quality ladies I saw at the orphanage lottery, and I ponder at their being out on such a bitter day, and not in their houses beside a fire. Before long, the coach stops alongside the Thames, and where we alight, the usual rumpus of riverside life is strangely quiet this day. On the banks lie the land-bound wherries and in a few sit watermen with oars across their knees as if for warmth, their caps out for begging, as the river disabled by ice must have stopped their trade and their customary raucous shouting also.

Beyond them, the white-frosted river stretches easterly and my tutor guides me down to it. I have never stepped on frozen water and I ask, 'Is it safe? Will it not crack and swallow us up?'

'They say it is eighteen inches thick here, so there is nothing to fear.' He takes my hand and we step towards two men who take a coin from Mr Applebee as we pass into the fair proper.

Before us, the river teems with life and pleasing amusements. Tents have been slung up from bank to bank, ramshackle affairs of canvas and poles at chaotic angles, housing all manner of stalls, shops and entertainments. There are fairground booths, puppet shows and roundabouts; two men are engaged in a boxing competition, beside a whole ox being roasted and food stalls selling nuts, puddings, spiced buns, sausages and – my favourite – hot pies. My tutor secures his place in my heart by buying me one, warm and meaty and delicious. We eat and wander, watching the fair folk and their antics. There are many rowdy types gulping from mugs of steaming liquid and slipping on the ice, spilling their drinks and protesting, while young boys skid past them at great speed, running and sliding on the ice for fun. We pass by a strolling woman and her daughter carrying warm apples on their heads in baskets, calling their wares in duet, the sweet scent drifting like blossom in the cold air, soon mingling with the warmer tones of hot tea, coffee and chocolate from further stalls. We see a group of acrobats tumbling and a rope strung up between two poles along which a man treads without shoes, surely a trick of the eye, but no, he truly can walk upon it. There are printers and their presses selling slips of paper adorned with verses and the customer's name, as a memento of this extraordinary occasion of a frost fair, not seen on this river for twenty years or so. My tutor leads me in a leisurely manner, yet with a purpose, as he knows of one particular tent he wishes to show me.

'Prepare yourself, Dawnay, for now we are to see an unfamiliar creature. One that has fascinated you from an early age, I think.'

We stop in front of a tent with its flap closed. Before it stands a sign upon which are painted these words: *The Remarkable Beast of Africa*. My tutor pays a man who pulls back the flap and says, 'It is quite safe, girl. He is tethered.' As we enter, it takes our eyes a short time to adjust to the low light, and in the dimness a shape moves and I jump in fear. The shape sits down. It is thickly furred almost all over, dark and crooked, an animal surely, yet has the look of a small person. He has a collar around his neck, from which a leather lead is attached to a heavy chain, which in turn is bound around a broad beam in the back of the tent, so that he cannot move far, or escape, rampage and cause havoc. Yet he seems calm and quiet. He makes no noise. Before him on the ground are things for him to play with: a ball, a bone and a cup of water. He drinks from this cup, his upper lip protruding as if to help the liquid in. His feet curl round objects like a second set of hands; most useful, I think. His arms are broad and stocky; he sits on his rear with knees bent. His body is covered in shaggy, dark and dusky hair, while his face is paler and free from hair, as are the palms of the hands and soles of the feet. He picks up the bone and bares his teeth to give a brief gnaw. The teeth are sizeable, and two are pointed and look exceedingly sharp. I take a step back. His mood is peaceful, yet those teeth remind me that he is a beast after all. He puts down the bone and sits very still, in repose.

'What is it, Dawnay?' asks my tutor in a low voice. 'Can you surmise it?'

I answer in a reverential whisper, 'It is a chimpanzee.'

His face is quite like a person's, resembling an old man with large ears, a flat nose and deep wrinkles beneath the eyes, which are round, brown and expressive. When he glances from side to side, focuses on objects and people about him, I cannot help but wonder what he is thinking. And the moment when he looks at me, looks at my eyes for some time, I am thrilled by it and dare not move. I do believe there is a mind there that comprehends me, which is not idiotic or empty; which senses me as another animal, not simply an entertainment or potential tormentor. It is different from looking at a dog or a cat in the street, who are alien to us, as friendly as they may seem. They do not have human eyes, but canine or feline, and they think on meat and the tearing of it, or on running and catching, growling or purring. They are animals truly, as are the big cats and the birds I saw in the Menagerie. This creature seems to me utterly different from them, an intelligence in its movements and largely in its eyes which are undeniably kin to humans, to all of us, to me.

That day, my tutor and I lunch at my benefactor's and afterwards repair to the curiosities room – where we spend the afternoon each time we visit his house – and Mr Applebee reads to me articles of science and novelty from such learned journals as the *Gentleman's Magazine*; after which we study the artefacts, discuss their origins, make links between them, read of them, sketch them and write about them. This afternoon, I draw the chimpanzee I saw in all the detail I can remember. But I have trouble with its eyes and I cannot perfect it.

Seeing my trouble, Mr Applebee says to me, 'Copy mine. They are quite similar,' and he is correct. They are the same shape and even a similar colour, a kind of liquid brown. When I am done with my drawing of the animal I am pleased with it, I have captured something of it and we look at its likeness and are both quiet, both pondering.

Say I, 'Is it a joke by God?'

'What do you mean, child?'

'The chimpanzee. A kind of jest that God has made, which makes the creature so closely resemble us.'

'One or two learned thinkers have said that they are related to us in some way. A poet, Fenton, wrote not so many years ago these lines:

Foes to the tribe from which they trace their clan
As monkeys draw their pedigree from man.'

'Do you believe this to be true? That monkeys are our cousins?'

I want to giggle at such a picture – myself with a tail, hanging from a branch, playing with my monkey family – but my tutor's face is very serious and his hushed tones tell me this is not amusing. Then a question arises in my mind.

'But it cannot be that way, sir. For the Bible does not tell us so. The story of Creation says the Lord made every beast of the earth first and then made man afterwards: *in the image of God created He him.*'

Mr Applebee picks up a round, shell-like stone. 'As a boy, I had an aunt who lived by the sea in the west. Charmouth Bay it was, and its beach was full of these things. I would collect them and stow them in my pockets. I have told you before its name.'

'Ammonite.'

'Yes, and that it is a kind of sea creature. I told you it lived a long time ago. But that it does not live now.'

'Yes, sir.'

'There are men, Dawnay, who spend all their time looking for these curiosities. You recall the magazine article I showed you last week, wherein the capacity of Noah's Ark was minutely considered? There are many such puzzles and puzzlers seeking answers to them. Some of these men are of the Church, men of God if you will. They are looking for evidence on the earth of the Creation story. They look at ancient rocks and search underground for relics of those days. Some have found bones, giant bones, a hundred times bigger than the fossils we have in this room, a thousand times. Leg bones and beaks and spines, longer than rooms. Much larger than the elephant or even the whale. Where are they, these big-boned monsters? Are they hiding in dense jungles on islands we have not yet discovered, like that mysterious isle of *The Tempest*? Or, as some think, did they once live on the earth, yet from some unknown catastrophe they all died and did not procreate more, to die out completely and never again live?

'Look at this little fossil; a likeable yet humble gift from our Lord. But what, in fact, is it? Some people say that they are a strange type of animal that once lived underground. Others believe there was a race of stone creatures who walked the earth, perhaps the most peculiar theory. Men of God like to think that the evidence of bones in rocks points directly to the Deluge, the great flood that destroyed all corrupt creatures and people and only the righteous survived. Some of these men travel across the globe looking for these bones. But not everyone thinks they were once living creatures. Some say the rock itself makes them, that they are moulded by stone in the forms of creatures, by accident and luck. Just a whim of nature.'

'That is silly.'

My tutor smiles.

I go on, 'Good sense argues against it. These are clearly, most clearly, real creatures. That is, they once lived and now live no more. They were caught in the rock somehow, I do not pretend to understand how. But they were. I know it.'

'How do you know it?'

'Because my experience tells me so. When there are muddy puddles in the street and the sun shines on them, the water dries up and the mud goes hard. Perhaps that is what happened here. The rock is mud from the past, which was once wet. The sea flowed through it or over it perhaps, and then the sea dried up, or flowed another way.'

'Why would it do that?'

I reason it. 'The weather? Perhaps it was very hot. Or very cold. The sea froze, like the Thames. It froze and melted and moved itself in the process. Or it dried up in the heat.'

'Listen. There was an extraordinary man called Leonardo da Vinci, who lived in Italy around three hundred years ago. He became an eminent artist and inventor. As a young man he was engaged in the construction of canals and often dug up fossils of sea life, shellfish and suchlike as you see here. He believed they must have been carried inland by the sea, that perhaps the earth itself rose. We see this today in earth-quakes, the ground cracks and sometimes moves upwards hundreds of feet. If there were an earthquake under the sea, the earth would rise, the sea left below, and the sea creatures left in the mud would over time turn to stone.'

'But dead things rot away to nothing, especially when wet. I have seen this in the kitchen and in the rubbish heaps.'

'Clever girl. Yes, Leonardo thought of this too. And he speculated that the creatures decayed and left hollows in the rock. Later new mud flowed into these holes and filled them like a clay mould. Over time, these new mud shapes turned to rocks and left us with fossils.'

It is as if a cog has clicked into place inside my mind. 'That is it. That is the reason. It is obvious.'

He laughs. I think he laughs at me and I blush hotly. 'Do not mock me, sir. I am but a child trying to explain God's work.'

'I do not mock you, Dawnay,' he says, then wipes his hand over his eyes and stands up. 'Yes, you are a child. A very ingenious child, but still only young. And what I am telling you should not be spoken of. I have said too much already.'

'Indeed not, sir. You have not said enough. For now I wonder, why are there fossils of creatures who live no longer? Why were they not saved by the Ark? These giant creatures you speak of, these unicorns, dragons we have here in jars, these monsters. Perchance they were evil. Yet petty shellfish? Why were they not saved? And the old sinners, the men and women who were drowned in the Flood. Why have we not found their bones in the rock? Where are they?'

But my tutor is shaking his head.

I whisper, 'Are these *dangerous* words, sir?'

'They are, Dawnay. And you must not repeat them in company. You and I are safe to discuss such matters here, in this room, but nowhere else.'

'Or we will be put in the pillory and stoned?'

My tutor sighs and tips his head back, thinking of his next words.

'You see, there is a dangerous idea behind it, an idea that would change everything if taken as truth: *that the Bible may not be strictly true in every detail.* And the Church is very powerful in our society, child, and will not brook such blasphemous dissent. People have hanged for it, or worse.'

I feel the rope around my neck. But still I yearn to know more, to ask questions.

'*I will not tell a soul, sir.* Not a soul as long as I live.'

'It will remain in this room, then. Not even a word to the benefactor. He is God-fearing, despite his liking for rum. He would be angry to hear such ideas.'

'Not a word to anyone, Mr Applebee. On my brother's life.'

'So be it.'

At this moment, I look upon my tutor and thank God for him. He has opened the cage door these past years and set my thoughts free.

'You are most intelligent, sir, with the finest mind. Why then are your clothes so shabby and your situation in life so low? Surely you could have made more of yourself?'

Yet as soon as I have uttered it – believing myself to be helpful in my observations – his downcast eyes reveal I have insulted him and I am very sorry for it and scold myself inwardly.

'My life has run a crooked path, Dawnay.'

This is a response I had not expected, as I thought he would defend his position and quite rightly chide me.

'Why is that?' say I softly.

He thinks for a time and sighs. 'Circumstances conspired,' says he and that is all. He will not explain further and I am old enough now to know when to stop my questions and change the topic of conversation.

'Please tell me more, sir, of deserted islands thick with jungle that no one has ever seen.'

We are back on safe ground, yet I often think of my tutor's crooked path and what may have forged it.

7

For seven years we talk of such perilous things, but only in our curiosities room. When we meet at the orphanage, we study a more acceptable curriculum, of Latin, French, geography, botany, logic, art and architecture, the circle of the sciences, and other subjects acceptable to any onlooker far from our dangerous ideas. We cannot write these down, as we are afraid they will be found, especially at the benefactor's house. Despite their long friendship, I believe my tutor would be dismissed and his wife too. Thus the four walls of the curiosities room, the drawers and compartments and glass doors, the dead creatures in stone and spirits – oh, if they could speak! They would tell a long tale of blasphemous science that would have us sorely punished.

My life at the orphanage continues unaffected by such risky endeavours. Each afternoon I spend with Matron, where we train the younger girls in service. The weekly food rations I have arranged for my fellow inmates have earned their respect at last, and even some measure of friendship. Though my mind has outgrown many of them due to my good fortune, I do not seek to display it as I wish to avoid earning a reputation as proud. Instead, I engage in many a jovial conference with my asylum sisters on all manner of light topics, as well as playing knuckle-bones with the little ones. It is a relief to my overworked mind. Yet I do not relinquish education altogether in their presence; in fact, I have also – against the founder's and even Matron's knowledge – secreted writing materials in the dormitory and taught many a girl the art of letters. Most crucially, the extra food from Mr Woods has grown all the orphans straighter, and we have no cases now of scurvy nor rickets either. Matron was slow to accept it, keen as she is on the old remedies: cold baths, possets, snail tea and calomel. But straight legs and strong gums show her the proof and she agrees it in the end. We gossip and tend the house together, two old friends by now. While my education across the curriculum continues in the front room and my secret education in science in the curiosities room, Matron takes pains to teach me the most important lessons of life in our afternoon conferences.

'Move those knives this instant, Dawnay! You must never cross knives on the table, do you know *nothing*? It brings awful bad fortune.'

'I do not think I believe in luck. Or fate. Or any such thing any more.'

Her palms clapped on her cheeks, she exclaims, 'Does your tutor teach you nothing of the real world? I suppose next you'll be killing a money spider, or throwing milk on the fire. Even saying your prayers at the foot of the bed. 'Tis treacherous bad luck to do any one of these things, and you so blithe about them.'

I have not the heart to tell her I do not say my prayers at all any longer, at the foot of the bed or anywhere else. I can see Matron invests the accidents and happenstance of our lives with a significance I neither care for nor understand. I see scientifically; chance events are caused by a confluence of a hundred causes, neither directed nor asked for and in no way influenced by incantation. It is nature and its mysterious yet uncaring workings that drive our destinies, not luck nor crossed knives nor even God. That is my belief now. There are some black parts of the night when I hear the paupers' cart trundle past my window and think on my lost parents and stolen brother, when I suspect that God does not care for us at all, that He created the planet and set it in motion like a clock, then watches it fall to pieces with detachment. I do not share these dark thoughts with any living soul, not even Mr Applebee, who despite his radical leanings does speak often with reverence of the Almighty, and Susan would listen to aught I chose to tell her, but I have spied her praying earnestly for her son's safe return at the water pump, when she thought herself alone.

One spring afternoon, Susan's prayers are answered, for a brief time anyway. It is May of 1745 and I am around thirteen years of age. I arrive in the kitchen for my weekly, longed-for lunch and find a strapping young man slouching at the table, legs outstretched across the floor ending in square-toed black boots, over which Susan trips with glee and giggles like a girl. His face is framed by bushy side-burns and he sports a scrap of stained material knotted around his neck. His red coat hangs on the chair behind him, the pewter buttons glinting in the light from the fire. He smells of smoke, sweat and something else approximating roasted meat and bad eggs. Mr Applebee gives his son a good hard slap on the back, a manly way of showing his affection.

'Dawnay, this is my son, Owen Applebee.'

Applebee the younger laughs, as if this is a great joke, and in truth, before every statement he utters, he laughs the same, even when his words are in no way comical. 'How do you do?' says he and I say nothing. 'Shy, is it?'

'Not usually,' says Susan, fussing about his shoulders with a cloth, brushing away invisible specks. 'Speak up, child.'

'Are you come from the battlefield?' I ask.

'Oh, let the boy rest, for heaven's sake,' says his mother, buttering bread for his plate. 'No need to talk of battles.'

'Now then, Mother. The child can ask. And I am no boy any more and can talk of what I please,' says Owen with a broad grin. When he smiles, he is the picture of his mother – auburn hair and freckled skin – with little of his father about him at all. Perhaps in his eyes, that is all: wide, brown and expressive.

'I have been fighting under the Duke of Cumberland and am come directly from defeat in battle near Fontenoy. Tomorrow I go to see off the Young Pretender up north. I am stopping one night only with my family.'

Susan puts her hands on his shoulders. 'One night will have to do,' and then adds quietly, almost to herself, '*Thank you, Lord, for this one night.*'

'Enough of that, Mother. I am here, aren't I?'

Say I, 'You speak of defeat. You lost the battle?'

He laughs again and throws up his hands, revealing a rash of scars, a big red callus on his right hand and his fingers topped with a thick black line of dirt beneath the nails. 'We did! The truth is we *almost* won the day. We smashed through the centre of the French lines, only to find we were forced to retreat as our enemies rained cannon and musketry fire down upon our heads. The French had more cavalry and we had more infantry. Lots of heat from the French drove us back. We fought in our withdrawal though, and many French died, as well as our own.'

'Was it very exciting?'

'You feel the very life pulse through you. You are playing cards with death and so you feel your most alive.'

'I should like to feel like that.'

'You are not alone. There was a woman discovered in our company, only recently.'

'Surely not, son,' says my tutor. 'How can that be?'

'A soldier injured in the arm found his way to the wife of General Cumberland and then revealed *him*self to be *her*self. She'd joined to be with her husband, and when he was injured too and invalided home, she disclosed her identity so she could go home with him. Quite the tale about the regiments. No one had noticed a thing. Remember that we don't wash much. We don't see what's under our shirts too often. And mayhap she didn't have much under there to show!'

'Now, my boy,' says my tutor. 'There is a child present.'

'Yes, Father, apologies. So you see, child, there have been women in the army. Though I wouldn't recommend it. Must be a tricky thing to lie all the time, every day, and to live that lie. Any woman to try it would be a plaguy fool.'

His mother cries, 'Owen Applebee! Watch your words!'

The thought of dressing as a boy and running away this very night to fight the Young Pretender alongside Owen and the Duke of Cumberland's forces now seems to my childish fancy the only course my life can take. I worry it over in my mind, how I will find male clothes and how I will hide them. But my tutor must say something to Matron, for she keeps a close eye on me that evening and even sits outside our dormitory until I sleep. When I wake the next morning, I know Owen's regiment has gone and my chance with it. And would he protect me anyhow? I surmise he would not and would return me to my place here, so it would all be for naught.

The next visit I say to Susan how I envy the army life and she scolds me: 'My son's profession is a terrible beast that will tear at him if it can and pull him to pieces. So far, he remains intact. I pray he stays that way. You are only a child. Until you have your own, and they hand you the babe, and you run your fingers along its limbs to perceive that all is there and all is right and a wave of thanksgiving to God assails you and never leaves you – only then will you understand what the mother of a soldier suffers.'

But I do not comprehend and ignore her clucking ways. I dream of running away with the army for years to come. It is the idea of escape that is alluring, yet also the thought of living as a boy, as a man, appeals keenly. To escape the strictures of feminine dress and limitations – the narrow and small lives women live in our age – to escape that and be a swaggering man free to follow his own destiny, that is something to covet.

Once I am deemed fifteen years of age, my female existence catches up with me. I rush to Matron one morning with a great gout of red-brown blood at my thighs.

'Am I dying?' I gasp.

'No, of course not. You are a woman now. It will occur again from time to time. Perhaps once in a month. Those who eat quite well do bleed more often. Others with bad food and bad lives may not bleed at all. But you are one of the fortunate class. When it comes, it will last some four or five days and you must wipe it on your shift so that it does not soil your shoes, or my floor.'

Matron explains to me the hidden purpose of this bleeding. In my study of animals, I know of course the process of reproduction, the roles played by the female and the male. But I had no thought it need be accompanied by this gruesome bloodletting each month. I am certain female mice and frogs do not bleed thus. Or insects, though they may be too small to tell. Is it only humans who suffer this flux, only women?

'Stop daydreaming, Dawnay!' chides Matron. She then proceeds to speak of boys and men and their base desires for such a young woman as me. I have no interest in their cravings and tell her so. Not in that way. Only as specimens to study.

'But it is essential you know how to tell a good man from bad. You must think on finding a husband soon, Dawnay, or you'll be sent away for service before long. The founder mentions your continued presence with disdain. Most of our charges are long gone into apprenticeship by this age, as you know.'

'But I do not wish for a husband. For he will bring forth children and I have no wish for those either. How will I study with a baby at my breast?'

'Such talk is unnatural. And what choice do you have anyway? If you will not when you may, when you will you shall have nay. Marry soon or you'll be a mop-squeezer ere the year is out. And I fear such work will drive you mad, my dear, with your busy mind. A good husband might be kind and let you read a book from time to time.'

My tutor and I discuss it, how I can possibly continue my education when my fate falls one way or the other in the direction of service or marriage. He says he will think on it. But no further ideas are forthcoming. I begin to formulate my own plan, but keep it to myself for the moment.

I am called by my benefactor to his withdrawing room one summer afternoon, just before I am due to walk back to the asylum with my teacher.

'The orphanage has done its work by you and asserts you must find a position.'

'I know it, sir. And I have a proposition for you. This house is run admirably by your housekeeper Mrs Sturgis, your valet Mr Sturgis, and of course Susan . . . I mean, Mrs Applebee, your cook. But you have no permanent maidservant, sir. Just the girl who comes and goes, and is often run off her feet with the laundry and other rough work. I am thinking that I could work for you. I could manage the collection, dust it and take care of it, and help in the kitchen with preparation of healthful food for you, sir. And I can sew very well and be a kind of permanent seamstress for you. In return, I would require only a bed in the scullery or the garret, which I would put away in daylight hours. And I even know the art of wig keeping and could help your valet when necessary. Matron has taught me a thousand skills, sir. And if—'

'Enough!' cries Mr Woods. 'I have no need or desire for a lady's maid!'

'But sir . . .' The words catch in my throat, as panic rises there. To be sent away from this place, to lose my lessons, my discussions with Mr Applebee and chats with Mr Woods, my lunches with Susan, my afternoons spent in the curiosities room – it would not be an exaggeration to say at this moment I feel I will wither and die without them, or at least my mind will and all hope of happiness.

'Will you curb your prattling tongue for one moment, child? I wish to offer you something quite different. Now sit here, stop your noise and listen. You must know how very fond of you I have become, child, over the years. I am a bachelor and after me my name will become extinct. I wish to offer you a home here, for as long as you require it or desire it. You would have your own rooms and unlimited use of my collections. I would settle an annual income on you, so that you can continue your studies unabated. Legally, I would make you my ward. Our good friend Applebee alerted me to the idea and I agree it. I have become accustomed to our fireside talks, which provide a welcome escape from the rigours of business and the social whirl. I would miss them if you were to leave. I would miss you, my dear. This is to be your home, Dawnay, if you wish it. Well, child, do you wish it? Now will you not speak, when it is required of you?'

But I cannot speak, for I am afraid I will weep without end if I do.

'Why do you cry? Is it tears of joy?'

'It is that word, sir.'

'Which word?'

'*Home.*'

I take my leave of the asylum within a week. I am given the same brief ceremony all the other graduates are given, complete with a final meal of back bacon.

The founder stands me before all the other children, looks me squarely in the eye and pronounces thus: 'You are a singular girl, Dawnay Price, with some skills and facilities. Soon you will be of age. Endeavour now to remake yourself in the image of a good wife, for the female that wast the last and most complete of the creation was designed by Almighty God for a comfort and companion to mankind. As you grow in years, child, may you exert yourself to grow also in goodness. For your exit must every day draw nearer, and your proximity to the next world is beyond, and your inevitable farewell to the follies and indulgences of this world will be complete. Therefore, live every day as if you were to die at the end of it, and think on your salvation, for it will slip through your fingers if you do not handle it with care.'

Inwardly, I take from his speech a meaning I am positive he did not intend: that is, to *live each day as if I were to die at the end of it*, and therefore to live with reckless disregard for convention, regulation or fear of consequence.

Before I leave the house, Matron takes me aside and makes her own speech: 'As you know, I am a childless spinster. I have no delusions about my role here in this house. I prepare orphans for a life of service and I do so efficiently. But I am not made of stone. 'Tis a special child that wins my heart and none but you have owned it so completely. 'Twas the stealing of the quill did it, dear. Never have I seen such life and determination housed in a tiny frame. You do have a peculiar effect on people; as I think I told you once, even your namesake, the gentleman who found you, told me he had no interest in wretches until he saw you with his wig in hand that day and you looked him straight in the eye. I wish you well, Dawnay Price. I cannot guess where your clever head shall lead you. And I will be curious to follow your progress. But never come back here, never return to this place. It is not part of you, you are beyond it and too good for it. Never turn back, Dawnay. Off you go, now.'

I protest, but she will hear none of it. This woman has been a rough kind of mother to me, but a mother nonetheless.

8

Susan Applebee, my other mother, welcomes me to my new home. I am shown my room, my bed, my articles of toilet and, housed neatly in a wardrobe, some brand-new shifts and stockings, shoes with high curved heels and pointed toes, and dresses in a range of pastel colours she has picked for me. There is also a collection of fans. The wallpaper has been hand-painted in China and depicts blue birds amid flowers, leaves and berries. My dresser has serpentine drawers and placed on top are a china ewer and basin beside a soap dish decorated with light pink flowers. By the window is an escritoire with a drop front and mirror, and a dozen tiny drawers each with their own lock – I shall place my brother's note in one of those. The four-poster bed stands high off the ground with what appears to be at least three layers of mattresses and next to the bed sits a set of bed steps, with a chamber pot hidden inside. In a second dresser the top drawer contains powder, rouge, patches and lip colour neatly stowed in their own cubby-holes. There are two wig stands encased in narrow compartments on either side of the dresser, ventilated by silk panels in the doors. The fire is alight and I stand before it shaking my head.

Susan squints at me. 'Are you not satisfied, miss?' she asks with an ironic air.

'It is perfection. But I am not. I do not require this finery. I was never vain of my face. Nor did I yearn to wear silk dresses.'

'You cannot wear the asylum uniform any more. Now you must dress as a lady.'

'But I have no need for it nor interest in it. I cannot wear these stays with such boning, as the quality do, or these ridiculous shoes. I will not be able to bend across the desk or reach up to shelves. And where will I place my fan when I am about to screw together equipment for our experiments? What good would this lace apron be when I spill preserving spirits down it?'

'I know not. I only know Mr Woods will not have you shabby. He has a position to keep up. He likes his servants to go genteelly. And his ward likewise. He is a gentleman, after all.'

'And I am a natural philosopher, Susan. And I have my work to do.'

'You are a wilful stripling and will do as you're bid under his roof. Now change your clothes.'

A loud knocking comes on the door.

'Susan? Is the child there?'

'Stephen?' she calls. 'What are you thinking coming up here? This is not your part of the house.' She opens the door.

My tutor steps past her and beckons me hurriedly. 'Porpoises!'

'*What?*' we both cry.

'Porpoises, the sea mammals, spotted swimming up the River Thames. Come, Dawnay, quick! Throw on your cloak and hat. We may catch a glimpse of them if we run.'

So I am saved from tight stays by my persecutor's husband. We race through the streets and down to the river. Mr Applebee asks around and hears of the animals seen just downstream. We rush along and then see a crowd of people pointing by the riverside. We push through and find a post by the water's edge. We spot the porpoises breaking the water, their curving fins cutting through the choppy brown waves. Around and about them, the watermen are whooping and bashing the water's surface with their oars.

'Fie!' yells my tutor. 'Desist!'

'Stop it!' I join him. 'You will kill them!'

We are met with a barrage of oaths. But the porpoises are oblivious. They are so nimble in their medium they twist away from the boats and leap from the water. The crowd gasps.

'What a piece of work!' says my tutor and we cannot help but dissolve into laughter as we watch them sport with the watermen and fly through the water with graceful celerity, upstream. We and others follow them for a time, but then it seems they tire and turn about, heading downstream away from London and, we hope, to the open sea.

'Where do you think they are going?' I ask.

'To the Channel. They are not usually of fresh water. I have known of them in Scotland, Ireland too. But rare here, very rare. Peradventure they were lost.'

'I hope they find their way.'

As I watch their lithe forms fleet away from us, an erstwhile feeling surfaces in the pit of my stomach – an old associate of mine I did not know I was still acquainted with, not now I have my home, my benefactor and my new life. It is the yearning for travel, for discovery, to follow those creatures of the sea, to leave this soiled city behind and see new places. Perhaps my early life on the streets, my years following in an institution, without an object to call my own – excepting my brother's note – is it any wonder I have a nomadic soul? Yet so does the Applebees' son, still away with the army, not seen for years, and he had a stable loving home and escaped it for the rough comforts of a red coat. Maybe it is born inside us, this yearning to be footsore, and in others resides the over-whelming need for a bolt-hole. But now that I have a home, I cannot take it for granted. I do not wish it gone, only to wait for me while I go on my adventures and then come back to it, like a patient wife. I wish to see the world yet not as those with riches do, the Grand Tour of young gentlemen who are ferried from antiquity to supper and back again. It is another kind of travel I want, to move through it incognito as those porpoises – be a part of it, invisible within it – not as a young lady with all the restraints that creates. Not even as a man; but as a creature, at one with nature, at one with the air and the sea. But there is no woman I have heard of who ever achieved that.

I settle in to my new abode and form an uneasy truce with Susan as regards my dress; she has found me stays without bones that they call jumps, usually worn by pregnant ladies and, now, female philosophers. And I will not wear the silly aprons, nor lappets that hang and get in the way or a bulky pad over my behind that impedes movement. I have one weakness only and that is for a blue-green lustring gown that I wear often, as its hue matches my mind's image of the ocean I have never seen. I do make some effort to look smart and allow my new lady's maid – Jane – to dress my hair neatly each day. She does coo and fuss about me, saying how my complexion is far too dark and not pale enough to be fashionable and how I must apply powder to whiten my face, which I steadfastly refuse. She also eulogises on how long and black my tresses are, and dark hair is favoured presently and if only I would allow her to dress it properly, in the new style – oh, what a fine head of hair it is! – and suchlike. But each day, I insist she pin it up beneath a neat cap, away from my face and away from experiments, and be done with it.

I spend much of my time that first summer in Mr Woods's garden. He has a small plot at the back and hires a gardener, Mr Dawes, and an apprentice, Paul, to keep it tidy. Planted in the earth and in pots and boxes are a variety of trees, plants and flowers that can stand the coal-smoke of the city, including in one corner a Judas tree and in another a London plane tree – most commonly seen on the streets, yet here is one of our very own; with its peeling bark that renews itself every few years, it resists the damaging effects of the sooty air that would suffocate weaker specimens. Flowers that thrive despite the bad air here include a range of lovely roses, as well as lilac, holly and honeysuckle. I quiz our gardener almost daily about the different species of plants, flowers, vegetables and fruits he grows in the ground, in the pond and the glasshouse. He tells me that at other times of the year he grows the bulbs of hyacinths, tulips and daffodils, as well as medicinal plants, such as mandrake and gentian. We discuss types of seeds, plant diseases and breeding. He is a gentle, kindly man and a good teacher, to myself and Paul; needless to say my childhood fears of apprenticeship fade when I see Mr Dawes's patience with the boy.

I collect insects – butterflies, ladybirds, beetles, honey bees, dragonflies – and small animals: frogs, toads, mice and shrews. I kill one of each and preserve them, others I perform dissections upon and thus learn something of anatomy. Some I have kept in cages or jars for a short time, fed them a range of foods, medicines and liquors to see which thrived, which grew sickly, which died. I have removed the limbs of some small animals, used poultices of different herbs and chemicals on the wounds, to see which subjects succumb to infection and death, and which survive, or if any succeed in growing back a leg. Jane says I am awfully cruel, yet Mr Applebee and I know what we are about. It is science and science is a deity to me. There is no right or wrong when it comes to the truth; there is the fact and the fiction, the truth and the error, and little else matters. Certainly not a shrew's comforts.

I am permitted the run of the house, yet mostly find myself in the curiosities room with my tutor, the kitchen with Susan, my bedroom with Jane, or in the garden with Mr Dawes. My benefactor still invites me into the withdrawing room for our chat, the same as we have done these past years, only it is nightly now, rather than weekly. He uses this time also to instruct me in the languages of Portuguese and Spanish, of which he has learned much in his dealings with these countries over the years. I use the Latin taught me by Mr Applebee to improve them. Mr Woods is often out carousing, despite his protestations more or less once each month that he will give up. He goes to the coffee shops for gossip and trade every morning, then to the dockyards to oversee his shipments, back for dinner each evening with me, and more often than not out for drinks with his business associates. When we talk I quiz him about his days on the sea, where he went and what he saw. He tells me his favourite thing was jaunting between the islands that lay near Spain and Portugal, where he tried all the classes of wine and other alcohol he could lay his hands on. His drunken exploits proved his fortune, as he became such an expert in them that he set up his own exporting business and outsold all his rivals. And often he strays into the subject – tiresome to me – of how his riches secured his entry into polite society and how fortunate he has been to take his place within some of the finest households in London.

'Soon you must enter society, my dear,' Mr Woods exhorts me. 'Always shut up in that fusty old room. You are such a winsome thing. Soon you will attend balls, and evenings of entertainment and suchlike. I will introduce you to the quality ladies hereabout and one fortunate day you will meet a fine young gentleman, perhaps one of a bookish bent to suit your talents, and you will marry.'

'But I have no interest in balls or evenings or drink or the ladies of Bloomsbury Square, or anywhere else for that matter, and certainly not marriage.'

'But this is quite unnatural, for a young lady or indeed any young person. I must say, I do wonder these days what is to become of our youth, as the men seem to sink into effeminacy and the ladies advance to boldness. It is all quite against nature, and we will in some horrid future bemoan the fact that the sexes will become quite the same, their characteristic and delightful differences become confounded and lost.'

As Matron before him, Mr Woods seeks to engage me in

matrimony with some as yet unknown bachelor. Yet neither understand I have no interest in such a union, as it would interfere and perhaps curtail permanently my ability to study and work. Nothing holds more value to me than that, and despite his kindness, my benefactor seems incapable of grasping this. I can see it frustrates him when I refuse to follow his advice, but the thought of submitting myself to marriage is akin to the pillory for me, and I will never do it willingly.

We engage in such squabbles from time to time, yet it upsets us both to cross swords over a topic upon which I fear we shall never agree. Thus, when I see the subject surface, I usually manage to steer our talks back to his travels, a more placid channel for us to navigate. I often ask him to expand on these islands he visited – what manner of flora and fauna inhabited them? Were they the same as those on the mainland, or how did they differ? And what kind of sea creatures did he see on his travels? I am becoming fascinated by the idea of situation. I spend the next years in this house devising a new theory of place. My experiments with my garden creatures and plants have led to me to think of our garden here as a tiny plot to us, yet a boundless realm of danger and opportunity for its miniature inhabitants. Its contents direct the lives of those who live in it or visit from other gardens or the streets, from the parks or the long river beyond. And it leads me to ponder the fate of islands, cut off from the mainland, and how their creatures manage their isolation so far from broader resources. How do they get there? How do they manage their abode? My life as a child from the street, to the institution, to this house has taught me that life thrives quite differently in different environments, given the right kind of food, drink and nurturing, or the wrong kind.

We hear news of Owen Applebee, that he is in North America, fighting the French alongside the Provincial American Forces. He writes to his parents that he has met members of the local American Indian tribes and mentions their bizarre dress and customs. But he is no man of science or even of poetry, and his words are frustratingly brief and give no detail of the extraordinary things he must be seeing. It is mostly filled with a written version of his usual verbal jollity and thick with references to his regiment – of Jack and Dick and Jim and their brave deeds and an officer who is a d—n fool *&c.* I recall I once wished to follow Owen all those years ago. But the army is no place for a natural philosopher – male or female; it is likely I possess the correct cool attitude towards life and death as a soldier needs, yet I feel I would be too distracted by my fascinations to pay much attention to fighting. And I have always been too interested in preserving life, rather than destroying it, as soldiers are required to do at times. Susan still prays for her son's return and my tutor still rails at the folly of army life and his son's absurd red coat. I do not care for his coat, only the liberty I believe he has and the sights he has seen on his travels – I am almost sick with envy at this aspect of his freedom.

In the year 1750, two curious events shake us up in London, quite literally. We have two earthquakes. In the first, the house rumbles and shakes for some moments. Mr Applebee and I know it for what it is and feel satisfied that we have experienced an interesting phenomenon. The second is somewhat stronger and sets the dogs off howling across the city; some say they saw fish jumping clear from the Thames. There is a great to-do about it when some merchants of doom predict a third will come in another month's time and finish us all off, due to God's wrath at the debauchery of city life. Panic sweeps the residents and hundreds of coaches flee in days. Thousands race to Hyde Park and camp there. Mr Woods comes home from his coffee house all in a fluster predicting disaster. My tutor and I watch this display of superstitious terror with the bemused eye of the philosopher and instead write up our findings of the natural effects of the quakes. A third one does not materialise and many return shamefaced. At times such as these, it is said to be fortunate to have the comforts of religion. But I find the opposite: that science, or rather the knowledge it represents, gives the greater comfort, as it explains the world to us and banishes delusion and fear.

By 1755, years of experiments, reading, taking notes and even my discussions with my tutor are proving frustrating. I feel as if I am slowly desiccating, transforming into a dusty specimen to be housed for posterity in this very room of curiosities.

I say to Mr Applebee: 'How can I truly study the nature of islands from a London town house?'

'You must read of what others have found, as you always have. You know Mr Woods allows you to buy any book or journal you wish. You are most fortunate.'

'But a true discoverer must study their subject *in situ*. It's no good, sir, I simply must travel.'

'It is not possible. It is unheard of, for a young woman. Even if such an unlikely event occurred, you could never go alone. Your benefactor is surely too old and fat to want to travel to some godforsaken island with you. And he has his business to attend to. Who would go with you?'

'Why, *you*, sir.'

My tutor falls dumb and does not speak of it for some days. I do not know if he broaches the subject with his wife. I know enough of my elders by now to bide my time when I want something, and wait for them to cogitate, turn it around in their minds and represent it to you as if it were their own idea in the first place.

Some mornings hence, Mr Applebee comes into the curiosities room, a pensive look in his eye, and I choose my moment.

'Will you put the idea to Mr Woods then, sir?'

'What idea is that?'

'Come now, sir. Our plan to travel.'

'I have spoken with your benefactor. He is intrigued by the idea. He even said he would think seriously on it, though he thinks you too young.'

'When I am believed to be twenty-three years of age? I am practically elderly. My life ebbs from me daily.'

'Oh, Dawnay, you selfish airling! Not all matters revolve about you and your desires.'

'I am very sorry, sir.'

I turn away. He has never spoken to me thus.

'No, dear, I am sorry. It is not your doing. Please forgive me. I have grave news. I received a letter some days ago that my son has been injured and returns home soon, an invalid. My wife and I must care for him. He has lost a leg.'

The house is quieter and the cooking indifferent, as Susan and her husband are away at home for several days, attending to their son. Mr Applebee asks if I will visit Owen there and I gladly oblige. On the walk through St Giles, we pass by the Roundhouse and see the hands of hungry prisoners thrust through the bars, hear their thin voices begging passers-by for food; and I shudder.

At the Applebee residence, Owen is stretched out in bed in the front room. One side of the mattress is raised by his hulking right leg, long and muscular as ever, the sheet clinging to it. The other side is flat below the knee, horribly flat, a wide expanse of grey sheet, where a man's lower leg should be. I cannot help but think of my legless shrews – and at this moment acquire a retrospective horror of what I did to them, the poor creatures. Owen's face is as grey as the sheet, thin and drawn; the life has gone from those big brown eyes and he appears trapped, hemmed in by his messy hair and his long dark eyelashes and the heavy curtains hanging behind him. A light has gone out from him and I fear it will never return. He does not wish to speak with me very much. He thanks me for my visit, says it is kind. But he will not look at me and closes his eyes to sleep. Susan's eyes are red and exhausted. My tutor is uncharacteristically quiet.

On our walk home, Mr Applebee says, 'I had hoped your visit might perk him up somewhat. I am afraid I was wrong. Perhaps I should not have brought you here, Dawnay.'

'I am glad you did. I have been a fool about army life. I thought it all fun and your concerns were nonsense. I have seen the cost of it now. The life it takes away.'

'He is alive, that is what Mrs Applebee says to me each night. He is alive, and that is our gift. They took his leg and now we have to persuade him that he still has his life. But he weeps in the night and says he wishes he were dead. We have to teach him that his life will be worthy, as it is to us. It will take us a long time, I fear, and we may never achieve it. But that is our role presently.'

I see my tutor has no place with me now, that his life will be at home. I ask my benefactor if he is providing for them, perhaps a stipend to help them manage Owen's recovery and physical needs. He assures me they are well taken care of and need for nothing. Once I know the Applebees will be well, I resolve on the course I must take.

9

I use my allowance to buy a compass and a map of the Iberian Peninsula. I study the problems of latitude and longitude. I scribble and sketch and plan. I discover that there is an archipelago of islands off Portugal known locally as the Berlengas. They are mainly uninhabited and replete with unusual flora and fauna. I have found my object of study.

I go to see my benefactor in the withdrawing room one Sunday morning, steeling myself for, at best, a lively discussion and, at worst, a bitter argument. I am so very fond of Mr Woods and hate to invite discord between us, yet I know I will battle against his refusal if it comes.

'I wish to travel to Portugal and study some of the islands near to it. I wish to go alone. I can stay with some of your contacts in Lisbon, but I do not require nor wish for a chaperone. It is the only course my life can take now, the only way I can develop my theories. I wish you to see the logic of it and help me achieve this aim. For if I stay cooped up in London, in this house – as dear to me as it has always been – I will lose my mind. I will not prosper. I hate to disappoint you, but you know by now I will never marry, never have a child. I will live single and devote my life to science but I cannot achieve my aims here. I need your help, as you have always helped me, to go out into the world and study it. Will you help me?'

'As you know, Stephen has already spoken to me of this plan. I considered it with him as your chaperone. But now that he is not available to go with you, Dawnay, I cannot see a way to do it. Decently, I mean. To do it decently, so that you are protected and seemly.'

'Sir, you come from very different origins to the place in society in which you now find yourself. You followed the call to adventure when it came, and now you have achieved your aims, indeed, you have surpassed them. Will you not afford me, your charge, your legacy, the same rights of accomplishment, to allow me to discover my own destiny? All my studies these years have led to this point. There is no alternative. I am a sensible and strong-willed person. I will require only that I am placed on the right ship, that I am shown the way to my lodging in Lisbon, and that a local guide can take me to the boat that sails for the island. If you can arrange those things for me, I will require nothing or no one further. I assure you, sir, I know precisely what I am about and no harm will come to me or to your reputation.'

'Ah, the optimism of youth. The arrogance of it!'

'Surely a virtue, sir. Better that than pessimism and drudgery.'

'But this plan of yours, to travel alone. It is most unheard of.'

'Not for a *man* of my age, sir. Only for a *woman*.'

'Precisely. For a woman, most uncommon.'

'And when do you recall me ever doing the common thing, sir? And you yourself have told me many a time that you have travelled widely enough to know that there are uncommon and strange things in this world unheard of in England. But that does not make them wrong, merely out of our experience.'

'You recall every word I speak – many of which I have forgotten long since – and use them against me!'

'Not against you, sir, but for my argument. A worthy argument, a righteous one.'

He shuffles in his seat and frowns, puts two fingers to his

lips and stares at the floor, his eyes glazed. Now is the time I must keep quiet and let him think.

He begins. '*If* we were to do it . . .'

'Oh, sir!' I cry in delight.

'Hush! I am merely presenting my thoughts aloud. Do not interrupt. As I was saying, if it were to be done, we would need a reliable ship with a captain we can trust to see to your welfare. A navy man ideally, though such a man might turn his nose up at providing passage for a young woman. And on arrival, I have several old friends in Lisbon who could assist you and make arrangements for you, and see that you are safe. For it is most important to me, Dawnay, that as well as satisfying your mind, I do my duty as your benefactor: to protect you, my dear. It is this that worries me most regarding this plan of yours.'

'Of course, sir – and you have my grateful thanks for that – but I assure you that I can look after myself quite adequately and . . .'

'All right, all right. I will make enquiries and I will look into it, Dawnay – ah, ah, now, now. That is enough. No *But sir*, no *and furthermore*. I will make my own mind up, young lady, as I always have. I will think on it. Run along and leave me in peace. You must exhibit patience now.'

But I have never been patient; it has no place in my list of virtues. That very night, I stay up late in the curiosities room, planning my route and studies from my maps of the islands. I am late to bed and rise late too, after a dream of a peculiar instrument I had devised which allowed me to observe sea life in the warm waters of the island. As I lie abed and design the instrument in my head, I hear Mr Woods go out early and say he will not return till this afternoon. I do not wait for Jane to appear with her pins and her finishes, instead throwing on over my shift only my jumps and a plain linen dress and leaving my hair to hang long about my shoulders.

I do not even wash my face, yet I have no fear of being seen. I will assemble myself before Mr Woods returns. I go downstairs to my desk where lie my plans from the night before, surrounded by the chaos of my papers, quills, ink spills, experimental apparatus, pot plants and my benefactor's jumble of curiosities. As I am sketching my design for the new apparatus, there is a knock at the door, which startles me. Nobody ever knocks at this door.

'Who is there?' I query, thinking it must be Jane gone bashful.

Mr Woods appears, sees my dishevelment and is taken aback.

'I did not expect to see you this morning, sir,' I say and both hands go to my hair, which I train over one shoulder like a thick rope. I shrug. It really is of no consequence to me, but I see it has unnerved him.

Mr Woods looks peculiar. As he stutters to speak and begins to turn, a figure steps boldly into the room behind him and stares at me. It is a young man, a few years older than myself, dressed with the smartness of a land-bound officer of the Royal Navy. He wears a blue frock-coat with waistcoat, breeches and stockings of pure white and sports a neat wig. A sword hangs from his left hip and he holds a gold-tipped cane in his right hand and a broad blue captain's hat under his left arm. He seems rather over-furnished for such a busy room as this. And I can see in his eyes that he is quite shocked at my slovenly appearance and the general chaos of the room in which he has unfortunately found himself.

'Dawnay, this is Lieutenant Commander Robin Alexander. Sir, this is Miss Dawnay Price, my ward.'

I think of providing the customary curtsey, but something about that officer's disapproving eyebrows decides me and I step towards him and hold out my hand. He stares at it, as if it were an old shoe served to him on a dinner plate. He takes it gingerly and I shake his hand in a manly fashion and feel his grip tightening, his skin cool and dry.

'Do you wish to put down your hat and your cane, sir, on my table here? I can move some of my things.'

Yet he is not able to reply. It is as if I have no voice, as if my appearance is so distasteful to him that I do not exist. He looks to his companion for some sign that he has not been hit on the head and is not now dreaming unsettling visions.

'Sir, should we return on another occasion, when circumstances are . . .' He runs out of words.

'No, no, young man. We are here to meet my ward and here she certainly is, surrounded by the very work of which I have spoken to you at length. Impressive, is it not? Look at the extent of her industry. Many a man of science has not achieved half as much by her age.'

I follow the lieutenant commander's eyes about the room and note that his grip on his cane slackens somewhat. He clears his throat.

'There certainly is a great deal of it,' he offers.

'Yes, well.' My benefactor wavers, looks to me, his eyebrows raised in some exasperation. He tries a new tack: 'My dear, I met Lieutenant Commander Alexander last evening at an entertainment and we spoke for some time about his next mission. He is to captain a small research vessel to Africa to produce naval charts of the north-west coast for reasons of trade or war. The ship will also take a variety of men of science to engage in their own studies, to return to England in six months' time. Yet on the way to Africa and on its return journey, his ship is to dock in Portugal, namely at Lisbon.'

I should have guessed sooner, yet until this moment I have no idea why this stiff young man has materialised in my work room. For a moment, I even entertained the unlikely idea that my benefactor thought he had found me a husband, to present before me the symbol of my resistance in order to win me round. I thank heavens it is not so and chide myself for doubting my benefactor; here he presents me with my chance for escape and I face it sleep-eyed and half-dressed. Mr Woods looks at me pointedly, a distinct air of disapproval about the eyes.

'When do you sail to Lisbon, sir?' I ask.

'Why,' says he, turning to Mr Woods as if *he* had asked the question, 'within three months at the outside.'

My heart quickens in my breast. I glance at my benefactor for guidance. He steps forward and invites Alexander to look at my studies spread out on the table.

I explain: 'Here are my maps for the Berlengas Islands.'

'We call them the Burlings,' he corrects me. 'They are most useful as landmarks yet can be treacherous when the fog is down.'

'Ah yes, thank you, the Burlings. They are ideal for my purposes. You see, I have been working on a theory of isolation. I intend to study the flora and fauna of these islands and test out my theories regarding the development of life in isolated situations.'

Lieutenant Commander Alexander looks and nods politely as I show my work. I cannot fathom the response of that organised naval mind to the sight of my scraps of paper piled in chaotic tumbling towers. I hope he can surmise that an untidy desk does not necessarily mirror an untidy mind, yet I shuffle the odd pile into a semblance of order as we speak.

'All I need to test my theory is to get there. I need passage . . . to Lisbon.'

He looks up at me, then at Mr Woods.

'I did not know you planned to travel, sir,' he says.

'I do not. But I have a proposition for you. My ward here intends to travel, whether I like it or not. And I would have her do it as safely as God allows.'

Alexander looked shocked enough at my appearance, let alone the idea of me on his very ship.

'In my experience, sir,' says he, in a subdued tone – as if by speaking a modicum more softly he might spare my tender ears the pronouncement he is about to relay – 'the people of

Portugal are uncultured and uncouth, and it is not at all the sort of place for a young woman to be gallivanting about on her own. I would strongly dissuade you from this course of action, for the good of the young lady, at the very least.'

'Come now, man!' Mr Woods laughs. 'I have spent many years with the Portuguese and I recognise no likeness in your description. It is perhaps your experience that has been jaundiced by never having left your ship and walked among the people of that beautiful land. Is it not the case truly, sir, that you have never actually spent your days on Portuguese soil?'

'Yes, that is true. But I have heard—'

'Well then, Dawnay will tell you – as will any natural philosopher – that direct experience is all. One can make assumptions in a laboratory, but the only proofs are to be found in the real world. I have faith in all men and faith in none in equal measure. I believe Miss Price to be more at risk of abduction on the streets of London than she would be on Portugal's picturesque islands or indeed in the better areas of Lisbon. When it comes to corruption, Lisbon is certainly no worse than London in this regard.'

Alexander nods and replies, 'I bow to your greater experience in these matters. But I must protest strongly on another account. This plan is most unheard of. The proposal that an unmarried young woman might travel alone to foreign climes? We have no facilities for ladies aboard our ship, or any ship for that matter.'

'Sir,' I interject. 'Forgive me, yet I must also protest. Let us all be honest. Your having visited here unannounced this morning and found me in a state of dishevelment may seem at first a disastrous occurrence for all involved. However, it has perhaps served us well. It should be apparent to you that if there is such a thing as a woman of science, then the evidence stands before you. I care no more for the traditional trappings of femininity than I do for a fig. My work is my life; it is that master I choose to serve in Portugal, and I need your kind assistance to relay me there. I will ask for no special consideration, no favours, no balderdash. I only require a bunk to sleep in, a place to store my equipment and papers, and some sustenance while on board. Once I am in Lisbon, my benefactor has many associates who can see to my welfare on arrival. All we ask of you is that you honour my ambition to work and to travel not only to further my own studies, but also to expand the reservoir of human knowledge. What say you, sir?'

During my speech, the lieutenant commander met my eye for the first time since his arrival. He listened intently.

'What a speaker, eh, Alexander?' says Mr Woods. 'Can you *fault* her? She should be in the House of Commons, what! Can you think of one good point against her? I never could. She is a force of nature! What do you say, man? Are we agreed?'

Alexander glances at my tables, my equipment and papers, at my benefactor, for a fleeting moment at me, before turning to Mr Woods. And then a remarkable thing happens. He actually smiles.

'Sir, Miss Price: I must admit you have won me over.'

'Huzzah!' cries my benefactor.

'You will not regret this decision, sir,' I insist, grinning broadly and hugging myself, in the absence of Susan or Jane to throw my arms about in joy, as I wish to do at this very moment.

Alexander even allows himself a shrug of the shoulders and a moment of laughter.

'I am a logical man, and the logic of your arguments won the day. I hope no one could call me an enemy of women, as I believe I have their best interests at heart. My desire to protect them from the harsh world is part of this earnest wish. Yet if any female can achieve a plan such as yours, then it must be you, Miss Price. I have never met a woman anything like you. I mean this as a commendation, of course.'

'It is of no consequence, sir. I only thank you for agreeing to my plan. That is all I am concerned with and is everything to me. Thank you, sir. I will be no trouble to you, I assure you.'

After a few more civilities, my benefactor shows out our new associate, with a quick nod to me and a gratified wink.

After he has gone, we laugh uproariously at our victory. And Mr Woods toasts our success with a substantial glass of port, in honour of my destination.

'To Portugal!' he cries, taking a gulp. 'And to Lieutenant Commander Robin Alexander, that whippersnapper of a junior sea captain, only recently breeched and already putting on the airs of a seasoned admiral. He is a good man though, reliable and sound by all accounts and I am certain he will ensure safe passage for you and I trust him in that. But I doubt you two will be friends before the voyage is out, or ever! I wish you good luck with him, Dawnay, the conceited skipjack.'

But I brush aside his insults. Robin Alexander will prove my fortune, as he is to provide passage for me to my greatest desire. I raise my glass of water and clink it against my guzzling benefactor's and say, 'To adventure!'

IO

I am to sail on His Majesty's Ship *Prospect*. She was once a collier, built in Hull, and was purchased by the Royal Navy and refitted as a research vessel. She has three masts, is full rigged and equipped with four cannons and ten swivel guns. She is constructed from white oak, elm, pine and fir. She is currently at Deptford, where she has been refitted for a scientific voyage, given extra cabins encircling the officers' mess to accommodate the men of science on board (and one woman of science). There is extra space too for use as workrooms and equipment storage. I will join the ship at Deptford, whence she will go to Falmouth for provisioning and to board the last remainder of the crew. We shall then set sail from Falmouth to Lisbon.

I have packed my clothes – simple, plain, functional – as well as my papers, key texts and instruments, all in one trunk. I have included some light walking shoes; a self-made list of Spanish and Portuguese phrases for unusual occurrences – my command of both languages is adequate for general purposes – and my compass; a book on marine life, namely the third volume of Albertus Seba's *Thesaurus* – a parting gift from Mr Applebee – and the instrument of my design I viewed in a dream, that a carpenter has since constructed for me: a magnified glass pane housed in a framed box, which I will use as a viewer for observing the shallow sea floor without having to place my head under the water. I have omitted from my case anything superfluous or overtly feminine. I am determined to travel as weightlessly as possible, just like those swift porpoises down the Thames.

It is time to say farewell to Mr Woods, Mr Applebee and Susan. We stand in the kitchen after a dawn breakfast of bacon and bread, as my ship is to leave early in the day to reach Falmouth in good time. My benefactor comes yawning down to the kitchen to find me.

'I hope I have been a good sponsor to you, my dear. I know there are days and certainly nights where I have behaved more like an ass than any man, where my consumption of spirituous liquors is concerned. But I hope you have felt some small admiration for me – now then, do not interrupt me, Dawnay, for you know you will go on and on and I will never finish my point. I knew from our first meeting that you were an extraordinary person. I know you will make your way in the world. But I feel I am losing a child. And though you are a young woman, I do still see that scrappy little wretch who turned up hungry each week and brightened my fireside with her stories of learning.'

'Thank you, sir,' say I and for the first time we embrace, as father and daughter might, as patron and ward, as friends.

I turn to my tutor and, despite the countless hours we have spent side by side, we are awkward and cannot find it within ourselves to smooth this parting. Instead, we shake hands in a rather solemn way, though we smile and my tutor nods; his large brown eyes shine with feeling, I think. Susan grows impatient and puts her arms around me and kisses my cheeks, saying, 'Take care, you mad girl. Don't dismay that young sea captain too much.'

I am conveyed to Deptford by my benefactor's coach and deposited with my luggage at the Royal Dockyard, before the Master Shipwright's house, fronted by plane trees, where a maidservant in her apron stands in the door shaking out the breakfast tablecloth in my direction. I turn away from flying crumbs and see opposite, across the wharf, a lofty pink-stoned building topped with a clock tower and fronted with the royal coat of arms on its façade. I remember my tutor told me this is the Great Storehouse. What a splendid site is Deptford Docks, with its pleasant architecture, small river craft and barges passing by, and, further on, the sight of the ribs of partial ships being constructed in their own personal docks. This area has a tangible history of seafaring, with the knighting of Drake by Queen Elizabeth aboard the *Golden Hind*. I understand here too Raleigh laid down his cape for her.

Beside me is a building dock, where I stare up at the ship that waits there. From the description my benefactor has given me, I think she must be my ship, the *Prospect*. I am told she is not an immense ship, yet she looks it to me, tall and mighty, proud and solid, a movable building afloat with windows and floors and a life on board. At the front under the bowsprit there is a figurehead of a mermaid, tastefully draped in wooden cloth to preserve her modesty, her hand raised and shielding her eyes as she looks out for ever beyond us to the horizon. I do not fancy myself important enough for it to be the case, but somehow as I gaze upon her, I have an inkling that she waits for me and me alone: nonsense, yet my true feeling. After all, we will be but the two women aboard this vessel on this journey.

As I soak in the maritime atmosphere, a boy of about ten years of age appears and asks if I am 'Mrs Price', and I nod. He arranges for my trunk to be brought on board, then leads me up on to the main deck and asks me to wait for him to fetch the captain. To stand on a ship's deck! To be far above the quayside, to look down on the men loading kegs on to boats or pulling oars in sweaty effort, to see the buildings shimmering in the glassy water, to throw back my head and stare up at the three tall masts sketched with hard lines against the blue sky, to gaze across the water to our way out to sea and to the commencement of our quest. I wonder if my brother ever stopped detesting his fate enough to enjoy his time on board, if he came to love it though it were his prison and took him away from me, his only family. I wonder if he came to worship his ship and the promise of the sea, in the way I feel at this moment. I fear I am romanticising it all; I will learn if I am soon enough, when we leave the safety of Deptford Docks.

'Miss Dawnay Price,' says a voice, and I turn to look upon our lieutenant commander. He is again smartly kitted out in full naval uniform, his white stockings shining and golden buttons glinting in the sunlight. Beside him stands a handsome woman impeccably dressed in high fashion: a gold and crimson silk gown – with bell-shaped sleeves, and ribbons, flowers and lace sewn about the neckline – and her light brown hair piled high in braids about her head and trailing gracefully down the nape of her neck. She is turned away from me and calling, 'Boys? Come now, boys.'

Brothers of around the same age as the cabin boy cavort behind her, pushing and shoving and snickering, yet turn and run to her on command. They are well trained and line up beside their mother with identical obedience. Though the same height and seeming age, they look quite different; in fact, one the image of the mother and the other the father, as if each face were copied by an expert portraitist. The left has the mother's hazelnut locks, while the right has shining yellow hair – so bright he seems to have sprung from the sun – and I wonder if our captain sports the same colour beneath his wig. The contrasted effect is disturbed by their having been dressed identically, in orange coats with open-necked cream shirts.

'Please allow me to introduce my wife, Leonora Alexander, and our twin sons Michael and Arthur.'

'Your boys are twins?'

'Oh yes,' replies their mother proudly, in a mellow and becoming voice. 'Born together. They are the best of friends and quite inseparable.'

'I am honoured to meet you all,' say I and sink low.

'What an enchanting young woman,' says the wife. 'I had imagined a lady of science to be dressed in breeches and frightfully ugly! But you are quite comely, my dear.'

'Many thanks.' I curtsey again.

'My family are on board to say their farewells,' explains Alexander. 'Please excuse us while they do so, thereupon I will show you to your cabin. We will be leaving shortly afterwards.'

I nod and the family turn from me. I feel myself dismissed. I go to the rail and watch the life of the dockyard go about its early morning tasks. Yet slyly I observe the lieutenant commander say goodbye to his family. I see her kiss his cheek and watch him ruffle his boys' hair, then the trio descend the gangway to the quayside, the wife floating as calmly as a swan and the boys running ahead; twins, yet not at all alike; quite an intriguing biological phenomenon. I look back to her husband but find him gone. Then I am summoned by the same boy as earlier, who takes me down a steep staircase and announces, 'The captain's cabin,' upon whose door he raps and waits, his hands clasped behind his back, feet apart, chin raised.

'What is your name?' I whisper to him.

'Noy,' he says proudly.

'Your Christian name?'

'Francis,' he says, with some suspicion.

'My name is Miss Dawnay Price. Shall we be friends, Francis? I know no one aboard and have never sailed in a ship. Will you show me how it is done and teach me its ways?'

The spell is broken and he grins broadly. 'Certainly, miss. I will!'

'My first question is this: how do we address your Lieutenant Commander Alexander? It is a bit of a mouthful, you see.'

'Yes, miss. Well, hereabouts we call him Cap'n Alex. Will that do?'

'That will do admirably. Thank you, Francis.'

The cabin door opens and Francis's face falls, his body stiffens and he pipes up, 'Miss Price, sir.'

'Yes, boy. Off you go.' He emerges without hat and closes the door to his room. I am only afforded the briefest glimpse inside and see a desk covered with maps and a variety of small instruments of his profession cast across the papers. I also note a red ribbon on his desk, and conjecture if his wife left it with him as a keepsake.

'Miss Price, please allow me to conduct a brief tour of this deck and show you your quarters.'

'Thank you, Captain Alex,' I say, giving a small smile and watching for his reaction.

But his face betrays nothing as he directs me to a door before us. Our brief tour shows me that there are to be four educated men on board, sharing two cabins. After a stay of a month or so in Lisbon on business, the ship will travel onwards to Africa for these gentlemen to pursue their studies and our captain his cartographical duties. I am shown my own cabin, next door to the cabin of our captain. It would seem he plans to keep an eye on me, when he can, as my benefactor would wish. It is a tiny space, a bunk against one wall, a small dresser opposite with a single cupboard below. My trunk, already deposited there, takes up most of the floor space. It is simple, plain and yet it is mine. I already feel attached to it. My little wooden home.

On the deck below us I am shown the cabins of the ship's surgeon, the master, the captain's clerk and the gunner, facing the mates' mess. An adjacent deck houses the remainder of the crew, such as the carpenter and his men, the sailmaker, the boatswain and his mate, the armourer and quartermaster, and a variety of other able seamen, more of whom are to join us at Falmouth. Captain Alex does not take me to any lower decks, I assume due to the proximity of the distasteful stink of the bilge that emanates from those quarters.

As he explains these details to me, I watch him speak and gesticulate, and I think of what my benefactor has told me about this man. This is his first command of his own ship. Lieutenant Commander Robin Alexander is ambitious, hoping to prove himself on this voyage. His father was in the Royal Navy, as were his grandfather and two uncles. He is the youngest of four children, the other three all sisters. What other path was there for him? He was born to go to sea. Next he will wish to be made master and commander, and then a post captain in charge of a large vessel. He must then prove himself in battle, upon which he will succeed to the Captains' List and have a chance of further illustrious promotion. Thus, he must be keen for war to break out as soon as possible. I think of Owen's leg. An ambitious naval man has a different outlook on such things than an ensign's mother.

He leads me back up on to the main deck, at which point we are met by a flurry of well-dressed men all talking hurriedly and smiling and pointing about, coming towards us. I conclude these must be our four Gentlemen of Science, late arriving and excited to be here. Introductions are made and thus I am newly acquainted with the following:

Mr Mathison, a cartographer, who is to help Captain Alex chart a stretch of the north-west African coast; around the same age as me, and in awe of the lieutenant commander.

Mr Kendall, a botanist, who is to study the plants of North Africa and bring back samples and seeds, a man in his fifties, who has travelled across Europe and retrieved many specimens on a variety of intrepid expeditions. I look forward sincerely to picking his brains for ideas.

Mr Piper, whose interest is in the peoples and animals to be found in the African desert; a dandy of perhaps nineteen years of age, whose dress is fussy and wigs the height of fashion, with a lot of money to waste and yearning for adventure. I wonder how he will cope with desert living.

Dr Hodges, a physician who wishes to investigate African

diseases and local remedies, an experienced doctor and
seasoned traveller, around thirty or so; he has a rather irritating
manner of looking away whenever someone else speaks, as if
no one but himself has anything of note to impart. Or perhaps
he is merely nervous.

I have some difficulty explaining my own interests to these
men, as I have no particular label. I am not a surgeon or an
astronomer, or another such recognised role. I say that I am
studying the flora and fauna of island colonies, and thus this
is accepted and I believe approved of. They are all men of
independent wealth and I think find it rather amusing that a
young woman is among them who presumes to know something of the world of science. We shall see how our first dinner
goes, where I may either be utterly ignored, or mocked gently
or investigated like one of their research topics. I am certainly
an object of curiosity to one and all on this ship, as evidenced
by the constant glances, smirks and downright staring I have
received from almost every man and boy on board – except
the captain – despite my austere dress. The fact remains I am
a woman in a man's domain and cannot escape it. I wish at
these moments I had the power of invisibility, or at least could
dress and speak convincingly as a man and therefore become
of no consequence. I reassure myself that at least on my
Portuguese island there will be few people and therefore fewer
eyes to gawk and gape at my ridiculous femininity.

I excuse myself from male company to answer a call of
nature in my cabin. There is a chamber pot secured under
my bunk for the purpose. It is a relief to know I will not be
required to point my hindquarters over the side of the ship
as I have already glimpsed an able seaman do. My stomach
churns and we have not yet set sail. I deliberate my choice
to take this journey: to leave the safety of Mr Woods's comfortable town house; to place myself in a world of men, wood
and salt; to be at the mercy of winds, canvas, the sea's moods
and the lives of foreigners. It seems my taste for adventure

is a child born to naïve optimism and foolish inexperience. As I squat on the pot, I look about for a receptacle in case I am to vomit. It seems my belly is a realist and is telling me in clear terms the risks I am taking in this lonely journey – alone, no friend, no ally. It was a rash decision and for a moment I almost blame my benefactor and even my tutor for not counselling me with more care, for failing to dissuade me from my rash course. But I know they are not to blame, that they would have needed to lock me in my room to have prevented me. I must face the fact that no one but my own self placed me here in this frightening journey into the unknown.

A tap on the door breaks into my misery.

'Who is it?' I squeak, stretching across to place my hand on the door in a sudden fear that someone will open it up to the unwelcome sight of me voiding my bowels.

'Only Francis,' says the boy. 'Cap'n says I am to be your boy, miss. Fetch and carry for you and whatnot. Can I assist you in any way, miss?'

I hesitate, yet see nothing will serve but honesty. 'You can help me in one minute, Francis, for I have a chamber pot to empty. Is this agreeable to you? Or I can do it myself.'

'Of course, miss,' comes his voice, the wood between us muffling it, yet perhaps I hear a catch in it, a hint of a giggle. 'I've done that for gents before, a thousand times. Hand it over when you're ready.'

'Thank you, Francis.'

The ship begins to move while I am busy. When I am done, I find a stoppered jug of seawater, retrieve a lump of soap from my trunk and wash my hands. I come out to find Francis standing stiffly, back to me, hands clasped behind as is his customary stance. He turns and grins, and I am immediately at ease and hand him the pot covered with a cloth. He takes it without a word and is off. Back in my cabin, I wash my face and look at it briefly in a hand mirror. My hair is neatly tucked beneath my plain, cream cap, my cheeks are wan and there are shadows beneath my eyes, betraying my sleepless night. I will have to do. After all, in my mind I am not female or male, I am a natural philosopher, a term that has no sex. I rush upstairs to the deck, to find that our ship has been floated out from the dock and is well on her way towards the sea. Now there is no turning back. I watch the seamen about their business, see the Gentlemen of Science throng near the captain and the master's mate discussing the weather, and confront my choice full face to the salty breeze.

II

It is three days' sail to Falmouth. I have heard of the dreadful sickness suffered by those new to the sea. My experience of it is curiously halved, as out of thrice I was sick as a dog on the first day, sick again the morning of the second, yet after lunch on that day I began to feel better and was quite well again on the third. This progress gives me hope that I will eventually obtain my sea legs and trouble the water with my vomit no further. During the worst periods, I have lain on my bunk and moaned, attended by Francis who discards my watery offerings. When I am feeling a little better, I get out my papers and read in my berth. I am considering the idea that I may conduct a search for fossils on the island itself or on the mainland nearby, as I have discovered from a recent account of this area that there are ancient remains dispersed about the local landscape. I wonder what I shall find.

Eating seems to aid me with my sickness, though some of the Gentlemen of Science choose the opposite view and eat nothing for the first two nights. Therefore dining is a solitary affair, from a tray brought to me in my cabin. The days have been overcast and close, thus little to see on board but louring grey clouds. And so I have taken my papers and maps to one of the scientists' work rooms and made further writings on my topic.

On the third day, we approach Falmouth and the wind falls. There is talk we will have to wait in port for days, if the weather does not rally. When we dock, I come upstairs away from my studies to watch the busy activity in port and aboard. I see the new crew arriving in dribs and drabs, helping to load up provisions into the holding areas in the lower decks. Some of the men are brought aboard stumbling, shoving and grumbling, by two midshipmen and the master with his gun about them. I realise these must be pressed men. My seasickness rises in my throat. These poor souls are shabby, sallow and slovenly, to a man. Not one of them looks well enough to fasten his own buttons.

I call Francis to ask to see the captain. I am led to his cabin, whereupon I am summoned to enter. He sits at his desk writing notes beside a diagram or two of waterways and coastal features. He puts down his writing equipment and turns to speak with me, still seated.

'Yes, Miss Price. You wished to see me?'

'Yes, sir. Thank you. I have just been watching the crew come aboard. Are there to be pressed men as part of this crew, sir?'

'There certainly are. Do not fear, miss. My officers and crew are well disciplined and will see they do not cause you nor a man else on board any mischief.'

'I have no fears for myself, sir. But I have a strong objection to the press gang as a method for the procurement of the crew of the Royal Navy.'

He turns from me and goes back to his quill, taking a penknife from his pocket and sharpening the nib meticulously.

'Life at sea is not an easy one, but it is a good career for any man. The Royal Navy does not have the luxury of a never-ending supply of willing seamen. Therefore, we are obliged to take from the streets the dregs who otherwise pollute it. And make them useful.'

'You remind me of the founder of my orphanage, sir.'

'Beelsby? Well, then I am pleased with the compliment. If indeed it was a compliment?'

'Indeed it was *not*, sir. I believe the practice of impressment to be wholly wrong. My brother was pressed as a boy and I never saw him again. It is theft, it is a kind of slavery, any kind of which I disagree with in the strongest terms possible.'

'Then please inform one of the crew if you wish to leave this ship here, and your trunk shall be deposited ashore at your convenience.'

I cross my arms and scowl at him.

'Do you wish to leave my ship, Miss Price?'

'I do not.'

'Then kindly allow me to run it as I please. I would sooner allow a Frenchman to advise me than a woman. Good day to you.'

I know now that my benefactor hit the mark about this infuriating bigot. I ought to hold my tongue for the present, but once we are out into the open sea and away from land, I should be able to speak to him more or less as I please, for I do not think even he would throw me overboard, woman or not. I am looking forward to *those* discussions.

Still docked in Falmouth, and our stomachs recovering, we are all formally invited to dinner with the captain that evening, as a full complement of officers and guests. All the Gentlemen of Science attend. As we are in port, the food is fresh and well-supplied and we are served florendine of rabbit with scalloped potatoes.

'This is an excellent dinner, Captain,' I remark and there are various noises of agreement around the table.

'Thank you, Miss Price,' says he and raises a glass to me before sipping, smiling in a genuine fashion. Perhaps he is surprised to hear me speak with approval.

Say I, 'I wonder what it is the men are eating this evening, the able seamen I mean. Do they have a similar spread?'

'They are furnished with the required rations prescribed by the Royal Navy for their station.'

'And what does that entail?'

'Perhaps,' says our captain pointedly and turns a cold eye upon me, 'you would like to retire to speak with our quartermaster, or even the cook?'

I smile sweetly at him and one of the young officers interjects: 'There is no need for Miss Price to leave us, sir, as I know precisely the daily ration of our able seamen, sir. If it be wished, sir, I can tell Miss Price, seeing as she is so interested in our life at sea.'

'As you wish,' mutters the captain.

I turn to the young officer, Leland by name, and say, 'Thank you and please do.'

'Now then, they have some salt pork or salt beef, which the men call in a colourful manner "sea junk". And there is beer. A little rum. There are dried peas and oats. We start out with some cheese and butter, miss, but this soon goes foul. There are molasses and hard tack always for every man. Sometimes the cook sells off the slush.'

'And that is . . .'

'Oh, the slush, miss? Why, it is the fatty dregs of boiled salt meat, skimmed off the bottom of the pans and sold as a treat to the men.'

'A *treat*?'

There is some clearing of throats around the table.

'Oh yes, miss. There is a roaring trade in it. Always sells out, every time.'

'Thank you, Leland, for your comprehensive reply.'

'My pleasure, miss,' he says, beaming.

I then turn my attention to the ship's surgeon. 'Dr Forbes, would you say the men are healthy aboard this ship? Or any ship upon which you have served?'

'I would say the officers are healthy. The men vary.'

The captain puts his wine down rather too quickly and heads turn. 'What I think Miss Price wishes to know is if our seamen are well provided for or treated badly on my ship. Is that not so, Miss Price?'

'I merely enquire as to the diet of the seamen. The awful disease of scurvy is rife in long sea voyages I understand, and yet no one has so far found a clear cause or practical solution to it.'

Dr Forbes concurs. 'That is true. I have been on long voyages and seen the ravages of scurvy. It is a revolting disease. There are many theories about its provenance or cure, yet as you say, miss, there is no foolproof method. Most of us believe it is related to the humours, or a blocked spleen.'

'Or a punishment from God,' adds Mr Piper. 'My personal view and that of many others, I dare say.'

'Yes, that too,' continues the surgeon. 'As for cure, some swear by tamarind or oil of vitriol. It is well known that idleness leads to scurvy, which is why one most often sees it in the lowest class of the crew; as they say, *those below the salt.*'

Say I, 'I have read a lot about this condition and have seen its dreadful consequences for myself at close quarters.'

Dr Hodges, our medical Gentleman of Science asks, 'And where have you seen this, Miss Price?'

'Did you know that children living in institutions, such as orphanages, have often suffered from scurvy? It is not only the disease of seamen.'

Mr Mathison chimes in, genuinely interested, 'I did not know that. I did not, I say!' and he turns to the faces around the table, clearly astonished.

Mr Kendall adds, 'So, gentlemen, we have ourselves a scientific mystery to solve. If the same disease is to be found among sailors and orphans, then what can be the connection?'

'As I said,' says Dr Forbes, 'a tendency towards idleness and the common occurrence of the disease among the lowest orders of society. Just the sort of child one would find in such an institution.'

I turn to Mr Piper and ask, 'And what have such as foundlings done to be punished so cruelly by God?'

Mr Piper sniggers and replies, 'I suppose you have been
engaged in charity work, have you, Miss Price? You are the
very twin of my younger sister, who wastes all the livelong
day doling out treats and grammar primers to the little
wretches. She comes back stinking of them. Quite repellent!
And I have told her that I cannot but think that we are of
a different species than the poor and no power but our Lord
can change a species. But she will go on with her meddling.'

Dr Hodges believes he has finished the argument when he
pronounces, 'And no good will such charity do any of them,
as they are born to it, will live in it, and die in it, and that
will never change. A man of science knows full well the order
of things in society mirrors that of the natural world. It is
fixed and immutable.'

I reflect upon my position. I wonder if it be wise to reveal
my origins to everyone around this table, none of whom is
aware of the shady circumstances of my birth. Yet I recall at
this moment that one man here is fully aware of the details
of my upbringing. I glance at him, to find he watches me.
He looks away instantly. It is pause enough for the conversation to move in a different direction and the moment to pass.
Captain Alex has not revealed me. I already labour under the
burden of being a woman in male company. He has spared
me from the secondary weight of being known as a low-born
foundling. And, though I am not ashamed of it, I am grateful
to him for that.

We wait for a change in the weather only one night. In the
morning, I stand on deck and my hair is loosened from beneath
my cap by a new stiff breeze. I pull my cloak close about my
shoulders and watch the bustle of Falmouth port and see the
last crates brought on board, and, last of all, a quantity of pig
iron to be used as ballast.

Captain Alex appears beside me and says, 'We have a fair wind today and will be under sail very soon.'

'That is good news.'

'Yes, it is very fortunate. Sometimes one has to wait days and days. But perhaps you would prefer that, Miss Price. I wonder if you are quite ready for this journey.'

'Do you question my resolve, sir?'

'No, I do not. I question if you go into it with your eyes quite open. I have not yet met a woman who does well at sea. One has to pander to their feminine needs and calm them in fierce seas. I have always considered the presence of women on board ship to be most deleterious to the ship's morale. They generally panic in times of trouble and the rest of the time serve as a distraction.'

'Perhaps you will allow that not all women are the same. Just as not all men are the same.'

'I do allow that, yes. I can see that in all respects you are an unusual woman. I can only surmise that your curious talents are God-given, a kind of highly uncommon gift for society: the woman of science. You are in fact a kind of aberration. You should have been born a man. Instead, you are God's charming mistake.'

He says this with a slight smile and perhaps I can discern a subtle twinkle in his eye. Is he sporting with me or can he be serious? 'A mistake?' say I.

'Yes, but a charming one,' says he and inclines his head.

Sport or not, I cannot resist but retort in kind. 'Well, I do consider sometimes if I were a kind of random error. A little like the birth of twins.'

'Twins?'

'Yes, a kind of blunder by nature, yet with *charming* consequences.'

'You are fully aware, Miss Price, that I myself have twin sons.'

'Of course. As I say, a delightful consequence of chance.

But what possible point is there in twins? What purpose could they serve? Other than to delight us.'

'My sons are not a *blunder*. They are a welcome gift from the Lord. My wife would be quite faint to hear them spoken of as *mistakes*.'

'Oh no, sir. You quite misunderstand me. I only remark that twins are very unusual and seemingly quite without purpose. In some cultures, they are drowned at birth, I have heard.'

'*Indeed!*'

He is quite beside himself. For a moment, I consider ending the discussion. But I remind myself that he started this, with his comments on my erroneous origins, and this insult – however veiled in playful irony – brought a little choler on me. I will not let him win, I simply cannot.

'Like myself, the clever woman. Not so very long ago, a woman with my knowledge and intellectual attributes would likely be sought out and accused of some witchcraft and hanged. In my case, there was a blend of intellect and opportunity. If I had not been plucked from the greasy stew of humanity and deposited in the orphanage, I would still be on the streets to this day, or else more likely dead, my fine mind gone with me.'

'Please do not forget that God directs all work in His creation. It is no chance you were plucked, as you say, from the streets, but His work.'

'Ah, but it was me who stole the founder's quill and taught myself to write. And it was this act that attracted my benefactor. There was nothing in either of my environments, be it on the streets or in the asylum, that naturally supported my keen mind. But I fought against the confines of my situation, and improved myself. Poverty is the enemy of the mind. One must fight a way out of it to achieve anything but mere survival. God does not help one to do this. The system of society is weighted against it completely. It is me who created this clever woman.'

Captain Alex's cheeks are now a high shade of pink and he glances about him. 'Miss Price, keep your voice down. Are you aware that you verge on *blasphemy*?'

'I am not, sir. I agree with you that my brain was a gift from God. But it is what I chose to do with it that belongs to me. And how I flouted my unfortunate circumstances – that of being both an orphan and a female – to become the person you see before you. I had luck along the way, kindness and help from good people, but it was my ambition that brings me here today. As does yours, sir, to rise in the ranks and make your fortune in war. Is it God's will that you are to rise through the killing of others? I do not believe so, but you are a good man and yet you need war to provide you with promotion. And I believe you were born with it, as a man, this male desire to conquer. It is perhaps this physical power – an obvious difference betwixt male and female – that has led to the subjugation of women. And that is why there are no statues to female thinkers of the past. You must admit it would be highly unlikely that I am the only clever female to exist in the history of the world.'

'No, there was Eve,' says he with distaste.

'Ah, Eve. Now that is an interesting case. Eve did taste of the Tree of Knowledge and could be said to be the saviour of us all.'

'*Saviour?*'

'Yes, for what would we be without our thirst for knowledge? It is what separates us from the beasts after all. I would rather that than paradise any day. Eve desired of the fruit of the tree to make her wise. She wanted to *know*. And I am no aberration: there are plenty of girls and women who wish to think, to learn, to know. But it is our society and the beliefs of the men who run it that keep women from thinking, from studying and learning. Any woman can do what I have done. Any woman with the right kind of mind. And what leaps could have been made already if all the world's women – or the poor, or the orphans, or any other powerless outcast – had been educated? Would the longitude problem not be solved by now? Or a universal cure for all? Including the dreadful scurvy? Scurvy is no punishment from God. Have you thought of improving your seamen's diet, sir? With a mixture of foods, with some pickled fruit and vegetable, rather than slush and hard tack? No wonder it is the able seamen and the pressed men who succumb first, sir. They eat rubbish and their officers eat like kings in comparison. What do you say to *that*?'

By now his face is thunderous. And I am quite out of breath.

'I say that you, miss, are the most infuriating and self-opinionated and insolent . . . *woman* . . . no, no . . . *person*, male or female – of any race or kind or shape – I have ever had the misfortune to meet. And the sooner we reach Lisbon, the better!' With this he stamps away.

I turn to the side and breathe deeply, watching the water lapping at the ship's side. It is restless and ancient, yet does not tire in its ancient restlessness; it wears its age lightly. I should learn a lesson from its longevity and stop trying to change the world in one argument. I scold myself, as my conversation lacked rational direction. My arguments were muddled into a hotchpotch with no clear point, and I truly allowed my emotions – namely anger – to lead some sections of the discussion. I must do better next time. And I really must stop rising to the bait of Captain Alex. He is quite clearly offended by me and everything I represent. For me, he is the epitome of everything I am fighting against.

12

That afternoon, we weigh anchor at Falmouth and proceed in calm waters. The sky is clear and vast and we have our first sight of a sunset since sailing. Indeed, it is the first sunset of my life wherein I see the horizon swallow the great fiery globe, and quite a sight it is. The seamen aboard are busy with their duties, yet we travellers are still and quiet with awe. It is a moment I have longed for since gazing from the orphanage window and my heart is glad. I am loath to leave deck for my cabin, even once the sun is long gone. I fall asleep that night bathed in the tranquillity of an ambition achieved. But in the night a storm arises. I wake from my fretful sleep to hear cries of alarm. I sit up and swing my legs about to stand, when the ship takes a heave and my trunk careers across the room and smashes into my bunk, inches from my feet. Say I, 'God have mercy!' and hear Francis knocking on my door.

'Miss, you lay still. Don't be afraid.'

I stagger to the door and open it. 'Good God, Francis! I suppose we shall all be lost. What shall I do?'

'It feels bad, miss, but we shall prevail. There is no danger. We have a land wind.'

'What is a land wind?'

'A wind that comes from the land, which will drive us out to sea. We shall be well when we have sea-room. Never fear and you lie still and do not leave your cabin on any account, miss.'

The boy leaves me. I sit on my bed and lash myself with

a scarf to a hook on the wall above it to stop myself falling out. The storm rages for hours and I hear one of the men scream and scream like a girl, which one I do not know – it could be one of the Gentlemen of Science, as it is in a cabin nearby, but some more screams come from above me – and I am startled by it and frightened to think that Francis had lied to appease me and we are all to be lost and those screaming men know it. But I act as I am told and do not leave my room. Once I put my head out of the door and hear the frightful rain beating down and the wind howling wonderfully strong and marvel at the power and force of nature. Yet the ship holds on and the dreadful tossing reduces to swaying and then to a more moderate swell. And finally there is another knock on my door and I call out, 'I am well, Francis,' and I open the door to find Captain Alex there, his wig gone, his hair sodden, plastered against his begrimed face and his clothes wet through. Yet he still stands upright and calm.

'I wished to inform you, Miss Price, that our ship is well out of danger by now and we are happily sailing away from the storm. Within hours all will be most calm.'

He attempts to right his dripping hair – which I see now is very fair and must be quite golden when dry – but it sticks up fearfully.

'You must change your clothes, or you will catch your death,' I say. He wipes his hand across his eyes and I perceive he looks light-headed and I am afraid he will collapse. I remember this is his first command and find myself full of sympathy for the frightful night he must have had, ensuring the safe passage of the ship, the heavy weight of responsibility on his shoulders alone for this first time as captain.

'Please, sir. Will you be seated?'

He closes his eyes and staggers against the door jamb to my cabin.

'Francis!' I cry and my boy appears clattering down the steps. 'Look to your captain!'

Upon which Alexander comes to himself and turns angrily to the boy, 'Get away with you!' turns on his heel and disappears into his own quarters, slamming the door behind him.

Francis hesitates, a look of shock and indecision clouding his features, and I say to him, 'Do not fret, Francis, but your captain needs rest and plain food, and fresh water to drink. Bring him some and see if you can persuade him to sleep a while. He needs it.'

'Yes, miss,' he says and heads off to the cook-room.

As the sea calms, I sleep a while. In the morning, I ready myself and come up on deck to find a brilliant blue sky. No one would guess of our tempestuous night. The seamen are about their business and the captain stands talking with Mr Kendall and Dr Forbes. They turn and greet me. I am about to ask the captain how he fares, if he feels better than when I saw him last. But I stop myself, as he must have done when orphans were slandered. I surmise he would not wish for the only woman on board to enquire after his moment of weakness – as surely he would categorise it – in front of the men of his vessel. So I hold my tongue. We are equal now, in that single regard if nothing else.

After the storm, our captain speaks to me only in company for several days, avoiding any opportunity for argument. He is highly courteous at all times and I believe our days of baiting may perhaps be over. After a week at sea, I am leaving my cabin one morning and he is coming from his at the same moment. I am about to give a quick sink and excuse-me, when he stops and breathes as if to speak, then falls silent.

'May I be of some assistance to you, sir?'

'About the night of the storm. I understand from Francis that you made no requests and no fuss. Francis called you very brave.'

I am thunderstruck to hear credit from him, almost at a loss for words. But not for long.

'I merely did as I was told. Francis said I was to stay in my cabin, and that I did.'

'It is said you were not sick and did not even cry out in fear. Not once. If only all our crew and our guests were so . . . so very . . .'

'Manly?' I reply, with a hint of a smile.

'I believe I owe you an apology, Miss Price. Please accept it, in goodwill.'

'I do, sir. I do accept it, most humbly.'

He turns to leave.

'And, sir?'

'Yes?'

'Will you accept my apology also? For behaving in such an uncouth manner during our argument. It was the behaviour of neither a lady nor a gentleman. I have a temper at times and have not yet succeeded in taming it. And I am sorry for it.'

'I do not pretend to agree with your opinions. Yet I would defend your right to voice them. Perhaps if you published your ideas, in more moderate and contained prose, you would find the audience you require. And deserve.'

'If it does not land me in the pillory.'

Captain Alex smiles. 'I cannot imagine that.'

'I can,' say I, in all seriousness.

'Miss Price, you mentioned to me that you had a brother pressed into service with the Royal Navy.'

'I believe so, yes. I was very young and it is a callow memory.'

'You say you have not seen him since. If you could give me his name, I would be happy to make enquiries for you in the naval records.'

'That is very gracious of you, Captain. But I am afraid I do not have his name, neither last nor first. I have no recollection even of my own name from those years, and that which I go by now was given me by the matron of my orphanage. Perhaps he was not even my brother, just a kind soul who cared for me. I have no proof of any of it, you see.'

'I do see. Without a name, it would be quite impossible to locate him.'

'Of course. But I am exceedingly touched by your solicitude in this matter. I have resolved that I will never see my brother more and that is that. To live a life of regret is a wasted life, is it not?'

'Agreed.' And he makes a short bow and adds, 'After you, Miss Price.'

We are at sea nine days further until we are told that we shall dock in Lisbon the following afternoon. I have seen little of the captain. His presence at dinner on the night in Falmouth does not become a habit and he is usually to be found talking with his men or in his cabin at mealtimes. His enquiry after my brother has warmed me to him and I would welcome some more discussion with him, yet it is not to be. On our last night aboard, I cannot sleep, too apprehensive of my landing tomorrow and what it will bring. I have lain awake for hours when there is a quiet knock at my door, so quiet I believe at first I am hearing things.

'Yes?' I answer just as quietly, in case I am wrong.

'Francis, miss. Cap'n wishes to see you.'

'Have I time to dress myself?'

'A little time, miss. But hurry.'

Never one to concern myself too much with appearances, I pull out my stays and simplest dress and throw them over my shift. My hair has escaped its nightcap, as ever, and tumbles everywhere inconveniently. I try to plait it away from my face as I follow Francis who holds his lamp aloft to light my way up the steps to the deck. My mind is perturbed at the thought of emergency. Why ever else would the captain call for me in the middle of the night?

I see him first standing by the side, his back to me, head tipped back, looking into the sky. He turns to me and beckons excitedly and it is then that I see it. Up in the black night sky, I see the waxing moon, very full and bright. Yet around it extends a faint halo and on each side, placed in perfect symmetry, are two smaller pale discs, shining dully and connected to the moon by the faintest of curved lines.

I stand beside Captain Alex and we both gaze at it without speaking.

'It must have a name,' say I.

'It does. It is a mock moon. Or some call it a moon dog. Astronomers have named it *paraselene.*'

'Why does it occur?'

'I have no clue. It is more usual to find it in cold places. But it is rare in any case. Very rare.'

'It is beautiful.'

'Yes.'

We stand for some time, unmoving.

'I hope you can forgive me, for waking you at such an hour.'

'Of course. I am so very grateful. Look at it!'

'I believed you would wish to see it. As a natural philosopher.'

I look about me and see only the sailors of the night watch. 'You did not call our Gentlemen of Science?'

And with a curious lilt, as if he does not quite understand the reason either, he replies, 'No. I did not.'

We stay there for many moments, beneath the benign light of the mysterious moon dog, the ship swaying lazily larboard to starboard, east to west, proceeding steadily south towards our landing-place.

The final leg of my journey is an agreeable passage, without the thick fog predicted by some on board that customarily hangs over the Portuguese coast. By mid-morning on a beautifully clear day, we passengers stand on deck and wait for the first sight of Lisbon. But first, we sail in sight of an array of islets, with one greater island and other smaller islets scattered about it. There are thousands of seabirds visible as dots taking off and landing from the smaller in particular, and visible on the main islet is a squat, irregular octagonal fort, all surrounded by vegetation – coloured apple green by the morning sun – spots of colour from other greenery and flowers and rocky outcrops, carved out by the restless sea.

Captain Alex arrives beside me and says, 'Miss Price, allow me to introduce you to your islands.'

'Those are the Berlengas?' I ask with gladness, as I did not know we would be able to see them on our approach.

'Yes, the Burlings. So, they will be your work for the next six months, I presume?'

'Yes indeed!' say I and gaze upon them, peering back at them once every man else on board has since turned away and looks for Lisbon once more.

By lunchtime, we are in sight of the rock of Lisbon, the famous Cabo da Roca. Here are broad cliffs that rise up hundreds of feet and cause cooing from the passengers. At the very top we see a small building perched, a hermitage that Leland tells us is the residence of a former English sea captain. In the distance, one can see the slopes of the Sintra mountains covered in clouds of woodland. We turn east for the land, following the coastline past small fishing ports and then we approach a massive and impressive scar in the coast, flanked by forts, where the Tagus River meets the sea. When we come near the entrance of the river, a local pilot comes aboard to take command of the ship to navigate her into the Tagus to the anchoring-place. He is spoken of as a *poor fisherman* and is rather mocked by the able seamen aboard, though to me he is my first sight of a Portuguese man, and I appreciate the flair of his long cloak thrown in a cavalier fashion about his shoulders and a tall cocked hat. It is said the passage through the channel is hazardous and only to be undertaken by the locals such as him who have the expertise to do it. Once safely past the river bar, Captain Alex takes control again and sees us up the final stretch.

All along the way on each side are dotted a range of forts, until we reach what those on board called Bellisle, the gateway to Lisbon. Another fort looms into view, this one grandiose with over a dozen cannon portals and thick walls ornamented with stone twisting ropes, spheres and ships; its name is the Torre de Belem, richly historical as it is the spot where Vasco da Gama set out to discover the sea route to the east and many other adventurers since, in the great age of Portuguese exploration. We are hailed from the fort and required to anchor here for a health inspection, in order to protect Lisbon from disease. Our seamen jeer and mock the inspectors and we hear from the master's mate that the sailors' tobacco is sometimes confiscated as contraband and thus the Portuguese inspectors are universally hated.

Once inspected and duly passed, we proceed quite close to the shore and see our first Portuguese coaches trundling along the main roadway into the city. We sail slowly by a raft of glorious mansions, monasteries, palaces and estates, jumbled alongside small white houses, the scene punctuated by windmills with linked sails like webs turning slowly in the sweet air. The land is filled now on either side by the patchwork outskirts of the city, by and by thickening into the jumble of waterfront life – churches, houses, a prison, and further on the buildings of the shipyards and the wharves, and another grander waterfront palace. Gathering all around us in the water bob and speed a variety of watercraft: taxis and fishing boats and cargo ships. The view from our ship of this city is magnificent and quite puts our London to shame, dirty and squalid as it seems beside this array of sparkling buildings. I have come here to study nature and yet I am presented with the height of architecture and culture, and find myself marvelling at the abundance of human achievement, something no animal has yet approximated, to my knowledge.

Caught up in the wonders of the view alongside the Gentlemen of Science, I am suddenly reminded that they do not vacate the ship here with all their belongings, as they will use the ship as a dwelling during their stay in Lisbon. But I am to leave it very soon, with all my belongings still distributed about my cabin. So I rush back to my cabin to find all my things have been fully packed by Francis. He is watching as my trunk is removed on the shoulder of a brawny seaman, who tells the boy to get out of his way in vulgar language. As I thank Francis, I see a melancholy gleam in the boy's wide eyes.

'I will miss you, Francis,' say I and the gleam transforms into two fat tears that roll down his cheeks. He looks away shamed, and wipes his face on his sleeve.

'Don't tell the cap'n,' he mutters and I swear I would never do such a thing.

'You will have adventures in Africa and I will see you again in six months, when the *Prospect* comes to Lisbon again, and I will be boarding for my return to England. I will need your help then as much as now. Will you assist me then, Francis?'

'With honour, miss,' says this sweet boy and salutes me fittingly. 'But do be careful. They're saying on deck that the French have been here in Lisbon some weeks past, their ships causing a stir in the Tagus. Keep your wits about you, miss.'

'Thank you for the wise advice.' I pat him on the shoulder, which he takes with some pride.

On deck, it is time to say farewell to the crew and the guests, who are very courteous and wish me well, while we are bustled on all sides by the unloading and loading of goods by our English seamen and the dark-skinned Portuguese dock workers. Before I descend to set foot on Portuguese soil, Captain Alex offers his hand and I shake it heartily, both of us laughing at the repetition of our first meeting.

'Here, you see that man there? That is the footman from the English Hotel, and he will take you to a coach that will transfer you safely to your accommodation. I shall ensure you are contacted directly we arrive back in six months' time. Do not wander off into the Portuguese wilds, Miss Price. Keep yourself most safe, will you not, and avoid reckless adventure?'

'I doubt it!' I jest, or half jest.

Here in the warm blue day I can see the pleasure he takes in his post of captain of this ship, and in the sights he must see on every journey across the seas. His eyes veritably shine with it.

13

My passage from the ship through the dockyards to a coach is not quite as savoury as the view from the river suggests. The muddy streets of Lisbon smell as badly as the worst of St Giles, especially as they bake in the mid-July sunshine. It is so warm that the ravens perched in trees stretch out their wings to cool themselves. The roads are teeming with men and women of black skin carrying out any number of jobs in the streets, coming and going from rich houses and poor, selling mussels and other foodstuffs in stalls and washing linen, not unlike the dark-skinned people I have seen about St Giles and the docks in London. Here they are somewhat more exotic, as some I see playing guitars and mandolins, while one dances in a rather shocking manner. Passing through are paler men of the cloth in their purple, black or white ecclesiastical robes – there seem to be priests everywhere one looks – alongside gypsies and peasants and gentlemen followed by their footmen in livery who wait for them by closed doors smoking cheroots; street vendors hawking fish, wheat, chest-nuts and rainbow-winged parrots; packs of wild-faced children running about the streets like dogs, of which there are also dozens; though apart from the poor women, there are precious few ladies anywhere to be seen on the streets, unlike my home city. I take this as a warning of its dangers and resolve to avoid studying too closely the human life on the streets of Lisbon, and instead aim to concentrate on my study of the safer territory of plants and animals of the Berlengas Islands at the first possible opportunity.

I arrive at the English Hotel, standing on the highest ground near Lisbon, nearest the sea. The road past the hotel is jostling with carriages and coachmen, and gentlemen on saddle-horses, all of whom convey a superior appearance as they go out together for an airing after luncheon. I take a moment to turn and look out across the city. It stretches across seven hills, beside the shining broad river. I would estimate one can see fifty miles across country from here. Such a contrast from the restricted dark views everywhere one looks in London. I had no thought that a city could have such a handsome prospect, despite masking its grubby nature at street level.

Inside the hotel, I meet the owners: Mr and Mrs Dewar from Northumberland, old friends and business associates of Mr Woods. We all speak fondly of my benefactor and they know well of his propensity for drink and we share a humorous tale or two. The hotel is frequented by a great deal of company: English, Irish, Scots and Welsh; gentlemen, ladies, merchants and servants. I am shown to my room, which is clean, with flowered walls and a comfortable bed. There is even an escritoire for my work. At the first opportunity, I ask Mrs Dewar to make arrangements for me to be taken to Peniche, the town from which I will be visiting my warmly anticipated islands. She reveals it is all arranged, after receiving word from Mr Woods to that effect some days ago. I am to be taken there tomorrow morning, after an early breakfast. And thus I only have a few hours to rest, prepare and wait for my first visit to Ilha Berlenga.

Before I go, Mrs Dewar presents me with an impromptu gift: 'Take one of my parasols, dear. You'll need it this time of year, especially by the sea. No lady wants to be turned brown, eh?' Yet as she says this, I see her frowning eyes scan my face and deduce she notes the natural duskiness of my complexion, though is too polite to mention it.

It takes all day by coach, with the horses rested three times on the dusty, potholed yet picturesque roads to the attractive coastal town of Peniche. Mrs Dewar has arranged for me to stay during the week in a small guest-house on a hill overlooking the sea owned by the sister-in-law of a wine merchant known to Mr Woods. She is a Portuguese widow of late middle age named Dona da Seda (in English, one could call her Mrs Silk), dressed in black from head to toe, though I know not how long ago her husband died. She is polite yet taciturn, and I welcome this; I know I will not be distracted from my work by this lady of few words. From this house, I will travel daily by ferry to the island, returning at night to eat and sleep. On Saturdays I will return to the English Hotel, where I am required to write my weekly diary, which is given to Mrs Dewar and forwarded to Mr Woods in England. Such are the minimal requirements laid upon me by my patron. He also wants to ensure I am well looked after at the hotel at least once a week, as the Peniche guest-house is plain in the extreme, with bare walls painted white, the minimum of furniture and no decoration of any sort, besides a crucifix on the wall above the low narrow bed. It is not without comfort though, and scrupulously clean. It suits me perfectly, far more than the hotel which, though congenial, would be far too sociable for collating my notes each evening.

In the morning, Dona da Seda brings me a simple breakfast of goat's cheese and bread. It is like my orphanage days, yet a good-sized portion, and this time I relish the plain food, to settle my stomach. She shows me the road I must walk down to the sea, adding the name of the man who will ferry me to the island – Horacio – the name of his boat and that he wears a red neckerchief. I carry with me a bag, in which I have my sea floor viewing box; three little boxes suitable for animal specimens; a book of thick paper for pressing plant specimens; a notebook and pencils; a leather water bottle and a simple lunch of figs, chestnuts and bread wrapped in muslin by my hostess. I wear a cap and carry my parasol to guard against the weather.

Squat white houses with red roofs line every street, while
every few houses I find one painted green, or pink, or a rich
terracotta, with yellow window frames or filigree ironwork
balconies, or an attractive image painted on the closed shutters, of flowers or fruit; on walls there are lines of flat fish
hung out on wires to dry in the sun, their black shadows
thrown sharply against the white walls by the bright sun. I
walk past an open workshop full of women and young girls
making lace placed over bolster cushions. I slow to peer more
closely and see that the lace is pinned on to the cushions in
elaborate designs, each thread attached to large clusters of
round wooden bobbins. The ladies nod at me as I pass.

'*Bela*,' say I and they smile. *Beautiful.*

'*Obrigada*,' they say and I walk on to the sea.

At this moment, I realise this is the first walk I have taken
without a companion in years. The first time since my street
days that I have been able to proceed, alone with my thoughts
and impressions, able to speak to people I pass; without
recourse to another, without care for another, without the
opinions of another to guide or hamper me. Nobody knows
me here, nobody expects anything of me or wants anything
from me. And I own a sovereignty over my life that heretofore
I have never had. For a moment only, I close my eyes as I
walk and feel the seaside air play across my cheeks and the
Portuguese sun beat down on me. I am truly free.

The sea spreads sapphire blue from the tumbling rocks of
the coastline, frowned over by an imposing grey fort. The
beach is butter yellow and soft, as I trudge across the sand
to find the boat I need, the *Gaivota*, or the Seagull to you
and me. I cannot see any names on the rowing boats lined
up on the beach but there is a fellow with a red neckerchief
beside one. He is waving at me. He confirms he is Horacio
and says that I must not be sick in his boat. He mimes vomiting
over the side to ensure I understand. He stows my bag, takes
my hand in his rough, calloused one and helps me step in. I

cannot see how this petite craft can possibly convey us all the way out to the Berlengas without dashing us on the rocks. I am about to question the wisdom of such a journey when I see he is rowing us towards a small sail boat anchored further out, *Gaivota* painted in white letters on her bow; and I think that for a person of scientific mind, I can be insufferably stupid at times.

Soon we are proceeding westwards, away from the Peniche harbour and out into the choppy seas. The journey seems endless, but perhaps is two hours or more. I vomit four times, I am glad to say over the side and not in Horacio's boat. Every time I am sick he roars with laughter and nods. I am annoyed the first time, but by the third I wipe my mouth and try to laugh with him. He tells me the return trip is not so bad, as the winds and waves act differently towards the mainland. This gives me something to focus on, as I hold my stomach and gaze ahead, willing the islands to race towards me and end this misery. I resolve that there is no way I can stomach this trip twice a day, five days a week, four weeks a month, and six months altogether. I simply cannot. When I arrive, I will enquire about a place I can stay on the island, for perhaps a week at a time, and resolve to stay over in Peniche on Saturdays and Sundays instead. My benefactor may not understand, as he has an iron stomach from his sailing days. But I cannot waste my study time and risk my health by undertaking this despicable journey twice a day. I vomit again, my breakfast all gone, my head light with hunger and exhaustion, retching emptily now. To think I strolled down the streets of Peniche this morning, the happiest woman in town, and now I am in misery: the costs of liberty.

At long last, the *Gaivota* arrives at Berlenga Grande, the largest island hereabouts. The mooring-place is at the foot of the fortress I had seen from the *Prospect*. The water in this cove is luminous turquoise, almost green, and crystal-clear. Ahead of us rise stately granite rocks painted red, yellow, pink and grey by nature and the sunlight. We dock by a short jetty beside a bobbing row of boats with oars, and I step out on unsteady legs on to thick clumps of bright green grass that curl round my shoes in fleshy tufts. Oh, how I love the land! Horacio passes me my bag. He tells me he will see me here when I am ready to return, but will come to find me if he tires of waiting. He says it all with a cheerful grin, then steps back into his boat, settles down on his back, folds his arms and closes his eyes for a nap.

I turn to my island. I retrieve my sketchbook, lunch and parasol, leave the bag on the jetty and spend this first day exploring the length and breadth of Berlenga Grande, getting my bearings. On my climb up to a headland, I pass by a small stone hut by a well. I look down the well and judge the water to be clean, as it smells sweetly. The dwelling looks like it was once used by a goatherd or some such thing, and needs a good clean out. But it has shutters that are solid and not rotten, and even an old stove and a fireplace. I carry on up to the very top of the highest cliff on the island and look out at my domain. I see clearly the three groups of islets that make up this archipelago: here is my island and its adjacent reefs, then nearby the rock that surely must have once been a part of this island: the Ilha Vela or Old Island, somehow cut off from here, by an ancient disaster, an act of God perhaps. Further off are two other island clusters: nearest are the Estelas and quite far are the Farilhões. They are home to many seabirds, I have heard, and to no people: a perfect menagerie, unadulterated by human interference. I will ask Horacio to take me to all of these, in good time.

I look to the fortress, which became so only in the last century, as it was built on the ruins of an ancient monastery. I think of the religious men who praised God here and tried to fight off attacks from enemies of Portugal, pirates and corsairs, often unsuccessfully; dying of untreatable diseases or falling from the cliffs, eventually driven away for good. I know there is a small garrison here in the fort, and there used to be some goatherds and fishermen; I contemplate why they chose to come to this island, away from the comforts of the mainland. I think of the people who made their way over here in ancient times, in boats far less reliable than Horacio's; perhaps on rafts, or even floating logs. And I marvel at the human need to explore, conquer and settle. I wonder how long we have been doing it, how many hundreds of years. Or, could it be, thousands? For now, there are no people evident from my viewpoint up here, and I feel I could be the only person in the world, the last woman alive. But I am surrounded by life. From where I stand, I feel the islands throb about me with independent existence, rich with industry and a battle for survival, against each other, against the pounding sea and the scouring wind.

14

The goatherd's hut will be mine. I am determined to have it for the duration of my stay, to reside on the island for some months and not to return to Peniche at the end of each week. After all, no one else makes use of the hut presently, so what is the harm? I go to see the captain in charge of the small garrison at the fort and ask him to arrange for a spare bunk and simple bedding to be sent up. He looks at me strangely but sees I am quite serious and does not refuse. He also agrees that his men will divert the course of their evening patrol to within shooting distance of my hut, in order to protect me. From what? I wonder. Vicious seagulls? When I tell Horacio of my plan, he clearly thinks I am insane and tells me so. He tells me there are a few malefactors incarcerated at the garrison and it is not safe. But I assure him I trust the soldiers there to guard them efficiently, at which he narrows his eyes and shakes his head. But he knows me enough already to doubt he will ever sway me, once I have set my mind to something. A few miscreants in a heavily guarded fort will never prevent me from my course of action, nor even the entire army of Portugal, I warrant.

Eventually I win round Horacio and he says he will enlist his wife's help in thoroughly cleaning out the hut and even providing some home comforts. We go back to Peniche and I purchase supplies of food, blankets, crockery, cutlery, candles and soap, Horacio agreeing to furnish me with more necessities from time to time during my stay. I tell Dona da Seda of my plans and she looks sourly upon them. I give her two letters: one for Mrs Dewar at the English Hotel – firstly to order for me some coloured pastels and more sketchbooks, for me to fashion accurate drawings of the wildlife I find on the islands – and the other to my benefactor in England, informing both recipients of my movements, for courtesy's sake. They may not approve either, but they are miles away and I am here. I am my own person and nobody can stop me. I have a mind to do something and – if it not be against the law of the land or cruel to another person – I will do it, and I will brook no objections on the grounds of what is normal, or usual, or even considered wise by others. If I hear protests, I question them carefully, I tease them to pieces and thereby destroy them, but gently. It is a method that seems to work very well for me, so far.

Pilar is the name of Horacio's wife; she is in middle age, like him, with the kind of face in repose that looks like it has never seen a moment's joy. On introduction, she tells me solemnly in Portuguese that she makes lace in Peniche and saw me that morning I greeted the ladies – that she would not have forgotten me, as a stranger in town is memorable – and she narrows her eyes at me in a rather severe manner. But when her husband tells her of my plan to live in a goat-herd's hut on Berlenga Grande, she considers it for a moment, then creases into mighty guffaws and we all fall into laughter together. She does not seem to think I am foolish; rather, she is enamoured of the challenge and accompanies us on the boat trip (she does not vomit once); she brings a broom, a mop, cloths, pots and pans, a blanket, and even a stool for me to sit on in my hut. We make light work of the cleaning, as Pilar reveals she speaks Spanish and is delighted I speak it too. My Spanish is much more fluent than my Portuguese, and she seems happy to converse in it again, though she tells me her native language is different. She explains that she was brought up on the island of Minorca and they speak a dialect there, but that Spanish will do for us. It reminds her of home.

She misses it still. Minorca became a British possession around forty years ago, and she remembers as a girl the English ships arriving. But she has surprisingly little malice in her about it, and said her family were glad when the English came, though there were families against it, who favoured one or other of the many invaders over the years. She came to Portugal as a restless young woman to visit relatives. She lived in Lisbon for a time and met Horacio, then moved to Peniche. She married Horacio at seventeen and the Lord did not grace them with children, so they live alone. She says she dreams of islands and envies me sleeping here.

Each evening I drift into sleep to the sound of the sea. Each morning I wake to the sound of the sea. I spend my days exploring and learning of my island's wildlife. I find I soon discard my parasol, as it seems always cumbersome and in my way; though my cheeks at first become a little sun-scorched, thereafter my skin seems to take to the climate here and bronzes quite unfashionably. The archipelago's relief is jagged with a flat central plain. No trees of any significance grace the scene, only a few stunted olive and fig bushes. There are a variety of seabirds hereabouts: yellow-legged gulls and black-backed gulls, petrels and shags and guillemots, storm-petrels and shearwaters. I watch the shags with their funny crests, yellow beaks and green eyes, bickering and complaining among themselves. The guillemots possess a strange calm, I think only due to their matt black faces and the curious white streak beside their eyes, which gives them the air of wisdom. There are black rats, probably arrived with mariners, and a curious lizard, bright green-yellow along the flank and back, mottled with black and brown patches. I know from speaking to Horacio that there are sardine and mackerel aplenty in these waters, as well as skate, eels and an ugly-faced fish, called by Pilar *el mero*, which some consider a delicacy. The flora is very appealing, with drifts of pink-purple thrift fluttering across the swells of land, flanked by yellow fleabane, and the rocks creep with a matting plant with delicate green florets which I believe is of the family *herniaria* or rupturewort. Pilar tells me that the odd thing is that these flora and fauna are quite different from those found in Peniche, as well as the red granite rock here being completely different to the limestone on the mainland – almost as if the island had been plucked from another continent and deposited here by a mighty hand, or perchance islands in the distant past did float across the seas, picking up curious animals and wind-borne seeds as they went.

There are numerous caves and hollows hereabouts. Some are on the other islets and thus far unreachable to me, yet I have managed to clamber into some on the main island. In one I find the floor strewn with old things: mounds of seashells, remains of fires and scattered piles of the bones of animals. I collect a few and examine them in my hut. It seems some of these bones may even be human. I consider how old they may be. Also I find several stones that seem too similar to be a coincidence. I would swear they have been fashioned in some way, flaked with perhaps another piece of rock to create sharp edges on both sides. They fit perfectly into the palm of my hand. And I could call up into my fancy the act of holding such a stone and cutting fruit with it, or even carving shapes into wood or bone, scraping, slicing, creating. It is a tool, I am sure of it. But what kind of people would need to use such a hand-made, lowly tool as this? Even the monks will have had cutlery, axes and knives. It must be so old it is beyond memory. I keep them all laid out in my hut and study them over and over, considering the hands that made them, and what their eyes did see in that distant past.

Once I have scoured the land of my island, I venture into the sea to study the life within it. At first I hitch up my skirts and wade into the shallows. I carry my glass viewer beneath my arm and peer down into the water for the first time. And what a world I find! Never have I dreamed of such a complete system of life so separate from my own, in this other medium, this water they have no knowledge of; they swim through it and yet have as little understanding of it as does a babe the air it breathes. I see flat rocks spreading out beyond me, home to a multitude of plants and creatures, a city of the shallows, buzzing with silent yet vibrant life; rather, it is silent to this outsider, looking in from the world of air, but I imagine within the water there must be a cacophony from all those tiny vivid inhabitants fighting for space, light and life, just as noisy as any London thoroughfare. Tiny fish dart between delicate plants constructed of waving fingers, spread across the rocks plastered with splashes of every colour I can imagine, strange jellied organisms – plant or animal? It is a mystery! – forests of tree-like structures spreading and contracting, moving in unison with every whim of the water, looking almost alive, sentient. I spend days looking at the reefs near to the beaches, up to my waist in ocean, my skirts sodden and salty. I scramble back to the beach and my bag, scribbling down notes and sketches of each new plant or animal I find, labelling each one with the names of the correct shades of colour, which I can later transfer into full drawings when my pastels and paper arrive from Lisbon.

In the evenings, I compare everything I have seen with the exquisite drawings in my book on sea life – how grateful I am to Mr Applebee for his gift – and find there are some species here not present in that volume. I imagine comparing them to all known species back at home, perhaps finding they are new to science, and the gratification of fashioning my own names for these enchanting specimens. To think, an animal or plant named by a woman, named after me! I swell with pride at the thought.

I soon grow impatient with my wading as I can see there is so much more to see beyond my depth. I venture further yet fear drowning. I anticipated this back in London and read a copy of the book *The Art of Swimming*; I have learned the techniques out of the water first, as the book suggests, practising in my room only when alone, as I look a fool doing it in the air. Now I begin to practise the arm and leg movements in the water, dabbling in the shallows to perfect my technique, and discover I am a strong swimmer. Within weeks, I have developed enough confidence to swim a little further out. Yet I want to go further still, so I borrow a small boat from the garrison and row myself out to quiet spots in deeper water, peering over the side of the boat through my viewer. Here I see even more stunning specimens of coral: bright yellow tree-like structures with white twiggy tendrils; a collection of terracotta tubes mottled with white-outlined red bumps; a pallid snowflake-shaped structure with transparent flowers that resembles an explosion of sparks. All these varied corals have one thing in common: though I am sure they must be plants, I have a peculiar feeling that they are thinking. There is something about the way they move, that they do not always sway with the current, but sometimes start as if in fear, and respond shockingly to outside intruders or even seem to engulf smaller creatures, as if eating them. It occurs to me that perhaps coral are animals, and not plants. But if they are, they are a form of animal without eyes or legs, or the other forms one associates with animals we know and love. If they are not animals, then they are intelligent plants, another uncanny thought.

One day I tire of my viewer and wish to see a broader area without it; thus I need to lean over from my boat and place my face close to the surface. But I stretch too far and fall in. I am submerged and weighed down dangerously by my ridiculous clothes, simple as they are. So I peel off most of them and discard them in the boat. I wear only my shift, feel my hair floating all around me on the surface of the water like a mermaid's; I tip my head back, spread out my arms and float on the surface of the cerulean sea, close my eyes and float, my

bare arms caressed by the playful water. This is the kind of
liberation I had not the wit to dream of in smoky, dirty
London, trussed up in stiff clothes and hemmed in by walls,
streets and custom. The water soothes and holds me like a
mother washes her child, like the babe in the watery womb.
I wonder if my mother knew me long enough to bathe me, I
wonder if she held me even. There are no answers to such
questions.

I turn and dip below the surface, open my eyes and through
the blur consider the riotous beauty of the coral reef and how
it came to be. This is a question I can contemplate. These
gardens are so exquisite that it seems as if they must have
been devised by a hand, created in order to be pleasing to
the eye; the whole swathe of them in all their stunning variety
across the reef seems designed by Capability Brown or some
such landscape magician, to provide the most harmonious
aspect. It may sound as if I am referring to the Almighty as
the architect of this undersea garden. But I am not; I have
an inkling that a human gardener created these displays, but
an ancient one, from our distant past. Perhaps the kind of
human who left their bones in those caves hereabouts. But
what kind of being could have produced such intricate beauty
as a coral garden, so long ago? And surely it would have to
be a human who inhabited the shore, or islands, if not the
sea itself; what, then, an aquatic human? I think of our smooth
hairless skin, our layer of fat, even the curious webbing we
all possess between forefinger and thumb . . .

Sometimes I believe the conjecture of the natural philosopher rests uncomfortably between enlightenment and lunacy.
I consider removing my shift to experience the water's embrace
on every part of my body, but I fear it would be my misfortune to be spotted by a patrolling soldier who would cite my
outrageous behaviour as evidence of madness and I would
be removed from the island. Swimming in a shift is bad
enough and I scramble back into the boat, spreading out my

sodden clothes and lying beside them in the sun to dry off, the gentle waves rocking me as I drift along the ridge of the reef. I could float out to sea and never be found. There are worse fates.

That evening, clothed once more, somewhat damp with bare feet and the tangled hair of a siren, I tramp up the grassed path from the shore to the hillock on which sits my hut. A movement catches my eye and I glance down to the mooring-place below. There is a sailing boat there, one I have not seen before. In it, a man is collecting his bag and stepping out, met by a soldier from the garrison. They salute each other and the soldier points upwards, towards my hut. The man turns and shields his eyes from the golden light low on the horizon. He looks up and sees me, barefoot and wild-haired in the dying sun.

15

I am so astonished to see Captain Alex striding up to me – smiling broadly, hatless, wigless, a bulky knapsack over his shoulder, ruddy-cheeked and windswept from his sailing boat trip – that I guess there must be very bad news to bring him all this way. The brief contemplation of this – or something – causes a prickly sensation to sweep from the top of my head to my toes.

'Is Mr Woods very ill?'

'Oh no, Miss Price, not at all,' he assures me. 'I fear I have distressed you.'

'I am so relieved.'

He places his bag on the ground and says, 'In fact, I come on an errand. I bring your colours. And paper. From Lisbon. For your work. And post from England. And some food, fine food you have perhaps not tasted in some time in your humble surroundings here . . . And I bring wine.'

Never was I so glad to receive a gift, and to have a friend to bring it.

'Well, Captain Alex, you are *most* welcome here!' I laugh and he is pleased. 'But where will you stay this night? It is already evening.'

'I am to sleep at the fort. It is all arranged. I will leave tomorrow afternoon. I was hoping that we might share a meal now, if it is convenient?'

'But I have no place to entertain you here, sir. No ceremony.' I hold out my arms and look down at myself, even more dishevelled than the first time he saw me, barefoot as I am.

'I am used to rough ways, at sea.'

'In your superior cabin?'

'It was not always thus. I began as a midshipman at ten years of age and lodged with the able seamen. I have seen my share of squalor.'

'Then my goatherd's hut will serve. Follow me.'

I clear the table of my studies and we lay out all his good gifts. He has brought cured ham and sheep's-milk cheese, custard tarts too and soft milk bread.

'I must admit I am quite stunned to see you here, Captain. I would imagine you to be in Africa by now.'

'We plan to sail in five days. And I have taken some leave. I came to the English Hotel in Lisbon, intending to offer to accompany you on a visit to the local attraction of Sintra, an appealing seaside location. But they told me there that you were in Peniche and also that some artist's materials had arrived for you. So, on a whim, I hired a horse to bring you your goods, stopping off to purchase some of the finest local food on the way. On my arrival your rather dour landlady informed me in imperfect English that you had decamped from there too, and were ensconced on your island for the week, only to be reached by a sailing boat voyage of several hours.'

'You went to far too much trouble, Captain, for me. All that travelling . . .'

'To be frank, Miss Price, I have enjoyed the whole experience immensely. I always find it invigorating to explore, wet or dry. The ride to Peniche enabled me to see the country and it was a pleasure to captain a small boat again, something I have not done since I was a boy.'

'I am glad. And I must say it is good to have some English company again. The Portuguese friends I have made are splendid people. But there is nothing like the sound of your own tongue.'

We devour the food in no particular order and glug on wine from a shared tin cup. He is clearly gladdened to see me enjoying myself; we chat amicably of Lisbon and its environs, the mishaps of the Gentlemen of Science on the rowdy streets of the capital, and also the grief of Francis who apparently is bereft without me to wait upon. Once we have cleared away our scraps, I replace my studies and collection of finds on the tabletop. Captain Alex picks through the objects I have found and examines them with close interest.

'When I knew you were to sail with us, Miss Price, and study fossils and so forth, I hoped very much you would seek out such as these. I anticipated that your work would serve to find evidence for the Flood described in Genesis. Tell me about these objects.'

'They are things I have found in the caves hereabouts. A kind of tool for cutting, I believe, very old. Animal bones, human ones also. Here – a piece of broken horn, perhaps goat or deer, and see here, lines carved in it, perhaps by a human hand: a circle with a half line in it. It seems too studied to be chance. Some examples of fossils I found in the rocks – here, some ancient sea creatures, caught in time, turned to stone.'

'Truly fascinating! Here we have clear evidence of the Deluge! These bones must have been of men who were killed by it.' He holds up a fragment of human thigh bone and says, 'He saw the Flood!'

'Or *she*.'

'Well, yes, perhaps,' he replies. 'He – or she – was one who committed wickedness and was destroyed by God, along with every other breathing, creeping thing. Seekers have found the bones of many destroyed creatures, such as the unicorn horn in your room in London, and the dragons' teeth, griffin talons: all drowned for ever. But it is far rarer to find ancient human bones. It is, of course, because they floated on the surface of the water and rotted, leaving no remains. How splendid that you have found some!'

I watch him, so sure of his words; he speaks as though each utterance were a fact, not supposition.

Say I, 'Some have said there was a series of marine inundations, not one single catastrophe.'

'Truly? But the Bible does not describe such events.'

'Some have looked at layers of rock, laid down in time, so that the deeper layers are the eldest. Fossils found at various depths do not resemble one another. Some think there was perhaps a different climate on earth at the time of the Flood. Or that there were several floods, as I say, to create these layers of animals.'

'Pure fancy,' states the captain with certainty. 'We have the evidence of the Bible and need nothing more.'

'You are a sailor, Captain. You surely recall your great predecessor Sir Walter Raleigh, imprisoned in the Tower.'

'Of course.'

'He wrote a history of the world there. He had sailed to the Americas, he had seen with his own eyes the hundreds if not thousands of new kinds of animals and plants as yet unknown in Europe. How could Noah have fitted all these species into the Ark? Raleigh was an admiral, he knew that even Noah could not have built a ship spacious enough to contain them all. He suggested that the animals of the New World did not have a place on the Ark; that Noah only saved the creatures of the Old World; that later those animals somehow emigrated to the Americas, and with the new climates they found there, changed over time and transformed into the new species we find there today.'

'That is one possible explanation, yes.'

'In the last century Matthew Hale devised the idea that the animals on the Ark were a kind of breeding stock, that they were formed of simpler animals that later developed over time into the complex range of creatures we see now.'

'Also possible.'

'So if animals can change over time, perhaps humans have changed too. Perhaps there was a time long before the Bible, long before the classical civilisations of Greece and Rome, where humans were more primitive; a simpler time, where we were not as we are today, where we were more closely related to the simpler forms of life on the earth.'

'No, no. That really is nonsense, Miss Price. We all know from the Bible that we are the descendants of Noah, a highly skilled and intelligent man, who carried the knowledge of his people with him and his family.'

'Then answer me this. You see this tool, this cutting tool held in the hand. Hold it, see for yourself, feel it. It was made by human hands, undoubtedly.'

'I have heard it said these ancient weapons are no more than thunderbolts, formed in storm clouds and rained down on the earth.'

'Which is most likely? Formed by cloud or by hand, chipping away with another stone – here are the strike marks, you see?'

'Agreed, most likely.'

'So, who made it? Why? Why not use metal? It works much better than stone, for cutting.'

'I do not know. Perhaps there was no metal on this island.'

'But men could have brought metal across from the mainland. They had boats, Noah the master shipwright would have passed down this knowledge to his descendants, surely.'

'True.' He is frowning now.

'There was an apothecary in London named Conyers, at the end of the last century. He found a stone axe like this, and some fossilised ivory which he concluded was that of an ancient elephant, that the beast had been killed with the stone axe, by ancient Britons.'

'What folly!'

'Is it? He surmised that these ancient Britons had not yet

learned the use of metal and used stone instead. More recently, the German historian Eckhart had investigated the burial-places of his ancient countrymen, and saw that the oldest tombs contained artefacts shaped only from stone or antlers, while the more recent ones had bronze swords, shields and ornaments, and finally the most modern had iron implements.'

'What does that prove, Miss Price? Only that some were richer than others, that they could afford to buy iron or bronze, while others could only afford the rocks they could find themselves.'

This seems a good point and he is pleased with himself, sure of himself, his eyes bright. But I am sure of myself too.

'I do not think so. They were of vastly different ages. I think that European humans have developed over time. That they were primitive once, knew not the art of metal working, yet changed and grew and learned about the world. Perhaps their climate changed – the floods I spoke of – and they were forced to change with it. Sea levels have risen and fallen – this is obvious from the sight of fossils of sea creatures high up in rocks hundreds of feet from ground level. It is also clear that different places on the earth have different kinds of animals living in them. Why is that? Here on these tiny islands live a range of creatures not found commonly in Peniche. Even the very rock itself is different. Is it not possible that animals on islands grow differently, according to where they live? That the weather, the plants and landscape surrounding them, their very situation may guide and change how they are, over great periods of time, over thousands of years?'

'But we know that the world is only perhaps six thousand or so years of age. And that the Flood happened only four thousand years ago. There is no time for this kind of change, surely.'

'If one accepts such a calculation, Captain. Based only on one book.'

'On *the* book, Miss Price. The divine word of God.'

'Perhaps the Bible just tells part of the story. God created the universe, set in motion the planets, the stars and our sun. De Maillet was writing, around the turn of our present century, that seeds rained down from the universe on the ancient oceans and animals grew from them. As the seas receded, some of these simple animals were forced by the change in their environment to breathe air. So amphibians and reptiles came into being. And over time, fins turned to gills, skin to down, scales to feathers, and a fish has turned into a bird.'

'That is the oddest kind of fancy.'

'It is written down. In a book. But of course, we should never presume to explain the whole of creation by reading only *one* book.'

He replaces the hand axe carefully upon the table. He is frowning again. He looks up at me pointedly, as if searching my features for answers to the questions I have laid before him.

'You are a very disturbing young woman, Miss Price.'

I smile at him. I take it as a tribute.

He turns away, coughs, then pronounces, 'I should like to view some of the caves where you found these objects. I would like to see what you have seen. Perhaps in the morning?'

'Better than that. I need a good sailor to take me over to the smaller islets out there. There will be caves there too, I warrant, undisturbed by modern people. Who knows what lies within them? Are you willing, Captain Alex?'

He knocks on my door just past dawn. I am already up and prepared, as I am every day here. I rise and sleep by the rhythms of the sun and moon. It is a perfect day for sailing: enough breeze, yet calm and warm. We begin with a trip around Berlenga Grande, and the captain manoeuvres his craft skilfully in and out of several sea caverns. One has the peculiar quality of turning your hand blue as you trail it in the water. One cavern is so enormous it undercuts the island from one side to the other. We go on to the nearby Estelas Islands and find them covered in seagulls, screeching in a cacophony of sound, some angrily screaming at us for invading their utopia, others mewing like kittens over their speckled eggs, laid in nests that cover almost every inch of the islands' surfaces.

I want to go further, the longer trip over to Farilhão Grande. I have asked Horacio before if he would take me, but he only makes brief visits here these days to leave my supplies and then he rushes back to his life on the mainland. 'One day,' he says, but he has not yet. My captain agrees, I think because he so loves to sail this little boat. The breeze is up and we whip smartly over there, guided expertly by his hand. But when we arrive, the wind is stronger still and it is too dangerous to approach the islets close enough to enter the caves. There is one islet much smaller than the others, a craggy rock that would take one five minutes only to walk its entire circumference. He keeps his distance, yet I can see, if the weather had served us better, that there is a landing-place on this tiniest islet of the Farilhões, from where a rough path ascends to a cave up above the sea line. I can see there are many fossils in the stone surrounding the cave mouth and even glimpse, between the bucking of the boat over the choppy waves, that there is something red, something black there, on the walls of the cave, at the very entrance. As if there were paint there, but surely this is a trick of the eye.

'Closer, bring her closer!' I call to him.

'I cannot. The weather is turning. We must go back.' He points at the sky and I see dark clouds ominous in the near distance.

A tightness in my chest grips me, yet still I strain my eyes towards the cave, soon out of reach and out of eyeshot, as we are buffeted by the stiff wind and turn about to make the queasy journey in return. By the time we reach my island, the approaching storm rains down over the Farilhões: a blanket of grey lines cuts the air and charges the sky. We scramble up to the hut and watch the storm move mighty and slow over the far islands, then drift out over the Atlantic, whipping up waves, to become some poor souls' problem in a lonely ship out there. We are spared. Then I realise how hungry I am and we go inside, shovelling in the leftovers from yesterday's supper.

'I think there were paintings in that cave,' I tell him. 'I saw colours and lines. I must return. I must! As soon as ever I can!'

'I wish I could take you again, but I cannot. I must begin my journey back to Lisbon within the hour, as we sail so soon. Will your Portuguese man take you? Is he a good boatman? It would be madness for you to attempt it alone. I think you are rash enough for such foolishness. Promise me you will not.'

'Of course I will not. I know my inadequacies and a-sailing is one of them.' I chuckle, though he is not laughing. 'In all my research of these islands, I know that there were no reports of those who lived here having ever painted in the caves. The monks certainly would have recorded it if they had done such a thing. If they are religious symbols, those of Christianity, then that will date it more recently. But if not, who knows when such images were made? It could be ancient, just like the other artefacts I have found hereabouts. It could be a great discovery!'

I am talking and eating and laughing all at once and he is watching me with a wry smile on his face. I slow down and chew my food in a more seemly fashion.

'I think I amuse you, Captain.'

'Quite the opposite.'

We fall mute, eating quietly, meditating in silence.

We finish our meal and then it is time for him to go. I walk down with him to his boat and we shake hands, as is customary for us now.

'Thank you for coming to see me. For my gifts.'

'I am impressed with your studies, Miss Price. I believe you carry out work of importance here. I do not pretend to understand it all – and I sincerely disagree with some of your conclusions—'

'There are no conclusions yet. I remain broadminded.'

'Quite right. A quality I could cultivate more within myself, as I know I can be low-thoughted. Thank you, Miss Price. It has been . . . illuminating.'

There are some passing pleasantries – wishing him luck on the next leg of his voyage, saying we would meet again in the new year for the journey home – and with that, Captain Alex climbs into his boat and sails away, back to the mainland, to Peniche, to Lisbon, and onwards to Africa. Perhaps I shall go there one day to study the apes. I consider his visit, I wonder why he came so far, yet mostly my mind is filled with when I will be able to get over to that cave again on the tiny islet off Farilhõa Grande, and what I will discover inside it.

16

The sea is much calmer than the day I went before, and Horacio is able to moor safely. I leap out on to a narrow platform among the craggy rocks of the tiny islet.

'Careful!' he shouts.

I brush away his fussing and hoist my bag over my shoulder. Inside are paper, pencils and pastels for recording anything I might see, as well as a tinderbox and candle lantern for lighting my way. If the cave is deep, it will be dark in there. I hitch up my skirts to begin the climb up the path. Oh, for breeches! I must ask Horacio to get me a pair, a boy's perhaps, due to my small frame. I do not know if he has settled down to sleep in the sun or is following me, and I do not care. I have my eyes up and ahead on the entrance to my cave. All along the path the rocks are encrusted with fossils – every kind of spiralling mollusc, domed shellfish and even the odd whiskery fish have been caught there in perpetuity.

I reach the mouth of the cave and stop in wonder. There on the walls are paintings, drawn in two colours – black like charcoal and a kind of reddish brown: they are fish, countless black-outlined fish with red gills and eyes, swirling and swimming over every lump and bump in the undulating cave wall. I see that some fish have been created from the natural shapes present in the wall itself, as if the artist stood, looked at the cave and saw the fish there in the mind's eye and used the pigment to fill in what the imagination had already created. They swim across the entrance to the cave, up over the arch and down the other side.

I drop my bag, light my lantern and step cautiously further into the cave. I can see that the entrance veers off to one side, and it does look like a deep and winding cave, perhaps with rooms further in, holding who knows what treasures. I touch the walls and as I move away from the roaring of the sea I see whiteness and feel wetness there; it is moonmilk, the milky substance that can at times be found on cave walls. Here and there the walls are drier and a colourless, transparent mineral has formed: ancient layers of crystalline rock. I reach the end of the entrance room and the beginning of a tunnel. On the left of this pathway sits a rock and atop it has been placed an animal skull. It has a long beak and at first I think it is a monstrous bird, but then I decide it may well be the head of a porpoise, complete with tiny teeth all the way along its 'beak'. The cave ceiling has dripped down on this skull for centuries, perhaps millennia, and the skull is encased in minerals to create a shimmering white sculpture. It seems no accident to have been placed there. It is like a welcome, or a warning.

I proceed, scanning the ceiling for more paintings, but there are none along this narrow passage, and I fear the fish are all I will find, as they were near the entrance and the natural light. Perhaps early people had no way of lighting such deep, dark places. As the tunnel narrows further, I feel the fear of any animal trapped in an enclosed space and my feet slow. The tunnel twists once more and the roof is low. I bend to crouch through and then in a moment I am surrounded by space and chill air. I stand, lift my lantern and gasp.

I am in a majestic cavern glittering with stalactites and stalagmites. Some have dripped down over so many years they have joined together in mighty colonnades. The floor is uneven with hundreds of bones and shells, more porpoise skulls placed in rows beside the walls, and to the right a pile of flattened pieces of stone with a depression in each, all shaped similarly, all placed carefully together, as if they represent a store of some precious object. I crunch across the floor as though tramping through a million eggshells, lifting my lamp high, and at the far reach of this cavern I see the lines of more paint gleaming on the walls. I stumble over there and see paintings of pointed ovals, striped all along and at one end of each oval a rounded head with an eye and upturned mouth. They are seals, unmistakably; and they are smiling. There are many of them, some painted in red-brown, some in white, overlapping each other expertly. The artists must have planned this scene, to break the line of each animal behind the next, to give the impression of depth, of an entire underwater herd of them; for they are swimming, not lying on the shore fat and ungainly, but sinewy and graceful. From the flickering of candle flame, the seals themselves seem to flex and move, and I can see these ancient artists – who surely must have had their own source of light to create this mural, perhaps a simple fiery torch held in the hand – will have seen the same as me, that the lambent shadows of the flame throw movement into these painted animals and make them weave and swim before your eyes. The seals congregate around another opening, a further pathway that leads deeper into the cavern, and so far from the entrance am I now, that without my lamp I would be in authentic blackness.

Down deeper into the cave I go, the walls glistening with moonmilk – silence, the sea acres away – in this inky darkness cocooned in thick rock walls older than time. There is one more cavern here, a final one, as there are no more paths leading from it; the belly of the beast. It is like a secret chapel, with its domed roof. And here is the most spectacular display of all: a hall of red-brown figures, stretching across every surface: women with floating hair, plump rounded breasts, wide hips that taper down to no feet – instead into the tails of fish. Swimming in the sea across the ceiling, dozens of them, some with children, also fish-tailed, grasping on to their mothers' long tresses for anchorage; some are clearly pregnant, their ripe bellies uppermost. I see more of them holding fish in their hands, some thrusting the fish between their teeth. Now I find some sitting on rocks, a pile of opened shellfish beside them: some are eating the mussels and oysters there, I can even see their tongues poking into the shells to retrieve the meat. There is one figure, larger than the rest, seated on a rock with white pigment streaming from her breasts, her arms outspread in welcome, surrounded by a complex design of fish, seals, shellfish and infants. Yet look down her full thighs and there is no fish tail, but human legs, like mine, and feet placed firmly on the ground. I look more closely at the figures surrounding her and I find some of them – particularly the children – have feet rather than tails; with some each foot is webbed, like a frog's toes. The great female herself has perfect human toes, no joining or webbing, no suggestion of fish or a sea mammal. And there above her head, the same symbol etched here in black that I have seen on the bone in my hut: the circle with a line drawn halfway down it from the edge to the centre; there are many of them here, all around the head of the mer-woman. Her face is turned to the left in profile, her mouth open as if speaking, and then I see the pattern in the chaos, that the figures surrounding her emanate from this point, that the swirl of sea life and mer-mothers and their babes issues from her lips, as if the whole picture is her song.

I examine each cavern in turn, from the deepest to the cave entrance. I sketch what I see and in looking closely, find more and more than I had noticed at first. Beside cracks in the cave wall in the deepest recesses of each cavern, there are handprints outlined in red – it looks as if each artist has placed a hand on the wall as a stencil then spurted paint perhaps from a reed on to the hand, leaving a trace around it. I hold my own hand up to many of these ancient prints and find my hand is of a very similar size. There are some much smaller, which must be the hands of children. Some of these are found very high up the cave wall, above my reach, which suggests an adult held the child while another painted its hand. None of the hands I see are much bigger than my own. Perhaps these people were smaller than modern humans. Or perhaps only women painted their hands and those of their children. Or is it possible that only women painted all these pictures, the fish, the seals and the mermaids? And then it strikes me: I have not seen one image of a male human anywhere in these caves. I look again to search for some swimming males in the cave of the figures, but there are none, not one. And it occurs to me now that the repeated shape I saw above the head of the great sea maid is anatomical; it is female, the sex of a woman.

In these caves, I have lost track of all time and might have been in here for hours. My stomach groans with hunger and I think I have stayed long past luncheon. I resolve to go out to reassure Horacio, but I am loath to leave. On my slow way back, I collect a few objects. There are fish bones and more skulls – those of porpoises and what may be seals, and more shells of many shapes. I collect one of the plates from the pile, as well as other stones from near to it, which seem worked in some way, chipped and formed into what looks like the head of a spear; I find some items made from bone, a kind of spoon perhaps, and a prong that could work like a fork and pierce meat; and here a small vessel, from which one might take a sip of water.

I have knelt for so long, scrabbling around on the floor, that when I stand, my legs have gone to sleep and I stumble, dropping my lamp and extinguishing the flame. The tinder box is in my bag in the cave entrance. I am left in the cave of the seals alone in utter blackness. I stop and a chill creeps upon me. I have the sensation I am being watched. Ancient eyes are turned on me, curious, wary. My scientific mind takes over and forces one foot in front of the next. Scrabbling about, I find my lamp. I reach out and feel my way along the wall with my one free hand. I can discern lines in the cave wall I had not noticed by sight – long curving lines in sets of three – they feel as if they were done in the moon-milk with the middle three fingers of the hand, then left to dry and set in the rock over the years. I follow these flut-ings; they lead me out of the seal cavern and into the long passage. They run, at shoulder height, in swirls and patterns, yet leading me on and on, to the cave entrance, and the light.

As I step along towards the first cave, I notice more mark-ings I had not spotted before, as they are in muted red and very subtle. They are so faint, as they are half-hidden behind a sheen of crystal, as if the rock itself had grown over them for thousands of years. They are dots, spots of pigment just above head height, arranged in patterns. There are rows of three dots, one above the other. Here, there is a faint outline of a box, with two dots inside it. There, a series of short lines side by side, like tally marks. At first, their positioning seems arbitrary, but then each configuration is placed beside a crack in the wall and follows its progress, like the handprints in the other caves. There is method here, sophistication, deep thought; more than an impulse merely to make a mark. I step out into the cave mouth and blink, blinded by the afternoon sun. I hear Horacio calling me, but I cannot fathom his words as I am not present, I am not myself; I am standing at the edge of a cave once inhabited by ancient ancestors, standing where they stood, seeing what they saw, and it fills my vision: the sea, the sea, the sea.

★

Now that I have made my spectacular find, I know what my purpose here must be. I attempt to persuade Horacio to travel to Berlenga Grande more often; indeed, if it were my choice, I'd have him convey me to my caves every day! Yet, we agree a compromise and throughout September and October he takes me there once a week. He is not interested in its contents; he tells me there are piles of ancient things scattered all over the coast near Peniche and he has no curiosity for them, they are only old junk. I spend each day fully in the cave, sketching and collecting artefacts. I arrange for my collections to be boxed and sent back to England. There are other curiosities in the cave I had not noticed at first: on some of the walls I find black scuffs and fragments of coal; it seems a torch was scraped there, to rekindle the flame. Were these later visitors to the site, or the original inhabitants? There are also small mounds of stones, not fallen from the ceiling, but collected by ancient hands and placed in ceremonial heaps, yet why they are there is a riddle lost in time. I study the flattened pieces of stone with a depression at the end of each one, and think and think of what purpose they may serve. I surmise I may have solved it: such things may have been primitive oil lamps, with the depression serving to hold the oil in which a wick would be laid. This would explain how such detailed work could be carried out, sometimes clearly using both hands, without the need for constantly holding a torch. It is conceivable.

In the long evenings in my hut, sometimes I come outside, wrap my shawl about my shoulders and walk up to the point where I can see the cave islet in the distance. I stare out to it and think about the people who painted it, who collected skulls and stones in it, who carried their lamps into the darkness and created beauty. Or is it more than that, a kind of message, for such as me, for their descendants, for the future? There are the fish first, then the seals, then the cave of figures – half female, half fish: the hybrid beings with webbed feet, all ruled over by one whole woman, wide-hipped and milky-breasted, a goddess of fecundity. And as I have observed, there are no men on these walls, not one; it is a triptych of the sea and only the women who came from it. Whatever can it all mean?

But I cannot stay to study these marvels for much longer. It is nearly the end of October and Horacio warns me that the weather turns much colder in the next month and is particularly unpredictable on these islands. Soon it will be too cold to sleep in the hut. I hate to leave, but I know I must. My benefactor agreed to six months only, and I must obey, this first trip at least. I plan to return to Peniche, take all my things with me, and work on my thesis at Dona da Seda's quiet guest-house for the remainder of my stay, with a brief trip to Lisbon for supplies first. I have to go myself as I would like to purchase a microscope, if one can be found in the city, and I do not trust any postal service to deliver safely such a precious item. I wish to understand the smallest marine animals, to complement my studies of coral and other life of the sea. I can also spend my days in search of ancient artefacts in Peniche and round about, if the country is cluttered with old things, as Horacio complains. And to examine the flora and fauna of the area, and compare it with the islands' life, take tiny creatures from the sea lapping the beaches of Peniche and study them under my microscope. It will be good to have some company again besides the screeching seabirds and distant soldiers of the Berlengas; there have been times when I grow maudlin in my hut and think on my lonely childhood and my lost brother and never-known parents and I hug myself and long for something. Yes, it will be good to return to civilisation for a time, even if it is only the taciturn company of Dona da Seda. I will write up my findings, adapt them into a kind of narrative that any reader can understand. Then back to England on the *Prospect* at the end of January. Back to wintry, smoky, foggy London. From there, to tell the world about my cave, perhaps? But only once I have decided what it all means.

Pilar comes to help me clear out the hut for my journey back to Peniche. I show her my drawings from the cave and she is fascinated, quite unlike her husband. She wishes to see the cave, but the weather is against us. It will be bad enough returning to the mainland, so Horacio refuses to attempt the trip to the Farilhões, much to Pilar's disappointment. When she sees the pictures of the mer-people, she registers no surprise, and instead nods knowingly.

'I have seen them,' says she, in Spanish.

I ask her what she has seen.

'*Sirenas*,' she answers. *Mermaids*. 'In the Mediterranean Sea around Fornells, on the north coast of Minorca. Fishermen and their families know of them. There are old, old stories of the women of the sea. I was in my father's boat, a very young child. I saw one, in the distance. I saw her tail flip out of the water, I saw her pale skin course through the blue water. And she was gone. But I saw her. My brother lives there still in our family home, fishes there with his sons. One day, he will show you.'

Pilar has a fanciful bent. She has often told me of folk remedies for illnesses, reminding me of my talks with Matron all those years ago, a comforting feeling that adds to my enjoyment of Pilar's company. But she seems quite sure of this, quite serious. I ask her more but she offers little detail as she eulogises her brother's family and says how she misses them and the white house where they were brought up. She tells me there are peculiar ruins on the island too, collections of stones placed one atop the other, the remains of ancient villages, as old as the moon, says Pilar.

'They made their own caves there too,' she adds. 'Dug them out of the rock. Left old bones in there. We would play nearby, but never go in. And there are beautiful sea caves too. A good place to trap a mermaid.'

She tells me that it is an ancient knowledge of Minorcan natives that mermaids used to frequent the waters there, not so much in these days, as the vessels that ply the shipping lanes have frightened them away. She speaks of the mermaids as of old friends, greatly missed. Could it be true, that there are real mermaids in this world? Are they a remnant of our own path to full humanity, a link to our marine past? I tell her I must go there some day.

'If only I could come with you!' she cries and takes my hand, squeezes it.

Say I, 'Why do you not? You could see your brother again. And be my guide. Let us promise it, Pilar!'

Horacio enters the hut and breaks the spell. Pilar stands and fusses with the last of my things. Her husband says the boat is packed, that he will take me to Peniche today and he has asked Dona da Seda to book passage for me in a coach to Lisbon tomorrow, on All Saints' Day. Now, it is time to leave. I weep silently in his bumpy sailing boat that takes me away from my beautiful island, my dear hut, my cave of marvels. I swear I will return and see it again, study it and protect it for future generations, so they too can see what I have seen, know what I know, and feel the joy of insight into our mysterious past on this earth. Horacio glances at me as I wipe my eyes and offers me a little gruff comfort. He says that I will miss my island and I nod. He adds that I too will be missed, that the soldiers saw me swimming from their lookout at the fort. I had wondered if they might, but the lure of the water overcame my reservations. I blush and look out to sea. He tells me they had a name for me.

'The English mermaid,' he says with a crooked smile.

The sky hangs low today. Soon we are enveloped in a heavy fog that beclouds our senses. Horacio mutters that the tide is late. As we approach the bay there hangs a sulphurous odour in the air. Tonight is All Hallows' Eve, and while my Christian brethren will remember their saints who have passed away, I will be thinking of our ancestors and their ghosts that haunt my cave, watching me, willing me to reveal their secrets.

17

It is the first day of November. My coach trundles along the high road to the English Hotel. We will reach it shortly. I have dozed on the way. I have dreamed of churches, of bells, many bells ringing out together. Then I recall it is All Saints' Day and all the churches of Lisbon and its environs are calling the faithful to prayer. My portmanteau is stowed away above me, but I clutch to my heart the cave notebook, wherein I keep all the sketches I made. It is too precious to me, and I have kept it about my person all the way. I awake from my bumpy slumber to a rough road. The coach is rattling uncommonly. I hear the driver shout out and realise the horses have halted, but the coach still jolts from side to side. A rushing noise surrounds us, resembling a hundred coaches and horses passing by. I look out of the window to see the earth itself shaking, as if the ground were rolling like the waves in the sea. Then a strange rumbling booms from beneath us, like a hollow thunderclap. To my consternation, I see a massive crack open up in the road beside us and the horses panic. They bolt and we take off at a terrifying pace. I am thrown to the floor of the coach. My notebook has flown from my arms. I reach for the seat to pull myself up, but an almighty crash throws the coach on to its side and I am thrown with it into the door.

My eyes are open all the while and life seems to slow to an underwater pace as I watch the world tumble around me. I think I must close my mouth, or the stones from the road

that are being flung through the window as the coach scrapes
along on its side will come into my mouth and I will swallow
them and die. Finally, the coach stops its forward motion
and there is a fraction of stillness. But around us the earth
rages and groans, and as I gather myself to climb out of the
window above me, the coach swings from side to side throwing
me about like a dried pea in a rattle. At last, I scrabble out
and fall to the road, whereupon I see a tall town house before
me swinging like a reed in the wind and rending into cracks.
The roof snaps and collapses on to the top storey, which
collapses in turn on to the next floor. And I know then I
must run, or I will find myself under that house when it
collapses completely. As I scramble away from my coach I
see that monumental stone lumps have landed on the front
of it, crushing the driver to death and horribly wounding the
two horses, who are lying red with spilled blood and whinnying in grievous agony. But I have no time to aid them, and
I race across the road to find all the houses are tumbling
down around me amid great cracks and noise. I see an archway
and run to it, thinking if I stand beneath it, I may be given
some small measure of protection. As I reach it, I see a
mother and baby emerging from an alleyway, whose wall
collapses on top of them; they are buried and surely killed
in an instant.

Along the road, fissures in the ground are spewing out
water and dust is flung into the air in gouts as if invisible
men with shovels were throwing it so. More people emerge
from the houses still standing and run into the street,
screaming and throwing themselves on the ground. Two
houses opposite bend so far over towards each other that I
see a man leaning out of the window place his hands against
the outer wall of his neighbour's house, before it swings back
again. The horrendous scraping sound of all the houses
grinding against each other is unearthly. Fallen masonry and
roof tiles litter the ground and as the road shakes they jog

about my feet like dancers. I look down the street and see another house collapsing, and yet another and another – one burying three chaises with chair-men and passengers – billowing out copious clouds of suffocating dust. As I cough and cough, I hear the rumbling begin to subside, to be taken over by the lamentable cries of the people. Then the world stops.

I have a moment to consider our situation. It is an earthquake. A hundred – no, a thousand – times worse than that which panicked London five years ago. But I have less than a minute to decide my next action, as the peace is short-lived and a second tremor commences. The ground starts to tremble once more and I spot an area further up the road where a building has collapsed, beside it an open space on a hill with no buildings around it, looking down across the river. I run over there as the quake begins again and I collapse to my knees on the hillock, holding on to the long grass. I look down to the river and see crowds of Lisboetas rushing to the water's edge, crying out to men in boats, some being pitched head-first into the water by the tremors and others leaping straight in up to their waists to escape the violent agitation of the land. Another brief respite brings a shocked silence for a second or two, soon filled by the shrieks of grief and terror of people all along the street behind me. Two women who have followed me to the hillock are rolling around on the grass clutching and striking at their breasts and each other, crying out, 'Mercy, my Lord!' A third tremor quietens them and again the earth shakes and ruptures itself, while I grasp hold of the grass as if the world itself were about to tip up and hurl us all into the Atlantic like playthings. What will my end be?

Time is confounded in a disaster. But I think a quarter-hour has passed since the quake began. When I deem the earth is at rest, I endeavour to stand, though my knees are weak with fear. The women beside me set to their screeching again and I stagger past them. In my shock, all I can think of is my notebook buried in the coach. I step into the road and look about me at the devastation. This had been a street of smart town houses on a broad way above the city of Lisbon. Now it resembles the sack of Troy. The air is thick with suffocating dust. I rub my eyes and cough it up, my nose streaming with smutty mucus. I stumble on up the street I had come down. Through the gloom, I can see at least that every house I pass has tumbled into a ruin. There is not one left standing. From the rubbage, one can discern the limbs and crushed heads of corpses protruding, and amid the heaps of the dead lie the dying, moaning in a piteous manner. I climb over the rubble to help a woman trapped beneath a heavy door, who calls out weakly, 'Help me, help me!' Another walking survivor appears beside me, a man of advanced years, and together we do our best to shift the door from her chest, but we are too feeble. And before we have the chance to find help, she has murmured her last and expires.

I walk on through the dust and find a man crazed with grief and panic, who rushes to me and begs me to help him find his child. We search among the wreckage that was once his house and all the while he cries out in misery and prays so loudly I turn to him and tell him to be quiet, but he is not listening. I think I hear a cry from the stones but he rants on and finally I must take his arm, he turns his face to me to protest and I slap his cheek. In his shocked silence, we hear a tiny voice call out, '*Papai!*' and again, over and over. We scramble over the rubble towards it and start to dig. I feel my hand touch warm skin and thrust the stones away until a small face is staring at me, cheeks ashen and smudged with filth, eyes dark and searching. The father digs around his daughter's head ferociously, as she weeps and cries out for him, and when she is finally freed from her tomb and swept up in his arms, the confused, pathetic sounds those two humans make as they hold on to each other is like nothing my brief and sheltered life has ever prepared me for.

I wander on, past other survivors mumbling, praying in hoarse voices, exhaling in bitter sighs and staggering about, many half-dressed, women with breasts exposed, injured dogs limping past and whining. Then I reach the ruin of my coach, lying in place exactly where I left it, except the horses are now dead, their tongues thick and black. I climb up into the open door and peer down. The inside is now coated in a deep layer of brick dust, so I lower myself in and scrabble around. I find my notebook intact and hug it to me and weep. I know I must present a ridiculous figure but in this moment I feel a modicum of comfort that at least my precious work is not lost. But the people, oh, the dead, the corpses in the ruins; I am distracted by anguish and screw up my eyes, will myself to concentrate. I search for and find the small bag I kept with me in the coach, which thankfully contains a leather water bottle and some bread and apples. I must think sensibly now and remember that we are in the midst of a natural calamity, where the normal routines of everyday life are suspended; it may not be an easy task to find water and food later. I sit inside the upturned coach and drink and eat everything I have to sustain me. I have not the strength to carry my portmanteau, so I resolve to collect this later and first make my way to the English Hotel on foot, at least to see if it still stands.

The walk would take me a matter of minutes on a normal day, on a normal street, with no obstacles in my path. But there are no roads any more. There is only rubble and more rubble, and the air gloomy with dust. There are no landmarks, no church steeples to remind you which square you are passing through, because the churches have all collapsed and the squares are all filled with debris. We are climbing over the roofs of houses, the world flattened as if underfoot a giant. People are stopping each other and asking, which street is this, which road is that? People who have lived here all their lives are quite lost. I only know the hotel is along this hill somewhere, so if I keep on the same level, with the Tagus to my right, I should find it eventually. Some structures still stand, though as I walk there are mild tremors that fling off roof tiles and destroy teetering ruins and send people scattering and wailing into the street again. I walk past houses where the ground floor has remained intact, even the first floor, but there are no exterior walls and people congregate in rooms open on all sides, calling for someone to help them climb down as the stairs have collapsed. I walk past those who are maimed and soaked in blood, a perfect mask of horror on their faces. And I think, How can I assist them? But what can I do for them? And to choose one is impossible, and there are so very many of them, countless souls wandering through the chaos like lost spirits, of which I am one, hollow and numb.

It is perhaps an hour before I reach the English Hotel. I am so thankful to see that it still stands. A tall tree has crashed into the roof on one side, but the structure of the building is largely undamaged. Buildings across the street have not been so lucky and there is general destruction here too. The coaches of the wealthy are crushed, dead passengers and dead drivers and their dead horses bestrewing the road. I turn away from the unspeakable sight and sob, my hand to my mouth as I enter the hotel to find it deserted. I decide to place the bag with my notebook and bottle inside behind the counter usually frequented by the hotel's owners. I do not want to be encumbered by it, or have it stolen from me by some rampant survivor.

I wander back outside, thinking perhaps that it is not safe to stay indoors, as I am familiar enough with earthquakes to know there may well be more tremors later. I cross the street to a grassed area that was once surrounded by orange trees, many of which have been uprooted like snapped twigs. I sit on one and gaze out at the previously stupendous view of Lisbon and its snaking mighty river. The scene is one of utter desolation. This great European capital is now nothing but a ruined heap. Everywhere one looks there are no churches, no convents, few palaces or humbler houses still upright. I look across to the unharmed buildings and it is now I notice a new feature: a broad column of dark grey smoke rising from one of the river-facing palaces that survived. Now I spot another, and another. Now, the lick of red as flames consume the roofs. Spirals of smoke billow from spots all over the city. Lisbon is on fire. For a mad moment, I think the earth itself has opened up and will swallow us whole. But I surmise it must be the kitchen fires and candles catching at the furniture and rugs and tapestries and whatnot, all fanned by a strong wind coming from the east. The smoke stacks are expanding fast, greedily feeding on the chaos, ballooning into inky-blue monsters puffed with flashes of crimson and orange, the flames fuelling their hideous growth. I see people sprinting from the fires, away to the river and I reach out a hand towards them as if I were a deity and could pluck them from the constant stream of terror pouring down to the banks. Then, the earth begins to shake again.

It is another tremor, this one as bad as the first. I throw myself to the ground and cover my head with my hands, hopeless I know, but there is no other cover to be had. The houses nearby collapse further into choking dust and I run randomly from them, catching a glimpse of the hotel roof caving in under the swaying tree that had landed there before, now tossed like a leaf on the breeze. I run down the hill, away from the hotel, looking for open space, instinctively heading towards the river though I know it is miles from here. The air from below brings ashes and sparks to choke me further and I realise it is madness to head downhill, I must go back up where the air is cleaner. People are scrambling from houses that survived the first quake, now shaken to pieces by this new tragedy when they must have thought they had escaped God's wrath. I trip over rocks and fall, hitting my forehead on the ground and almost fainting away. I touch my head and see blood mark my fingers. The sky is filling with dust tinged with an acrid heat emanating from the raging fires. The air is being eaten by flame. I know if I stay seated here I will share the same fate as those I walked by earlier, so I gather my last ounce of strength and force myself to stand up.

Choking and gasping, I turn and pelt back up the hill as fast as my fragile legs allow, and see a garden behind a ruined house with a family kneeling on the grass, holding each other and praying as the world judders. It is as if God shakes a fist at them in their simple devotion. As I approach, I see there is a priest with them, a purple-robed canon who stands up shakily and crosses himself. He shouts at me in Portuguese, 'Who are you? Where do you come from?' and I shout back, 'England!' as it is the only word I have in my mind. 'England!' I shout again – as if I could will myself back there and out of this catastrophe – and I look down at myself and realise what a shocking, bedraggled sight I must be: my torn dress, my battered legs with stockings shredded, my shoes gone – when did I lose those? – my hands painted with blood, my hair matted with ash and dust. I must look quite mangled. I stumble towards him and he shouts at me again, this time invoking the ire of God upon my head, the Englishwoman, the heretic. God has been provoked and we must call upon the Blessed Virgin to intervene. He holds up a cross and tells me to kiss it, kiss it! I back away. He follows me, gesturing to the sky and pointing at me, then the house in whose garden he has been praying succumbs to God's fury and collapses behind him, a pile of stone falling atop him and he is gone. All at once the quake subsides and everything stands still once more.

I stare at the ruin where the priest is buried and the family appear from the garden. They are shrieking at me. I cannot understand their words but their faces are masked with hatred. In my shocked state, I watch them as I used to study insects in Mr Woods's garden, curious yet detached far above them. Over their shoulders, I glimpse the river. It is wildly heaving, as if a sea monster is about to breach the surface. Then I see the wave. It is a wall of water, as tall as a cliff, heading directly for the Burgio, the small island in the middle of the entrance to the Tagus. The vast wave swamps the island completely, then proceeds down the Tagus and tosses the vessels up and whirls them like sycamore seeds. It swiftly approaches the shore, boats carried atop it, on their sides or upturned. The quayside in every direction heaves rows deep in people and the river itself is swarming at the edges with others who have jumped in to escape the fires. Involuntarily I lift my hand and point, as the wave engulfs the quay and all the souls standing on it. Thousands of Lisboetas disappear in an instant. I cry out, 'No, no,' and shake my head, that what I am seeing cannot be, it cannot be. I cannot stop shaking my head. As the water floods into the streets, I see people tossed in its flow along with weighty pieces of timber, casks, barrels, household goods and other detritus from the wharves. The boats lifted and pitched by the wave smash into the ruins of buildings and I watch as sailors and passengers are hurled into the water, while a few leap out and grab on to objects to prevent their destruction, yet are swept away by further waves. The shore is flooded twice more, accompanied by the clamour of those souls not yet drowned as they flee uphill to escape the wave's assault and its deadly cargo of fast-flowing rubbish. Then the flotsam is sucked back out as the water recedes – roaring, tinkling, creaking, squealing and crashing – and the river becomes a bubbling mass of entangled ships' masts and beams and ˙twisted knots of sails, shattered roofs and tree trunks and wrecks of huts and houses, swirling ribbons of wheels and doors and window-frames and countless reams of many-coloured litter; and bobbing and spinning among the rubbish, scores and scores of floating corpses. In the space of just over one hour, the beautiful city of Lisbon has become a ruined, burning, floating graveyard. Every element has colluded in its utter annihilation.

18

When I have seen my fill of it all, I turn away, somehow disgusted by my complicity as observer of the horror. I trudge back to the hotel. One end of it has collapsed, but the lobby is intact, as are many of the rooms. There is no one inside. I collect my bag, cross the yard at the back to find the kitchen and fill the bag with bread, fruit and cheese from the cupboards. There is a well in the yard outside and I bring up a bucket of water to wash my face and try to get some of the dust out of my hair. The water runs red and then black with the blood and the muck. I fill my water bottle, drink it down, then fill it again before going back inside to search through the rooms for women's clothes I can change into. I find a suitably sensible dress and stockings to fit my frame. I find hairpins and a cap and tie back my damp hair. I locate a pair of shoes, too big for me, but they will do. All the while I am aware that I am stealing, but in the aftermath of this disaster it is as if there are no rules or laws or culture any more; the world has come to an end and started anew. The owners of this food, these clothes, these pins are most likely dead. If not, I believe they would not begrudge me a little help, as I hope I would not them if our positions were reversed.

I find a downstairs room that does not appear to have a current resident, hide my bag under the bed, lie down and I am asleep before I know it. I am found hours later in darkness by Mrs Dewar, the owner of the establishment. Her face is smudged with black from the ubiquitous smoke and her hair somewhat dishevelled, yet other than that she appears unhurt and quite bright.

'Why, Miss Price. I am astonished to see you here! Are you well?'

I clasp both her hands in mine. 'I am so glad to see you, Mrs Dewar!' To see a living person, and a known face, a friendly face, is unutterably moving to me, and my voice catches in my throat and whimpers a little.

'Oh, my dear. There, there now. Don't fret. Oh, your head, it has been wounded! Oh, my dear!'

'I must tell you that I borrowed some food from the kitchen and this dress from another room,' I confess. 'I will pay for all of it, I assure you.'

'Oh, don't fuss yourself on that account, my dear. Let me fetch something for that head of yours. Besides, we have just this minute come back from the city where we went to find our family and friends after the first quake and already there is terrible lawlessness on the streets down there, enough to make your hair curl. There is looting and raping and, oh, dreadful things. You stay here with us, miss. Safer up here on the hill. The troublemakers are too idle to walk all the way up here. Oh, Miss Price. The sights I have seen today, the people suffering. And the city is utterly racked. How will we manage? What will our livelihood be? Even though Mr Dewar says the tourists will come to see the ruins, like they do in Pompeii and Herculaneum. They will flock to see it, he says. But food, and firewood and supplies. Who will supply us, Miss Price? I fear for our future, I really do. Now, I said I wouldn't do this. I must steel myself. No, my dear. I am not the one with an injured head. Let me help *you*. Stay there. I won't be a moment.'

As I await her return, I can hear Mr Dewar and an assortment of English-speaking guests traipsing in from outside, sharing stories of damage, destruction and death. Mrs Dewar dresses my head and makes it sting, fusses over me somewhat and asks if I would like to stay on in this room, for which I thank her. I accompany her to the kitchen, keen to be useful. There are no servants here. I help make tea for everyone and prepare food. The men are outside burying the dead. Mrs Dewar tells me several guests were leaving the hotel this morning for a day trip when the quake started. Those were the crushed coaches I saw outside. She says all the hotel servants rushed away to find their relatives and they have not seen them since. Somehow she must get word to the families of the deceased guests, but no ships are permitted to leave the Tagus – to prevent deserters or looters leaving with their bounty – so what will happen to the postal service? As we work, it is comforting to listen to her babble on, yet periodically I find tears running down my cheeks, though I feel no emotion. I see the same happens with Mrs Dewar and at times we glance at each other and shake our heads in disbelief.

Say I, 'I was in London for the earthquake in 1750. It was nothing like this. Nothing. And what a fuss they made then.'

'This was like something from the pages of the Old Testament,' says Mrs Dewar. 'It will always be remembered.'

That first evening I spend with the Dewars and the few other surviving guests before the fire in the sitting room. It is cold at night here in Lisbon and I think of all those out there shivering under the empty skies, homeless, half-dressed, injured, hungry and thirsty. But I hug myself and stay put, as I have no more strength for strangers this night and have come to know that self-preservation is the strongest force extant. I tell my stories of what I have seen and the other guests tell theirs. One had been buried under rubble for hours until he found a way out, almost choked to death by powdered lime he can still taste in his mouth. An Irish guest had been in his office in the Baixa, ran outside at the first tremor and lost his brother in the mêlée; he has not found him yet, though he scoured the ruins until the fires came. I hear that thousands are homeless and all the canvas and wood has been burned up in the fires so nobody can make any shelters. Some noblemen have been opening up their mansion gardens to the destitute and handing out refreshments, cloaks and blankets and the royal family are camping in makeshift tents in the grounds of the palace. A Scottish lady had seen a few half-hearted soldiers appear in the street and tell some looters to clear off in the name of the King but were met with mockery and missiles, whereupon they retreated and nothing of the law has been seen since. Another guest had been over two hundred yards from the river-front yet had found himself up to the waist in water when the great wave came and was only saved by grasping hold of a flagpole.

We speak of how there seemed no pattern to rescue or death, that some had been killed by water or saved by it, or safe in basements where others had been crushed by them – no rules to learn from if there were ever a next time. Mr Dewar tells of the scenes in the main piazzas, like the grand square the Rossio, where thousands had rushed after the first quake to create a scene of mania resembling the final judgement day, numberless souls dying and wailing, and the survivors in their religious fervour were seen to smite their breasts and beat their faces until their cheeks were swollen and bruised hideously. The churches had been full as it is All Saints' Day and thus thousands of worshippers were killed as church towers and steeples fell down by the dozen and crushed them; even so there seemed to be priests everywhere shouting at people to repent of their sins and performing absolution for hundreds of crazed followers, ranging around with groups of dazed zealots forcibly baptising those who are not Catholics, harassing the dying – and I remembered the canon who came at me with his cross and thought I had dreamed it, but I think it must have been real. He is dead now, buried under that house. His God did not save him.

Everyone starts at the sound of an explosion coming from the city. We rush outside to hear two more, and Mr Dewar conjectures it must be fire reaching the gunpowder stores on the waterfront. We all stand on the grass and watch the fires burning in zigzags across the scene and listen to the punctuated cries of women and children. I fear I will not sleep tonight. I fear nightmares. The flames light the sky and turn it almost daytime, cinders float on the air and fall down like drizzle, and the tremors continue, more gentle now, but constant, three or four an hour all this evening. I expect it to continue well into the night, as if the earth shudders at its rage and somewhat regrets it. Nobody speaks more – there is nothing left to say – and, one by one, we slink off to bed, though my prophecy is proven and I lie awake until dawn.

In the morning, I help to prepare breakfast as the servants have not returned and perhaps never will. At around nine o'clock, we see there are boats coming up the Tagus to rescue survivors from the flames. We watch but soon I cannot bear to see it, for the chaos ensuing on the waterfront as people fight to get aboard is too horrible. Mr Dewar points out that the fire is spreading from the Customs House and has caught the stacks of timber, now billowing out smoke horrendously and making the people scatter and scream. I turn away – shaken, sick-hearted and ridden with guilt at the constant sounds of terror – and sit inside alone until luncheon, writing a long letter to Mr Woods and the Applebees, attempting to describe this catastrophe as best I can, though I omit the ghastliest details to spare them. They are heart-wrenching sights I dearly wish I had never seen, thus I have no desire to inflict them on my friends. I assure them I am well and very lucky to be so. I cannot finish the letter at first though, for I come to the part where I am to state my immediate plans and honestly cannot end the sentence. If the *Prospect* arrives as planned at the end of January, then I will return home on it, of course. But what until then? I cannot stay here. What of Peniche? Will it have been as damaged as Lisbon? Earthquakes cover hundreds, perhaps thousands, of miles, they say. Peniche is but a few hours from here, and, for the first time, a personal chill ripples through my flesh as I think of Horacio, and Pilar and Dona da Seda. And the Berlengas. What damage could the tidal wave have caused there? Then I remember my coach, crushed with my bag secured to it. I had forgotten it utterly. It is as if everything before the moment of the first tremor has been wiped clean from my mind.

I find Mrs Dewar and ask her about my belongings. She arranges for her husband to take their mule – which survived by escaping to a wood nearby and returning dusty yet unharmed a day later – to find my coach and see if he can retrieve them. I ought to offer to accompany him, but I cannot bear to see the ruins of those streets again. He returns later that afternoon with a grim countenance and a bare-backed mule.

'All gone, Miss Price. I am sorry. Looks as if it were all looted. There have been no burials up yonder and the stench in the streets is awful, just awful.'

I thank him for his pains and consider my position. I have the clothes I stand up in, stolen from a dead guest. I have a small bag and a water bottle. I have access to my benefactor's money in a bank down in the city, which may have burned to the ground or been flooded. I have my precious notebook, filled with drawings of my cave. Thank heavens I saved it from the wreck. Thank heavens I have that at least. And the rest of my belongings are in Peniche, as well as a strongbox in Dona da Seda's cupboard, with the last of my Portuguese money therein. All damaged, destroyed perhaps; and my land-lady and friends, will they be well? I must go back there, as soon as I can get passage. I must see for myself.

I have to wait for almost a week before transport can be found. Just finding food is hard enough, as the price of bread and other staples has inflated to ridiculous proportions. Luckily the Dewars were well stocked with supplies before the disaster, but these will not last in excess of a few days more. And within a day of the quake there have been soldiers on the roads out of Lisbon stopping labourers and other workers from deserting the city, as they are needed for construction. Mr Dewar has found me a Portuguese merchant friend of his who is returning up the coast to his family; they know not if he has survived, so he is keen to get up there. He will drop me at Peniche free of charge. I take a tearful leave of the Dewars, and thank them for their kindness and assure them I will see them again soon. Mrs Dewar agrees to post my letter to Mr Woods – which I finished with a summation of my immediate plans to return to Peniche – if and when the ships start to leave the Tagus again.

The merchant collects me at dawn in a clean yet basic horse and cart. He is not talkative and informs me only that we will not be stopping on the way for any reason, as he has heard Barbary pirates are massing off Cascais (three miles down the coast) and will invade the city within days for the purpose of capturing Christian slaves for the markets in North Africa. I have heard enough extreme rumours these past days – such as cannibalism rife in the city – to ignore most of them. I do not argue, but make sure I bring plenty of victuals and I use the chamber pot in my room before we leave, in case the journey is long. The day's trip takes us fourteen hours. The roads are often blocked and we have to manoeuvre round countless obstacles. At least many of the corpses have now been removed. We see squads of soldiers commandeering the locals to bury those not yet accorded that right. I am surprised to see how many buildings have been left standing after the disaster, though I would say half are gone. All the way along the coast road the homeless appear from encampments made from carpets, sailcloth and any other found fabrics strung over vines, poles, ropes and tree branches, cooking over small fires, roasting what look like rats or doves or other wild food. To see the environs of Peniche and the sparkling sea gladdens my heart and I find myself praying – to a God from whom I now feel wholly disconnected, as if from a family feud – that my friends will be thriving here.

The merchant wishes me well and I alight, walking the final stretch to my goal in the twilight. There is certainly damage here, crumpled houses and huts, yet not nearly as bad as Lisbon. Dona da Seda's guest-house is standing and complete, thankfully. But what of the lady? I knock on the door and upon receiving no answer, try it to find it open and I call out. I hear a weak reply from her sitting room and enter. I find her sitting with her leg sheathed in bandages upon a stool. Her face when I enter is a picture. I have never seen her smile so, or smile at all, since I first met her. She is so pleased to see me alive, well and returned. Everything she has heard from Lisbon has been bad news. She knows they brought the soldiers from the Berlengas fort, as well as those from Peniche, and sent them up to Lisbon to keep law and order. We talk for a long while about our experiences. She was out in the town when the quake began and some masonry fell on her leg. The doctor says it will heal but she must rest it. I vow to take care of her, though she says her daughter and son-in-law do come by to bring her food. I was not even aware she had family here! We have not spoken more than a few sentences these past months. The same could be said of Mrs Dewar and certainly her husband. It is curious how a disaster brings folk together. I ask Dona da Seda for news of Horacio and Pilar – have they lost their boat, is their home intact? – but she has heard nothing of them, confined to her house. I resolve to find my friends and see if their livelihood and hearth have survived, but on the morrow, as it is night-time by now. We sup together and swap our grisly stories. I sleep fitfully that night and dream of the *Gaivota* and Pilar's fish stews she would sometimes bring me at my hut. And of mermaids.

At first light, I walk down to the sea past the house where the ladies of lace are usually found, yet it is shut up today. The beach I arrive at in shock. There are no boats to be seen, unless in pieces. Driftwood and dead fish besmirch the shore. There is no sign of Horacio's rowing boat or the *Gaivota* further out. And I do not know where my friends reside. I double back and return to the lace house, knock at the door and wait. I hear there is movement inside, and a kind of moaning, a deep low sound, most distressing. Then the door opens and one of the older lace ladies stands before me, her face a picture of desolation. She does not speak, simply looks at me. I ask her in Portuguese about Horacio and his wife Pilar. Is Pilar here? Or is it possible for her to direct me to their house? She seems unable to speak and another woman comes to the door, her daughter it must be as she calls her Mother and ushers her to sit down. She says, 'We are suffering. We have lost husbands, brothers, sisters. About fifty altogether. And all our fishing boats. Many rushed to the beach to escape the falling houses, but then the wave came and drowned everyone on the sand. The bodies were swept out to sea. We cannot even bury our dead. Horacio and Pilar were there. They are lost too. They are dead. So many are dead. We cannot help you. I am sorry.'

She turns from me and closes the door. My good friends are drowned, their bodies lost to the sea. I pace slowly back to the guest-house to find Dona da Seda asleep in her chair. I go to my room and sit on the bed. I close my eyes. My mind is like a shattered mirror. Shards of memory – cruel and happy – fall in a jagged heap. I believe my mind is broken. I cannot fathom how to mend it. Each rational thought I attempt is swamped by brutal visions of what I have seen and what I know.

My good friends, washed out to sea. Their fear when the wave came, trying to flee perhaps, their feet slipping in the soft sand, but too late, too late. The roaring of the wave as it crashed ashore, the screams of the people who thought they were safe on the open sand. My friends: loyal sailor Horacio, the bonny boat he manoeuvred so well; his hat over his face as he slept in the sunshine; his humorous look as I would appear barefoot at the boat sometimes with a fish for his lunch, caught on my coral garden ventures; and kind, attentive Pilar, her mop and broom and dusters; the thoughtful gift of the stool for my hut, which stands now in the corner of this room, brought back from the beloved island; her wrinkled fingers poring over my notebook, her haunting stories of the mermaids of Minorca.

Plans, I exhort myself, make plans. The only thing I can think of to do now is sail to the Berlengas. Seeing my island again would be my only consolation. Somehow, I must get over to the Farilhões. I want to see my cave. But with all the fishing boats destroyed, how can I? Perhaps Dona da Seda knows of someone else, anyone, whose boat has survived, which I could charter to take me there, to my island, to my cave. I simply must see it, I simply must, today.

Oh, my friends, my good friends.

I hang my head and sob. How could I have been so cold about the thousands who died in the city? Is it only those close to us who deserve our pity? I scold myself for not helping enough, for escaping. But it is not my fault. I did not cause this. If God made this happen – this quake, the inferno, the wave, all this suffering and sorrow – then I *hate* God. I used to think God set the world in motion, then watched it play itself out, looked on as folly followed disaster. But how could He stand there, in His unending wisdom and goodness, and let it happen, cause it to happen even? Punish the innocent and guilty alike, the looters and rapists surviving while Horacio and Pilar die, their lungs soaked in brine? If there is no God, if it is all a story, a lie, then I hate the earth for its stray cruelty. I hate it so. I put my faith in people now – not the earth and not the heavens – I stake my claim with humanity.

If only I could see again my ancient paintings crafted by clever, hopeful, human hands; they are sacred to me and would bring me solace, would give me peace. I bury my wet face in my pillow and waul my lament. All that was sweet and soft in my life here has turned to briars and thorns.

There is the clip-clop of a single horse on the path outside, then footsteps approach the house. I sit bolt upright and wipe my streaming nose. Someone is knocking, now banging on the door. Who would come to this house, so early, on horseback? Why do they knock so urgently?

'Miss Price, are you there?' an English voice calls from outside. 'Miss Price!'

19

Captain Alex – this man I had seldom thought of, had not wished for, and yet when I see him, it comes to me that he is the one person I want to see, who can understand what has happened here and who I can truly talk to, with no pretence and no expectation. How I know this is mysterious to me, yet I feel the strongest urge to take his hand and hold on to it.

'Captain,' I manage to say and I am aware of myself and my blemished appearance, yet I recall I was always thus dishevelled in one way or another with him, and he never seemed to mind it. 'You have surprised me once again.'

'I am so very, *very* glad to see you, Miss Price. So well, I mean.' His face is concerned at the sight of my wretched eyes, his hand slightly raised as if to provide comfort. He is dusty from his ride and bronzed from his time under the southern sun. 'That is to say, unharmed. You are unharmed, are you not? But I see there is some damage to your forehead. *Are* you quite well?'

'I am, yes. I did escape unharmed, more or less. Others suffered much worse fates than mine. The worst fate, for too many. I saw it all. I saw everything. But how on earth do you come to be here, in this place? You were in Africa until January, were you not? Please, come in.'

He thanks me and I briefly visit my landlady, to find her still asleep. I carefully close her door and turn to the captain in the hall. There is nowhere in this small house to take him other than my room, so I suggest we go for a walk. I feel quite faint standing in that darkened hallway, and almost run to the door to open it for welcome air, the scent of citrus trees and the sea. I find a bucket for his horse and we refresh it with water. We stroll among the golden streets of Peniche, I leading us to avoid the lace cottage, which I cannot bear to see again today, and down towards the ocean. I ask him again how he comes to be in Portugal.

'I was near Morocco when the quake struck. We were moored near Tangiers and there was a veritable commotion in the sea, rising and falling almost twenty times that day. When we went ashore, we saw it was an earthquake and the damage it had wrought. I took the decision to sail the *Prospect* up the coast and on to Portugal, to see if our allies required any assistance, if the disaster had affected them. And we found, as you well know, that the worst hit was Portugal, and Lisbon itself. We docked in the Tagus and my men have been instructed to take aboard any English guests of quality who require a passage home. We can only take a few, as you know we are not a huge vessel, yet we will do our best to provide aid to refugees. They will need to journey with us to visit Africa once more to pick up our other guests, yet once that is accomplished, we shall all sail home together.'

'And our Gentlemen of Science? Are they safe?'

'As yet, I do not know. They are all within the interior and I have had no word. We will find out next month, if they are waiting at Casablanca in December as planned. Though we hear the port there has been so damaged by the earthquake, I do not know if we will be able to dock. I will arrange for them to be met there at any rate, and they can travel overland to meet us further down the coast if necessary.'

'But how did you come to be up here, in Peniche?'

We have reached the fort and decide to sit a while on a wall nearby it in the sunshine, my back to the beach so I cannot see its ruin. There is not a person nearby. Since half a hundred of their citizens have been lost to the waves, the townspeople seem to be staying away from the scene, behind closed shutters.

'My ship at rest in Lisbon, I came up to the English Hotel. I wished to tell you that you could come aboard immediately, leave Lisbon and live on the ship for the next month or so, until we returned home. The owner of the hotel told me you were here. I came to relay the message.'

'You could have sent a letter by courier. You did not need to come all this way yourself, on horseback no less.'

He is staring at his hands as he listens, wringing them, a kind of dry washing. I have a notion about him and I want to ask him a question, yet I fear the response. Fear it, or welcome it, I cannot tell. This puzzle of a man has come to me at a time when I am in no fit state to solve him.

'Why did you come here, Captain Alex?'

He looks up and his hands stop. 'I could not leave it to chance. I had to see you – that is, I had to see you were well.'

'I am glad you did. I am glad you are here.'

I turn towards him and we are face to face. I know he sees the grief in me and his eyes pity mine.

'My friends were killed here – the fisherman and his wife. Drowned.'

'Oh, my dear.'

For a still moment, both of us are at a loss for words.

'Have you seen death?' I ask him.

'I have.'

'Death from misadventure; horrible death?'

'Indeed. On a long sea voyage, one of my first, as a boy.'

'Tell me of it.'

'Are you sure?'

'Yes.'

'We were part of a fleet, searching for a rich prize, a Spanish treasure ship. We attempted to round the Horn and met a great storm, with mountainous waves and perpetual terror.

We feared we would be sent to the bottom, as men were dashed to pieces against the decks or sides of the ship and another sent overboard – he was a strong swimmer and we saw that he would continue sensible for a considerable time longer and would be wholly aware of the horror of his hopeless situation. Thence came snow and sleet which cased our rigging and froze our sails and then the storm calmed and we thought ourselves saved. But we had miscalculated longitude and were terribly lost. Some of our squadron had disappeared and we found ourselves alone and incapable of repair or replenishment.

'The scurvy came soon after, beginning with the able seamen. Large discoloured spots dispersed over the whole surface of the body, swollen legs, putrid gums. The poor wretches would swoon or even die on the spot at the least exertion of strength or the slightest motion. Shiverings and tremblings and an uncommon lassitude of the whole body; and a tendency to exhibit dreadful terrors. Then ulcers and rotten flesh festering. Perhaps the worst effect is when the scars of old wounds reopened, broken bones dissolved, from injuries perhaps suffered years before. A day did not pass without a man dying. Some of the dead were sewn into their hammocks and thrown overboard. But as the sickness progressed, there were not enough hands to do the labour and thus the corpses were put in the hold, where they washed about in the bilge and filth, or left on deck. Eventually we found landfall. But by then, two-thirds of our crew were dead and half those left were young boys like myself. There were hardly enough of us to stand by the sails and so the ship was torched and we joined another. She had been a beautiful ship. She burned all night and when the flames reached the powder magazine, it exploded at dawn. I was ten years old.'

He falls silent.

'I am sorry I spoke of scurvy so on the *Prospect* that night,'

I say, my voice quavering. 'It must have been distressing for you to think of it.'

'You were not to know. I never speak of it.'

'Thank you for telling me.'

We sit quietly for a moment.

'Miss Price, I want you to know that I have employed your suggestions of an improved diet for the men aboard the *Prospect*. I have ensured they receive fresh food whenever possible. And there have been almost instant results: notwith-standing their improved health, their regard for me as their captain has, it seems, doubled or more. The whole mood of the ship has lifted and I would wager a considerable sum that no scurvy will be found aboard my ship, if we are able to continue with the same healthful level of provisions. You were right and I was wrong.'

In times past I would have crowed. But at this moment I have no inclination. I say dolefully, 'I am glad of it.'

'What happened to you in Lisbon, Miss Price?'

'It would not aid me to talk of it.' I say it not unkindly, but with fatigue.

'But I do *so* wish to help you.'

I am gazing out across the bay and I realise my eyes are scanning for boats there.

'Perhaps you can, Captain,' I say. 'I need to see my island again. The cave we saw from your boat? It did have paintings inside, the most miraculous things you could imagine. Ancient paintings, very old. Beautiful, extraordinary. I need to see if any damage has been done there. I need to see if my cave is well.'

'You speak as if it were a person.'

'If you saw it, you would understand. But this is a town in mourning. They have lost some of their men and all their fishing boats. If you could find a boat, perhaps in the next village along, you could pilot me to the island and we could see.'

'And if I could organise this feat for you, will you come

with me afterwards, back to Lisbon, to the ship, where it is safe?'

I consider this. What had been my plan? Something hovers in my mind, an as yet unformed resolution that murmurs its dissent, yet for now I have no clear answer.

'I may do. I do not know for sure.'

'I will persuade you, methinks. Come. Let us waste no time. I will fetch my horse. You will rest and I shall see what I can find.'

He is gone an hour only. I speak with Dona da Seda on my return and we share some delicious cold soup. I change into my sailing clothes and wait in the small garden in front of the guest-house until the captain comes back, his horse swiftly trotting up the street.

'I have found us a boat, in Peniche. It belongs to the mayor. He was most pleased to make my acquaintance as an English sea captain and readily agreed to lend it to me.'

'And I have found you some luncheon.' I hand him some bread and dried pork, which he devours on the way to the mayor's quay. It is away from the main beach, and though some of the boats are damaged here, many are intact.

'A sandbar protected this side,' he explains as we climb in. Soon we are away, a rolled-up blanket – in case the journey is chilly – and my small bag beside me, filled with food and drink for our trip, my lamp and tinderbox, and some paper and pencils to record anything new I find. I have an intuition this will be my final visit to my cave for some time. A change is coming. We talk little on the way, as the breeze is strong and whistling. As we approach Berlenga Grande I look up to see my hut standing proudly and my heart lightens. But all around the coast of the island I see there is damage, egregious damage in places. I know its inlets, caves and shapes so well – I have paced and mapped it mentally for months – that I note where every rock has altered. They have been smashed by force, some caves have collapsed and stacks have been created where once there were arches. We veer north towards the Farilhões and head for the cave islet. I realise there are no animals here. All the squawking seabirds have gone, not one remains. As we get closer, the same damage is visible here and I am nauseous as Captain Alex steers us into the mooring-place beneath my cave. Already I can see that we are in the wrong place, that this must be the wrong islet, for there is no path, no cave, just a ruin of rocks.

And I shout at him, 'This is not correct. It is another islet.'

'No, no. This is the one. Where we went before.'

And with horror, I see a few fossils in the stone below the rock pile. This was once my cave.

'No, no!' I cry and pull off my jacket, ready to jump in and swim to it. He grabs my arm and pulls me back, then brings in the boat. I scramble out and do not wait for him. I can make it a few steps up the path, but no further. I peer into the ruin to see if a way can be cleared. I hitch up my skirt and begin to climb over rocks, but they slip and I cry out. He is below me, shouting for me to stay still. I ignore him and try to climb further, but the rocks come sliding down in a tumble and I land on my back on the path, my hands grazed and my pride wounded. As I lie looking up, I see that the very roof of the cave has been crushed, that there is no cave any more – there is nothing left of it, only broken shards and lumps of stone. Then his face is before mine and he is scolding me.

'You could have been hurt, killed!'

'My cave, *my cave!*' I howl, turning my face from him into the sandy path, tears streaming off my nose into the dust. His arms about me, I stand; but my knees are weak, not from the fall but from the dreadful knowledge that a thing of rare and unique beauty has been cruelly smashed to pieces. And this is the feather that will break my back;

it was all I had left and my hope and spirit seem crushed beneath it.

'My dear, my dear,' he says and holds me. 'There will be other caves.'

'You do *not* understand,' I scream at him, pushing him away. 'There was nothing like it on this earth. It was singular, a *miracle*. And it has been destroyed, wantonly ruined by . . . by what? By your vengeful God? For what purpose? It held the secrets of our past. And now it is gone. Oh, it is gone, it is gone for ever.'

He holds me while I cry, though I have shouted at him. In silence, he leads me to the boat and sails us to Berlenga Grande, past the empty fort, whose soldiers have been dispatched to the mainland. We are alone in this place. He takes my hand and draws me out on to the quay, puts his arm about me and walks me up the hill to my hut. It is empty too, except the bare cot in which I used to sleep to the sound of the sea. Inside, every glance reminds me of my friends, my cave, my happy times on my island, and my eyes brim again. He takes my hands and squeezes them. I look to him.

We watch each other for a moment, the eyes, the hair, the mouth. And we kiss.

'*Dawnay*,' he whispers.

We kiss again. The second such kiss of my life.

'A beautiful name. I have spoken it, over and over, these months. Like a blessing. *Dawnay*.'

To hear my name from his lips, it is like honey on the tongue. No one has ever said my name this way, so soft and sweet.

'The orphanage gave that name to me.'

'Beautiful though. Because it is yours.'

Another kiss. There has been a life of twenty-three years, without kissing like this. And I have wasted my time.

And when we fall on each other it is as if we fight and

when we lie together we move as one curved creature and afterwards we half sleep, half wake, breathing deeply, surrounded by the suspirations of the ocean.

20

We are wrapped in each other and the blanket, as the November wind whistles about our hut. I am lying in the arms of my love and nobody could be more astonished than myself. My head buried in my work, my heart beating only to sustain life, I did not see beyond myself, I did not know my love until he kissed me.

'Will you call me Robin?'

'I will not. You are Cap'n Alex to me and always will be.'

'But I want to hear you say my name!'

'Then you will have a very long wait.'

'Is there any subject upon which we agree?'

'I doubt it.'

We glare at each other, then smile.

'If you will not say my name, then speak to me of other things. I love the timbre of your voice. It is like music to me. Tell me about your work. Tell me of the paintings in the cave.'

I explain them in all particulars, trying to convey their splendour and importance.

'How do you know they are ancient? Surely they could have been made by local children, very recently. They sound quite infantile.'

I pull away from him and sit up on my elbows. I am quite naked and yet have no shame, no sense of propriety, indeed I delight in it, and his nakedness also. Here, on this island, we are like the last two people on earth, or the first.

'Oh, you are so belligerently ignorant at times! Many of the paintings are embedded in translucent minerals. It has formed over them. It takes an epoch of time to form such layers. And what is more, they are surrounded by ancient objects on the ground, covered in aged moonmilk, such as the animal skulls and cutting tools formed from rock.'

'If you are correct, then there will be further caves across the world. It is simply a case of finding them. This cannot be the only one.'

'Then that will be my task. To search for them and find them all.' A fleeting image occurs to me of myself on Robin's ship, sailing the seas together, yet I dismiss it as beyond folly; I do not wish to face the future just yet.

'I believe if anyone can, you can. But for now you must return safely home to Mr Woods's house. And if you will travel in the future, find yourself trustworthy and experienced male companions, to protect and cosset you. The world is a perilous place. Especially for a young woman, and one with such beauty as yours.'

And he kisses me again and again. But the thought of returning to England after the destruction of my work and the loss of my friends is sadder than I can bear. To be in London, to attempt to prove to the scientific establishment my theories of cave paintings and the history of humans – but with no evidence, no facts, no proof. Only the scribblings in my notebook and a ruined pile of rocks in the Atlantic. No one will believe the word of a mere woman, a young one and a foundling at that. I will be ignored at best, vilified, mocked and even imprisoned at worst. But my proof was there in that cave, yet now it is all gone, as if it were a figment of my mind, a dream. I feel as if all my work has been for nothing. As if a mighty eye saw my work and was displeased by it, and a mighty hand plucked me from it, dropped me down amid disaster and smashed my work to pieces; as a lesson to me, as a warning.

'Are you sad?' says he.

'I am fearful.'

'Of what?'

'Of God.'

'We must all be fearful of God at times. But why now?'

'I believe I invited His anger. My work, my theories, my thoughts. Perhaps they are blasphemous, truly evil. He punished me for it. He brought forth a great wave to destroy my cave utterly. He cracked the earth open and wrought disaster on this place and thousands of souls were killed by it. I fear Him, how I fear Him!'

I weep and I am held.

'Hush,' says he and soothes me. 'Hush, hush now.'

When I am quiet, he looks at me keenly. 'You are the brightest and best woman I have known in my life. You have a gift the like of which I have never imagined in a female. Cleverer than most men I have heard of, let alone women. I believe this talent is God-given. And I do not accept it could be twisted to do the devil's work. You are young and a little hot-headed, but there is no evil in you. I know you will use your brain for good ends, to enlighten us, to enrich our store of human knowledge. Our Lord could not ask for a better example of everything He intended the human mind to be, so lofty, so separate from the base creatures, mankind made in His own image.'

And though his manner is comforting, his argument frightens me further, as I know – and this I have told no one – that the most secret part of my theory thus far concerns precisely this: that we are not distinct from the animal kingdom; that we are intimately connected to it, as cousins are, siblings or even children. But I cannot reveal this to him or anyone. And so I keep myself quiet and bury my face in his warmth and seek peace in him. We sleep that night entwined, two heavy lazy fellows.

We must return to Peniche in the morning. We are surprised to find a familiar face awaits us at my guest-house. It is the midshipman from the *Prospect*. He salutes his superior officer and retrieves a piece of paper from his pocket, which is read then conveyed to me by Captain Alex.

'I am to be promoted to master and commander, to captain the frigate HMS *Fox* currently docked at Lisbon. I am to arrive there as soon as possible to take command of it and another officer will pilot the *Prospect* back to England.'

Though he is taken aback, I can see pride in his eyes, and excitement. Yet as he hands the paper back to the midshipman and glances at me, I believe I see confusion there, even regret. He addresses me quite formally, in the presence of his – perhaps suspicious – colleague. As for myself, my throat is tight and I feel somewhat sick. Yet also there is a strange lightness about me I cannot explain. I am as confused as him, that is the truth.

'Miss Price, do not concern yourself for your own arrangements. I will ensure safe passage for your return to the *Prospect* where a haven awaits you.'

'Do ships sail from Lisbon to the Mediterranean Sea?'

'I do not know where my orders will take me. It may well be to Gibraltar or further afield. Perhaps even to the American colonies.'

He clears his throat and shuffles; it is clear to me he wishes he could say more.

'I request the information on my own behalf, Captain Alex. I wish to journey to Minorca and enquire if I am able to sail there from Lisbon or if I require a different port.'

'You wish . . .? *Minorca*?'

'Indeed,' I venture, glimpsing a modicum of amusement at the corner of the midshipman's mouth. 'I intend to continue my studies there. I only need passage and supposed I may need to travel further south to obtain it – perhaps a port such as Faro, perched as it is at the southern end of the country, would be suitable.'

He dismisses the midshipman and instructs him to wait

at the fort by the beach, that he will meet him there when ready. He does not need to explain himself to a subordinate. He watches the man go, glances at the guest-house to see there are no windows open and bids me follow him to the side of the building, where we are sheltered by lemon trees and privacy.

'Now then,' says he, 'this will not do. This absolutely will *not do.*'

I retort, 'You must know that there is nothing you can say to dissuade me, once I have made up my mind to something. I *will* do it.'

'Here it is again. This stubborn refusal to see sense. My dear, conflict is coming to these parts. France is edging us ever closer to it. Perhaps in a matter of weeks, Europe will be at war. You must come home, as soon as you are able. It is said this war may not be resolved for many years. You are young and you will have to wait.'

'I will not wait! And I will not be told, by you or any man, what I can or cannot do! It is my life and my choice. I do not presume to direct your actions. How dare you make free to dictate mine!'

'It is not me who dictates. It is the state of affairs that surrounds you. To put on blinkers and ignore the danger of your circumstances would be half-witted. I always suspected that most women are children of a larger growth. And here is my evidence! I thought you had more wit than this.'

'Minorca is owned by the British. It will be quite safe, I am sure. War is the business of men, not women. Life goes on in wartime. And so will I.'

He furiously shakes his head, even raises a fist and clenches it.

'Will you blaze with me, sir?' I ask, unable to suppress a smirk. 'You are most quarrelsome and hot!'

'Do not mock me!' he spits. 'Do you care nothing for me? Do you?'

He takes me by the shoulders and kisses me very hard. My body cries out for his, but I will not be used roughly and I step back from him.

'Now we see the truth. The man possesses the woman, even one not his wife. Or believes he does. But you are misguided, sir, if you think you own me or my direction. And the question of how I care for you: it is an insult to the memory of yesternight to say I care not. But whether I do or do not makes no odds with your plans. You are to captain a new vessel, most likely to sail to war. Your feelings for me will not stop you. And I will not dutifully trot to London and await your pleasure there, while you fight the French and on rare visits home father more children with your wife and appear at my door from time to time for entanglement. I have a life, sir, and I will live it.'

'Foolish pride! You think I wish to control you?'

'I do, sir.'

'It is your free will makes me love you. It is your life I wish to *protect*, not direct. I want you to be safe, away from harm, as I would my own child.'

'I am not your child. I am a grown woman.'

He turns from me and grasps at the roots of his hair, stares at the ground and paces away a few steps. My eyes fall upon his form, the long curve of his back, the straight solid fullness of his thighs and his beautiful sunburned neck. It is then, in the heat of my self-righteousness, I must face the likelihood that we may never be alone again. He may even die in this war. Never more to feel his body against mine, around, beside or inside it.

I go to him and embrace him, kiss him over and over.

'Robin,' I murmur.

We are in shadow, beside a white house in Peniche, Portugal – yet we are nowhere and we are all alone, the world slipped away.

★

Time returns, and, with it, responsibility and the future. We discuss our plans. He knows he will not dissuade me and does not try. He will escort me to Lisbon, find me passage to Minorca, then he to his ship and I to mine. We will try to write letters, yet we need an intermediary we can trust. It cannot be anyone who knows him. It must be someone in my camp. But who? Mr Woods would not approve, and in a drunken mood may open a letter; and then we are lost. No, and even Susan Applebee is quite clear on virtue. There is no safe, private way for us to correspond.

Robin says simply, 'The moment I am able, I will discover your whereabouts, and I will come to you. Do you believe me, my love?'

'I believe you would do that. I do.'

We go inside and I quickly write a letter to my benefactor, explaining my plans and begging his approval and continued funds. I shall ask Robin if he can see it finds its way to England. So it is arranged, and I pack all my things up. I take my leave of Dona da Seda, who bids me well. I cannot think I will ever see her again and this pains me, though I have no particular attachment to her; her wrinkled face and black mourning dress bind me to Peniche, its soft-sanded beach, the *Gaivota*, the ladies of lace, my friends dead and gone, and my islands.

It is then I realise my plan to travel to Minorca is the correct one. It had been brewing silently in my mind these past days and yet did not voice itself until I said it to Robin outside. What I seek there, I cannot quite explain. There are islets ripe for study, that is true. Yet there is more to it. I wish somehow to pay homage to my friend Pilar, honour her death in the place of her birth, and investigate her stories of mermaids. This latter part is rather far-fetched, I know, and I do not put much stock in it. I recall my childhood wonder at the pages on mer-people in one of my benefactor's volumes, where these creatures were illustrated faithfully and described in as much detail as the trout or the pike or any other English fish. But my tutor told me they were so rare that it would be a miracle to see one and witless to search for one and I vocally concurred, though secretly I harboured thoughts of seeking my own mermaid one day. The magical memory of it beckons me there at least, and I would rather be in Minorca than London any day of the week. And I cannot stay here.

We leave Peniche for Lisbon at midday, the sun warming the roof of my coach. The midshipman rides a nag to my left, Robin his horse to my right. I cannot resist but look out of my window to catch sight of him flanking me there, and he smiles at me, his eyes burning. I withdraw and close my eyes, shake my head. What a muddle we are in. He is a gentleman, a husband, a father; and ambitious, employed by that conservative bastion of society, as were his father and father's father, spending his days in the wooden kingdom of a ship. I am a foundling, a spinster, a learned woman and thus open to ridicule and mockery, no property or possession of my own, a nobody. It is all impossible. But we knew that yesterday, and loved each other nonetheless.

21

Robin is true to his word and does indeed arrange passage for me. As I had feared, we are not to be alone again. We approach Lisbon through constant heavy showers, trundling through the fragments of the city, where many Lisboetas still reside in shambolic encampments ankle-deep in wet mud; yet some have returned to live among the ruins of their former homes, unable to accept their destruction, or perhaps simply tired of living beneath canvas or carpet. Many houses are propped up with giant planks of timber and goats sheltered in the empty ruins. As my coach makes its way through, I am keenly aware of travelling over land that houses thousands of carcasses, who perhaps starved to death in the end, rather than being crushed or suffocated by smoke or burned by fire, and it makes me shudder to consider the vast mausoleum the city has become and what multitudes of spectres must haunt it at night.

Robin's farewell is played out swiftly at the dockside and in a suitably platonic manner before the crew of the *Prospect*. They watch the arrival of their once captain, as he stops at the wharf to take his leave. There is only a moment when he takes my hand to assist me in alighting from the coach and he squeezes it so hard I gasp. We share a glance blurred by the rain, with not a moment to stop as he escorts me a few steps to a new coach bound for Faro. Robin has assigned a marine from the *Prospect* to accompany me, who guards my coach on the journey and arranges overnight accommodation on the way. He is a beefy fellow and does his duty (though

I do hear him carousing with two of the guest-house maids, sharing some bottles of strong wine late into the night). I remember I have not told Robin of my destination once in Minorca and charge the marine with relaying this message to his captain, that I am heading for the village of Fornells on the north coast of the island. But whether this news will reach Robin before he takes up his new command is doubtful, though the marine assures me he will do his best, most politely. He also guides me to my ship, a Portuguese merchant vessel with a scattering of paying passengers that calls at Minorca and the other Balearic Islands before it sails on to Corsica, Sardinia and further afield. I am sorely tempted to stay on board and see these other spectacles, but I know there will be time for that in my future.

The entrance to the Mediterranean is through the Straits of Gibraltar, also known as the Pillars of Hercules. It is said the Roman hero smashed through a mountain to forge a path, thus creating a channel through the middle, with half a mountain remaining on either side, in Spain and in Africa. The legend also suggests a warning was placed here, at the end of the Mediterranean, that 'nothing further lies beyond', as past the entrance to their sea was the unknown world, and there be dragons. Our ship enters the strait at dawn, with the sun blooming gold and fiery at the horizon as we pass by Europe to port and Africa to starboard, each peak looming through the sea fret. With a strong westerly wind we make good passage, yet are soon surrounded by a jumble of other vessels going to and fro and narrowly avoid several collisions, all accompanied by a cacophony of insults from our sailing companions in a variety of languages.

I survey these sights with barely a pinch of the sense of wonder I used to own, as I realise my mind is filled with these sights and sounds, yet my body is haunted by him. It is a physical necessity. I have not possessed true closeness in my life, not ever. I have no memory of it with my brother, though it may have been there. I have no memory of it with anyone, and now I understand how much a person craves it and I want it again. I did need it all those years. And yet never having it, I did not understand what a basic requisite it is, as flavour to the tongue, music to the ear. I consider the way mammals nurture their young, the infant cradled, clinging on to its mother, a circle of protection and warmth, physically manifest. It is a yearning ache for closeness and it hurts me inside. Robin may infuriate me, with his pomposity and sureness, his arrogance and patronising ways, but oh, how I ache for his body and his love. And the knowledge I will not have them again, soon or ever, is sour. I must train myself to forget him and live without him for good. I make my resolution as I watch the Rock of Gibraltar recede and see my past go with it. But the rock will still be there, solid and shiftless, whether I choose to lay eyes on it or not.

The winds change and delay us somewhat on our journey up the Mediterranean, yet on the morning of the third day we dock safely at the western port of Ciutadella at Minorca. The capital of Port Mahon – changed from this place to that by the English to suit themselves – lies to the east and would be more convenient for travelling from, yet here is where our Portuguese merchant captain decides to allow us to alight. It is such a pretty port of turquoise water, surrounded by a crowd of white houses and a clutter of boats everywhere one's glance falls. An imposing fort of golden hue built upon tall foundations peppered with dark green weed sprouting among the stones dominates the harbour wall. Around and nearby it loiter a rash of red-coated English soldiers. Somehow the sight of my countrymen does not stir me, and I make my decision to ignore them. It gladdens me that I will not be based in Port Mahon, as it is the headquarters of the British army, and I wish to be invisible, without nationality, without allegiances. I only wish to be myself in this lovely place. The stone of this town, of a light caramel hue, verily glows in the

sunlight, and behind it one can see a tumble of church spires
and municipal buildings in this same golden material, dotted
with the white brick and hexagonal sails of windmills,
composing a beguiling vista through which I would love to
pace its narrow cobbled streets and see what I can see. If only
Pilar could have stepped off this ship with me and indeed
been my guide, as we once held hands and daydreamed.

But I will not spare the time to enjoy its pleasures, as I am
keen to journey presently to Fornells, where Pilar's family
home is situated. I find some of the inhabitants of the wharf
speak English. I attempt to use Spanish to impress them, only
to recall that – as my friend once mentioned – the inhabitants
of this island speak a curious dialect of Catalan called
Menorquí. It has some similarities to Spanish and Portuguese,
and we get by with familiar-sounding phrases such as *Bon
dia* which perhaps any western European might understand.

I find a genial driver who seems particularly pleased with
me for speaking Spanish rather than English at least, and
despite the fact that he would not as a rule drive as far as
Fornells, he agrees to convey me all the way there. It will take
the whole day, he warns me, so I had better purchase some
victuals to take with me. I do so – fruit, bread and fried fish
from quayside sellers – and I fill my bottle from an ancient
water carrier who is wordless and toothless. My driver loads
my luggage on the back of a sturdy cart joined to four feisty-
looking mules. '*Sedon*,' he says to me, as he pats the seat
beside him, sounding for all the world like a creole version
of *Sit down*, and I conjecture how much the recent invasion
of the British has already influenced culture and language
here. They say there are Friesland cows hereabouts imported
by a British governor from a few years back, from whose rich
milk the Minorcans now make a tasty cheese. Less salubrious
is the gin production I have heard of in the east of the island,
the worst of English habits imported to satisfy the thirst of
British soldiers stationed here. I hope sincerely it does not

ruin these dusty paths as it has the gin-soaked streets of our cities back home. I pull my shawl around my head and shield my eyes from the glare of the sun, my hand bumping against my forehead as we lump along the sandy, rutted roads.

After a time, I spot a curious object on the horizon. Across the landscape, to the south of the road we use to traverse the island, is what can only be described as the tidiest pile of stones I have yet seen. It is only as we approach nearer that I see it is a building of some sort, not an accidental pile at all. It is a broad, rough circle of boulders, some of which are built up one atop the other, to create an almost oval wall of sorts. I can see there are olive trees – somewhat stunted by the fierce wind blowing through them – and other vegetation growing all around and between the stones, so that perhaps this was once a walled structure with even a roof, yet neglect and nature have overtaken its grandeur and created this rubbly ruin. Of course, this must be one of the ancient sites Pilar told me about.

I ask my driver in Spanish and we converse simply, in our half-Spanish, half-English with a smattering of Menorquí.

Say I, 'You see that old building over there? Can we stop and see it?'

'We never go in them. We stay away.'

'Why?'

'Ghosts.'

My cheery driver frowns, gees up the mules and will not stop. Further along the road I see another such structure. This is more extensive, with longer walls, what look like caves in the rock and a peculiar construction of boulders, which for all the world seem to have been balanced one atop the other almost like an archway or pair of stone columns. I simply must see that cave, but I know my driver will not turn for it, and I must be patient. Yet my loss at the Berlengas has made me fearful and obsessive. I half expect this site to be gone if I come back tomorrow, though it has sat here for generations. I keep my eyes on it and seek out answers in its eccentric forms until the land rises, falls and hides it from me. I will go back.

On our welcome approach north to Fornells, I look up to see the castle of Sant Antoni surrounded by scrubby ground, patches of brave green shouldering dusty yellow soil; I have since read of its history, built against the Barbary pirates about a century ago. From there the small outpost of British soldiers must possess the ideal panoramic view over the bay of Fornells and the village nestling beneath them, with the Fornellers going about their fishy business and the goats clambering in herds across the landscape. Some houses are brightly white-washed, neat and well-kept. I spot a cormorant preening its oily feathers, then diving into the clear blue sea – the clearest I have ever seen – with patches of marine life here and there beckoning me to examine them later with my glass viewer. There is an attractive mixture of white and golden rocks, green plants clinging resolutely beneath the strong sea winds that have bent some trees to the ground. We pass a pretty church amber in the sunshine.

My driver deposits me at a reputable guest-house owned by a lady from a place he cannot remember, which he attempts to explain is English but not English. I suspect she is from Scotland, yet on entering the Hotel Cardiff I find the lady is Welsh. Her name is Mrs Meredith and she greets me with kindness. She has a room spare and by late afternoon I am fed, watered and situated in a small yet comfortable room overlooking the harbour of this sleepy fishing village. I sit at a table beside the window and write a brief letter to Mr Woods, informing him of my new address and location. I tell him I intend to stay here for six months, until early summer. This is vague enough to give me some time to decide for myself what my plans are. Truth be told, I have not a clue what I shall be doing by the spring. My experience in Lisbon has taught me that plans too long in advance are pointless, as the future may crack open in a moment and devour you, most literally, plans and all.

I leave my room, letter in hand, and Mrs Meredith offers to arrange postage of it tomorrow. I thank her then ask if she knows of a local fishing family called Cardona, specifically Pilar's brother whose name I was told is Mateu. She says rather imperiously that she has little to do with the local fishermen, but directs me to her fishmonger who she says deals with such people. This man does know Mateu Cardona. He sends his boy to accompany me, a dark-eyed scallywag with a cheeky gait who runs too far ahead of me around corners, then pokes his head out to see if I am yet lost. But I can run too, when I need to. We arrive at a row of houses two streets back from the sea, the accoutrements of their trade to be seen all along the street, with old nets being mended by women seated on stools and gossiping in the dying sun. The boy points to them, turns on his heel and runs away, the little scoundrel.

They raise their heads and stare curiously as I approach. Once I begin to speak in Spanish, their faces light up and nod, though one young woman giggles at me, as perhaps my Castilian pronunciation sounds odd to Minorcan ears. We converse in a mixture of Spanish and the strange nuances of their Menorquí. I ask if they know of this man, that I knew his sister in Portugal and wish to pay my respects to him and his family. 'Pilar?' they say, 'Pilar, Pilar!' And they laugh in recognition and I know I am in the right place. One woman stands and approaches me, smiling. It is at this moment I realise something I had not thought of: perhaps Minorca felt the distant effects of the earthquake and yet it is very likely that none of these people will have heard of Peniche's disaster. And almost certainly they will have no knowledge of Pilar's death. And the fact occurs to me that I will be the harbinger of this hateful news and I must give it without delay to her bereaved brother. How stupid of me not to have foreseen this, to have been so caught up in my own affairs and desires that I have forgotten how sluggishly intelligence travels. I have arrived here far quicker than the news trundles through continents, and I wish I did not carry it to this lovely place. I now regret my hasty choice to come here. Would it not have been better for him never to know? To imagine his sister, if he thinks of her at all, happy in Peniche with her fisherman husband? I must choose now, to tell the horrible truth or keep it my secret.

The woman tells me her name is Francina and she is Mateu's wife. He is about to return from fishing with their two sons. She asks me, 'How is Pilar?' She tells me they were friends, as girls, that she has not seen her for thirty years or more.

And I am torn, whether to tell this good woman first, or save it for the brother. But I am saved from my indecision as the tramping of boots resounds at the end of the street and a group of men come down greeted by the women with indifference. I ask Francina if her husband is among them. And she nods, taking my arm and leading me towards a man with white hair and an ample moustache covering his mouth. He looks older than Pilar yet has young eyes, green like hers and glinting.

Francina explains who I am. All the men have stopped now to stare at me and listen. But then Mateu brings his own surprise. There has been news, he tells the rapt audience about him, from the Portuguese ship that brought me. Word has taken a day to travel across the island and now all talk is of the disaster that afflicted Lisbon. Mateu questions me politely: was I there, in the centre of the earthquake? They did indeed feel it here, yet it sounds as if it were quite weakened by distance. How did his sister fare? Did her husband lose his boat? The women sewing have ceased their work, and wait to hear what the curious Englishwoman has to say. I stand in this cobbled street, Pilar's family home behind me, her brother, his wife and their sons leaning forward to hear my news. I wish to say that Pilar is well and sends her best regards and love. But I cannot.

'I am very sorry to tell you that Pilar and her husband Horacio died in the earthquake,' say I in Spanish, and a gasp ripples through the assembly.

Mateu frowns and glances at Francina, who shakes her head, her hand covering her mouth.

Mateu asks me, 'How did she die?'

'Mateu,' says his wife, as if to warn him from seeking too much.

I mean to say in peace, she died peacefully. But I cannot lie, and yet I cannot speak the words. I open my mouth to say it and stop.

'Please, young lady,' says Mateu.

'After the earthquake, there was a great and terrible wave that came across the sea. Pilar was on the beach with her husband.'

I need say no more. It is understood. People begin to mutter and comfort each other. I stand alone and do not know where to look or what to do with my hands.

Then Francina takes my hand. 'We are very glad you came.'

'But I bring such awful news,' I reply softly, as if it were my doing, as if I were the cause of the earthquake and I come carrying my shame.

Mateu adds, 'Then we are glad it was brought to us not by a stranger, but instead Pilar's friend. We are glad it was you.'

He bows deeply and retires into his house. He is clearly moved and I feel I must remove myself. Francina kindly offers that I should stay for some refreshment, yet I thank her and make my excuses to go. She asks me where I am staying and says I must come to visit them again soon, under brighter circumstances. With that, I leave Pilar's family to grieve. I came to this lovely place with knowledge of their country-woman, so long gone away and now, out of nothing, there is news. But it is fearful news, of the worst kind. I feel I have infected this street with bad tidings.

The next day, I wander mournfully on the local beach. I pace across white sand strewn with curious balls of fibrous material I believe must be washed up by the sea. I bring my usual bag of specimen collectors and my viewer. I remove my stockings – to the surprise of some nearby fishermen who grumble and point at me. But I am used to being the odd foreigner – indeed, the English mermaid – and I paddle to the edge of a reef. Beyond it, I can glimpse the edge of a captivating underwater meadow of swaying seaweed, bright green clumps aligned along a channel with ribbon-like leaves almost as long as I am tall, swaying elegantly in the water. I believe the balls I see on the beach may be the desiccated foliage of this seagrass. Its genus may be the *zostera* described by Linnaeus, yet I am not sure, so I make a quick sketch and write a brief description. My viewer also affords me a clear view of red coral, crustaceans and molluscs, and even a blue spiny lobster scuttling to hide from me. It is true I have brought sadness to this place, as I have carried my own within me. But there is such vivacity here, I feel somewhat renewed and sleep that night with visions of ocean gardens replacing my customary recent nightmares of destruction and death. Instead, I dream of life.

22

I spend the next two days similarly surveying the coast, notebook and pencil to hand, recording my first impressions of the local flora and fauna. Over breakfast on my fourth day, Mrs Meredith hands me a note delivered very early this morning while I still slumbered. It is from the Cardona family and they are inviting me to lunch at midday. I walk over there slowly in apprehension. When I arrive, I believe there remains a subdued tone to the street's inhabitants, yet at the sight of me, all I see are respectful and nod, smile and greet me most decorously.

Once inside the Cardona home – simple, comfortable, clean and painted bright white, just as Pilar described it – I am made to feel most welcome by Mateu and Francina. From an awkward first few moments – where I feel Pilar stands in the midst of us like a haunting – a slow yet steady stream of questions trickles from them, about how I met Pilar, of her home, her habits and Horacio – whom they have never met – and from Pilar's nephews, two or three very particular questions about the construction of Horacio's boat and how well it sails, which I endeavour to answer, casting back my mind to happier days on the gay *Gaivota*. During this latter delightful interrogation, Francina has been busy in the kitchen and soon returns with steaming plates of the most marvellously scented food.

It is a Sunday and I am treated to what I am told is a traditional Minorcan Sunday lunch. Francina tells me with regret that we will not be having the English *bifi* with *grevi*, and there again is that curious mish-mash with English I have heard before. There is something endearing about it, yet I would not wish this lovely island to lose its unique quality in subjugation to an alien culture such as my own. Let us hope the two cultures enrich each other, indeed like a fine gravy, and do not repel, like oil on water. We eat a delicious stew made of lobster, served with thin pieces of toasted bread and small potatoes. There are clams too, eaten with lemon, and curious crustaceans that appear to be a barnacle of sorts, the kind of animal an Englishman would turn up his nose at, but the flavour is quite good. The delight of eating and sharing good food seals our ease with each other. And by the end of it I am as fat as a belly-god, only to be told there is dessert: a kind of nougat mixed with almonds, and soft pastry cakes that melt on the tongue. The kindness and good nature of the Cardona family is exceptional; though they are not poverty-stricken, the simplicity of their dwelling shows how little they have to spare, and yet they feed me like a queen and keep bringing more. After the sweets, Francina offers me a small, tasty plum and she says in English, 'Never Saw Plum.'

Whatever can she mean?

Say I, in Spanish, 'Would you like to learn English?'

'No, no!' she says. 'An Englishman, the governor here, ten years ago or more. He was in the market in Máo and he saw a woman selling fruit. She asked him, "What do you call this plum in England?" And he said, "I *never saw* it in England." And from that time on, everyone calls this fruit the Never Saw Plum.'

How we laugh! This curious procreation between my country and this enchanting island is most diverting. I begin to feel at home here, though it is a far cry from the squalid streets of my youth.

After dinner I offer to assist in clearing away the platters and so forth but I am refused, so ask instead to speak with Mateu. I am eager to explore the coastline hereabouts and need a kind of Horacio to help me. I know how busy these fishermen must be – and I wonder for a moment if it is somehow inappropriate to ask – yet as soon as I moot the idea of a boatman to assist me with my studies, Mateu assures me he would be honoured to take me. Not every day, of course, but once or twice a week. I explain to him my work on islands and he nods gravely. He says he can take me out to broad beds of the local seagrass, which are flanked by rocky outcrops rich with sea life. It is then I ask him about Pilar's mermaids.

He lifts his eyebrows, pauses a moment, then tells me we can look, but that these creatures are hard to find nowadays. He adds, 'The English have frightened them off!' He uses a lovely Spanish word for them: *doncella*, meaning a pure young woman – maidens of the sea.

I ask him, 'Do you believe they are real? Have you seen them?'

Francina has overheard our conversation and joins us. She adds, 'There are surely mermaids in these waters and have been for ever. Some are helpful and kind. They have married our men. Others are cruel and lure ships to disaster. When I was a child, they said there were giant sirens near here, male and female, who would rise high above the water and make a terrible screaming sound when boats came near. And some even came to shore and dragged two men and a woman into the sea and drowned them.'

I shake my head with appropriate awe. Yet I consider this may well have been a cautionary tale to frighten little Francina and her friends, to keep them away from the dangerous tides. I turn to Mateu to see what he makes of all this.

He shrugs. 'I have seen something in the water,' he says. And no more. He does not chatter, like his sister once did, as if his heavy whiskers discourage it.

We sail the next day in an attractive boat Mateu calls his *llaüt*.

There are many of these to be found about Minorca, so I surmise they must be a traditional vessel of the island. He tells me he builds these boats with his sons and sells them at a good price, and now I understand how a fisherman can provide such a good meal as I had yesterday. He is clearly a skilled craftsman, as this neat little boat cuts beautifully through the blue waves, swift and true. He takes me to the next headland to the west and we dabble about the adjacent reef, my viewer affording me – and an ever more curious Mateu – some wonderful views of the abundant sea life. I see a blue lobster again and Mateu tells me this is what I ate in Francina's delicious stew.

We head towards two tiny uninhabited islets. Mateu tells me this is where he and his family have seen flickers of tails in the water in the past.

'I am not a fool,' he says, a slight twitch of his moustache showing he is amused by the thought, not annoyed. 'I think the mermaid is most likely a child's story. But there is something here, sometimes, in the water. Something we cannot name. From time to time.'

We sit, drifting fitfully on the currents, for a while. We have brought food: cheese, bread, spiced sausages and a tasty sweet concoction of breadcrumbs and cinnamon baked by Francina. We eat in silence, pensive, watching the waves, scanning the islets. Time passes. I *will* something to appear in the water. Yet I know it will not. I am not that lucky.

After a day at sea, I trudge back exhausted to Mrs Meredith's guest-house and collapse on my bed. I can neither stir leg nor arm. I sleep, woken only by her feisty knocking to rouse me for supper. She has sent out a rabbit for roasting in the local baker's oven and I devour it hungrily. I adore the simple yet hearty food here, the fresher than fresh food of the sea and the sugary rich treats Francina bakes for me. I adore the crystalline water, the emerald seagrass swaying and the blue lobster clambering about its reef. I adore Minorca.

These winter months I sail to the islets twice a week with Mateu. We wait and watch, yet see only fish in the waters. I ask to land on an islet and we spend time at several different ones. A curious fact reveals itself: there is a species of lizard living on these islets, and Mateu tells me that it is not to be found anywhere on the main island. On closer examination, I discover that the lizards one finds on each islet are slightly different. There are variations in colour and pattern on the skin of each separate lizard, yet within each tiny landmass the lizards are all the same. For example, on one all the lizards are tan mottled with black patches. On another, they have a green tail and a dark brown body; others have aqua patches beneath the chin; one islet is home to only black specimens, while some are striped and more still are spotted. It is as if the Creator grew burthened with tedium at the idea of one single lizard species when painting the island of Minorca and thus decided to mix up His palette and experiment.

I make sketches of each variation of lizard and paint them in watercolours, and sit in the evenings by candlelight in my guest-house mulling over the differences. One could explain it with the idea of a bored deity, many would agree. Yet I am not satisfied with this. Why would there be a different sub-species of lizard on each little island, each with its own markings? What else differs between the islets? Is the vegetation distinct, the colouring of the land itself marked differently? Does each lizard fit its situation neatly, unable to conceal itself successfully anywhere else? Does it *need* to conceal itself? Does it have natural predators – perhaps birds of prey? Such questions fill my mind, requiring answers and producing more by the day.

When Mateu is busy working, I spend the rest of my days exploring the ancient sites of the island. I hire a cart and mule and show myself around, following directions from the local people. My mule I christen Horacio, as he is good-natured and has a comical aspect yet soft sweet eyes, and he likes me because I feed him apples for treats. I visit the ruins I saw on my first day, as well as several other walled constructions made in a dry-stone fashion. Some are almost complete as dwellings, containing rooms, windows, and doorways constructed with a colossal coping stone placed to form a lintel. Inside, I am disappointed to discover there is no decoration, though there are a few bones and artefacts, such as carvings on small pieces of stone, decorative rather than figurative. When I find my first of these and pick it up, I feel it almost vibrate in my hand with pride in its own history, though I believe it is rather my hands trembling at this thought. There are also more extensive ruins, with walls running around and towers set to guard the inhabitants. Small details suggest a domestic situation, such as a water basin.

The evidence of these architectural endeavours suggests a more advanced ancestor than those in my Berlengas cave. These people knew how to build, though their art is not half as accomplished as the cave paintings. However, there are sites here that seem more about ceremony. There is one where a tall pedestal forms the shape of the letter T, from two slabs of rock. It is not a door gone awry or any such error – it has clearly been designed that way. And nearby is a great single stone standing tall, with a massive hole excised from near its top, like an ancient eye glaring over the land. What curious purpose these stones once played is beyond my imagination, at present. It is as if the Berlengas artists were painters on rock walls and the Minorcan artists were sculptors of the rock itself. I have heard tell of monuments like these in England – in the West Country, I recall – and resolve to see them for myself. At the base of one of these mighty Ts, I find a few terracotta objects: small bowls and drinking vessels, half buried among the scree and vegetation.

Within some of these ancient hamlets, I find my sought-after caves, but there is no painting or decoration here, only that some have been enhanced by a built entrance surrounding the cave's natural opening. There are carved caves here as well – too numerous and uniform to be aught but human-made – high up on the cliff-face above a cove. The climb seems impossible and is infuriatingly tantalising. I have asked and asked around the locals but nobody knows of a safe way up there and they seem quite impenetrable. I stand land-bound and eye them, listening to the sea, watching the seabirds above that chatter and jibe at me in their swooping flight. If only I could follow them.

In January, I receive a letter from my benefactor:

My dear Dawnay,

I am much relieved to be in receipt of your letters from Lisbon, Peniche and Minorca. To see your words formed by your own little hand gives me much succour, as you are a world away and seem very tiny and distant in my sight. When I read of your plan to travel on to Minorca, I was extremely displeased at your extravagant conduct and it seemed an unworthy journey. Yet, I have enough self-knowledge to recognise that this is largely selfish as I do so miss our fireside conversations and your cluttering presence in the house. I never married because, as they say, it were better to dwell in the corner of the house-top, than with a contentious woman in a wide house. But you are my anchor, my child, and I do feel your absence and think myself a poor sort of being. As is my lot, I continue to suffer from a long list of mortifications regarding my health and also social endeavours – (I have again embar-rassed myself in public with drinking too much bumbo) – which only your presence could soften. I realise now that I was foolish to imagine that a few months in Portugal would be enough for a restless mind such as yours, and I was not surprised to hear that you wished to extend your odyssey.

But I am highly concerned about your safety, my dear

girl, as your lucky escape from the ravages of the earth-
quake has shaken me to the core. We have received more
reports of this late dreadful event and London talks of
little else. Clearly it was the most grave judgement of
God's wrath inflicted on sinners. Many say that it was a
punishment for the idolatrous ways of the Portuguese, but
you know I do not agree with such extreme views of any
foreigners (excepting the French of course) and I do not
believe it was proof of God's particular anger towards
Lisbon but instead that such an event reminds us all to be
circumspect. Whatever is, is right, as the quake awakens in
us a truly Christian spirit towards the suffering of our
fellow man, and in this way the earthquake can be seen as
a good thing and thus, all is well.

I did however lose some significant stock and funds in
the disaster too, and for this reason have some concern
over financing your travels indefinitely. Do not fret too
much about this last point, but be aware that you must
return in the summer at the latest, as you have promised.
Somewhat more frugal times may be ahead, unless Lisbon
recovers itself more swiftly. There are also rumours of
imminent war with France which some do not take
seriously but I know the French of old and I do not
underestimate their capacity for double-dealing and down-
right viciousness. Therefore, I urge you to return home
sooner than your desires may wish, and be safe here with
us for good.

All best regards and love to you, my dear, and keep well
&c.

M. Woods

Post Scriptum: I almost forgot to mention our old friend
Lieutenant Robin Alexander came to visit me the other
week. He is now a master and commander with his own
frigate to direct. He was in London for a few days to visit

his handsome family and then was off to blockade the
French. He asked after you, my dear. I do believe he
admires your work and says it is extremely fruitful. It is
only his good word of it that prevents me from becoming
too disappointed with you, as I understand from him that
you have been working very industriously and not wasting
your time in the sunshine.

And by the way, did you retrieve any relics from the
ruins of Lisbon, such as melted coins? They sell very well
or would be an interesting keepsake.

To hear of Robin! I smooth the letter carefully on the table
before me and stare at my lover's name. To hear that he is
safe and well – or was then – that he thinks of me and made
a special visit to speak of me with Mr Woods. And my dear
benefactor, his rambling tone moves me so very much – despite
his chiding and his outrageous viewpoints and ridiculous
signature almost obscured by pretentious flourishes and folde-
rols – that I find tears rolling down my face at the thought
of him, of England, of the Applebees, even of Matron. Of
home. Yet I fear I may have to disappoint my benefactor again,
as I do not wish to leave this place soon or in the near future.
But, guided by the real nature of my situation, I must admit
the lack of finances may force me home.

In February, news rustles around the island that the British
garrison has put out a call for local volunteers, from their
base at Fort St Philip at Port Mahon. It is well known that
the soldiers live in squalor there and some have taken their
own lives in their misery. It is said only two dozen locals
have volunteered to join them. Many Minorcans tolerate the
English here, and some speak in romantic terms of the French
and even with nostalgia for the Spanish, but I believe the
truth is that they simply wish to live their lives peaceably
on their own island, and have no interest in the intrigues of
their overseers, whatever nationality they are. It does make

me query, though, for what purpose the garrison may require more men. Perhaps I ought to return to England sooner than I planned, but first I must complete my studies here satisfactorily.

By March, the waters are warming. Mateu says he will take me to a spot along the coast, new to me. He says there is a sea cave near Aranel d'en Castel, where something has been spotted in the water this past week. We go there and wait. We go again the following week and wait. Mateu naps beneath a hat, just as Horacio did. Spring flowers are blooming on Minorca: scrambling pink convolvulus, asphodel, buttercup, narcissus and red poppy. There are already tiny irises poking through, which will bloom in the coming months. Soon I must leave this place. A slight breeze gets up and the water turns unsettled.

'*Per allà,*' says Mateu. *Over there.*

There is a glimpse of something. Out in the blue, our eyes dazzled by the sun. Nothing. Then a plash and a switch of something breaking the surface, closer. I grab my viewer and thrust it into the water, swivel round to see if I can catch sight of it moving underwater. I spy a blur of movement in the corner and I drop the viewer.

'There!' cries Mateu and points to the sea cave behind us.

There is something in the water, beneath the surface, quite still. The shadow of the rock obscures it. I steal a glance at Mateu – as I know he will try to prevent me from what I am about to do – and I throw off my outer garment and slip into the water. I hear Mateu shouting at me but I am not listening. I am under the water, eyes open, swimming towards the rock. It is gone. I turn a complete circle under the water, swim deeper. My lungs are crying out for their medium of air. Then I spot it, some yards away from me, side on, undulating. Blurred yet quite distinct, a creature. Pale, curved, forearms dangling. I simply must have air or I will faint. I race for the surface to gasp and return, but the choppy waves hurl me back and as I turn to see how close I am to the rock I feel myself smacked against it and the water turns red with blood from the back of my head. I wish to dive again but arms are about me and Mateu is dragging me into the boat. He is scolding me in lively Menorquí slang and I have no idea what he says, and care less, as I beam and beam and say to him, 'I saw her, I saw her!'.

The blood dries stiff in my hair and I cannot comb it or allow it to become wet for a week. Mrs Meredith says so, or the wound will open again.

'One of those fishermen hit you with a rock. They want their wicked way with you, they do.'

'Nonsense,' I insist and smile to myself. *I saw her.* But what did I see? There was no long flowing hair, no breasts that I could discern. But it was a shape wholly unlike any animal I have ever seen, not fish, porpoise or whale. Something – or other.

Once my landlady agrees my head would be safe to be wet again, I fairly run down to the Cardona home and I am made a fuss of by the ladies. I assure them I am quite well and eager to get back in the boat. Mateu agrees and along comes Francina. She would like to see the *doncella* too.

We sail out again to the same sea cave. Mateu reveals he has visited several times this week already, but seen nothing. My hopes fade. We wait for hours. Francina is bored. I see glances between them, hinting we should return. Then we feel a tap under the boat. We all look at one another. There it is again, another tap. We throw ourselves around to look over the side and see a mass in the water. It is huge, long, pale, curved, its forearms hanging before it. A flat tail projects backwards, as round and large as a serving platter. Its head is bulbous, its snout tapping curiously against the boat. I hear my friends chatter away beside me. I have lost my viewer on the previous trip, so I ignore what I know they will say and, as before, slip over the edge to come face to face with my mermaid.

It is grey as an elephant. Small dark eyes, widely spaced, consider me sleepily. A circular snout twitches with white whiskers. Its fat body is as round as a wine cask. It swivels one forelimb back and forth, back and forth, as if beckoning me. It lifts its head until its nose just breaks the water, sniffs the air then lowers again to regard me. A graceful way to capture breath. I need it too and tear myself away to surface. I see the faces of Mateu and Francina shouting at me and I sink again, to find my new friend has lost interest in me and is floating serenely away into deeper waters. I swim after it, yet despite its bulk it moves effortlessly and is soon far away and impossible to catch. I watch it go with sadness and fondness. It is no mermaid. There is nothing human there. It may be related to the porpoise or whale, perhaps a type of seal or walrus. I recall a picture in Applebee's encyclopaedia of something found near Russia in recent years, a sea cow. My creature has those gentle, bovine qualities. It is certainly no mermaid. But my, it is marvellous.

For days after, there is much chatter between my Minorcan friends and me about the creature and what it is. We are all agreed it does not resemble our traditional ideas of the mermaid, yet I can see how, from a distance, its pale colouring and curvy form – quite unlike the sleekness of the porpoise – could be mistaken for a human female. It occurs to me in these discussions that these folk memories of peculiar creatures – from mermaids and sea monsters to dragons and ogres – could simply be animals that once lived alongside humans yet died out like the disappeared fossils one finds in rock; that is, perhaps giants and ogres were a folk memory of early humans; dragons a kind of early reptile; mermaids a mammal who tired of land or whose environment altered through earthquake, volcano or other disaster and fled to the sea, changing over the years – as Raleigh conjectured – into limbless sea creatures, perfectly adapted to their medium and quite helpless on land, as would be our sea cow. It is a sad thing to think our folklore may be lost to science, yet I believe too that there are countless more species hidden in the seas and forests and deserts of this earth that we have not stumbled across as yet, awaiting us, innocently living, reproducing and dying in utter ignorance of us and we of them. There is much more to look forward to.

I am taken out several more times in March and early the month after to our cave to look for our aquatic friend, but it does not return, not once. I spend my evenings sketching the sea cow – if that is what it is – comparing it to other animals it resembles – under the sea and on land – from whales to seals to hippopotami to elephants. I write notes on the ancient dwellings scattered across this fair isle and compare these with my cave notes. I begin to place my notes and drawings on the floor. I use dried seagrass, available in abundance, like twine to fashion diagonal connections between the pages, a visual representation of my thoughts. I begin to see patterns there. I scribble down series of thoughts. I formulate my theory. I am on the cusp of something new, and it thrills and frightens me in equal measure.

I sit on my bed and stare at the patterns on the floor, sometimes for an hour or more without moving. Mrs Meredith thinks I am going queer. She complains that she cannot sweep the floor and she and I quarrel about it. What has more importance, after all? Yet I do consider of course that the cleanliness of her establishment is her work, as my papers are mine. Still I insist they must not be moved.

One morning, there is a harsh knocking at my door and I step across the display to reach the door, in readiness for more debate and open the door, finger raised to say, *Now then, my dear lady*. But she is shouting through the door: 'Miss Price!' she cries.

I open the door swiftly and ask, 'Whatever is the matter?'

'The French are here! The ships have been seen, out there. The French are coming to Minorca! To invade!'

23

I am running up the hillside to the castle of Sant Antoni, and see the British soldiers there rushing to and fro in their brick-red coats with a flash of yellow, a flurry of panic. They are gathering their equipment and readying to move out, chattering and pointing out to sea. I look and there are the French ships – a dozen or more – traversing the horizon in a stately armada. I call to a young soldier and tell him I am English.

'What of it?' says he and turns to ignore me.

'But what will happen? What should I do?'

'Not my business, miss. You do what you like. We're off to Mahon to bunk down. Best hope we have is to stick it out there till the navy come, if the buggers ever do.'

'Are you not to defend the island?' say I, with some disgust.

'Look here, there's only three thousand of us. You see those ships? There'll be twice that or more of them. We haven't got a hope.'

And with that, he trots off down the hill with his comrades, some of whom were already on the road shambling eastward. The navy, he said, *the navy*. I turn and watch the French ships sail smoothly on south. They look as if they are heading for Ciutadella. I turn and make my way over to the Cardona home, but nobody is there. Perhaps they are all gone to see the new invaders.

I return to Mrs Meredith and ask her, 'What do you think we should do?'

'Do? I'm not doing anything. I'm staying here.'

'Should we not try to leave, now, while we still can?'

'I'm not leaving. I buried my husband and son here and I won't leave them for the French or anyone else, thank you.'

'I am sorry to hear of that, Mrs Meredith. I did not know.'

'No reason you should. They were carried off by a malign fever, ten years ago now. Fair broke my heart. But I picked myself up and made this guest-house pay and here I am. You go if you want to. But I'm staying put, I am.'

Later that day, I finally find Mateu and Francina. They tell me the British have sunk a fireship in the harbour at Port Mahon and their engineers are destroying the houses in St Philip's Town. We hear too that the garrison has been driving in all the cattle they can find and have begun to break up the main road from Ciutadella. One could not leave the island now, as both ports are blocked. I am stuck here and must make the best of it. I ask my friends how they feel about the imminent arrival of the French on their island and they are equivocal. Francina explains Minorca is at a crossroads of many powerful nations and thus will always be trampled as one or the other passes through. They are accustomed to being stepped on.

Mrs Meredith simply carries on as usual, excepting the extra supplies of necessities she purchases, just in case.

The next day, I ride my mule cart over to the highest point on the island, the Monte Toro, and climb up it. I know from previous excursions that a good view of the port at Ciutadella is attainable from here. I am not alone, and find myself sharing the sight with several locals. We watch as the French ships are unloaded and their officers disembark. There seems to be little animosity, with many Minorcans eagerly assisting, and there is even music and singing to entertain the new arrivals, which sets my nerves on edge.

Later I tell Mrs Meredith what I have seen and she replies,

'They're all Catholics over that way. They don't like the English much there.'

'Where?'

'In that Soo-da-della. Port Mar-hon is full of Protestants, so they won't get much welcome there. Lucky for them they landed where they did.'

This puts my mind a little at rest, but only a little. How the local people respond to the invasion seems to me crucial in how it will be resolved. I perceive my position here is tenuous at best. Robin was right. War was coming and I chose to ignore it. As a natural philosopher, my mind is trained to see clearly, but it cannot withstand my own choice to ignore what I did not wish to see.

In the following days, there is little evidence that anything has changed on Minorca, up here in sleepy Fornells. We hear that the British ships at Port Mahon are preparing to leave, hopefully to return with a stronger fleet. This feels like desertion, again, just as the soldiers here ran away, whatever their reasoning. Surely the British ships could have stayed and used their guns against the French army as it moved about the island. They could have done much damage this way. I say this to Mateu, but he sensibly reminds me that they would soon run out of ammunition, and in the end would be forced to sink themselves in the harbour and be good for nothing. The tactics of war are beyond me, I see this. Fort St Philip is now packed with every British soldier on the island, shut up and ready for a siege. The French have tried to advance from the west, but the broken road has slowed them. We hear instead that they have sent their siege train by ship and landed at Cala Mezquida in the east.

The next day we have our first meeting at close quarters with the French soldiers; they cut a stark figure against the blue sky with their milk-white coats and black tricornes. They

arrive by road from Port Mahon and take Sant Antoni for
themselves. I keep to my room and venture out not at all. I
do not wish to be revealed as English. I hear the French
language drift across to my window from time to time and
it sounds like verse. But I do not have any romantic concepts
about these people and their invasion. They say there will be
no looting, but who can trust an army's word? News from
Port Mahon is that the governor – a fellow in his eighties
called Blakeney, apparently cheerful yet bed-bound due to
gout – has received dried fruit as an offering from the French
commander the Duc de Richelieu and in return has sent some
bottles of English beer. After this civility, they have decided
it is high time to begin fighting.

Over the next fortnight, I hear daily reports that the French
are building batteries on the outcrop of La Mola, opposite
the British entrenched in Fort St Philip. Now the guns will
begin and time will tell how long our army can hold out until
relief arrives. My only hope now is that the Royal Navy will
come and the sooner the better. The artillery duel begins in
the first week of May. Purple vetch, borage and the aptly
named French honeysuckle are blooming in arcs across the
island, as the guns of Richelieu and Blakeney blast at each
other across the bay. For two weeks, our days are peppered
by the boom-boom-boom of this battle held at arm's length.
I try to work, sifting through my notes on the early peaks of
human endeavour, of art and architecture, while a few miles
to the east the culmination of our development takes the shape
of a mass of men hiding behind rocks hurling fire at each
other. I wonder if we have progressed at all from the days we
lived in caves.

I tire of my self-imposed gaol and begin to venture out.
The French garrison up the hill keeps themselves to themselves, and, anyway, they do not know me or where I am
from, as yet. I visit the Cardonas and go for walks to watch
the late spring flourishing. One day, Mateu and Francina

come with me and we walk in silence for some time. Then they stop and say they wish to talk seriously with me. Mateu makes a kind of speech, and Francina nods her assent throughout. He says that they do not know what will happen, what the French plans are for their island. They do not fear for themselves, but they think I should leave whenever I can.

'There is no way,' I protest in their language. 'Where can I go? How could I get there?'

Mateu clears his throat and replies, 'If the English come, and if you ask me to, I will take you in my boat to an English ship. They may think we are spies, they may fire upon us, but I will take you, if you ask me to.'

'I would not ask you to put yourself in danger.'

Francina says, 'For Pilar's friend, we will do it.'

I take her hand and say, 'I am sure it will not come to that. The English will arrive soon and drive out the French, I know it.'

But I fear this is a dream, based on a fleeting liaison with a Royal Navy officer – and thus a soft ideal of what our brave mariners are capable of – and not the hard facts of the craft of war. Will the navy come? What if the French threaten English shores with invasion? Surely all will be needed there, and Minorca must be sacrificed for the greater good. But what will the British public say if Minorca is lost? Perhaps the navy *will* come then. Oh, the agony of not knowing. I continue my daily walks and stand on any outcrop I can find to stare west at the sea, at the horizon. If French soldiers approach me, I excuse myself politely in Menorquí and hurry away. My dark colouring assures I blend in with the locals.

On the nineteenth day of May, I am strolling through the village when one of the Cardona sons comes racing down the street on horseback. He sees me, turns his black horse about abruptly and calls to me. He shouts across the road and a cart rumbling by drowns out his words. I rush across to him and then I hear it: 'The English are here!'

The British fleet has been sighted off Cales Coves on the south coast of the island, the very spot where I stood and looked up at the ancient caves carved from the rock. My heart leaps in my chest and all I can think is, Will he be there? Will Robin's frigate be one of them? It is a slim chance, at best. There are British ships stationed all over the world: in India, the West Indies, in North America. He could be in any one of those far-off places, quite easily. But the last I heard was from Mr Woods, that his ship was to blockade the French, which would mean the Channel, or perhaps even the Mediterranean. And from where would the navy amass their ships to form a fleet to relieve Minorca? Surely those nearest by, surely those already in local waters or along the way here. I have tried to put this idea from my head since the French arrived last month; I have forced myself not to think of it, not to hope for it. But now, now our ships are here, here in Minorca, perhaps I can allow myself to imagine Robin at the helm of one of them, gazing up at the ancient caves and wondering, Is she here? Is my Dawnay here and is she well?

I wish to jump on my cart and rush down to the south coast, but it is a day's journey and by the time I reach Cales Coves the ships will have moved on. The word is that the English fleet is heading for Port Mahon, to relieve the garrison by landing more soldiers, and thereafter will engage the French fleet. So I repair to my room and wait for news. It soon comes. That afternoon, we hear that our fleet has rounded the islet they call Aire – I envy the lizards there watching them sail by – and now the ships are to be found becalmed under the lee of the island. By nightfall, we hear that the fleets have spotted each other, but as neither wants action at night, each has stood off and they are waiting till morning to fight. Then I will take my cart and mule at first light and go down to Port Mahon to see what I can see. What on earth I may be looking for I do not know, as I am ignorant of ships, and of what manner of vessel my Robin would be on. But I cannot sit here and wait.

I begin to ready myself for bed this night, clearing away my papers, washing my face. I am about to undress when I hear a tiny noise. I think, It is an animal in the rafters, tap-tapping. But it goes on, and there is method to it, a rhythm. It is at my window. I go to the curtains and open one. And there is a face at my window. For a moment, I am taken aback, thinking the French have come for me, but I realise in the next instant that I know it, and it is the round young face of my old naval friend, the boy Francis. Here, at my guest-house, in Minorca! Has he abandoned ship? Or has he been sent?

I open my window and he climbs in. We execute this in colluded silence, as if we carry out this deed every day.

'Oh, miss! I'm plaguy glad I found you!'

'Tell me everything, Francis. I will not be angry with you, if you are a runaway.'

'Oh no, miss. It's nothing of the sort. I've come due to Cap'n Alex.'

A wave of emotions – elation, desire, then fear – courses through my very fibre and I struggle to compose myself.

'Is he here? Is he well?'

'Oh yes, he's here and he's very well. Don't fret.'

Relief floods my senses and then confusion. What does he know of us? Oh, do I truly care in either case? Francis is our dear boy.

'Tell me everything.'

'Can I eat, miss? I've been on the road all day across the island and am fair fainting from lack of drink or food.'

He is breathing heavily, pink-cheeked and perspiring. If he came from Port Mahon or nearby, it would have taken him hours to get here. Poor thing. I first give him a glass of water from my dresser, then tell him to keep silent as I open my door. I tiptoe to the kitchen – my landlady already abed – and find bread, meat and Never Saw Plums for the boy. I watch with exasperated patience as he simultaneously gobbles and apologises for doing so. Then, at last he speaks.

'I am come from Cap'n Alex's ship, HMS *Fox*. He is a commander now. At Lisbon, he took me with him from the *Prospect* to his new command, as I believe he liked me a little and wanted a friendly face. So we goes back to England and then in the Channel, then we was called to this sea to relieve Minorca. We arrive this morning and three ships, including ours, is sent ahead to signal the garrison. We get so close into the shore that Cap'n Alex has to get the boats out to tow her clear. But before he does this, he gets me aside and tells me I'm going to take one of the boats and go ashore on my own. And I nearly fall over with shock, but then he tells me it is a secret and I must tell nobody but that Miss Price is here, on the island, and he has a slip of paper with the name of your village written on but I don't know my letters so he tells me what it says and makes me say it over a few times so I won't forget it. And he gives me a plan of the island and a compass and shows me the route to take. Then he gives me a few coins and tells me I must get ashore and hire a pony or suchlike and go up to the north of the island and find you. It took me all day, but I didn't get lost once, and when I got here I said to a number of locals, "Englishwoman?" but each shook their heads or hurried away but then one man nodded and led me down a couple of streets and I put my hand in a fist ready if he was leading me a merry dance but then he stopped and he pointed to this window here. Thus here I am, miss! Oh, and Cap'n Alex says I must bring you back with me.'

'Then there is no time to be lost!' I cry and stand up, to ready myself and pack. 'I have a cart and mule ready.'

'No, miss!' says the boy and holds up his hands. 'Not yet. He says we must wait.'

'Wait for what, for heaven's sake?'

'For the battle to be done, miss. Tomorrow morning our fleet will engage the French. We are about evenly matched, more or less. It will not be an easy fight but there is a bit of confidence we will win the day. But no one can know for sure, and the captain doesn't want you on board in such a case, with the danger of battle, if we are damaged, or even sunk, or he is killed.'

'Then that decides it,' I say and begin to gather my things and pull out my box.

'Whatever do you mean, miss?'

'That if there is a chance he may be killed on the morrow, I must go to him tonight. Do you understand me, Francis?'

He blushes then, a strapping lad with magenta cheeks. 'I have a notion.'

'Will you help me then?'

'But it's not that simple, miss. The fleet will have moved away south for the night by now, and we cannot reach it by the rowboat I left onshore. It would take us all night. We'd need a proper swift sailing boat.'

'And I know the very one. If I can persuade a friend of mine to take us, under cover of darkness, will you be able to direct us to the *Fox*?'

'Yes, but miss, the captain was very clear in his instructions, he was. Not until after the battle. That was his express direction.'

Meanwhile, I am almost packed. 'And I will follow my own direction, *with* or *without* you, my boy. You know me by now a little, I think, and that I will do what I will. I hope it will be *with* you, Francis? Will you help me?'

I am knocking gently on the door of the Cardona home, past nine at night and the moon is shielded by cloud. Mateu blinks at the door, his face creased with sleep. Fishermen are abed early and rise early. He glances down, sees my travelling clothes and notes the unknown boy beside me.

'Now,' I say.

Mateu nods.

24

I have never sat in a sailing boat at night. The air is chilled and the scenery spectral. We proceed through a cloudy night and listen to the snap of the canvas filling with breeze. I am wrapped in a thick blanket donated by Francina – who, in farewell, kissed both my cheeks so kindly and placed about my shoulders one of her own woollen shawls edged with Minorcan lace – and I am grateful for it, for the air is damp and cold, and when the sea mist descends I shiver until it lifts. Before we left, Mateu had nodded towards Francis and said, 'Do you know the boy? Do you trust him?'

'His captain is a dear friend of mine. And I would trust this boy with my life,' I had said, and Mateu had looked at him pointedly. Then, that broad moustache lifted in a smile.

'He has my wife's name,' said Mateu, and this seemed to settle it for him.

We have been sailing for a long time. We are fortunate to have the luck of the wind, and it drives us south down the east coast of the island. As we approach Sa Mola, and the French battery, Mateu carefully alters our course to take us out to sea further, where we are safely shielded by the mist, so the French on guard do not spy us. We pass by Fort St Philip and the English soldiers safely cocooned therein. Soon, Francis shifts over to me and whispers, 'Tell your man we're near. It's south-south-west from here.' I translate, and Mateu nods. He has not spoken a word since we embarked on this journey. He steels his face against the night and what may come next. Within perhaps a half-hour, the ashen shape of a sail looms in the distance, then another, and another. We have found the British fleet.

'That one, there,' – Francis points – 'you see on the far right?'

Mateu guides us out to sea, away from the eyes on watch. Again we are lost to mist, but need to turn sharply to come round to our objective. Now is the crucial moment. We must get in close enough to call to the watch, to alert them to our presence without being fired upon. Francis puts his finger to his mouth and whistles, a curious pattern of toots, designed to identify himself I suppose. We hear shouting but cannot discern the words.

'Able seaman Francis Noy!' he shouts. 'Permission to come aboard.'

'Noy, you clodpate!' comes a voice and I can see a man on deck, leaning over the side, with a gun pointed straight at our boat, but the fog descends once more and he is hidden from us.

'Permission to come aboard,' Francis says again, 'with an English lady escaped from the French. Captain's orders.'

'In the middle of the damn night?' calls another voice.

We are very close now. My eyes strain through the mist to see the men on board. I can only see vague shadows moving, then the fog lifts and I look up into the face of Captain Robin Alexander. As he sees me his eyes open wide with elation, quickly altered to business: 'Permission granted,' he says and I look at Mateu, who nods. He knows all is well. We come closer and Francis gestures to me to stand up. First I turn to Mateu; it is time for goodbye and I have so much to thank him for, yet I do not know how. But somehow, this man of few words has always understood me – just as his sister did before him – and I need explain nothing. He can see it in my face, and, as is his way, he nods and smiles.

'*Adéu, doncella,*' says he and I grasp his hand in thanks.

Then Francis helps me step over to the rope ladder hanging

from the ship. I hand my blanket and shawl to the boy, grasp my skirts in one hand to sweep them aside and place one boot firmly on the bottom rung. I am stepping up and swaying somewhat, determined not to lose my grip. I do not fear accident as much as humiliation, if I fell and got a soaking or landed on poor Francis and broke his nose. There are hands grabbing my upper arms and in a trice I am swooped up and landed on deck, almost toe to toe with my Robin, dressed casually in dark breeches and white shirt, without hat or wig, and I must force myself to stand upright and not fall into his arms. I do not know what his men have been told of me, but I suspect Robin's reputation depends on my discretion and fortitude. So I bow my head and give a quick sink to the captain.

'Thank you, sir, for allowing me aboard.'

'You are welcome, Miss Price. I will show you to your cabin. Your luggage will be brought to you. You must be very tired.'

I feel his hand at my arm and hear whisperings and grunts from the seamen on deck as I am led to the stern of the ship and some steps down. We enter a commodious room, a table and chairs at the centre, covered in scrolls of paper, pens and inkwells, a jug of wine and glasses. And I hear the door close behind me and we are in each other's arms and kissing, kissing.

'Darling, my darling,' he whispers. 'You were meant to come another day.' He holds me and looks at me, at my mouth, my hair, as if he cannot quite believe his eyes. 'After the battle, when it is safer. Francis has proved himself quite the idiot.'

'Do not blame him. He explained it to me perfectly. It is I who chose to come now. I knew the danger. But how could I wait? To know you were here, only a matter of miles away. I could not wait, I could not! Do not be angry with Francis, or with me, my love.'

And we kiss again and fall into each other.

There is a knock at the door and we must stand apart. I swiftly walk to the window that stretches across the entire width of the stern, affording a view in all directions. I gaze out at the nothing of fog and night, the door opens and men have brought my box and my bag, my shawl and blanket, and are instructed by Robin to take it through to a room off this one, where I spy a cot and desk, covered with more papers.

'But Captain, that is your night-cabin, is it not?'

'I am to bunk with my first officer this night, Miss Price. I am more than happy to give up my room for an English lady who has so bravely evaded our enemy. It is our pleasure and our honour to accommodate you here.'

A speech for the seamen's benefit and I thank him. When they are gone, I ask him, 'What do they know, Robin?'

His face falls. 'Nothing. I have told them nothing, not even Francis. As far as they know, you are an Englishwoman requiring rescue from the island and that is all. This is most irregular and I could be in a lot of trouble for doing it.'

'My dear!'

'No, it was my choice. I took the risk. It is on my head.'

'I would do nothing to endanger you, Robin. Will there be repercussions? Should we call back my friend in the boat?'

'No, no! You are not going anywhere. My men I believe are loyal and respect me. They know of my credentials, of my hard experiences at sea, and they honour me for them. And I am fair with them and not overly harsh and they know it. I feed them good victuals, provide a clean and airy ship – as far as I am able – and a promise of reasonable and prompt payment for any prize. There may be grumblings about a woman on board, especially the night before battle, but I do believe they will keep their counsel and all will be well. But we must be careful and circumspect and never act in the way of lovers about them.'

'Of course. You must go. You have been in here far too long already.'

He stands and gazes at me, shakes his head. 'It is a miracle to have you here with me now.' Then his face changes and his stance stiffens, as if we are not alone. 'But there are battle plans to discuss, and I must see my officers. It will be light soon and I believe the admiral will call for us to come into formation very soon.'

'I wish to be useful. I wish to help during the battle. I have knowledge of anatomy. I could assist the surgeon.'

'You will stay in my night-cabin over there and sit on your bed like a good girl and do nothing of the sort. *That is an order*. I cannot be fearful for your safety while I am to carry out my duty as captain of this ship. You must promise me you will stay put in that room and not move. For once, Dawnay Price, *do as you are told.*'

'I will,' I say, and dutifully oblige. For the moment.

Robin goes to his men and I to the night-cabin and sit on the cot for a minute or two. Then I cross to the desk in here and look at the maps spread out upon it, one titled St Stephen's Cove and another Sandy Bay. I think of him studying these maps and making his plans; in charge of the actions of all these men aboard, who look to him for instruction and wisdom. I swell with pride at the thought of it, though I know he is not mine, he belongs to another. I will not think of her now. I leave the cot, sit by the window in the day-cabin and watch the sky lighten and the fog begin to thin. I listen to the ship coming to life, the thumping of heavy boots on deck, the banging of doors, the shouting and coughing of many men about their business, and the slap-slap-slap of the sea against the hull. I have had no sleep all night and I cannot keep my head from nodding. I plod to the captain's bunk and lay myself down, wrapping Francina's blanket about me and nestling my cheek against Robin's coverlet. I can smell his scent there, familiar, desirable. In moments, I am fast asleep.

★

I am woken by Francis, gently, who holds a bowl of porridge. The ship is moving and I start up from the bed.

'It's all right, miss. It's time, now. We're getting into line.'

'What will happen next? Explain everything to me.'

'We are a twenty-four-gun sixth-rate frigate and we accompany a ship-of-the-line, the *Defiance*, under Captain Andrews. We'll line up opposite the French and we'll be trying to get in the right place to fire our broadsides at 'em. The French will likely go for our rigging and try to cripple us as they like to hit a fellow then run away. But we'll do our best to dodge 'em and bring 'em down, miss.'

'I want to be helpful.'

'You eat now.' He ignores my offer. Robin must have spoken with him. 'I'll keep coming to check on you. Stay here, though, won't you? Captain's orders.'

I am ravenous and shovel in the cold oats. I come into the main room and look out through the window to see one ship to our left; to the right, a magnificent line of ships extends out to more than a dozen in ragged formation, all sailing forward together, the men climbing on the rigging and toing and froing over each deck. I am filled with the thrill of the sea, and suddenly understand the appeal of a life in the Royal Navy. It is a spectacular sight to see these sculpted wonders whipping over the waves and it fills me with awe at the ingenuity of humans, who can use their minds to create a machine of such clever industry. I cannot stay put in this room when there is so much to see. I resolve to sneak up the stairs to the deck and peek out. I am determined to be an ocular witness of my first battle at sea, at least the beginning of it. I am not afraid. I am too curious for that. I venture up the stairs and peer over the top, ready to duck down if spotted and trot back into the captain's cabin. I look up to see a set of square-rigging, much grander than Robin's old command. Here there are four stupendous sails on each mast and acres of criss-cross rigging creating an elaborate complication of rope. We are moving quite swiftly and as yet, there is no panic in the air to suggest imminent danger, so I take my chances with the captain's wrath, and decide to venture up to the top step and step cautiously out on deck. The sun is high in the sky, so I must have slept all morning.

My eye seeks Robin first and there he is, standing with other officers, dressed in his full uniform: dark blue coat with white facing stripes, blue breeches and white stockings. His face in repose wears an aspect of relaxed good humour, as if he were attending a fête, not a battle. I see him nod at a companion's statement and reply, 'Indeed. I never saw a finer line.' Around us men are hurrying about, making final preparations for what is to come. There are small groups of men positioned at different parts of the deck, heads back surveying the sails as if ready to make quick adjustments. Some are soldiers armed with muskets who finger and tinker with their weapons, then begin to move into positions. Officers are shouting orders and word goes fore and aft. Below I can discern the sound of many men moving heavy objects across floors, perhaps sea chests or tables, perhaps for the surgeon and his mates, or the men who arm the guns. All hands are now ordered to their quarters. Robin calls an order, which is repeated by a bellowing voice below thrice: 'Load double shot.' Behind us is the island of Minorca, beyond us the mighty line of French ships. I can see the scarlet flash of the French officers' uniforms and a stabbing fear in the pit of my stomach reminds me brutally that they are the enemy, we are at war, and they wish to destroy us.

A boom from away to our left signals the first cannon shot. I turn on my heel and fly down the steps. I hear Robin's voice shouting more orders, and though I am fearful, I cannot leave this spot and hide, a coward cowering in bed. I sit down on a middling step and listen to the deck from here. I hear the cannons play and clasp my hands tightly. There is more shouting and then I hear Robin has moved, closer to my hiding-place, and is saying, 'Good God! What can the admiral mean?' And other men are shouting and cursing. Robin again: 'Now is the time: he must make all the sail he can and fall in with the enemy!'

'What can be happening?' I hear another officer shout. 'You on the quarterdeck, all of you. Take good note of the admiral's movements. Be witnesses!'

Then another voice: 'Cornwall has broken the line!'

An almighty racket of gunshot breaks out, as the fusiliers give volleys of small arms and I duck my head and cover my ears. I feel a hand tugging my sleeve and find Francis with a face like thunder impelling me to return to my station of bed-rest. Once safely ensconced on the captain's cot, I ask the boy, 'What on earth is happening, Francis? Is something amiss?'

'It is madness! The admiral tacked too late. So our sister ship the *Defiance* crowded on sail to draw abeam of her opposite French number, but the admiral is holding back at the other end of the line and signalling that all should do so, when we are in the perfect position to fall in. And Captain Cornwall of the *Revenge* has gone against orders and attacked. Now three ships are on the *Defiance* and we must manoeuvre to . . . hold on, looks like we're keeping back.' He runs to the window and calls, 'The French have sheered off! I told you they do that! Stay here, miss. If you please!'

And with that, off he races up the steps and I creep from my room to see more, but the whole window is masked by thick dark grey smoke and I can see nothing through it. But then looms the shape of a French ship only a few hundred yards from us and the cannon fire explodes above and I am sent tripping back to my refuge and behind the night-cabin door. The roar of the cannons is all about us and there is a loud crack above and something enormous crashes on the deck. Is it a mast shot down? If Robin was below it! I cannot bear to leave this room and I cannot bear to stay. I force

myself up, up, up the steps and peer through the smoke to
see a section of mast has indeed struck the deck and men are
pulling it to one side and then I see my Robin's blue-coated
back – thank heavens! – and he turns aside, shouting to another
officer, 'We cannot! You see my hands are tied!'

A mariner approaches him and says, 'Just the mizzen-
top-mast, sir. No more serious damage.'

Then a hearty cry goes up from many men: 'Huzzah!
Huzzah!' and a voice cries, 'The French are hit!'

And another, 'No, 'tis the *Defiance*. Cap'n Andrews is down!'

A waft of black smoke billows across the deck and I lose
sight of everything. I hear Robin's voice: 'Cut away that rigging.
Port tack.'

'We can't make headway,' shouts another voice. '*Defiance*
is flung up in the wind.'

'Gap in the line!' comes from high above, perhaps a man
up in the rigging above the smoke, which descends once more
and causes my eyes to sting and weep. I creep back down
and sit abed, listening to the lessening reports of gunfire and
the now more distant rumble of the cannonading and perceive
the battle may be waning, hoping against hope that this smoke-
filled nightmare is finally coming to a close, or at least a pause
in the engagement. At last, the firing falls quiet for some time
and it seems it has ceased.

Francis appears.

'You all right, miss?'

'Yes, but how is the captain?'

'Oh, he's all right. He's done so very well for his first action.
All the men are singing his praises. And all are cursing the
admiral.'

'Did we win?'

'Nobody won, miss. The French are heading north-
north-west. We're coming round in case they renew the action.
But it's coming on dusk soon and we'll lose the light. I think
it's over.'

Francis is breathing heavily, his cheeks blackened with smoke, his clothing dishevelled and his hair a fright, but his eyes are alight with excitement and I do believe he is having the time of his life.

'I'll bring you some supper soon. Must get back up now.'

I wait a while then go up myself. Men are clearing up all over the deck and making repairs, coughing and chattering, the carpenter and his assistants at work among the ruins of the mast, the officers arguing about something, hands raised, at the bow. The smoke has dispersed and the sky is dark blue, fading to night. Robin appears beside me, his face a picture of exhaustion and elation.

'Are you well, Miss Price?' asks he.

'I am. And you, Captain Alex?'

'Yes indeed. We will sup together soon with the officers in my cabin. You must be very hungry.'

'And you. Francis said nobody won the battle, is that correct?'

'That is a matter of great debate. I will explain at dinner. You will hear some hot opinions, I am sure.'

We are seated around the captain's table and eat a hearty meal of chicken with vegetables and gravy. The bread is somewhat coarse but a small glass of wine is welcome and I am happy, beside me my Robin and inside me the warm secret we share. Now that the imminent danger is passed I can bask in his nearness. His fellow officers are all engaging fellows, kind and courteous, seemingly pleased of my presence and the excuse to show off in their stories of battle bravery. Yet soon the discussion descends into an argument over the decisions taken by their much-maligned leader, one Admiral Byng.

'But what on earth was he playing at, lasking like that?'

'He allowed our end to be much punished. Andrews is dead, for God's sake. And Noel's leg shot off. But the *Ramillies* has not one injury or an inch of damage.'

'It was cowardly, by God.'

'Have a care.'

'What else can one call it? I say what I see.'

'It is only the good seamanship of the rest of the line that prevented an outright disaster. The crippling of the ships' rigging in the centre held up all the ships astern of them and that is why the gap opened up. Thank God our brave colleagues closed it, or we would be in French hands tonight, or dead.'

'The French fought well, one has to admit it,' says Robin, the first statement he has uttered for many minutes. I receive the impression that he is holding back, particularly on the conduct of his superior officer. He restricts his comment now to the French and says nothing of the admiral's tactics. 'Galissonnière showed fine judgement. He used his van most wisely to disable and muddle their opposites and then retired at the moment we began to develop our firepower. He could have exploited the gap and tried harder to cut through our line, but perhaps his instructions forbade him from taking the risk. And that is why they retreated when they did.'

Many heads nod in assent and droop in thought.

'Gentlemen,' I say and all heads lift, 'am I correct in concluding that the battle has ended without any definite advantage to either side?'

'Well, I don't know about that,' says a lieutenant and there are various blustering noises.

But Robin turns to me and says, 'You would be partially correct, Miss Price. One could say we had the best of the action, disgracefully confined as it was. But one might also assert that if our rear in general had done their duty but indifferently well, we could have won the day. And now, this evening, the French fleet lies between us and Fort St Philip, we have landed no relief force on the island and we have at least half our ships damaged, several hundred incapacitated or killed, and Minorca still lies in the hands of the French. What the admiral will do next is anybody's guess.'

All at the table chew silently, or take a swig of wine, and one young officer nibbles on his thumbnail.

Say I, 'But I know that *this* ship fought bravely and cleverly. Never have I seen such comradeship, order and resilience as that displayed here today. I believe every man on board the *Fox* did his utmost.'

'Thank you,' says Robin, smiling subtly.

'Hear, hear,' says another. 'To Miss Price.'

'To Miss Price,' say all and raise their glasses.

Robin still smiles at me behind his swilled wine. But his eyes are dreadfully tired and I see he is gnawed with fretfulness about the ignominious action he has taken part in today, and what on earth will happen on the morrow. And I wish for a moment alone with him, so that I can kiss his eyelids closed and caress his cares to sleep for a time, away from the odious remembrance of this day.

We do not receive our moment, however, as he must attend to ship's business late into the night and I go to his bed and sleep all night alone, tossing and turning and dreaming of cannon fire and of Robin. He is not mine – he belongs to his ship, his wife and his sons – I know this. But it does not prevent me from wanting him, however wrong it may be.

The next day, some of our crew are engaged in working hard to repair what is possible to do at sea, while others run the ship as we are sent on an errand. Two of the ships – the *Intrepid* and the *Chesterfield* – have parted company with us in the night, so we go looking for them. Though I ache for time alone with Robin, I must say that to spend time with him amid his colleagues, to see him at work and at ease in his most fitting environment in command of such a grand vessel, is so enjoyable that my frustrated desires are kept at bay and I find myself blissful. I cannot predict what will happen in the coming weeks. I know our days together are finite and will be cut short, maybe very soon. And so I luxuriate in this one, a sunshiny day of sea air and porpoises spotted off the bow, of activity and the bright shouts of men cutting the swish-swash of the ever moving water; and over my shoulder, whenever I wish to turn, the comforting presence of my beloved Minorca, nestled in the azure Mediterranean. But what will become of it, now that it seems our admiral has played his game of war so badly? And I feel a pang in my heart when I think, I will look back at this day, perchance from a grey street in London; I will recall what it was to be truly happy, how it ebbed away from us and was lost to the tide of time.

25

That same day in the late afternoon, I meet with Robin in one of his few free moments on deck and insist that I be removed to a smaller cabin and the captain make full use of his once more. He arranges for his first officer to share with another, while I am allocated this small cabin for myself. My effects are moved in and I welcome the smaller space, as I felt swamped in the captain's cabin and a veritable usurper. Also, I am hoping that now Robin has his own cabin once more, he may well have the freedom to leave it in the dead of night and visit me. And indeed he comes to me that very night, at two bells. We do not speak one word. Our bed sheets are much tumbled. He has to leave soon after to avoid detection. I have no dreams at all and sleep wonderfully well. He comes again the following night, and the night after that. During the days we are all decorum and propriety and Miss Price-this and Captain Alexander-that and at night we are silent and all is of the body and nothing else exists on this ocean.

The next morning at seven bells, the admiral calls a council of war. Robin is not present, as only the captains of the ships-of-the-line are called, and not those of the frigates. By evening, we hear that the decision has been made to return to Gibraltar straightway. There is general scandalous disapprobation of such a move. Voices are heard complaining that the Minorca garrison has not had a sniff of us to bolster and comfort them in their hour of need, and now we are to abandon them. The mood in the ship is characterised by decided resentment. I cannot believe it to be so. To leave my cherished island, when such a collection of His Majesty's ships are here, ready to beat the French again? What can be the thinking behind it?

On deck that evening, I ask Robin what he makes of the admiral's choice. Around us, his crew go to and fro, attending to their roles, some clearly listening in to see what their captain makes of this latest scurrilous order from above. The admiral's decision is not only crucial to the interests of Minorca and to England, but also to this one woman and how long she will be able to spend her days – and nights – with her lover. There is a heat amid us so thick one could almost reach out and grasp it. I listen with care to Robin's words but have to force myself to concentrate, as all I can think of at this moment is preventing myself from slipping my hand into his breeches.

Says he, 'I have been told that all the captains in the council of war agreed on the main question: if there was no French fleet, could the English fleet save Minorca from the French army? The answer was no, to a man. We have not the number of troops to succeed.'

'But surely they could have landed some soldiers to help the garrison?'

'It was felt that the troops were needed to defend Gibraltar.'

'Are the French to attack there? Is there proof of it?'

'I know not of proof. But the council agreed that no man could be spared. Though it is rumoured that the bulk of the French army in this region is on Minorca, and therefore cannot be in two places at once. And that the French transports are all busy fetching supplies from Toulon, and therefore could not be available to bring troops to Gibraltar. But those are only rumours.'

'Do you feel Gibraltar is at more risk than Minorca?'

'I do not know. But you must remember too that we suffered losses in the late battle, and many repairs are needed. We have enough victuals for ten weeks, but are very low on our boat-swain's, gunner's and carpenter's stores.'

'You agree with this decision, then?'
'I follow orders, Miss Price.'

The next day, we make sail to Gibraltar. Robin tells me the
journey will take two to three weeks or thereabouts. Each
evening we dine with the officers, and play at some cards –
the sound of the sailors singing on deck might drift in – and
I speak lightly of my work (keeping my more controversial
ideas to myself; I am learning not to bluster through this
world as if it owes me its ears). I am charmed by the manners
of Robin's colleagues and begin to comprehend the cama-
raderie that exists between men in a life at sea. There is clearly
a tremendous fondness and respect demonstrated by the men
for their captain. Robin and I attempt to engage in nothing
that could interfere with that respect. We eye each other surrep-
titiously whenever we are near and the air sparks between us
invisibly. One day strolling on deck I hear a seaman whisper
as I pass, 'There goes the captain's doxy.' I expect they say
much worse below, but it smarts nonetheless.

Robin cannot come to me every night, and those when he
does not are long and unsettled. As well as the beautiful silence
of lovemaking, as time goes on we begin to take time to
whisper to each other, before he repairs to his cabin. We do
love to talk – and argue – as ever we did. I tell him of my
'mermaid' – the sea cow – and wait for him to mock me and
my theories, as he habitually does. But he does not.

'I do not know if there are sea people or not. A captain I
once knew from the Isle of Man swore he caught a mer-child,
which from the waist upward had a human form, but the
rest was like a fish, with a tail turning up behind; the fingers
were joined together by a membrane and it had green hair
like seaweed. He said it struggled and beat itself almost to
death in his net before escaping and swimming away at great
speed. I myself have never spied one. But I know enough of
the sea to say that there are such curious phenomena within

it that neither you nor I nor any man on earth can say he knows it all. To exemplify, there is a fish that was thought to be a sea serpent. It is exceptionally long with a red crest and fringe that runs all the way along it and looks as much like a Chinese dragon as one could want. And I know that once hundreds of these reclusive fish beached themselves in the Far East one day, only hours before an earthquake and giant wave afflicted that very region, as if they knew well that the quake was coming.'

'I thought you would scoff at me, hunting for sea maids.'

'I do like to laugh at you, for I love to see your eyes blaze when you are angry with me. But, on this occasion, we can agree. As the Psalmist wrote: "They that go down to the sea in ships, and occupy their business in great waters, these men see the works of the Lord, and his wonders in the deep." And that is what you do too, my love. We are engaged in similar enterprises, in that respect at least.'

'You adore your work, do you not?'

'I do indeed.' He smiles at the thought of it.

'It is as if you were born to it. I cannot imagine you doing another thing in this world.'

'Nor me.'

There is a moment where we consider this fact and then glance at each other, his smile gone.

Another night, we play a game of the imagination, where we pretend there are no rules, no restrictions or regulations, and we can make any choice we wish of what will happen next, of where to go and what to do with our time. It begins happily enough, as he thinks up such trifles as, 'I wish a plate of roast goose would appear before us this instant, served with apple sauce and a calf's heart pudding and green sallet,' and I add, 'Or a steaming bowl of Francina's lobster stew with a plate of her sweet little cakes to follow.' Then we move on figuratively from this room and project our desires out into the world.

Says he, 'I wish I could sail this ship to . . . to Cephalonia, an island near Greece. It has a beautiful prospect. There we would descend into my barge and row to shore, find a tavern and eat olives and shrimp and drink wine, and from there we would rent a small room with white walls and a large soft bed and I would make love to you all evening and we would sleep until the afternoon, when we would climb up the hills to the highest point and then stroll down under the shade of the trees and feel the sea breeze. Even on the hottest August day, there are refreshing sea breezes there, and one is never hot, or uncomfortable, or the slightest bit homesick. And I believe, if time stopped, and the world did not turn, I could live there blissfully with you, my love, until the end of time.'

I kiss him ardently for that.

'And you,' says he, 'what is your heart's desire?'

'I think you have said it all. As long as I could do my work.'

'No time for work. Only for love,' and he caresses me most delicately.

'But I would miss my work,' I muse, but instantly know it is an error, for we are wrenched out of our dream and back to our true station here, stealing moments on a British man-of-war headed for Gibraltar, at war with France, and Robin seals it by saying, in a low, gloomy tone, 'And I would miss my sons.'

A fortnight has passed and the ship will arrive in Gibraltar within ten days or fewer. Our time passes in days of charming discourses, nights of anticipation, yearnings met or unfulfilled; an intoxicating mixture of which I will never forget the heady yet infuriating sensation. I will the ship never to reach her point of disembarkation, but the wind and the waves sweep us onwards. Our night conversations change. The real world encroaches too often.

'There is a question betwixt us,' says he. 'I do not know how to phrase it.'

'Nor me to answer it.'

We lie in each other's embrace and I screw my eyes shut to force it out. But there it remains. I sit up.

'Do you love your wife?'

'I do not.'

'Why not?'

'That is a strange question.'

'Why did you marry her, if you did not love her?'

He shakes his head. 'Is it possible to be so clever and yet so naïve? I married for position. Her uncle is high up in the Admiralty.'

I am quiet for a moment. 'That is a cold fact.'

He looks worried. 'Do not think ill of me, Dawnay, please. Many have done as I have. Our parents arranged our meeting when we were but sixteen years of age. It was a match advantageous to all. We had little say in the matter and we found each other amiable, at first.'

'And now?'

'She and I have been fortunate that I am away from home as much as I am. We cannot support more than a few days in each other's company.'

'I am not so naïve as you think. I am aware that an Act of Parliament is needed for divorce. And even if it were possible, such a move would ruin your career.'

And there it is. The question betwixt us.

I continue, 'We were quite sensible of our situation, even on our first night together on the island. We knew it then.'

'We did,' he answers quietly and watches me, frowning.

'Thus it must be approached with logic, as befits a sea captain and natural philosopher.'

'Indeed.'

'Thus, we conclude that our relationship has no future, no possible role to play in our lives. For you seek promotion and cannot risk a scandal, and you have your boys and must see to their prospects also. And I have my work, and once returned to England I intend to seek publication. And cannot risk my work not being taken seriously – at best – and at worst, being painted the whore by London society.'

'That would never be. I would not allow it.'

'You speak from your heart and not your mind. You know it to be true, as I do. I possess not your lucky heritage. I am trying to make a place for myself in this world. I did not have it carved for me at birth. We are mismatched creatures, you and me.'

Robin sits up and hangs his head, grasps hold of his hair, as he is wont to do in moments of emotion.

'My love,' I try, but his head sinks lower.

Says he, 'What will become of me, I cannot think.'

The time of our parting comes stealthily and sits between us, an indolent, dead weight. There is one night left before we arrive at our journey's end. We shut out the world and lie together hours longer than we usually risk. We promise not to talk. But he cannot help himself and says we simply must discuss our prospects, yet I beg him to refrain.

'We have done this,' I remind him, 'and there is no way for us.'

'How can you relinquish us so easily?'

'Easily? How dare you! You believe this comes easily to me?'

'No, but I *could* come to you, in London. Whenever I am on leave, we could find a way. I could come to you and find you, we could snatch moments together. It would be better than nothing, better than a life without each other at all.'

'No, it would not. It would be slow torture. It would spoil and ruin our lives.'

'Then at least we could correspond, to begin with. Let me write to you, and you will write to me. We can read each other's words and I can touch the paper your hands have touched.'

'No, not even that. I will not do it. I will not waste my life waiting for you, for the moment you deign to send me a letter or visit my chamber. You will not come for months, years even, or, worse still, you will die at sea and nobody will think to tell me, until I read it in the newspaper and mourn your death alone, a nobody with no connections, no family, no home.'

'But you have a home!'

'I do not! I do *not* and never have. It is pretence only. Let us pretend once more, shall we? I wish my brother had escaped from that tender in which they impressed him and come back to me and found me and we lived together always. Or that my parents never abandoned us and we were brought up in a loving home; poor or otherwise is of little consequence, as it is *love* that a child needs more than any other one thing, a loving family. A father, a mother, and twin boys secure in the knowledge that their father adores them.'

'I do adore them but . . .'

'But nothing further. That is how it should be, how it must be, and I would hate you if it were not. You love your sons and would never abandon them. You have no idea how fortunate you are, how fortunate your boys are, and your wife.'

'But I am *yours*, Dawnay.'

'Falsehood!' I am white with rage now. 'I have *never* had a thing wholly mine, not one thing just for *me*, for *myself*. I cannot have you and therefore I will not wait for you or yearn for you. I will make my own life. I will put you out of mind and I will forget you. Do you hear me? Even now, I have *forgotten* you.'

And I weep and weep – as I have not since the days at the orphanage – and he holds me hard and fast and is silent, and we hear four bells and know it is dawn and he must go.

On arrival at Gibraltar, the order comes that the fleet will make ready to exert all haste in repairing itself in order to return again to Minorca. But my place here is over, and I am to be transferred to a merchantman back to England.

Robin explains, 'As it is wartime, your ship will sail in convoy with several other merchantmen under the protection of a forty-four-gun man-of-war. You will be quite safely relayed to England.'

I must shake hands with Robin on board and we nod our heads politely – watched complacently by his junior officers – I thanking him for his kindness, he praising me for my bravery and other such meaningless banalities. Though he does hold on to my hand a little too long and I feel the loss of it terribly when we are forced by convention finally to let go.

Says he formally, 'I imagine we will meet again in London some day, when I am on leave.'

'And when do you think that might be, sir?'

'I could not say, Miss Price. I am required elsewhere. But I will visit with my good friend your benefactor again one day, and peradventure I will see you there.'

'Perhaps,' say I, and I wonder if his eyes ache as do mine when we stare at each other, and if his heart aches at the imminent moment of parting. I am sure of it, I am sure he is racked by it, and it breaks my own heart to see him suffering.

But there is a moment where we are both aware that no one about us seems to have a close eye on us – though ears may be listening – then he grasps my hand again and encloses it between his own, and tenderly says, 'I have not forgotten you. Nor will I ever.'

The flurry of activity at the quayside prevents any further private moments or even longing looks, and I must content myself with the pleasant goodbyes of his officers and men, who seem genuinely sorry to see me go. The saddest face is that of a boy who has never done well in hiding his feelings: Francis Noy. He is charged with taking me to my new ship home, and his round cheeks are fiercely red and his eyes start with tears again as he shakes my hand goodbye.

'Be a good boy, Francis.'

'I will, miss. I always will.'

'Look after Captain Alex, won't you, dear?'

'I most certainly will, Miss Price.'

'Don't let him be hurt, injured or be in harm's way.' My tears come now.

'Of course not, miss.'

And I feel I am to say to Francis everything I wished to convey to my love.

'Do not let him die, Francis. Never, *never* that.'

'Never, miss. Oh, God save you and be safe. I never did like his wife, you know. She's too proud. Goodbye, Miss Price.'

And with that he is gone, and I turn to my place in line to board a tender bound for the ship home. No more for me the ships-of-the-line and frigates of the Royal Navy. I am ordinary now. And I am alone again.

26

On the 28th day of June 1756 the British garrison under Blakeney surrenders to the French on Minorca, after a heroic siege of over two months – and the island is lost. Admiral Byng is ordered to return to England and on his arrival in Portsmouth is arrested immediately. During these events, I am to be found heading for England on the most repulsive, badly run and deficient ship that ever sailed the seas. Our captain is a buffoon, the winds are set against us at every turn and the sailors are used to practise a foul range of oaths and imprecations. Everything is sordid, disease-ridden and sickening. There is a store below of rancid cheese that the captain will not hear of being thrown overboard, which stinks out the entire ship and can only be escaped by leaning over the side and filling one's nostrils with the salt air of the sea. My neighbour in the next cabin has an insufferable toothache and cries out all night of her woes and who will save her from this prodigious pain and they say in her ravings she has broken the whalebone of her stays in two – yet there is only a pretty young fellow on board playing at being a surgeon. The captain is a numbskull unable to comprehend the squalor of his own ship and the degenerate nature of his men; he crows at dinner of how he saw a ten-year-old murderer pardoned in court and brought the wretch on board to serve him, only to find him drunk the next day and have him flogged soundly; he boasts of what an orderly ship he runs and, when we are stilled, insists that the wind will at any minute come about fair, and he is always wrong. And much other nauseating cant does our perfidious captain spout, too tedious to mention, as well as turn on me a lascivious eye, at which I barricade my cabin door with my baggage when I am abed.

Two days out from Gibraltar, we sail into fog so thick we lose sight of all other ships in our convoy, including our man-of-war. We hear shots fired and all passengers cry out and there is much consternation. Where is my Robin now? Our hopeless captain assures us this is no corsair here to attack, rather it is another ship from our group signalling its location and we shall soon discover them. As with all his other promises, he is mistaken and we see no more of our convoy. We emerge from the mist a week later, off course and drifting aimlessly. We must make our way alone now, in warring waters.

We are almost two months at sea and I fear I will turn distracted. The only moment of respite is the sight of a volu-minous cloud of white butterflies fluttering past the ship on its way south, which lifts my spirits momentarily in awe at a thousand fragile wings making such an epic journey. I had not suffered a moment of seasickness since the *Gaivota*'s first trips, and yet on this journey I find myself vomiting copi-ously several times a day. In my delirium, I come to believe I died at Gibraltar docks and this ship is my boat to purga-tory, which I rave at our surgeon-quack. He does at least agree, being a young man of hitherto fine manners and rather appalled to find himself in such a revolting posting. He gives me some small help and ensures I eat broth when I am able and brings me raisins too, but he is run off his feet with the other passengers and mostly I shift for myself. I miss my boy Francis exceedingly; there was so little of ill design or ill nature in him, he is a rare friend and I feel his absence weigh upon me.

I never thought to be glad to see London, but I am so relieved when the Thames is first sighted that I weep overboard and my tears mingle with the river's flow. Our ship is weeks past its estimated arrival and thus I know no one will await me at the wharf. I must find my way to a carriage and manage to stay standing long enough to hire a post chaise to rush me home. I am told later that I arrive at the door pasty and talking gibberish, whereupon I faint in the hallway, though I have no memory of this. I am carried to my bed and sleep for many hours. I recall Susan Applebee coming to me and it is gratifying to see her benign face again. Within two days of comfort and broth I am sitting up and feel quite well. Mr Woods comes in to see me and we have our first proper talk since my arrival in England.

'In your absence, my dear, I have had a most melancholy time and missed your company exceedingly. I have in consequence embarrassed myself with liquor on too many occasions. But what am I to do? If I go out with my associates or in society, I must drink as they do or they will label me a poor singular fellow. But I always had my happy home to return to, with my dear Dawnay to speak with on the morrow. But this past year – yes, a year, you cannot deny it; and it was meant to be only six months or so – I have lived with constant worry about you and sincerely regretted my decision to let you go. Now you should know that I will not be funding any more travels for you around the world; no, indeed, I will not. You are aware, I believe, if you received my letter? You did? That the Lisbon disaster harmed me financially and so will war with France; now we all must take care in pecuniary terms. So it is that, even if I did not miss your company so much, my dear, I would not be able to afford to fund your adventures for much longer.'

After this oration, we fall into our old habits of chatter and talk affably of the sights I have seen. He is most enthralled with my sea journeys and not so interested in the islands I visited or even the earthquake or the battle for Minorca. It seems he misses his days at sea, as his particular interest is directed at which kinds of sails, boats, ropes and cables and suchlike each ship I sailed in possessed. I do my best to answer him but fear I disappoint him as – when his eyes might have been looking inward at the ship's fittings – mine were usually outwards, to the sea, the sky or the land, or else to a particular sea captain.

The curve of his neck to the bare shoulder as he kissed me.

Next I am visited by Susan, who ushers out Mr Woods. 'Do not vex or upset the child,' she chides, as if I am still in infancy, and insists I must rest.

'Travelling does not agree with you, my dear.'

'Oh, it was a bad ship home, that is all.'

'You are thin and whey-faced and you look sick. Did you catch a tropical disease of some sort?'

'I was not in the tropics, Susan. Please, I am fine and will thrive again.'

'There is a sadness about your eyes. Is it so heavy with you to return to us?'

I cannot speak of that. 'How is Owen these days?'

'Ah well, he is much improved, thank you.' Her face lights up. 'He is so nimble on his crutch and peg now, and is even courting a woman of good family. She likes my Owen's handsome face and humorous manner and so does not seem to mind his absence of leg. She is the young widow of a gunsmith and now Owen works in that business too, with a brother of hers who trains him in the craft. It is a business that one seldom wants bread in and is rather ingenious, requiring a steady hand and skill with wood and metal. He always had good hands, my Owen. He does well.'

'I am so very pleased to hear it.' I feel much revived by such good news. It quite lifts my spirits and delays the moment when Susan will look at my eyes again and ask me what ails me in my heart.

A knock on the door signals her husband has arrived to talk with me; though she tries to dismiss him, I bid he enters. He sits beside me and his wife leaves, shaking her head in disapproval. We exhibit our customary shyness with each other regarding our mutual fondness, yet I see from his searching eyes he is concerned for me and, I believe, glad to see me safely home.

'So, my dear, you escaped for a good year or so,' says my tutor. 'Did you wish to stay away longer?'

'I was compelled to return.' Then I recall a conversation my tutor and I had once, many years ago, and a certain phrase he used with me when he chose not to explain himself. '*Circumstances conspired.*'

'I see. Do you wish to speak of it?'

'Not in particular.'

'Very well. But did your work proceed well? Did you learn much on your trip? Was it valuable to you?'

'Oh indeed, exceeding much. I did learn a phenomenal amount. Almost too much to comprehend the true breadth of it all. I need to collate my notes and look upon them with eyes afresh, in order to coalesce them into something mean-ingful. I believe there is importance there. I intend to begin today.'

'There is plenty of time, you know.'

'I always feel as if time is tumbling away from me, Mr Applebee.'

'You may call me Stephen these days. You are not a child any more. You are an adult now.'

'Perhaps I am.'

'Undoubtedly. In your character, your demeanour, I believe you are altered.'

'I am a year older. And now I must begin to earn my living.'

'Whatever for?'

'I must publish in order to earn money, as Mr Woods has said he will not fund my travels again. And indeed I must travel, as I intend to go to Russia to study the sea cow, to America to look at the fossils of giant mammals, and to the island of Sumatra to find an orang-utan to examine or otherwise Africa to look at apes.'

'Mr Woods believed your need to travel would be cured by this sojourn.'

'Did you believe that?'

'Not for a moment. Can I assist you with your work?'

'You must! I need your sound eye and powers of reasoning. I have something of note here, yet I am unsure as to its full significance. It concerns the progenitor of all humankind.'

'Is that all?' says Stephen and he laughs.

We begin the next day. When Stephen is not attending to his other pupils, he arrives as soon as ever he can to assist me. We spend the next week or so with all my findings from the painted cave of the Berlengas and the ancient structures of Minorca, as well as my labelled watercolours of the varied sea life of these islands. We read through my musings, rearrange and discuss them, tease out the arguments. One afternoon, we have everything arranged in neat piles all over the table in the curiosities room, and all the artefacts are gathered in groupings alongside findings we already possessed for comparison. We stand back and stare at our pattern of work. Stephen takes off his wig and wipes his brow with it.

'Are you unwell?' say I.

'I am nervous.'

'The truth should not make you anxious.'

'Indeed it does. I believe there is much work of value here. There are studies of coral polyps, molluscs, sea grasses and your sea cow here that would be of great interest to those who survey the plants and animals of the oceans. Also your study of the animal life of the islands – particularly those curious lizards of the Minorcan islets – educated ladies would enjoy reading such things. You would do very well in creating a short book examining the flora and fauna of these islands and I imagine a publisher might pay you a small advance for such a work. But as to your other work – that concerning the cave, the drawings therein, the ancient structures and their architects, your theories about their conception; indeed your ideas regarding the history of humans – Dawnay, I must urge you strongly *not* to attempt to publish your findings.'

'How can you say such a thing? You, of all people, Stephen? My tutor, my friend in natural philosophy?'

'It is because you are my friend that I advise it. I am certain you will not get a publisher who would risk it, as both they and you could well be arrested for blasphemy. Do you not recall the publisher in the pillory? Your theories about the Flood, and Creation, the earth creating itself through earthquakes rather than God's hand? And your ideas of how the paintings suggest the breaking down of our social hierarchy, of placing women on the same footing with men, the orphan on the same footing as the King? Seditious libel! And you could be accused of treason too! I certainly could not involve myself, as despite Owen's recovery he still lives with us and relies on us for much of his maintenance, and may always. I cannot risk arrest or prosecution.'

'But do you *agree* with my arguments, Stephen?'

'I cannot disagree wholly. They are compelling and worthy. But what matter is it if I agree with you? Just because you are right, it does not mean society will agree with you, especially the authorities. Consider Galileo. You may think we have moved on from his time in this modern age of rational, scientific thought. But the crimes of blasphemy and treason remain and are very real. Let us be clear: we are talking of the pillory, of prison, or worse.'

'Very well, if there is to be no publication, then I can seek out a scientific institution and deliver a lecture on my theories.

Surely they would be well received by like-minded intelligent people?'

'That would be worse! To publish anonymously is dangerous enough. But to stand in person and deliver your ideas from your own mouth is fat-witted! You would be likely lynched and taken to the law on the spot! I could even see it causing riots in the streets. The English love a good riot and seem to need no excuse nowadays.'

'I do not believe that men of science would allow such a thing to happen.'

'You expend too much faith in natural philosophy. Remember that many geologists devote their studies to the search for evidence of the Deluge and to prove the Bible correct, not to disprove the existence of God! And besides, all the scientific institutions I know of do not accept women, even to listen to lectures, let alone give them. Most scientific men are devout and devoted to both their God and their King. They will not stand by as either are called into doubt, let alone rubbished and done away with, as the natural consequence of your theories suggests.'

'Perhaps a letter to the *Gentleman's Magazine*? An anonymous one?'

'They would never publish it. The editor would most likely reply that their magazine would never be a conduit for ideas of this nature. Unless you toned down your arguments. Even then, I would expect furious replies from clergymen.'

'I do not wish to tone down my arguments, or what is the point of publishing at all? But surely there must be another forum, however small, that is ready to hear such ideas and discuss them sensibly? We cannot be the only ones on this earth.'

'There may be one or two at most, possibly in France? But we are at war and contact is impossible. You must be patient, Dawnay, write up your work thoroughly, thoughtfully. Continue your studies. Omit all reference to these dangerous, modern ideas. And you may find in a few years that society changes enough for you to share your theories.'

'A few *years*?'

'What causes your desire for instant satisfaction in this regard?'

'Because of what has been lost, what has been suffered. Everything I have been through, to complete this work and bring my ideas into being.'

'What have you been through, Dawnay? Will you tell me part of it?'

'I do not wish to speak of it. It is . . . private.'

'It may help you come to terms with it.'

'I have come to terms with it. The work is my answer. The work is all. And what was the point of it all if I keep silent? If I play the coward? I will not waste my life in waiting for society to catch up with me.'

'Patience. You have *never* possessed this virtue. It comes with age and I'd hoped you might have developed some by now. You scribble patterns in the sand and see the tide come and wash away your prospects and you believe all is lost. But think not in the daily movement of the waves on the beach, think instead of the mighty cliffs above, of years of erosion, the layering of sediments, of eras not minutes. Develop a new way of viewing your life, Dawnay, or you will throw it away in rash decisions.'

But I am compelled and spend the next month writing up all my notes from Portugal and Minorca into a coherent whole, or a kind of scientific paper, and I do not omit one thought, one idea, however dangerous Stephen considers it. I work alone and I am filled with a frenzy for it. Stephen advises me to slow down or I will make myself ill. I confess only to myself that I do feel weak at points, thus I eat more and more and gain a little flesh. But no matter, as it is all fuel to my work. I have opened up the boxes I had sent

back to England from Portugal containing the ancient artefacts recovered from the Berlengas and I spend many tactile
hours examining them, at times moved to tears by the memories they revive. In all this time, I hear nothing of Robin.
Nothing.

The bulge of muscle in his upper arms, taut and spherical as he
lifted his body to lie atop mine.

His absence is a fact and I must resign myself to it. My work
fills my mind, my days and all my waking hours. It is only in
sleep that my dreams torture me with exquisite memories and
I awake almost every day, knowing that my pretence is futile
and I am sick with love for this man. Work is my cure and
so I resolve to sleep as little as possible. I work all day with
wool in my ears to block out the street noise and often into
the night by candlelight, one time singeing my hair on said
candle when I fall asleep at my desk.

By September I am ready to seek a publisher. I do not
reveal to anyone at home my business this day, as I leave
the house and seat myself in a coach, and direct the driver
to each address I have written on a piece of notepaper: a
list of publishers, who I visit unannounced, one by one,
clutching my precious manuscript. I have listened to
Stephen's warning, but I believe there must be educated
men out there who will not condemn me immediately. I
resolve, before I enter each publisher's establishment, to speak
conservatively of my ideas, to begin cautiously and reveal
only snippets, to gauge their reactions before I reveal my
true theories. And thus I do the round of all the most pres-
tigious (and several of the much less so) publishers in
London. I am greeted with politeness and condescension.
Stephen was right inasmuch as some are quite interested in
a book detailing the flora and fauna of Minorca in particular,
now that this Mediterranean jewel has been lost to our nation.

One expressed the desire to create a picture book of my watercolours, in order to please a female audience, while another asked if I had truly written a book or else plagiarised it, as 'no lady could understand so many hard words'. Others are polite yet immediately dismissive, and do not attend to hear even a word of my work, as they are not taking submissions at present. I spend several hours at this toing and froing and by the latest rejection I am heartsick and hungry. There are several more on my list, but I do not know how much more stamina I possess and resolve to visit only with the one individual whose establishment lies in my path back to my benefactor's house.

His name is Simeon Graybourn and his is one of the smaller establishments, next door to a physician. The one-room office is at the back of the building, facing on to a busy square, where the windows rattle each time a post chaise passes. He has no partner in his firm, only a young assistant, who today is away from the office. Mr Graybourn is good-natured and affable, and every wall of his room is clothed in shelves jammed with books and papers, while more teetering papers occupy much of the floor space, as well as a haphazard collection of oddments – perhaps sent by correspondents – of adventitious objects, such as a dried piece of scaly skin here and what appears to be a leg bone there. It brings to mind my own study and I am at home at once. I begin with my account of the islands and he is attentive. He asks me searching questions about my ideas behind my finds. I begin to tell him of my experiences abroad: I touch upon the cave paintings, the ancient structures, the movement of the earth, fossils and mermaids.

When I am done, he rests his chin on two fists, his elbows perched on his knees. He sits this way for some time, thinking.

'Miss Price, you have told me a variety of fascinating things about your travels. You have dropped tantalising hints at ideas that have been sparked in your mind. You have quoted to me from great thinkers of the past. But I do believe you are tiptoeing around your subject. I do believe you have something to tell me, something buried within that pile of papers you cosset in your lap that you have not yet passed to me, though we have sat here more than an hour. And so, I would ask you to tell me what it is you really want to say. I am quite sure by now that I am about to hear something quite extraordinary from you, something quite new, and I am quite out of patience. Will you please, in as few words as you can muster, expostulate your theory to me, and explain what you are really trying to tell me?'

'Do I have your word that everything I am about to say will be kept confidential, for the time being at least? In particular, that my ideas and my name attached to them will not be repeated to another living soul, without my full written and signed permission?'

'You have that assurance, miss, and my hand as covenant on it as a gentleman.'

We shake hands. He continues, 'And you must say it all, without pause, and I will not interrupt. I wish to get to the heart of the matter, Miss Price.'

I sip from the glass of water he has poured for me, then begin.

'These are the truths postulated by myself concerning the origins of humans, that is, of man and of woman, and their place here upon this earth. I put it to you that the earth is far older than the Bible suggests. Perhaps millions of years as opposed to thousands. Earthquakes, resultant tidal waves, volcanoes and other catastrophic phenomena can explain the changes that have taken place in the history of the earth, such as the rising and falling of sea levels and the distribution of evidence as to the ancient animals that once lived upon this earth and yet do not exist any more; namely, fossils. I believe that fossils were living creatures that expired, whereupon sediments were laid down upon

them and in time their forms became rock. Such finds age
in correspondence with their depth, thus the lowest levels
of the rock are the most ancient. These levels show a development of fauna over time, from more simple organisms
to more complex ones. Thus, this law of nature explains
the development – perhaps from their origins in the seas
– from tiny animalcules to the zenith of the animal world,
humans.'

Mr Graybourn coughs and is about to interject, perhaps
even contradict.

Instead I say, 'Please, sir. You assured me, no interruptions.'

'I did, yet . . .'

'I believe if you give yourself pause, and listen to the full
argument, your queries may well be answered in the telling
of it.'

'Very well,' says he, nodding. 'Proceed.'

'Now, I was speaking of humans. Man – *and woman* – are
but another step on this ladder of life, which resembles that
of a spider's web rather than a straight line, in that each
animal group split off – according to where it found itself
living – and developed along its own lines. For example,
just as the lizards of the Minorca islets developed different
markings to disguise themselves in their own environments,
each branch of the animal kingdom developed similarly
according to its situation. I contend that there was a branch
of monkeys, and then chimpanzees and other apes, who for
reasons as yet unknown to us – perhaps to do with the
unsuitability of their location – moved into the shallow waters
of the oceans, lost their hair, except that on their heads, for
their infants to cling to, began to walk upright, developed
a layer of body fat not unlike seals and sea cows and other
mammals of the sea – and for a time lived mostly in the
water.'

Graybourne's eyebrows sit high enough to leave his forehead. 'Rather far-fetched?' he muses.

'Not if one considers not only the physical evidence of the strangeness of humans – why do we walk upright and have so little hair? – but the evidence I found in the cave. I conjecture that this period in our development was documented on an islet off the coast of Portugal, but was destroyed by the earthquake, yet seen by this witness and, who knows, perhaps other local people have seen it too. This evidence suggests a society redolent with the myths of mermaids – a kind of folk memory of our ancient sea-going past – whereupon the female of our species dominated and the male was subordinate. There is a possibility that these artistic females – shown by their exquisite cave paintings – even manufactured coral gardens and thereby created the origins of the reefs we see today. Perchance some land-based people remained on the mainland who were developed from apes – hairy and stooping, tree climbers and dwellers on all fours – while island-based humans developed from the fish – hairless and smooth, graceful, long-legged as swimmers – and eventually came ashore and mated with the land humans and created the hairless, upright apes people have become today.'

My listener's eyes grow as big as saucers and his mouth is set, it seems, in disbelief. As I say it aloud, it does sound outlandish. Yet I steel myself with the thought that many have gone before me in the history of science and discovery, and spoken new ideas that appeared as preposterous fiction, yet over time were proven as true as day follows night.

I forge onward with an alternative argument: 'Or it could be that the land conditions improved and humans returned to it. With their newly found hair loss and upright posture, they were forced to seek out shelter, such as caves, and new ways of finding food – as they could not run efficiently on all fours as they had once – and therefore were forced to develop new ways of living, seeking out static food – such as agriculture and animal husbandry – and creating new ways of carrying food. Since their babies could not cling to their fur any more, as they had none, the mothers needed a hand free, and this led to the development of pottery; likewise weaving, and the design of clothes in order to keep their naked bodies warm. Their search for safe grounds and new forms of food led them away from the shores and out into every corner of the globe; they were able to do this as at one time all the land of the earth was of one piece, and earthquakes and suchlike did break up the pieces later.

'When caves were not readily available, these early humans created their own by building structures such as those found on Minorca, and used their bigger brains to create artefacts of beauty and use, such as oil lamps, painting implements, stone axes and so forth. Indeed all these changes and developments show that the history of humankind was not always one of male over female, or even female over male, but more often a history of equality of the sexes. Not only that, but that in times before the long-term settlement of humans in one place, there was no division into rich and poor; and no requirement to protect the rich from the poor as is the defining social structure of our own time; and crucially no need for a leader, a hierarchy of any sort, and thus no divine right of kings.'

Graybourn's wide eyes have flickered to the window, as if expecting an angry mob to appear there at this very moment. 'My dear lady, you are dangerously close to—'

'Please, let me finish. If this web of life is taken as the model of life on this earth, therefore the logical conclusion is that there is no need for a designing hand, an overseer, or even a mind to create it; that the system functions perfectly well on its own; indeed, that there is *no need for a creator at all.*'

'Miss Price!' cries Graybourn and throws up his hands. But I hold up mine to silence him.

'I *must* finish, now that I have started. I must be heard.

You see, as a species, we have developed a complex form of communication that we call language, and we have married language with thought and thus created ideas. And perhaps our most ambitious idea was that of an almighty creator, a father figure, who would watch over us always and protect us from harm, but only if we fear Him and serve Him, and that the fear of the loss of Him is too great to transgress, and the fear of becoming an orphan in the wide world is too dreadful to contemplate, that this story of our Father has become one that dominates our lives and even our thoughts, and all is coloured by it. But if we accept the fossil record, the evidence from the effects of disastrous natural phenomena, the similarity of different animal species to each other and therefore the likelihood of a parentage and relation between them . . . surely, this is strong evidence to suggest a denial of the very existence of God. And if we discard the Bible's version of events as no more than legend, and if we lose this conception of God as the Father of everything, we will not become orphans, but instead will discover that we are connected with all life upon this earth, and always have been, and always will be, and that we are not and never will be *alone*.'

'My God,' says he. 'They'll have you whipped.'

I say nothing to this.

Graybourn stands and removes himself to the window. He stares out of it for a time at the street below. There is no mob there, no angry priest or magistrate. Only the trundling of waggons and the shouts of hawkers. London ignores us. 'And what is the name of your paper? Does it have a title?'

'It does. I have named it *The Orphan Myth*.'

He stands for a time longer. I feel serene. Saying it aloud has had the effect of a dam of thought bursting; the release of ideas pent up and under pressure for so long that a mighty flood has saturated the land of my senses and, once the deluge has passed, the waters of my mind are calm, and still, and at peace.

Graybourn then turns to me and says, 'No one in London will publish this. No one in the British Isles would dare do it. Even in France. My God, don't you know Voltaire is constantly on the run from one country to another, just to escape arrest and imprisonment for his writings? And they are not half as insane as this.'

'You believe my theories are insane.'

'No, I do not. I believe they are eminently sensible, most of them, at least. I'm not sure about the coral gardens or the mermaids. But the rest of it? I believe they could well be a breakthrough of significance. But there is no way that I or anyone else can publish this. You must realise that?'

'I have been advised of it.'

'Then what is your business here, Miss Price? What on earth do you hope to achieve? I could have been an unscrupulous man, a devout zealot who would cart you off to the nearest magistrate. You are most fortunate that I am not. That I will not speak a word of this to anyone. And I strongly suggest you follow the same course. What possessed you to speak of this to me today?'

'I am forced to. I must earn my living. I need funds in order to travel and continue my work. And thus, the only skill I have is to write of my studies and to have my writing published.'

'Show it to me,' says Graybourn and reaches out for my manuscript. With reluctance, I pass it over. He seats himself and begins to read, whispering salient words, nodding his head and scratching the bristles on his chin. 'Why, Miss Price,' he says, once he has leafed through its entirety, 'you write beautifully. And I have a proposition for you.'

'Is it within or without the law?'

He guffaws, then carefully neatens the manuscript and passes it back to me gently, with great care, which act warms me to him. 'It is within the law. Listen, I will pay you to write. Not about such rhetoric as this, but other topics of scientific interest. There is a new audience out there hungry for popular science. Our public are more literate than ever, and our ladies – as you are evidence – are hungry for texts that explain the nature of things in clear, precise and lovely language, just as you possess. You and I could make a good living together, as I commission topics of interest from you and you produce them to this high standard. Does the idea appeal?'

'It does indeed!' It is the first broad smile I have given in weeks.

'And in no time, you should amass the money you need to go on your travels, collect your necessary data, and continue your private work – your most secret work, I would advise – gathering evidence to prove your more, shall we say, controversial theories? And in the meantime, you can write for me travel journals of your adventures, as the public lap those up too. Are we agreed?'

'Oh, yes!'

'And you are quite free, quite unattached? No husband in the offing to keep you chained to the hearth, no child at home awaiting its mother's attentions? I need to know that you can dedicate your full attention to it, that each piece once commissioned will be produced swiftly and efficiently, and that you do intend to go travelling again as soon as you are able? I would need such an assurance to enter into a contract with you.'

'Quite so, sir. Nothing, absolutely nothing, stands in my way. I am utterly free.'

'Then, Miss Price, if that is your name—'

'It is!'

'Then we shall make money together, I warrant! And who knows, one day, when you and I are old and doddering, we might be able to publish your real work.'

'Bless you, Mr Graybourn, thank you!'

And I stand up to shake his hand jovially, yet my eyes mist and hand trembles and down again I sit, with a thump.

'Whatever is it, Miss Price? Are you well?'

'What hour is it, Mr Graybourn?'

'Why, it is nearly three.'

'Ah, I have not eaten since breakfast, that is all. I have been so caught up with my visits to publishers that I have not dined. I must repair home now and do so.'

But I cannot stop my hand from shaking, and I curse myself for being so weak. Perhaps it is a throwback to the appalling sea journey I undertook, the month of work and occasional sleep, or even some ill-defined sickness as Susan suggested. I take another sip of water to steady myself and resolve to stand – which action occasions my head to ache violently. I so desire to quit this stuffy office – my word, it is insufferably hot in here, my cheeks are burning, my stomach, chest and armpits are drenched with perspiration. I try to speak, to ask that my coach be hailed, that someone assist me, and then the room tips. And all I can think is that the earthquake has come again. I fall, there is a tremendous blow as my head hits the floor and then there is nothing.

I awake on a chaise longue in a room with dark brown panels. I hear voices, distant. My head aches appallingly. My dress is damp with sweat. My throat is as dry as straw and I cannot speak for a moment. In my silence, I hear mutterings from male voices somewhere behind me. I think I discern Graybourn's voice and another, older, deeper one.

'Do you think?'

'It is possible. Her weakness, the shape of her abdomen, despite the rest of her body being so slim.'

'She is unmarried.'

'Well then, I shall not treat her. Or her *bastard offspring*.'

I gasp and turn my head. And then an older man with a long peruke wig looms into view.

'She wakes.'

'Where am I?'

Mr Graybourn's face appears above. 'You fainted, Miss Price. We transported you to a physician's room in the next house.'

And my publisher's face disappears and is replaced by the peruke, a stern and disapproving scowl upon his face.

'You must get yourself home forthwith and *look to your condition, miss*.'

On arrival, I slink to my room and sit on my bed, the truth of my condition glaringly evident before me in the modest dome of my belly. Again, my sense has been blinded by attention only to my work, yet inside me, a secret was burgeoning and I was too clever in my stupidity to see it. I stare at it, this new shape, this new life lodged in me, this part of me, of Robin, of us. A wave of nausea rises in me, yet mingled with it is bliss, pure bliss, soon replaced by terror of what will come to pass. I place my hands over it and stroke it, as I know for certain that whatever comes, I will defend it with my very life and no harm shall come to it, to her, or him: my child.

The door opens – Susan rarely knocks – and she looks to my face, then my hands placed just so on my belly.

'Oh, Susan!' I cry. 'What is to become of me?'

Nothing is said for some minutes. Susan holds me and rocks me, as I clutch on to her clothes and wet them with my tears.

'I thought it,' says she. 'The moment you came home from your travels, I suspected it.' She was always wiser than me, even with all my book learning. 'Where have you been today, to see *him*?'

'No! No . . .' I sigh. 'If only I could.'

'He is far away? Not dead? Or a foreigner? Not a foreigner, Dawnay?'

'Oh spare me, Susan, please.' I turn from her and wipe my face on my sleeve. 'I will never tell of it, so do not ask me.'

She is quiet for a moment, then asks, 'Was it conceived . . . in joy, or by force?'

'In joy! Oh yes, in joy.'

'Good, good.' She is thinking. 'I will not ask you again who he is, as one day you will tell me, if you wish to. But is there a chance that he could come to you, before too long, and marry you?'

I shake my head forlornly. 'If his situation were altered, or had never been what it is, there would be no happier union. But no, he will not come to me and we will never marry.'

'Oh, *Dawnay!*' she scolds me and stands up. 'Could you not have chosen a single man, one who could stand by you? You did not think on it at all?'

'I did not *think* at all. I simply loved, that is all. I did not choose it.'

'Oh, why have you been so stupid? Now there is nothing I can do to help you.'

Susan turns and stares from my window, rubbing her palms together slowly. Now she has gone from me, I feel the isolation of my position, and know I am alone in this, that indeed it was my choice, my folly and yet my delight. I alone chose it, and I alone will face it.

'You are disappointed in me, perhaps even disgusted. I know that.'

'You know nothing,' says she. 'And I know everything you are feeling at this moment.'

'I do not think so, Susan.'

She turns and comes to me, sits beside me and takes my hands. There are tears in her eyes. 'There is much you do not know, despite your great store of knowledge. Stephen was once a curate. You did not know that, did you? When I met him, he had a good career before him, a nice living in Marylebone and he delighted in it, a renowned expert in scripture and a marvellous preacher of God's word. But I was just a cook and there was no chance for us. No educated man would ever marry beneath him, marry a servant. But we loved each other, and we defied it all to spend secret time together, and I grew heavy and then we knew. He left the Church – his one calling, his vocation – and Mr Woods helped us, gave me a position in his home and secured a teaching post for Stephen. Thus Mr Woods is our benefactor too. He did not approve of what we had done, in fact he railed against us and was quite red-faced about it. But he and Stephen are boyhood friends, a bond that has never been broken, and he did not want to see his friend live in penury. He knew that Stephen loved me and would never leave me. Thus, we married and Owen was born soon after. Stephen became a struggling tutor, but in general a happy one, with his wife and son and a home full of laughter and books. Yet I know he thinks on his lost career, and mourns it, from time to time. It was only when you came to us, and I saw the pleasure and solace he took in your lessons, and as you grew, your discussions and the work you undertook together, that I saw something of the fire in his eyes I had once seen in his regard for the Church. And I thank you for that, Dawnay.'

'Oh Susan,' I cry and we hug each other. 'That was his crooked path!'

'What is this?' Susan frowns.

'Nothing, nothing. I mean to say, what a very fine man your husband truly is. And a devoted wife and mother you are. And I am a fool.'

But Susan sits up straight and grasps my shoulders, forces me to straighten myself too.

'But you are no fool, my girl. You are the cleverest person

I know, or Stephen knows, or has ever known. So put that great intellect of yours to use, and devise a plan to save yourself, your work and your child. What are you going to do, Dawnay? Think on it and *solve* it.'

27

The beach at Charmouth is littered with fossils. Every few steps, if one knows what to seek, one can pick up an ammonite or suchlike and pocket it, only to find another a few steps on. I have quite a collection now, placed on a high shelf or in heavy drawers so Alexandra cannot find them and pop the smaller ones in her mouth, as she is wont to do with all little objects, unchecked. Other fossils can be found too, though harder to locate – I have found some examples of a marine animal with feathery arms that I do not believe has yet been named. Also, I have three prized examples of small fish, one of which Alexandra found on one of our beach wanders and it was marked in domestic history as the occasion of her first word: 'Fish.' When I sit to sketch and paint my finds, she helps with a pencil stub on her own notebook and scribbles snail-shapes, rainbows and smiling faces to entertain me. Her hair is golden-brown with sparks that shine in the sun, like the fool's gold we sometimes find in the Charmouth rocks.

The same month my daughter arrived in the world, Admiral Byng left it, executed on board ship in the Solent. When she was born, her hair was bright copper, yet within weeks it had thinned and fallen out. When it came back, it was white blonde, now fading to honeyed tones. Her face is so like that of her father, it pains me and gives pleasure in the same glance. My daughter has my eyes at least, green-blue. They began very dark, watchful and curious, then lightened over time. She fed badly in her first weeks, and was forever at the breast. But I could not satisfy her. I began to search out goat's milk, or sheep, whatever I could get daily from the Charmouth dairy, which I would boil and cool first, in order to destroy any animalcules present. I would spoon it to her, later slow-cooking oats until mush then pushing them through a sieve and mixing this with warm milk to satiate her infinite hunger. I believed myself a failure for being unable to provide everything she required from my own body – what could be more natural than feeding your own baby?

She slept for short bursts, then would wake again hungry, never enough time for me to rest or think or complete a single task. When awake, she would howl if I left her for a moment; she required a constant perch on my left arm from where she would survey her kingdom; and if put down would rarely sleep easily and required jiggling and comforting and singing at length before her eyes would finally droop and close. Even then, she would not sleep soundly and would wake at the slightest excuse, so I took to wrapping Francina's shawl about me tied with a firm knot, and placing the baby inside it swaddled against my breast, and there she would sleep longer, to the sound of my heartbeat. My back ached as a consequence, and my left arm seized from months of carrying the load, but these were her happy places, and I would not deny her. It was a constant and well-matched battle for attention between mother and daughter – a siege of long days and longer nights – and she was always the victor. (It occurred to me as I continued my chores with the child safely stored at my breast that this method of carrying one's baby is an example of technology invented by a female surely, back in the mists of time, weaving slings from plant materials; as well as most likely inventing pottery, agriculture, medicine, botany, the spinning of cloth, animal husbandry and even butchery, the use of pigments in decoration and art, methods of cooking *&c*. The list is long.)

When she was around four months of age, I began to mash up bread with milk, then potato, carrot and turnip, or any vegetable I could get hold of and cook to softness. From the moment she started to eat, she was a changed child. She slept for longer and longer, without crying out. Once she was weaning, and I preparing all her food, my feelings of failure evaporated, as I was in control again of her sustenance, and was able to gratify her at last and watch her full-belly smile as she settled down for afternoon naps. She moved from my bed into her own cot and – though she always wanted a bedtime song or story – she would happily close her eyes and sleep all through the night, allowing me my first uninterrupted stretch of deep sleep for half a year or more. I had my first dreams in months, many of my brother, of memories long forgotten, sparked by an intuition I cherish that my daughter seems to carry his aspect. Often I dreamed of Robin, and awoke feverish, then melancholy, the recollection of a hundred tender passages of our love filling my head.

Those early months I look back on and shudder: a wasteland of trouble and loneliness. After my discovery, I kept it from my benefactor as long as I was able. Susan was my rock, took great care with me and insisted I ate properly and regularly with much rest. Two weeks after my meeting with Graybourn the publisher, I had given up all hope of that acquaintance and was desperately trying to formulate a way to support myself and the child, when I received a letter from him. He turned out as good as his word, and said he had no interest in my personal situation as that was my business, and instead wished to renew our discussions in terms of my willingness to write for him, as soon as I was fit and able to do so. I met with him and we agreed I would write during my pregnancy

– and after the birth – then I should decide what I could
manage and inform him when I was good and ready. I told
him how exceptionally accommodating he was and when I
asked him why, he kindly stated: 'Because you are an exceptional person, Miss Price.'

Thus, I had my security and, armed with it, I approached
Mr Woods one afternoon and told him my news.

I received a customary, blustering lecture along these lines:
'*You*, Dawnay? Not you! The last I would ever have suspected
of being guilty of such an act. I believed you the most virtuous
of your sex, never one for dances or cavorting, or drink or
intrigues; always dedicated to your work and the pursuit of
reason. This behaviour I can hardly brook. What would the
quality think of me? Oh, but what can be said of passion in
these reckless days? How careful we must all be of ourselves
in this particular, when we daily see good women – hitherto
good at any rate – falling into the abyss in this reckless
manner . . .' And so on, and so on.

Once he had calmed himself somewhat, he demanded the
identity of the scoundrel, which I assured him would never
be revealed and would remain my private knowledge as long
as I lived. He ranted some more and grew red in the face
– just as Susan once described to me – but soon saw I would
not reveal it, and so gave up that fight. Next he insisted he
had the answer to my grievous situation.

'You will go into the country for your confinement, and
upon the birth, you will give up the child to a good farming
family or suchlike, and you will return here as if nothing had
happened, and London society will be none the wiser. And
life in Markham Woods's house will return to normal, with
no more talk of travels or babies or other such nonsense and
we shall live quietly and happily together until the Creator
deems my time is done and after that, you may do as you
please, though I do hope, Dawnay, that you choose the righteous path of virtue and perhaps it would be best for you if

you remained a spinster and devoted your life to science. Yes, that would do very well indeed.'

And he closed his eyes as if the matter were settled. I expected this; to his credit, my benefactor has always done his best to serve my interests, to guide and persuade me, yet often has lacked insight into the true nature of my own heart. I waited for him to glance at me, upon which act I merely said, 'Indeed, it will not do at all,' and left the room to pack.

But where to go? The dark streets of London confined my senses and I wished wholly to escape them. I wished to breathe clean air again, as I had on my islands. But I could not afford to go abroad and required to bc in England at least to send my work easily to Graybourn and receive payment promptly likewise. A childhood memory of Stephen Applebee, collecting fossils on his boyhood beach, reminded me of Charmouth and my mind was set. It was far away enough from London to avoid the scandal Mr Woods feared for his own place in society and his business. It was said to be a beautiful part of the country and it provided on a plate a subject for study: the fossil beach and coastline thereabouts, well known for its ancient finds. And most of all, it was beside the sea. I missed the sound of the sea. It washed a measureless store of flotsam memories for me and I wanted to be beside it once more. I yearned for it.

It seemed a superior plan. To Charmouth I would go – and not to give the baby up, as my benefactor supposed – but instead to make a life there. To live simply, with my child, to write and earn a living, to study fossils and work. I called myself Mrs Price and wore widow's weeds for a time, to smooth relations with the local people. But I had not prepared myself for seclusion. I had not predicted the intense isolation of being a new mother, with screaming child, and no other meaningful person with whom to share it. Alone, without friend or comforter, only a housekeeper named Betty

Dawlish from the village to assist twice a week with household business, and no ear to listen, no friend to embrace,
no partner to offer solace. I ached with isolation in the pit
of my stomach, in the empty chambers of my heart; I breathed
loneliness. I had spent many days alone as a child and younger
woman and never once did I feel the stark seclusion of those
days; I was left as a lighthouse on a rock, or a folly on a
hill.

As the child shrieked and would not sleep, as the hours
went by – days like weeks, weeks like aeons – I felt myself
losing my mind, at the worst times, holding the child coldly,
believing it hated me and wanted to ruin my life, tempted
to throw it down, or across the room, or into the sea. But
enough reason remained in my addled sleep-starved mind
to stop these impulses, and verily I did no harm to my child,
though I dreamed of it sometimes; not of hurt, but of silence,
of simply one moment to think, to listen to the birds, the
sea, to be myself again and not only this servant of an
imperious infant, to be Dawnay Price and not merely Mother,
to be at peace. That first month there was snow in April
– universal deep snow and such weather never recalled by
the oldest person hereabouts – and I struggled to keep the
baby warm, but she detested swaddling and fought to escape
it. We were trapped in the house, unable to go for walks in
the icy air. I lived in fractions of hours. The harsh white
light of the wintry weather taunted me with its bleak clarity
of view: this is your choice, your life now. There were no
soft greens, fringes of leaves or even tight buds to soften
it.

When the child was two months old, a knock came at my
door and I opened it, babe on my arm as ever. Standing
there were the Applebees, Stephen and Susan. I wept at the
sight of them, upon which Susan took the baby and bade
me sit. She handed the child to Stephen and set about

making tea with sugar for us all, an expensive treat they had brought me as a present. I was in heaven, sitting with them, drinking the fresh, sweet, hot tea and watching my old friends take over, understand and give me much needed aid.

'It has been so very hard,' said I to Susan.

'It is for everyone,' said she. 'But anything worth having is fought for. Your children make you earn your love for them through sacrifice. But once won, it resides in your heart and your soul, and no one can take it from you.'

My friends' arrival lifted a great weight of sorrow from my weary shoulders. They would do any kind office for me. Susan shared many wise and helpful thoughts about motherhood. Stephen brought talk of the outside world and developments in science. At last the burden was shared, and I was able to discuss matters other than milk or sleep or excrement, topics suited to the adult brain and not the infant body. They stayed for a week and as my mood improved, I took pleasure in waiting upon Susan for once, preparing good food for her and serving her, as she had done for me so kindly in our past; after all my training with Matron as a maid-of-all-work and with Betty's help, I have become quite the housewife. I made a currant tart and plum pudding, which Susan praised and they both ate with relish.

Stephen and I went for strolls along the beach, Susan very contented to be left alone with the child, ushering us out. We discussed my work, my publisher, the secret ideas I continue to formulate. I told Stephen I had changed my mind about coral gardens: that now I believe coral is a collection of many animals, sentient and predatory, not the design of ancient peoples, but architecture created by animals. And furthermore, I now doubt the existence of mermaids. The cave of the great sea maid I believe was not a depiction of nature, but a metaphor for it. It has occurred to me that the paintings were a kind of genealogy, these ancient people's ideas of creation: the simple beings of the sea first – even the fossils of shellfish in the walls leading up to the cave play their part in this procession – the fish at the entrance, leading on to the mammals next – the seals – and finally the half-mammal, half-fish humans in the final, deepest cavern; as if they wrote a book on the walls of a cave, rather than parchment or paper; *as if they are writing their own Bible*.

Stephen listened carefully, then I said to him, 'You know by now that I am aware of your past career, that once you were a man of the Church. I hope I have not offended you, in any of my ideas, my rantings against religion, my current theories. If I have, you have not shown it for a moment. But I would expect nothing less from such a gentleman as you, Stephen.'

He smiled, then replied, 'There can be no offence taken by a person who seeks the truth. My mind had grown and changed alongside your own, Dawnay, and I have learned to question my old accustomed ways of thinking. It is only to the good that you too seek to question your own theories. The scientific mind must cast beyond the moon, into unknown territory, and thus may take a wrong turn from time to time. The trick is to recognise it and instead choose a better path to knowledge, just as a natural philosopher should.'

The Applebees' visit was medicine to me. When they were leaving, I begged them to stay, though I knew they could not. Their son Owen was by now married and set up in his own home, doing very well; so they are more at liberty than they once were. But life intervenes and they must return to theirs and their work, and I had to resume the life I had chosen also. The days after their departure were my loneliest yet, and I missed the comfort of their company in my very bones.

And motherhood returned to me as a trial and perpetual vexation.

Yet, as the first months waned and spring proper came, as the child settled, as I grew to know Betty more, as I ventured out into the village, down to the beach, discovered the wealth of ancient life in its rocks which I had suspected but was overwhelmed actually to lay eyes on: all these gradual processes – requiring time, patience and faith – began to tell on me and ease my sense of solitude.

I remember one grim day, when Alexandra had not slept for over fourteen hours and I was near distracted with exhaustion and half weeping, half racked with anger and complaining bitterly to Betty of all my troubles, she waited for me to quiet down, then said, 'One day, you and your girl will be the best of friends. She will be your helpmeet and your darling.'

And I looked at Alexandra and my eyes brimmed with tears of joy – a deep knowledge settled then and told me: now, you have it, now you have a person in this world who is for ever connected to you. It was not that I owned her, never that, as since the earliest flutterings in my womb I knew she was other, she was herself and – though a part of me, though of me – she was completely her own person and would go her own way in life. But that she would always be my daughter and I would always be her mother. And nobody else in this world – not now nor for ever – holds that station but *me*.

Now we live through simple days, a plain cottage within the sound of the sea, ordinary food and drink, happy uncomplicated days together. We always have a fire, even in summer. I like a good fire. Sometimes, news of the war with France is spoken of in the village, and papers come from the capital with news of notable battles and victories for the British. But I do not pursue news of the war, or the navy, or seek out news of a certain person, as I have my new life now and resolved I would put my past behind me, and so I do. I look only to the deep and dim past of ancient time and forward to the unravelling future. The latter is a new sensation for me, as I was always too impatient to consider the far future, only the present moment, as Stephen knew too well of me. Yet since I have had a child, my outlook of the years ahead stretches out beyond my life to hers, and to her children, and her children's children, and beyond – a line of mirrors reflecting mirrors into eternity. It is parenthood that gives one the longer view. It is a relief to think of another before oneself. Alexandra and I are two stars side by side, forever orbited by others yet never moved from our own fixed station in the sky. I work and she plays; I read Voltaire and she paws at picture books and the alphabet. We talk, I tell her about the birds and beasts, the way people are, draw her pictures of islands and apes and sea cows – try every day in some small measure to feed her unquenchable thirst for knowledge. She is three years of age and luminous with life.

It is a pleasure to look upon her and see that wishful inkling of my brother. His note to me I have kept all these long years and framed behind glass and put on my dressing table. I show it to her from time to time and tell her, 'This was a present from your uncle, my brother.' Just saying the words fills me with pride and sadness in equal, exquisite measure. The loss of him, the silhouette where my mother should have been, and my father more shadowy still – these blank spaces, this hollow in the heart of me, I see now it has driven me onwards, to seek, to find, to be found. For years I harboured a fantasy that my brother would track me down to the asylum, would speak to Matron who would surely recall me, would find his way to my benefactor and appear at our door one glorious day. I pictured his face, his features lengthened by age and hard experience, yet his eyes the same as those I knew as an infant, that smiled kindly upon me. But it never came to pass. I know it never will. Yet I still dream of his face from time to time and wake in serenity. Alexandra has inherited some of his character too, methinks. She is certainly kind and tender, like him, bright and quick too.

She knows how to wield a quill, one of my first gifts to her once she could hold a spoon. No child of mine will be deprived of writing, however young. I continue to write, part for my living – books on my past travels, on my drawings of the natural world, and more recently on children's primers in science – and in the evenings, once Alexandra sleeps, I write my own private ideas. One day perhaps the world will be ready to hear my hypothesis; it may have evolved sufficiently to accept it from a woman and an orphan, even. But for now I do not attempt to broadcast my dangerous ideas, as I will not threaten my daughter's future by willingly risking her mother's place by her side, of removal to the pillory or to prison. I'll be damned if she might ever know the smallest part of what it feels to be a foundling. I have made more than simply a domicile for us here. My child came into the world in this little house and will always know it as her birthplace. One day, I intend to travel again – to see those exotic creatures I imagine in unknown lands – and Alexandra will come with me. Together we shall seek evidence for my theories in hidden caves and hollows, jungles and oceans, as yet unexplored, undiscovered; beyond the edge of the map, where the sun sets. Yet wherever we journey, like a shell on her back, my daughter will carry the memory of home.

One late March afternoon in 1760, a week or so after her third birthday, we are rambling on the beach, Alexandra running ahead as ever, stopping to hold aloft fossil prizes to show me then placing them in the bulging pocket I have sewn on to her smock for just that purpose. There is a warm breeze this day that blows the surface of the sand in rushing waves upon waves, as if alive – a bright shadow on the sea-damp surface. A figure arrives way down at the end of the beach, near the great dark cliff that looms above us; come from the coastal path, it steps out on to the mingled pebbles and sand. Clothed in a dark coat and broad tricorne hat, Robin Alexander stands on Charmouth beach and scans the scene, his head turning this way and that among the other strollers and fossil-seekers this bright spring day, and then he finds me.

As I walk towards him, he stands straight and serious, not moving. Only as we approach – as Alexandra curves in her circuit and runs to me, hands me the fossils she has no room left to store, then is off again on her own aimless path – can I see his eyes turn to her, a golden-headed ball of energy whisking this way and that with the sea breeze, crunching across the pebbles and talking to the clouds. He watches her, cannot take his eyes from her every move, and only when I am close enough to see there is white in his hair now, and that his left arm is shorter than his right, that indeed his left hand is missing, does he turn to me and meet my gaze. We stand apart, almost four years and convention between us.

'Are you angry I have come?' says he.

The sound of his voice, the tone of it, how I had practised the timbre of it for many months in my head, until it faded and at last I had forgotten its exactitude, and now to hear it again is like song.

'Never that. Does it hurt you?' I ask, looking at his arm.

'Not any more.'

'How did you lose it?'

'In a mighty sea battle, at Quiberon Bay.'

I had heard of it. Last winter, our navy had routed the French and put paid to their invasion plans once and for all. 'Our local lord put on a day of festivities in Bridport.'

'Did you attend?'

'I did not.'

Years of painful separation and we speak of such trivialities.

Say I, 'Thank you. For fighting for England, for keeping us safe.'

'I did my duty.'

'And did it exceedingly well, I warrant. Can you continue, as a captain, I mean, with your injury?'

'It is possible. There is an understanding that I could retire honourably, take up a position on land, in Greenwich or suchlike. I have had my fill of war.'

'How fares your family?'

'My wife is well. She is very active in society. My boys are now fourteen and have entered the navy, insisting that they serve together on the same ship, against my wishes. They are hearty, brave boys, but they will not be parted for all the world.'

'They are twins. They are bound to each other.'

There is a fervent silence between us and we may gaze upon each other. I dearly wish to touch him. I take a step forward.

Says he softly, 'All is dust and ashes without you.'

Alexandra squeals as she has found a sandworm and is dangling it for my approval.

'Be kind to it,' I call.

Robin stares at her, then looks to me. 'You are married now?'

'You do not know?'

He glances at Alexandra again.

'How did you find me?' I ask.

'I went to visit Woods. He said you had moved to the country, to the West Country in fact, to pursue your studies of the natural world. I do believe he misses your company exceedingly, as he reminisced at length about your younger days. I could extract no further information from him as to your exact whereabouts, without raising suspicion. But as I was leaving, the cook pulled me aside and handed me a slip of paper, your dwelling written on it. We did not speak one word. Excepting that you are here, I know little else.'

'Dear Susan . . .' I muse, then turn to watch my daughter

frolic in the encroaching tide. I look to Robin. 'She is my daughter. Three years old. Her name is Alexandra.'

He watches her. 'She is beautiful,' says he.

'She is yours.'

I have a rowboat we use, Alexandra and me. I have become quite the sailor these three years. On summer days when the sea is warm we slip over the side and I teach her to swim like a fish. Now we take off our shoes and stockings and Robin removes his boots too, swiftly and with no delay; he has become accustomed to a single-handed life. The three of us – barefoot and laughing at the cold sea slapping about our toes – push the boat into the water and hop in. Robin takes up the right oar and I the left, and together we propel ourselves smoothly out into the grey-blue waters of Charmouth Bay.

Says he, 'I miss the sea terribly. One day, I would like to pilot scientific journeys again – as we did on the *Prospect* – further away, to the South Seas perchance. I would require natural philosophers to accompany me.' He looks down at his daughter. 'Of any age.'

She pulls out her fossils from her pocket and lays them all down in a row in the bottom of the boat in an order only she understands. I sit and watch them both, my heart full.

We come to silence. We drift.

'Who are you?' says Alexandra to Robin.

He looks to me, and I nod.

'I am your father.'

She shoots a glance at me and I smile.

Says she, 'Will you stay with us?'

'I wish to,' says Robin. 'Very much.'

'Do so then,' says Alexandra and turns back to her fossils.

It is easier for us than for him. He yet resides in a world fraught with ticking minutes and wagging tongues, past regrets and future restraints. Alexandra lives in the endless present of childhood. I have always been the outcast: a foundling, a woman, a thinker. Once I sought to join the crowd for approbation, existing on the edges, looking in. Now I have geological time as my lens. It has brought me great peace. I recommend it to you.

AUTHOR'S NOTE

Here are some thoughts on the varied historical aspects of *Song of the Sea Maid*.

Women in C18th science

Readers may like to seek out the excellent and mind-expanding book *Hypatia's Heritage: A History of Women in Science from Antiquity to the Late Nineteenth Century* by Margaret Alic, to learn about the hidden history of women in science. There were several models and antecedents of Dawnay Price in the C17th and C18th, including such important figures as Émilie du Châtelet, Sophie Germain, Anne Conway, Lady Mary Lee Chudleigh, Lady Mary Wortley Montagu, Mary Somerville and Margaret Cavendish. Many of these women are largely forgotten by history, and arguably this is largely because they were women. They had a lot to fight against to be allowed to work, let alone be recognised. Émilie du Châtelet once wrote:

> *Judge me for my own merits, or lack of them, but do not look upon me as a mere appendage . . . I am in my own right a whole person, responsible to myself alone for all that I am, all that I say, all that I do. It may be that there are metaphysicians and philosophers whose learning is greater than mine, although I have not met them . . .*

And as Alic writes:

> From the earliest times women contributed to the

development of scientific knowledge, yet most of the women in this book remain unknown – even to historians of science – and most of those recorded here were women of privilege; as such, they represent only the surface of the history of women in science. Thousands of other women scientists have undoubtedly been forgotten forever.

One of my main ideas behind the novel was this: what if a poor woman made an important scientific discovery in ages past? Would this idea be heard or remembered? Charles Darwin, a century after Dawnay, did not develop his wonderful ideas in isolation. His work built upon that of many others over the centuries; for example the past scientists and their work that Dawnay discusses with Applebee and Robin – all of these are real and documented. Darwin was a man of independent means who was able to put forth his ideas, eventually, though of course even in his age he met with considerable obstacles. Yet largely he was the right person, in the right place, at the right time. Dawnay Price – an C18th woman and orphan – was the wrong person, in the wrong place, at the wrong time. The reader may like to consider how many other important ideas have been lost throughout the history of humans which were likewise thought of by the 'wrong' people, and this may well continue to this day.

The very helpful historian Dr. Gillian Williamson also told me that the concept of ideas coming before their time affords other examples in Dawnay's era. For example, in Gillian's words:

'In the *Gentleman's Magazine* there was a letter on the dangers of tobacco-smoking linking it to lung cancer – which obviously got nowhere for centuries. There was also a physician who said that puerperal fever swept through lying-in hospitals because it was spread by doctors' unwashed hands – this was thought inconceivable since the doctors were gentlemen and the patients of the lower orders . . .'

Cave art

Dawnay's caves are my own invention, yet they are based upon some existing finds, such as drawings of seals, mermaids and red dots, and the presence of primitive oil lamps and skulls embedded in calcite. To date in 2014, very recent discoveries suggest that women played a significant role in cave painting. Female handprints have been found at many cave art sites surrounding key paintings. I carried out my own small (and highly unscientific) survey to get an idea of how modern humans imagine their ancient counterparts and almost every respondent pictured a male painting cave walls. Yet there is little or no evidence that this was the case. Research in this field – largely due to the rarity of finds – you might say is in its infancy. What other hidden caves may be out there to reveal to us more secrets of our past? Whatever is found, it is to be hoped that the interpretation of this evidence is free from gender bias and represented as such when it is reported and analysed. For issues of how researchers of both sexes have interpreted ancient humans, see *Women in Human Evolution* edited by Lori D. Hager and *The Descent of Woman* by Elaine Morgan.

Dawnay's sea cow

Readers who know anything about sea cows may wonder if they used to frequent the Mediterranean, as they certainly do not nowadays. The truth is that remains have been found of prehistoric sea cows in the Mediterranean region, but there is no evidence that they inhabited this area in the C18th. Thus, this is artistic license. However, Steller's sea cow, a large species found near Russia, which Dawnay mentions, was discovered during Dawnay's time and soon after promptly became extinct. I wished to use Dawnay's sea cow as an example of how, in the 1750s, there were still many species of animal not yet widely known even by expert naturalists, and also there were many mythical creatures that were still widely believed to exist. Most of the references to mermaids in this novel are taken from contemporary 'sightings' of mer-folk, some of which were published in highly respectable journals such as the *Gentleman's Magazine*. I hope the reader will allow me some license in placing a creature in a sea it has not frequented for some time. After all, just because there is no evidence available for something, it does not mean it never happened . . .

Robin and his ship HMS Fox

As scholars of the Battle of Menorca 1756 will know full well, there was no frigate present named HMS *Fox*. I did not wish to usurp the real captains of the ships involved and unceremoniously dump one overboard to be replaced by my fictional character. Therefore, I chose to insert a fictional ship into the battle. I suspect, however, that an extra frigate such as Robin's would have been most welcome to a fleet not as full as Admiral Byng would have liked it. Byng's fate in this novel is, sadly, all true and alluded to by Voltaire in *Candide*.

The Berlengas Islands

The flora and fauna of these islands has been rendered as accurately as possible, reliant upon research into the C18th inhabitants. However, there is no evidence of a painted cave on these islands – this is fiction. Yet, a cave has been found since near Peniche that contained a variety of artefacts and evidence of early humans, so this area of Portugal is a fitting one for Dawnay's quest.

Lisbon earthquake

This natural disaster was well documented at the time and I have used a variety of sources to provide details of what happened. Luckily for the English-speaking researcher, there was a range of English people in Lisbon at the time who wrote detailed accounts of what happened to them and thus provide invaluable resources for the modern reader.

Orphanages

There were several such asylums set up in the C18th, particularly in London. See the Coram Foundling Hospital, which now has a museum dedicated to it. This was established a little too late for Dawnay's purposes, yet several aspects of the orphans' lives were gleaned from here, as well as other less positive institutions of the time.

Markham Woods as benefactor

Mr. Woods is an example of a type of self-made, wealthy man in this era who turned his money to good use. Thomas Coram (of the Foundling Hospital) is one and there were many others, who used their benevolence – some with good intentions and others less so – to fund various charities or adopt those less fortunate to improve their lot. Other examples include Jonas Hanway, who founded the Marine Society, whilst Thomas Day adopted two orphan girls in order to educate them in how to be 'good wives', which unsurprisingly did not end well for anyone involved.

Women on ships in the Royal Navy and elsewhere

See the fascinating book *Female Tars: Women Aboard Ship in the Age of Sail* by Suzanne J. Stark for details on how women sailed the seas in this period. Also, *The Ordeal of Elizabeth Marsh: A Woman in World History* by Linda Colley is a wonderful account of a lone female traveller in the 1750s who was taken prisoner aboard a Moroccan corsair ship and makes

Dawnay's adventures seem positively tame. I read this book after I had written the novel, yet was gratified to see that Dawnay was not the only woman to strike out unaccompanied upon the seas in the mid-C18th.

Porpoises swimming up the Thames
This did happen in Dawnay's time and was documented by witnesses.

Frost Fair
There was indeed a Frost Fair on the Thames in 1740 and at other times before and since.

The Menagerie
There was a zoo of sorts at the Tower for many years, through which a variety of exotic and sad beasts passed and were seen by avid visitors.

The English Hotel, Lisbon & Mr. and Mrs. Dewar
This establishment did exist in Dawnay's time and was run by the Dewars. However, my characterisation of the Dewars and their dialogue is entirely of my own creation.

Lizards on the islets of Menorca
All of the varieties of lizard described do exist and you can go and see them today if you wish.

C18th prose
Many aspects of current language use that we tend to take for granted – such as punctuation and paragraphing – were not fully standardised during the C18th. Therefore, writers such as Daniel Defoe, Henry Fielding, Laurence Sterne and Tobias Smollett used aspects of punctuation and emphasis in varying ways. This is complicated by the fact that the texts were then at the mercy of the compositor, who also made

decisions regarding its layout and presentation. In creating my own C18th narrator, I decided to use this point of flux to my advantage and make my own choice of rules to follow and to disregard, in order to give the flavour of C18th prose, hopefully without alienating the modern reader in the process. It is also worth noting that – as this narrative is told in the present tense and in the first person; a kind of stream of consciousness style – that it is not entirely necessary to approximate the C18th prose style, as it is not meant to approximate a written text as such. However, I did feel that the reader might find it appealing and interesting to experience a way of presenting prose that is more contemporary to the period than that provided by modern texts.

The aspects I have chosen to include are:
- single quotation marks used for speech marks, as opposed to double
- use of the dash and semicolon to extend the length of sentences and convey thought processes
- sir/madam/miss all use lower case as the initial letter
- says she as well as she says
- using *&c* for etc.
- the spelling of Menorca as Minorca
- Italics used for several reasons: names of ships, books and magazines, as well as use of Latin and foreign terms or speech to signify the written word; and for adding emphasis to certain words and phrases. In terms of emphasis, this can be where dialogue words require stress or accent in their pronunciation; yet it has also been used to draw the attention of the reader to particular words and phrases of note, as Defoe often did.
- It may be interesting for the reader to note that I have chosen to omit some commonly used aspects of C18th prose, as I personally found them to be a little too distracting for the modern reader. These include: the use of capitalising the initial letter e.g. Thus my Pride, not

my Principle, my Money, not my Virtue, kept me Honest; use of an apostrophe and the letter *d* for past-tense *ed* endings e.g. ask'd; italics used to identify speakers and names of places e.g. *say I*; they went to *London*.

Particular thanks must be extended to Dr. Helen Williams, Lecturer in English Literature at Northumbria University, for her assistance in all matters relating to C18th prose and literature; also to Dr. Gillian Williamson, for suggestions of amendments to anachronistic vocabulary and phrasing.

ACKNOWLEDGEMENTS

Many thanks to:

Jane Conway-Gordon, for reading the first draft of this novel in a day and loving the moment where they scrub Dawnay and 'find a little girl'.

Suzie Dooré, for saying yes – again! – and to two books this time! And for her excellent and sensitive editing, as ever.

Francine Toon – who also edited the first draft and did so beautifully, particularly regarding her happy memories of Portugal.

Dr. Gillian Williamson for reading the first draft as an historian and providing amazing notes and advice on so many aspects of the period, from mermaids to doctors, the *Gentleman's Magazine* to benefactors, and jumps to frock coats; Tim Hitchcock for raising the book at the Long Eighteenth-Century Seminar at the Institute of Historical Research and thereby putting me in touch with Gillian, and Denis Judd for suggesting Tim in the first place!

Dr. Helen Williams, Lecturer in English Literature, Northumbria University, for her extremely useful help on aspects of C18th prose.

Dr. Jane McKay for suggesting I look at Prufrock and helping with the final title of the book.

The staff at Burton Constable Hall, Fairfax House and the Foundling Museum, for fascinating glimpses into all things C18th.

The Caird Library and the National Maritime Museum at

Greenwich, for assistance with research relating to Robin's ships and the battle of Menorca.

Samuel Johnson's House and curator Celine McDaid, who discussed the particulars of Johnson's abode and era one sunny August afternoon.

David, Donna, Emily and Alex Chadwick, for providing perfect room and board during my London research trip, with great conversation and lovely dinner, as ever.

Russell Beeson for expert botanical advice on plants that would resist the coal smoke of London and on the flora of Menorca.

Dorothy Judd & her friends, who sent me pictures and descriptions of Portuguese islands.

Marie & Kevin Porter and Adele Webster, who supplied meals, cake and child-minding when I really needed it, during the writing of this book.

Clare, Dave, Lucie, Clarke and AJ Wingate, for all your interest and support for my writing (especially AJ).

To everyone who kindly answered my survey on attitudes towards early humans and cave paintings, including Simon, Mum & Russell, Dorothy & Denis, Pauline Lancaster, Kerry Drewery, Francine Koubel, Sheila Houghton, Cathy Smith, Brenda Taylor, Emily Chadwick, Richard Morris, Jennie & Rick Grieve, Robert Chadwick, Jon Chadwick, Kim Doyle, Pete Wall and Chris Sutcliffe.

Early readers – Simon, Mum, Marie, Kerry, Dorothy, Pauline, Francine K., Lynn Downing, Sue White, Josie Gray, Theresa Roberts, Alexis Hepworth, Ann Schlee and Kathy Kendall – whose support and feedback are hugely appreciated and valued.

To all the book bloggers and other lovely people on social media and readers who have attended events, who have welcomed the idea of this book and said they're looking forward to reading it – thanks for your support and here it is!

Emma Daley, Laura Macdougall, Alix Percy, Naomi Berwin,

Jack Dennison and everyone else at Hodder, for their efforts in all things promotional.

Staff at Waterstones Grimsby and Lincoln, as well as all booksellers wherever you are, for supporting me as a writer by stocking my books – I salute you.

To Morag Lyall, copy-editor extraordinaire, for reading with such care and spotting the tiniest of errors and biggest of clangers. Let us dedicate this novel to the six sons . . .

Samantha Blake at the *Cleethorpes Chronicle* and Laura Crombie at the *Grimsby Telegraph* for their help with publicising events and kindly documenting my career so far.

To everyone at the Edinburgh International Book Festival, for nominating *The Visitors* for the First Book Award 2014, welcoming us to your beautiful city and wonderful events, and providing Simon, Poppy and me with one of our best weekends ever! And a special thanks to Mum, Robert and Suzie for coming.

To Tink and the hedgehogs, for entertainment purposes.

Last and the opposite of least, my favourite people – Poppy and Simon – for ceaseless love and constant support. Heartfelt thanks to Simon – AKA my lovely fella – for all the thoughtful searching for C18th reference sources, for expert photography on our research trips, for reading the first draft first and for keeping the faith in my work always and for ever. And to Poppy for drawing the best front cover design for *The Edge of the Map* . . .